ROGUE FRONTIER

JASON KASPER

SEVERN RIVER

PUBLISHING

Severn River Publishing
SevernRiverBooks.com

ISBN: 978-1-64875-639-9 (Paperback)

ALSO BY JASON KASPER

American Mercenary Series
Greatest Enemy
Offer of Revenge
Dark Redemption
Vengeance Calling
The Suicide Cartel
Terminal Objective

Shadow Strike Series
The Enemies of My Country
Last Target Standing
Covert Kill
Narco Assassins
Beast Three Six
The Belgrade Conspiracy
Lethal Horizon
Congo Nightfall
Rogue Frontier
Final Strike

Spider Heist Thrillers
The Spider Heist
The Sky Thieves
The Manhattan Job
The Fifth Bandit

Standalone Thriller
Her Dark Silence

To find out more about Jason Kasper and his books, visit
Jason-Kasper.com

To Julie

SDMT

"I know not with what weapons World War III will be fought, but World War IV will be fought with sticks and stones."
-Albert Einstein

"Our team's motto is 'Fast and Loose.' Welcome to our world."
-Worthy

1

Qasbo, Sindh Province, Pakistan

"Hey, space cadet."

Ian looked over his shoulder, then turned in his seat—a rickety foldout chair facing the wall of the Toyota HiAce panel van now threading its way westward through the remote Pakistan village.

He was met with a smoldering gaze from Cancer, who sat atop the bench on the opposite side of the cargo area.

"What?" Ian asked.

"I said you better not fuck this up. And you weren't even paying enough attention to hear that, so—"

"Come here," the intelligence operative cut him off.

Cancer rose and stepped toward him, keeping his head down in the van's jostling interior, eager for a confrontation.

He leaned in close enough for Ian to speak without being overheard by their teammates in the back.

"Do you remember," Ian said quietly, "that time I told Reilly how to treat a collapsed lung after someone got shot?"

Cancer thought for a moment.

"No."

"What about when I gave Worthy advice on his close-range speed shooting?"

The grizzled sniper was silent then, beginning to get the point.

"Or," Ian added, "when I tried to educate you on how to make a sniper shot at twelve hundred meters? Remember that? No?"

He paused a beat before continuing.

"That's because I don't lecture people on anything that's not my area of expertise. 'But why, Ian?' Because everyone knows how to do their own specialty better than I do. So they don't need me to tell them how to do it, do they? Which is why I find it fascinating that you've got the audacity to do the opposite—especially when I could at least take a swing at doing any of the above myself, while seeing you try to work my equipment in cross-training was like watching a monkey try to read a roadmap. Need I go on?"

Cancer found his seat on the bench, shifting uneasily as Ian glanced at the others.

Reilly was watching him over the dogeared pages of one of his mindless military thriller novels. How the medic could possibly continue to read that kind of fictional drivel after doing the real thing himself was a mystery to Ian.

Worthy, meanwhile, was in a state of Zen-like calm, watching the van's progress on his phone's satellite imagery with a look of peaceful focus.

The only disturbing thing about the scene was everyone's attire, or lack thereof; instead of the usual tactical kit that was currently stowed in stash bags at their feet, they wore civilian clothes with, as a final affront, concealed pistols as the only weapons to their name. That detail alone lent the entire scene a surreal quality, particularly given how utterly vulnerable they'd be if compromised.

It was a far cry from their usual arrangement—no member of the team rode up front to supervise their driver. For one thing, this wasn't an area where they could risk having an American spotted in the passenger seat. And for another, in this case their driver needed no supervision.

Ian turned back in his foldout chair to face the wall of the van. Sure, he'd just told off Cancer for perhaps the first time in their history together. But the inner truth remained that he *was* nervous. The energy was very different from that which usually preceded his team raiding an objective. It wasn't that the stakes were higher. Far from it, in fact.

Nor was it that he wasn't used to being the critical intelligence link between finding a target and his teammates unleashing their considerable tactical acumen once the objective had been located. He'd done so many times, and likely would many more.

But this time there was no objective to raid. As a result of Pakistan's steadfast restrictions in allowing Americans to assist the stated mission, there would be no opportunity for his team to launch themselves into the breach of a well-defended target.

There was only him.

As the van made a right turn onto a dusty side street, the driver called back with the overemphasized "t" of the Pakistani accent.

"One minute."

Ian lowered the lid of a compartment concealed within the van's siding, letting it rest atop his lap. A keyboard was now at his disposal, and the exposed cutout above revealed an array of screens. He activated the master power and let the assembly boot up, then tapped the digital interface to home his systems in on the relevant frequencies and networks.

There was a directional component to all this equipment that he'd dial in once the van was in position. For now, however, his focus was on minimizing the time from that stopping point to fully monitoring his area of concern—there was no telling how long they'd have to wait for a communication intercept, whether hours or days, but in the off chance that one transpired immediately, he had to be ready. Ian donned his headphones as the van pulled to a stop, keeping one earcup tucked back on his head so he could hear his teammates.

Pakistan was an operating environment unlike any the team had known before. A contentious border with India was marked by the disputed territory of Kashmir, a flashpoint for numerous conflicts. The country's western frontier, especially along the border with Afghanistan, was covered in vast unregulated regions that served as havens for various militant groups, including the Taliban. And Iranian influence was not-so-subtly woven into Pakistan's socio-political fabric, especially in areas like Balochistan and Sindh Province where the team operated now.

Ian turned a knob to orient the directional aspect of his communications intercept equipment to the west, aligning it with the Kirthar Mountains.

The desolate expanse held countless recesses and hidden valleys, concealing enclaves that provided a near-absolute cover for militant forces to disappear as if swallowed by the earth itself. All of this was inaccessible to the team in every way except one, and Ian performed a final check over his systems to ensure everything was up and running.

Satisfied at last, he sat back in his chair, secure in the knowledge that he now monitored twelve phones and three radio frequencies in a targeted network, all of them the product of extensive CIA analysis on the secondary and tertiary networks surrounding the one man they'd come here to find.

The van's ignition turned off, engine dying to a muted quiet in the cargo area.

Cancer announced, "All right, Tahir. Hand over that product you picked up for us back in Khairpur."

Tahir Qureshi removed his sunglasses as he turned in the driver's seat, which was located on the right side of the vehicle in an orientation that Ian had never gotten used to and never would.

With a somewhat rotund figure cunningly obscured by his broad shoulders, the man's thick build exuded an aura of undeniable strength. His face was marked by a thick, jet-black beard and sharp, discerning eyes, his stare radiating alertness and an intelligence that seemed to pierce through every word as he bristled with defensiveness.

"This," he said, patting a bag on the passenger seat beside him, "is not *product*. It is Aseel jumbo, premium quality, the pride of Sindh Province. You will find nothing finer in all of Pakistan, I promise you this."

Worthy noted, "You seem pretty confident."

"Confident enough," Reilly added darkly, "to mean you've already had a taste."

With a noncommittal shrug, Tahir admitted, "How else would I confirm?"

Cancer sat up, his back ramrod straight and an edge in his voice. "No wonder you're in a good mood. But we paid you a thousand PKR for a full kilo, and we better be getting a full kilo."

Tahir corrected him, "You paid me to *acquire* a kilo. My cut, however, is half."

"Half?" Reilly cried. "HALF? That's highway robbery, and you know it."

The Pakistani man's eyes narrowed, and an icy silence fell over the van's occupants.

"These are my terms," he said resolutely, face solemn. "You either accept them, or get the fuck out of my country."

Ian and his colleagues were used to working with CIA-vetted local assets who took orders rather than gave them. Governments of the nations they operated in typically had no idea the team was there in the first place, much less why...which made a formal diplomatic agreement all the more maddening, as was the Pakistani-mandated assignment of a "minder" from their Inter-Services Intelligence agency, or ISI.

And while Tahir Qureshi's supervisory capacity made him a pain in the ass, he did possess an immensely useful superpower. He had a multifaceted network of informants and deep-cover operatives spread along Pakistan's many unregulated frontiers, any of whom he could call upon for route reconnaissance and, more importantly, safe locations for the team to travel between. The trip from Islamabad to Qasbo spanned two days and three nights, doubling the time of a single road trip—but they'd also arrived undetected to the lawless militias controlling much of the territory in between, and that was an advantage that four white Americans couldn't get any other way.

Worthy pointed out the obvious.

"There's one of you, Tahir, and four of us."

"What are you going to do," the driver leered, "threaten me? With your pistols?"

Ian winced, remaining silent as Worthy dealt with the slight.

"That restriction is your government's fault, not ours. Let's not forget we're trying to help your country eliminate the embarrassment of a rogue general—the least you could have done was let us bring rifles."

"If you had simply provided the ISI with your, shall we say, unique 'capabilities,' you would not even have to be here."

Tahir was referring to the Toyota HiAce panel van they occupied now, a vehicle whose nondescript exterior was the only normal thing about it.

Signals intelligence intercept systems were seamlessly built into the vehicle's framework. It had antennas disguised as a roof rack and direction-finding equipment masquerading as front and rear bumpers. Hidden compartments in the cargo space housed cyber surveillance tools including IMSI catchers and Wi-Fi interceptors, all meticulously arranged to be concealed at a moment's notice. This entire array was powered and cooled by a specially modified, near-silent electrical system, transforming the van into a covert mobile listening station that was more or less invisible to the outside observer.

The van's base price was forty grand before the CIA's Armor and Special Programs Department had modified and equipped it at the cost of 1.2 million taxpayer dollars, making it more valuable than the annual GDP of the entire district it now occupied.

And since none of that equipment could fall into enemy hands, the van had a built-in self-destruct mechanism by way of thermite devices that would incinerate the interior of the vehicle in seconds.

Reilly blurted, "This isn't some kit you pick up at RadioShack. It takes years to learn this stuff."

An abject lie, Ian thought. He'd provided rudimentary cross-training to his teammates in the span of a week, and by now everyone could man his surveillance seat with reasonable proficiency in the event Ian got killed—or, at least, almost everyone. Cancer remained somewhat vexed by the equipment, falling behind even Reilly in his attempts to grasp its operation.

Tahir issued his mocking response.

"You underestimate the ISI. And for your sins, you have a babysitter and no rifles. Well done, America. Well done."

Cancer shot back, "It wasn't our agreement to broker. And if it was, I damn sure wouldn't help you unless we got to do the takedown."

"My country has perfectly capable soldiers, thank you. You find our man, and Zarrar will take care of the rest."

After a brief pause, Tahir added smugly, "And perhaps they will be so kind as to allow you a look at their objective once it is secure."

Zarrar Company was the Pakistani Special Service Group's elite counterterrorist unit, though the designation of "elite" varied widely outside major Western militaries. Even if they were good enough to capture their target alive, Ian thought, the man could just as quickly be released on the basis of political connections.

"We'll see about that," Worthy muttered.

Tahir was either oblivious or willfully ignorant to the subtext of accused incompetence in the pointman's reply. Instead, he chastised the entire team.

"None of you have reason to complain. This work is your job, is it not?"

Ian groaned.

The unenviable truth was that no, conducting technical surveillance most definitely was *not* the team's job. Ian's, perhaps, but not his team's writ large. It was perhaps the greatest indignity of the many on this mission. For the first time in the history of Project Longwing, their role was to locate a target and then sit back and watch while the Paks kicked in the door. There was no shortage of intelligence outfits that were born and bred for such a role, but current geopolitical considerations restricted the effort to forces completely unattributable to the US government.

Which, of course, Ian and his fellow CIA contractors most definitely were.

Reilly replied, "Doesn't mean we have to like it."

"Nor do you have to like my terms," Tahir sagely noted. "But if you want the product, then I keep half. Or you could try to find some on your own, and overpay for the *gobar* they sling to tourists."

A few seconds of tense silence ensued, with the standoff finally ending when Cancer admitted defeat.

"Fine," he said. "Keep half. But if you ever come to the US, you better believe we'll remember this shit."

Tahir was undaunted.

"If I ever find myself in the US, you will not have to threaten me. Just hand me a gun and I will gladly pull the trigger myself."

Ian turned his gaze to the displays before him, listening to the crinkle of plastic as Tahir's package changed hands, each team member taking a sample.

Reilly was the first to comment, his voice dancing with delight. "My God...this is the best we've had yet, by a long shot."

"Top of the line," Worthy added. "I'll give you that."

Cancer was next, his enthusiasm audible despite his words.

"Not bad. Better be, since we paid double. Ian, try this—"

Ian pulled both earcups into position instead, hearing the chime of an incoming call to a phone on the secondary network he monitored.

A burst of static preceded a local greeting from the recipient, followed by a rapid-fire string of Urdu spoken with an air of authority. There was a final verbal exchange, after which the call ended as suddenly as it began.

Ian watched the display before him fill with ten-digit grids denoting the exact location of both speakers, a small light shifting from yellow to green as an indication that the recording had been successful. His first "audio grab" of the team's mission to Pakistan was complete, having transpired and ended within minutes of arriving into position. That alone made it a lightning strike of intelligence, the kind of thing he could've easily missed if their last stop on the journey had involved so much as an extended piss break.

He was still totally uncertain of what the conversation entailed; a stationary cursor continued to blink on his screen, and Ian felt a jolt of elation as the AI-generated translation began appearing in racing rows of text.

High Tower orders you to meet him at the command site. Depart for Barakahu at sunrise. Your reservation is at Indigo Heights under the name Saadullah Khan. Wait there until you receive the next call. He will send a driver for you.

Ian's elation transformed into surprise, and then total confusion.

He knew exactly where Barakahu was, but for all the wrong reasons.

The man they hunted was referred to by a variety of monikers, of which High Tower was one. He had abundant reason to choose the nearby Kirthar Mountains for his exile: there was no government presence or law enforcement oversight, and the terrain was sufficiently prohibitive to frustrate the most dedicated of search efforts. Most importantly, he was shielded by an entrenched system of tribal customs that would provide early warning and safe relocation, all while remaining within a few hours of Larkana and its attendant urban facilities, communication networks, and transport links.

So why, Ian wondered, would his target forgo every one of those advantages to move twelve hundred kilometers *closer* to the heart of government operations and surveillance in Islamabad?

Ian looked up to see Tahir watching him from the driver's seat.

"What was it?" he asked urgently. "What did you intercept?"

The man's sole purpose was to report everything to the ISI, and the longer either side of that equation possessed the information Ian had just gleaned, the greater the chance of a leak and, consequently, their target fleeing with ample advance notice.

Ian allowed his shoulders to sag.

"False alarm," he said dismissively. "Couple guys arranging a goat sale at the Gorakh Hill Bazaar."

Before Tahir could probe further, Ian reinforced the reverse bluff by pulling off one earcup and saying, "All right, let me have some of that product."

Cancer held out a bulging plastic shopping bag. Ian peered inside and selected a single dark amber date from the pile within.

He took a small bite, chewing slowly.

"Well," Reilly asked expectantly, "what do you think?"

Ian swallowed the morsel of date and considered the question before responding. "Flesh is dense and meaty. Caramel, with a hint of molasses."

Nodding eagerly, Reilly added, "And a subtle, almost imperceptible nuttiness?"

"Yeah. Yeah, I'd say that's exactly right. Surprisingly complex flavor profile."

Tahir slapped the dash in triumphant self-congratulation.

"I told you," the ISI officer said, checking his side-view mirror. "Aseel jumbos are the best in all of—"

The monologue ended when he fired the van engine and shifted to drive, accelerating with the words, "Gentlemen, we are burned."

Cancer donned his pistol belt and armored plate carrier along with his teammates, after which the sniper scrambled into the van's passenger seat.

"Hyundai Tucson," he called to his teammates as he checked the mirror, "multiple occupants, trailing us at fifty meters."

He whipped his head toward Tahir and asked, "His security force?"

"Baloch separatists," the ISI officer corrected him, wheeling the van onto the village's main road. "Insurgents, very dangerous."

"ECM on," Ian announced.

The van's electronic countermeasure jammers were designed to disrupt the triggering signals that activated roadside bombs, creating a hundred-meter bubble of relative safety.

But at the moment, they served the more pressing role of blocking any cell phone connectivity for the men following them now, at least one of whom was more likely than not attempting to call for reinforcements.

Worthy passed his phone to Cancer with the words, "Left turn half a click ahead. Right side, engine trouble, we take them from the six."

Cancer accepted the device and analyzed the satellite imagery of the village. Normally it was his job to come up with the tactical plan, but being down a man had promoted him to ground force commander.

The road they were on proceeded to a Y-intersection, where an adjoining side street ran northwest. Both sides of that street were filled with residential homes surrounded on all sides by mud walls—depending on how tall they were, any of them could mean viable cover or an insurmount-able obstacle.

He scanned the imagery for the dismount location Worthy had speci-fied. It had to be just beyond a turn so his men had time to hide before the enemy vehicle rounded the corner. The only viable option was a single footpath between compound walls that ran from the side street to the main road.

Worthy's assessment had been spot-on.

Cancer handed the phone back and ordered, "Tahir, take the next left—stop at the first footpath on the right. We're going to dismount there and hide in the alley. Drive another fifty meters and stop, put your hood up, and pretend you've got engine trouble. Once they pass us, all you've got to do is buy some time until we pop out behind them and drop everyone."

"'Drop everyone?'" he replied. "With your *pistols*?"

"Thanks to your fuckin' government, yeah. Just do it, and do it before any more bad guys show up. Their phones are blocked, but that's not going to help us if there's any survivors. We need to take them all out at once, and do it before they stop the pursuit and wait for reinforcements."

If Tahir had previously suspected the team's primary role wasn't technical surveillance, Cancer thought, then the coming engagement was going to remove all doubt.

Before he could so much as speak the words "bug out bag," Worthy handed Cancer his backpack. Every team member carried a similar one for such an event, filled with layers of clothing for changing appearance, food and water, mobile chargers, radios and spare batteries, even more pistol magazines than they carried on their person, and an emergency supply of Pakistani currency to bribe their way to survival.

"Left here, then floor it," Cancer called, threading his arms through the backpack straps and cinching them down as Tahir negotiated the Y-intersection onto the side street. As soon as the van was concealed from the Hyundai's view, he floored the accelerator, leaving Cancer to scan the scene that followed.

The road ahead was lined with mud-walled compounds shielding buildings with sun-baked exteriors. Dusty vehicles were parked haphazardly along the uneven edges and scraps of trash littered the ground, caught in the sporadic gusts of wind that swept through the lane, stirring up small whirls of dust. The footpath between compound walls on the right was barely visible against the monochromatic backdrop, and by the time he spotted it, Cancer was shouting.

"Stop, stop, *now!*"

Tahir slammed on the brakes, forcing Cancer to brace himself with a hand on the dashboard. The van stopped and began to lurch back on its frame as he flung the passenger door open and leapt onto a section of hard-packed sand below, hearing the rear cargo doors slam shut in unison with his own before he took off at a run toward the footpath.

The van was on its way forward a moment later, tires rumbling as

Cancer closed the distance with a three-meter gap between compound perimeters. As soon as he cleared the edge, he flung himself against the south wall, making way for his remaining three teammates to spill into the narrow channel. Reilly was the first to arrive, followed by Ian, and finally Worthy, the last man crouching behind Cancer as he knelt and drew his Glock 19.

A pistol was of little assurance given what was about to go down. They each had four spare magazines on their pistol belts, four more on their plate carriers, and still more in their backpacks. All that sounded like a lot until he considered the fact that each of those munitions was a 9mm handgun bullet, while their opponents likely had 7.62mm assault rifles and all the thirty-round magazines in the world.

He heard the van come to a halt down the street as Tahir followed his instructions to the letter, followed by the Hyundai completing the turn and accelerating toward them. No instruction was needed for his teammates— once the enemy vehicle had passed their position and stopped, and the slamming of doors indicated its fighters had stepped out, Worthy would take point while the other Americans fanned out behind him. Instinct and reaction would take over at that point, with the team using parked cars as cover to slay everyone besides Tahir and searching the Hyundai before loading up in the van and making their escape.

But something else happened instead.

The enemy SUV didn't pass by at all, instead making a high-pitched squeal as it stopped short of the alley. Cancer faced a moment of disbelief as he breathed in the earthy aroma of mud walls punctuated by the subtle stench of accumulated trash, and he listened intently to hear the Hyundai's doors opening and closing.

And that was his plan fucked, he thought. The van's sudden stop must have kicked up a cloud of dust that the enemy had identified easily enough, and rather than remaining focused on the now-obvious diversion of the van itself, they were wisely countering its recently vacated occupants.

Sneaking up on the enemies' six was now out of the question because their fighters were about to close with his current position. If all four Americans ran down the footpath back to the main road, they'd be shot in the back. But if all four stayed where they were, they'd be on the losing end of a close-range gunfight while the enemy driver could simply reverse his Hyundai out of position, escape the jammer bubble, and make a phone call that would lead to everyone's death, including Tahir's.

Cancer's only solution was to split his forces, with two men running down the alley to circle the enemy's rear and two men remaining in position to cover their retreat.

"Ian," he whispered over his shoulder, "you're with me. Worthy, Doc, head up the path and link up with the main road. Haul ass back to the side street and come at them from behind."

The only acknowledgement he received was when the latter men rose and broke into a run, leaving Cancer and the intelligence operative to feverishly look about to find covered fighting positions for the battle ahead.

At first glance, there was only one in the form of a weathered, overturned wooden cart atop a pile of straw and broken pottery. He nodded toward it, causing Ian to relocate. Cancer was about to follow when he identified an indentation in the mud wall behind him, a natural alcove just deep enough to wedge his body into. At this point he was more concerned about mutually supporting fields of fire than he was with his own cover and concealment, and he darted into the space before taking aim back toward the street. Ian and his cart were just behind him and to the right, providing a fallback position, and that was all the preparation they had time for when the first Baloch separatist appeared.

He stopped at the corner of the compound wall and took aim with an AK-47, his clothes a patchwork of local fabric and military surplus. His *shalwar kameez* was brown, and worn beneath a rudimentary tactical vest laden with pockets and ammunition. Worthy's and Reilly's footfalls were still receding down the alley to Cancer's rear, leaving them totally exposed to the newly arrived enemy fighter.

Cancer fired three rounds in unison with Ian, the opening salvo splitting the quiet of the village and echoing in the narrow corridor.

The first bullets hit the fighter's torso, puncturing the worn fabric of his tactical vest and breaching the flesh beneath. He staggered forward against the rough mud wall, his expression a mix of shock and pain, as more rounds followed, each one sending a jolt through his body until he slid downward. His weapon clattered to the dusty ground, a prize that

Cancer desperately wanted to recover in order to tilt the odds in his team's favor.

But that was where any element of surprise, along with their luck, ended.

The dead man was replaced almost immediately by another fighter, this one blasting an automatic weapon at them before they had time to shoot. Cancer pressed his body further into the alcove, suddenly aware of how shallow it truly was, as bullets snapped and hissed through the air and embedded themselves in the wooden cart. He caught a glimpse of a third man flitting across the space ahead, surely taking up a position at the far wall from which he'd very nearly have Cancer dead to rights.

A break in the automatic gunfire revealed the sound of the van engine revving and receding into the distance, which served as the first indication that Tahir had lost his nerve and fled in their million-dollar surveillance vehicle. With the electronic jammer on, there would be no way to call and coax him to return for a pickup—stealing the enemy vehicle was now their only way out, and would require them to kill everyone first.

The day just kept getting better and better.

Cancer fired two rounds at the first sight of the newly relocated enemy shooter, apparently missing with both as a roar of shots came his way, stitching along the mud wall and eroding a sizable chunk of the already scant cover to his front. Ian was slinging rounds with the man on the opposite side, the roar of gunfire deafening until it lapsed altogether.

Visually clearing the space ahead to confirm that both enemy fighters were absent and likely reloading, Cancer retreated to join his partner.

He rounded the back and shouldered Ian out of the way before taking aim off the left side, barely having time to do so before their two opponents were back in the fight, blasting away at the cart. Cancer only had time for three shots before being forced behind cover, the continued incoming fire assuring him that his trio of bullets had missed altogether. Pistols were little better than throwing rocks in a situation like this, leaving himself and Ian in sheer survival mode. A third rifle joined the fray as an unseen fighter filled the gap between his first two comrades, and all that remained was for them to begin their advance.

When that occurred, Cancer and his teammate would be able to drop one or at best two before succumbing to their own annihilation. He reloaded a fresh pistol mag in preparation for the inevitable, then shouted to Ian over the incoming fire.

"Reload, they're coming for us."

As his teammate complied with the order, Cancer found a particularly grim thought crossing his mind.

If Worthy and Reilly didn't complete their circuitous movement and round the corner onto the side street in the next ten seconds, he and Ian were done for.

Worthy sprinted down the road with his Glock in hand, his plate carrier worn tight and backpack straps cinched down as his long strides hammered against the sand and loose trash below. The temperatures of Pakistan in December peaked in the low seventies, but he was already sweating from his continued hasty movement.

He and Reilly had followed the footpath to its end to reach the main road that they traversed now, and were damn close to rounding the corner leading back onto the side street where the enemy vehicle had stopped. Worthy was immeasurably grateful that he'd selected their dismount position for exactly that possibility, allowing them an alternate avenue to flank the separatist fighters from behind.

But nowhere in his hasty planning had he considered that two of his teammates would remain pinned in the alley during this maneuver, and judging by the volume of automatic fire echoing through the village, that unexpected detail may well be their undoing.

The intersection with the side street lay a few meters ahead, and Worthy's priorities were clear enough. A right turn would be followed by immediately gunning down any visible enemy at the entrance to the footpath, an engagement in which every fraction of time and accuracy could be the difference between saving Ian and/or Cancer, or condemning one or both men to a violent death in the wilds of Pakistan.

Reilly scarcely entered into the equation, at least for the time being.

Judging by the medic's steadfast prioritization of raw strength over cardio, Worthy was easily outpacing him toward the objective area. Besides, he thought, his own abilities with a pistol were far beyond not only Reilly but the entire team. Worthy's experience as a competitive shooter had seen to that, and racing sprints between points of cover while accurately engaging targets was as second nature to him as breathing.

In shooting competitions, however, the targets didn't have assault rifles, and they most certainly didn't shoot back.

Worthy slowed his footfalls just enough to come to a stop at the corner of the mud wall, where he pivoted right and ignored the entirety of the side street to direct a laser focus at the outlet of the footpath. He identified a pair of fighters at first glance, leveling his Glock at the closer of the two and firing a trio of shots.

Only one of the rounds found its mark, striking the man in the shoulder and sending him scrambling behind a pickup before Worthy could finish the job. He loosed a trio of bullets at the next man, who was only just then becoming aware of his partner's fate—all three shots missed, one of them sparking a puff of dirt off the mud wall mere inches from the fighter's sternum before he, too, dove behind the parked truck and vanished from sight.

Worthy was on the move in a flash, speeding forward to the rear bumper of a Suzuki sedan to his front. It wasn't much of a forward bound, three meters at most, but every scrap of ground mattered now. He reached his covered position and leaned past a rear quarter panel pitted with flecks of rust, trying to confirm whether any of the opposing shooters were approaching the footpath and finding instead only the exposed legs of a man who must have been downed by Cancer and Ian.

He reloaded while shifting to the opposite side of the vehicle, then took aim down the street. Out of the corner of his eye, he caught a flash of movement. Reilly was circling behind him, heading toward a parked car on the opposite side of the road. The gunfire had momentarily ceased, and he knew Worthy was covering his movement.

The Hyundai Tucson sat stationary near the center of the main road, representing another potential hiding spot for enemy fighters that Worthy assessed and discounted out of the sheer urgency of two confirmed and currently unseen shooters who were reacting to the new threat. There may well have been one or maybe two more that he simply hadn't spotted yet, and it was only then that Worthy noticed his team's surveillance van was gone. Unfortunately, that detail meant it was probably speeding back toward Larkana with Tahir panicking behind the wheel.

He filed that piece of information away with no further thought beyond the Hyundai representing their fastest means out of the area, provided the engine block didn't get shot out in the imminent crossfire.

And provided, of course, that his team could locate the keys before any separatists within earshot of the firefight-in-progress arrived on the scene.

Worthy slipped down the driver's side of the sedan, utilizing its angle relative to the enemy ahead to obtain an oblique line of sight over the hood.

The front and rear sights of his Glock aligned without effort, the pistol bucking twice in his hand almost before he consciously identified the partially exposed torso of an opponent leaning beyond the edge of the pickup ahead.

Both rounds punctured the truck's side, leaving Worthy with exactly one pistol hit out of eight rounds fired. If he was faring so poorly, he thought, then the rest of his team was having a *really* hard time.

He ducked out of sight and glanced at the Hyundai SUV to his front left, intending to relocate there only to find that Reilly had beaten him to the punch. Now their situation was even more dire than it had been—they were matched if not outnumbered by the remaining enemy, of which only one was wounded and all of whom possessed far superior weapons due to, out of all things, the sheer fuckery of diplomatic restrictions. They nonetheless had to close with and eliminate the fighters without the benefit of support from Cancer and Ian, who may well be dead by now, before having the slightest option of escape.

Worthy considered reloading, decided against it, and committed to pitting his skills and training against the separatist fighters in the span of one second.

Darting forward to the pickup, Worthy slid to a stop behind the rear bumper.

He dropped to both knees, planting his free hand on the dirt and lowering himself to the ground until he was in the prone, one leg cocked, cheek resting against his right bicep with his pistol aimed beneath the truck's undercarriage.

The first shots were near instant, unscripted, his sideways view lined up with the Glock's sights as he fired at the visible fraction of a man's leg. One bullet found its mark—not much of an achievement given the close range —and the sudden fracturing of a tibia caused the target to collapse on the ground to receive another three rounds that, without question, killed him.

Worthy was transitioning to a second set of legs before the man scampered out of view, revealing the boots of a third, more distant fighter who likewise vanished in the opposite direction.

Pushing his way out of the prone and to his knees, Worthy prepared for his next move—climbing into the pickup bed and engaging in a life-or-death elevated shooting match to finish the fight.

But that plan evaporated as automatic fire blasted through the truck's windows, an undoubted precursor to enemy shooters rounding the vehicle, probably from both sides simultaneously, to take him out for good.

Worthy stayed low and moved back to the Suzuki, darting behind the rear bumper and reloading. His audacious advance had served to remove one opponent from the fight but nothing more, and now he and Reilly were back to square one.

Reilly took aim over the Hyundai's hood, using the engine block as cover as he drilled bullets toward the front of the pickup in an attempt to cover Worthy's retreat. The pointman's suicidal charge and firing from the rollover prone had succeeded in putting down one of their opponents, which was more than Reilly could say for himself; although he'd sent rounds downrange at every fleeting sight of an enemy fighter, not one had yet scored a hit.

A separatist shooter abruptly fell backward beside the pickup, landing in a writhing crawl that ended with three additional shots from the direction of the footpath. Cancer or Ian or both had achieved the kill, the first indication that either of the men was still alive, and any sense of relief that knowledge afforded was eclipsed by what Reilly saw next.

He pivoted left in reaction to a fighter who appeared out of nowhere, now standing in the road and taking aim at Reilly with an AK-47 whose buttstock was already seated securely against his shoulder. The first shots would come within a fraction of a second, and by the time the medic dove behind cover, it would be too late.

But the instant this realization crossed his mind, a blur of white came screaming down the road, the surveillance van a chariot of fury that struck the man's backside before Reilly had time to blink.

The effect of a 5,000-pound vehicle moving at highway speeds impacting a human body was astonishing.

Reilly watched with muted alarm as the man's body was launched at an angle toward him, sailing airborne with incredible speed. He'd lost control of his rifle somewhere in the process, the AK-47 twirling in wild cartwheels while its owner completed a stuntman arc over the street—there were no flailing limbs, the man having been turned into a quadriplegic the moment his entire spine was shattered.

He hadn't lost control of his voice, however, making a groaning wail that rose in volume as he approached Reilly. For a moment the medic thought the separatist fighter would still finish the job and kill him, not by rifle fire but by knocking him down like a bowling pin and breaking his neck in the process. He launched into a sideways run with the thought that this entire scene was like something out of a cartoon, the spectacle expanding in time until the man's body blasted into a mud wall to Reilly's left, striking with head, chest, and pelvis in that order at a spot two meters off the ground.

That served to end the protracted moaning noise, turning the fighter into a mass of flesh and splintered bone that ricocheted off the wall and landed in a dusty heap as the van swerved around the Hyundai SUV and screeched to a halt to his right.

Spinning in place, Reilly popped two rounds into the mangled corpse to achieve his first pistol hits of the day. He looked up at a door swinging open in a compound wall only to see three huddled children peering toward him with great curiosity. Lowering his Glock, he offered a friendly wave.

The door swung shut.

By then his teammates were spilling into the road, stripping rifles and magazines off fallen enemy amid scattered pistol shots to ensure all of them were indeed dead.

Reilly approached the former human pinball before him, intending to take his ammunition and instead finding that both magazines strapped to his front had been visibly warped in a losing battle with the mud wall.

He moved to the rear of the van instead, flinging open the cargo doors to allow his teammates to enter. They leapt inside cradling the captured assault rifles, Ian followed closely by Worthy and, finally, Cancer, who breezed past while providing his own personal take on the grisly death of their final adversary.

"Fuckin' airborne demolition derby," the sniper said as he climbed aboard, leaving Reilly to follow suit and slam the doors shut as the van accelerated forward.

Cancer ordered, "Take us straight back to the highway, then north to Larkana."

"And the mission?" Tahir asked from the driver's seat.

"Van's burned," Cancer replied. "The mission's scrapped. We're heading back to Islamabad."

Reilly offered, "Thanks for coming back."

Tahir was incensed at the slight against his honor.

"I never left," he thundered. "Did you expect me to run men over using mirrors? I had to turn around."

"Just the same, thanks."

Reilly didn't mention that the van's speedy return had saved him from imminent death. After all, he didn't want Tahir getting cocky.

Worthy nearly shouted at Tahir, "That would have been a hell of a lot easier if we had rifles."

"We do now," Cancer noted, handing out the AK-47s and magazines they'd lifted off the dead fighters.

Accepting one of the weapons and stuffing two mags into his pockets, Reilly found himself floored at Tahir's unapologetic response.

"You have your orders," the ISI officer shot back, "and I have mine. One of them is the same—you do not use rifles. If you violate that order, I *will* report it and my government *will* eject you from Pakistan."

Following the rules was one thing, Reilly thought, a compliance his team had never been particularly skilled in, but Tahir's inflexibility in the wake of what had just happened was nothing short of staggering. The medic wondered if he'd be such a stickler right now if it had been him fighting for his life in the streets instead of his American charges.

Worthy almost laughed.

"Tell you what," he said, replacing the magazine in his AK-47 and pulling back the bolt to ensure a round was chambered, "if we get compromised again, how about you show us just how easy it is to shoot with a pistol while we wait in the van?"

Tahir said nothing, leaving Reilly to direct his thoughts toward bigger issues.

Now that adrenaline was fading, he grew increasingly crestfallen that after all the mission preparations for intelligence gathering, to include his being increasingly confused by Ian's attempts to explain the surveillance equipment's operation, all had come to naught shortly after their arrival to Qasbo.

He asked no one in particular, "So, that's it? Like, we're mission complete? Time to go home?"

"Maybe," Ian acknowledged, "but not necessarily. Let's see if the Agency can drum up anything that will help us."

It was then that Reilly noticed the intelligence operative giving him a surreptitious thumbs up, with considerable intensity in his gaze. Had the slippery little bastard actually intercepted something of value in the moments before their compromise?

Reilly nodded enthusiastically. "Right," he concluded, then swept his gaze across the cargo area with mounting concern.

"Hey," he protested, now maneuvering between his teammates to search the floor, "what happened to our dates?"

2

CIA Headquarters
Special Activities Center, Operations Center F2

"There's no reason for Raza to be in Barakahu," Wes Jamieson declared, speaking loudly enough for his voice to echo in the operations center.

"And yet," Andolin Lucios calmly pointed out, "that's exactly what the call indicated."

"Maybe they suspected surveillance, or someone in the ISI tipped them off. They could have simply been trying to pull our team away from the mountains, possibly for Raza to relocate."

Chen watched the dialogue play out with both amusement and interest, leaning back in her chair at the highest seating tier of the cavernous office area. Everyone else in the OPCEN followed her lead in remaining silent, many of them shifting at their desks to watch the ongoing confrontation. This wasn't the first such debate between the two men, and was very unlikely to be the last.

They were perhaps the two most central figures in the Project Longwing operations center, Jamieson as the operations officer and Lucios heading up the intelligence desk. The opinions of her other staff primaries came into sharp focus at key times when communications, aerial infiltration or exfiltration, or, God forbid, legal considerations were at the forefront of her planning and considerations.

Working under the purview of her primaries were groups of analysts and specialists in their respective fields, all of them doing the legwork required to keep the ground team's operations running smoothly, or at least as smoothly as a heavily compartmentalized targeted killing program could manage.

Lucios re-entered the verbal fray, first acknowledging and then deflecting Jamieson's latest theory.

"We can't rule out an ISI leak, but we've got to follow the intelligence. Especially when we've got no other option."

"The other option," Jamieson pointed out, "is to restage the team at an alternate location outside the Kirthar Mountains. Maybe they get something and maybe they don't, but I'm reluctant to bet the farm on a single audio grab."

Chen silenced them both by asking, "Jamieson, are you playing devil's advocate, or do you genuinely believe the call was deliberate counterintelligence?"

The operations officer turned to face her, his face resolute and unyielding. A background in the Marine infantry would do that to a man, she thought, and if not that, then his prior service as a paramilitary officer in Ground Branch would.

"Either/or," he replied. "But we have to acknowledge the fact that if we pull out of Sindh Province now, the ISI's not going to let them return. Our decision now will determine if we get closer to Raza or lose him again, so we damn well better—"

A new voice came over the speakerbox then, gravelly from the satellite communication from the other side of the world.

"*Raptor Nine One, this is Cancer.*"

Chen lifted her hand mic.

"Cancer, Raptor Nine One. Mayfly here. Send your traffic."

"*Be advised,*" he continued, "*we were compromised by Baloch separatists at our initial surveillance site. One engagement, four EKIA, we're all fine. Current location is Larkana en route back to Islamabad. Did you receive our audio grab?*"

"We did."

"Yeah, well, I hope it justified the price of the van. Because that's all the intel we'll be able to provide anytime soon."

She took a moment to process both declarations. If the team had a skirmish with an insurgent force resulting in four enemy killed in action, they were lucky enough to be alive. And that at least somewhat tempered the fact that their first surveillance foray had ended nearly as soon as it began.

"Is the ISI tracking this information?" she asked warily.

"Of course not. We're keeping it close hold, and when there's something for us to act on, it needs to come through your channels so we have some plausible deniability with Tahir."

Not just a smart play, she decided, but the only one.

"What did Angel have to say about the grab?"

The response would determine whether or not her staff was on the right track about what the captured information did—or did not—represent. While her OPCEN had the final say, the team had their own intelligence operative in the form of Ian Greenberg, and his interpretation of the raw data was usually just as good as the staff at CIA Headquarters.

Cancer hesitated a moment before responding, *"It's either a really good red herring, or something big is about to go down."*

Nodding, Chen transmitted, "That's about where we're at, too. Stand by."

She lowered the hand mic, letting her gaze drift across the front wall of the OPCEN and the many digital screens it contained.

One of them showed an official portrait photo of Kamran Raza, the fifty-four-year-old Pakistani man her team was now tasked with finding.

Raza was clean-shaven, cheeks full and hinting at a bit of extra weight that softened the edges of his otherwise strong jawline. Dark and reflective eyes held a calm, assessing gaze, projecting an air of quiet strength and thoughtful poise.

More notable was his uniform, a khaki dress coat laden with medals and crossed by a green and white sash. A stiff collar displayed bright red patches adorned with insignia, the epaulets hosting a trio of badges. The image of lifelong military service was completed by a peaked cap, black visor marked by gold embroidery, front displaying the emblem of the

Pakistani Army, national crest of crescent and star surrounded by laurel leaves.

Below the photograph was his last rank and job title.

Major General, Deputy Director-General SPDF.

The Strategic Plans Division Force was tasked with safeguarding and protecting Pakistan's extensive nuclear materials, and Raza's placement there was responsible for the CIA-assembled portion of the dossier data filling the rest of the screen. Of particular note was his implication in selling uranium enrichment technology to North Korea, along with the codenames of CIA dissemination operations to distribute that information on the global stage after the Pakistani government refused to act, and the date of the subsequent disappearance that elevated Raza to Target Number Four in Project Longwing's target matrix.

Chen scanned the history of his exile that included intelligence reports confirming he was still in Pakistan, and then narrowed his location down to Balochistan Province. Then tantalizing leads that he was somewhere in the Urak Valley with increasing fidelity, right up until the moment he disappeared once more—coinciding, as was the case with nearly every Project Longwing target, with the targeted killing of an international terrorist figurehead in Yemen.

Thus far only Raza had reappeared, or at least probably so, three weeks earlier.

Multiple reports placed him in the Kirthar Mountains of Sindh Province, two of which were from highly credible sources. The location was consistent with the same factors that he'd relied on for protection in the Urak Valley, namely tribal affiliations, geographic inaccessibility, and an utter lack of control by the Pakistani government writ large.

Why would he depart such a stronghold for the outskirts of the national capital where he had once served? And what of the command site? What exactly was there for him to command?

Those final two lines of inquiry, she realized, held the key to her decision.

She announced to the OPCEN, "If the audio grab is a deception ploy, it means Raza is either still in the mountains or relocating to remain in hiding. We may find him again, we may not."

After a beat of silence, she continued, "If it's genuine, however, we're looking at something else altogether. The ISI has his wife and children in a safehouse in the hopes that he'll attempt communication and reveal his location. Since that hasn't happened by now, it never will. If Raza had any chance of restoring his legitimacy, I could see him making that play, but he knows he'll never see his family again. That means if he's taking on command duties, it's for revenge or profit. Either or both of those point to the same thing, which is that Barakahu represents the leading edge of a major terrorist operation. What that operation could possibly be, I have no idea, but that's our greatest threat, and that's what we're going to keep our team focused on."

No objections from her staff, not even Jamieson.

She went on, "For now, we take the intel at face value. I want us to gather everything we can on the messenger and recipient of that call—who they are, where they are, full tracking on the movements of the recipient's cell phone and any other communications devices that are co-located at any point in time. The hotel, what was it?"

"Indigo Heights," Lucios supplied.

"Right," Chen said. "Find out everything we can about who's been staying there and for how long, what dates they arrived and departed. If they're using it as a gateway to funnel the call recipient toward Raza, then it may not be the first time. Set up a full exploitation of the hotel, digital, cell, security cameras, everything we can.

"Next is Barakahu and the surrounding area. Scrub it for data to the best of our abilities. If there's a command site, there will be an uptick in FM, cellular, and/or satellite communications. So we start with aberrations in electrical usage and go from there. Unless I'm missing anything."

"Done," Lucios noted. "And we'll give it our best, but anything we can remotely accomplish for Barakahu will pale in comparison to what the team can glean with the SIGINT equipment in their van. I advise they canvass the town to pick up any abnormalities as a backstop to whatever we find, and between us and them we've got a chance of dialing in on a key location."

Jamieson added, with a tone of foreboding, "If there is one at all."

"Okay," Chen concluded. "If Barakahu turns out to be a ruse, it'll have been a damn good one and I take full responsibility. Given the alternative, I hope I'm wrong. But from this point on, we're all-in."

Raising the hand mic to her lips, she transmitted, "Cancer, this is Mayfly."

"*Go ahead.*"

"Inform your ISI minder that we've got nothing to go on at this time. Move back to Islamabad as planned, but don't get comfortable—you're going to receive orders for roving mobile surveillance in Barakahu. Your goal and ours is to locate any and all possible command sites. We'll send you a cover story, and anything that either of us finds will be kept out of the hands of the ISI until we've got a definite fix on Raza. If that occurs, we'll notify the Paks at the last possible second to mitigate the risk of leaks before they conduct the raid. Zarrar Company is on standby for time-sensitive targets, and it won't take them long to get there."

"*Music to my ears,*" Cancer responded, which should have been the end of it.

But instead, he concluded the exchange with a final question.

"*Any word on when Suicide Actual will be out here?*"

3

University Hospital
Charlottesville, Virginia

I crouched between my wife's legs, hearing her ragged and frantic breaths, panting, groaning, through the chaos around me.

My first glimpse of my son came in the form of a tiny skullcap slicked in blood.

"Crowning," someone announced.

A woman beside me spoke calmly. "I'm going to work the baby's shoulders out, and then it's all you."

"Okay," I managed, making room for her to reach past me in preparation for the inevitable.

I had, of course, asked to catch the baby.

Nothing after that point had made me second-guess the request—the onset and continuation of labor was exhilarating, save the grief-stricken concern over my wife's anguished cries of what sounded like unspeakably grueling pain.

And while I was already a father, this was my first experience with childbirth by a long shot. Having adopted my daughter, every step of this journey—from Laila telling me she was pregnant, to her increasing physical discomfort over the following months, to rushing her to the hospital when she went into labor—was a first-time experience for me.

Laila unleashed a guttural yell at the nurse's next order to push, and I watched the OB/GYN beside me guide the tiny head that appeared out of the birth canal, then begin maneuvering his shoulders to either side like she was rocking a grapefruit in her hands. I'd been in my fair share of wild and rowdy situations in combat, traveled the world, and endured horrific violence on both the giving and receiving end.

But this—*this*, right here, right now—was unquestionably, without the slightest doubt, the craziest shit I'd ever seen.

"Dad, go ahead," the doctor said, moving out of my way.

I reached forward with both hands, accepting the newborn infant as the rest of his body appeared, so greasy slick against my neoprene gloves that I was afraid for a moment I'd drop him.

Instead I lifted him toward me, inexplicably transfixed by his cries. The open-mouthed squalls, delivered between the trembling lips of a newborn, were heartbreaking and exquisitely beautiful at the same time. Never before had I felt such an urge to comfort a fellow human being.

At some point in those first seconds with my son, somewhere between seeing my own face in his wrinkled features and hearing him shrieking to the full extent of his tiny lungs, my entire world shifted on its axis.

A primordial impulse came over me then, some powerful surge of hormones that bonded me with this child for life. It wasn't the peaceful glow that I'd often heard described, but rather a swell of every emotion I'd ever felt underscored by raw, primitive aggression—I would kill, fuck, fight *anything* in the world to protect this infant, a tiny human who instantly assumed the same elevated status as my daughter by the simple fact that he now existed in the world.

I held the baby, one hand cradled behind his head and the other cupping his slick buttocks, mind wild with a madman's glee. This was the biggest event in the history of the world, I was certain of it, and I barely registered the nurses clamping his umbilical cord in two places.

They took the baby from me and someone handed me a pair of medical shears, the same thing I'd used to slice the blood-soaked clothes off fallen men to expose their gunshot wounds. While I was more than familiar with the shears, I'd never used them to slice through anything but fabric and gauze—cutting my son's umbilical cord felt like working the blades through a piece of chicken, but there was nonetheless a sense of freeing him from the womb entirely.

When I received my son again, I swiftly moved along the side of the birthing bed, eager to deliver him to his mother's arms.

Laila was on the last reserves of her strength, both pale with exertion and immeasurably composed at the same time. I laughed hysterically as I set the infant atop her chest, letting her cradle him, sensing that she was infinitely more deserving of this honor than I was.

Repositioning myself beside her, I kissed my wife on the forehead and saw that a deep calm had fallen over her. She was still breathing heavily but her face and her smile were serene, perfectly natural, as she gazed at our son, whose cheek was resting on her breast. He'd stopped crying at the very sight of his mother, and weighed against the connection between them at that moment, I almost felt like an impostor—but the thought vanished amid the emotions that surged through me now that the three of us were united in a way we never had been before.

Every infusion of adrenaline I'd ever had, every BASE jump, every gunfight, totaled nothing more than a minor sugar rush compared to the overwhelming love and euphoria I felt at this moment.

My wife looked immeasurably at peace as she watched our son and he watched her.

From my slightly elevated vantage point, however, this was all just the calm in the center of a churning maelstrom—nurses moving with practiced efficiency, conducting procedures whose purpose I couldn't begin to fathom, one of them holding a comically large biohazard bag that continued to fill with what appeared to be blood and mucus in mind-bending quantities.

The sheer intensity of all this was so powerful that I couldn't begin to grasp that it was a universal human experience, something that continually occurred all over the world since the dawn of man. It felt like I was stepping into some ascended realm of understanding known only to those who'd had a child—most of adult humanity, I realized, although it still felt like Laila had just accomplished something sacred, unique.

"I can't believe this," I said, delirious with joy. "You did it."

"*We* did it," Laila corrected me. "I love you."

"I love you too," I replied, laying my head against hers, and together we watched our son squinting back at us.

My son slept fitfully in my arms, occasionally writhing within his swaddle, head clad in a light blue newborn beanie that the hospital staff provided. My chair wasn't the most comfortable, but it nonetheless allowed me to alternate between watching the baby in my lap and my wife sleeping in the bed of our dimly lit maternity room.

Or maternity suite, I corrected myself.

Laila worked in the hospital as a pediatrician, which garnered her VIP status the moment we'd left the delivery room. A steady stream of her colleagues had entered to meet the baby and deliver flowers, and as a result the suite looked and smelled like a rose garden. Every flat surface was crowded with vases supporting bouquets, and as a gift from the hospital administrator, a bottle of sparkling grape cider and two plastic champagne glasses.

My wife's parents had also stopped by during visiting hours, bringing with them our daughter, Langley, who couldn't have been more thrilled at the arrival of her baby brother. Between that and the medical checkups for Jackson and his mother, the entire day had been one endless turmoil of activity that left me with precious little peace and quiet to bond with my son. And for someone who'd never held a newborn, I had adapted remarkably well to this latest transition.

A few hours earlier I'd dutifully performed my first-ever diaper change, but by now I felt like I'd been caring for this child my entire life. Cradling him as he slept felt like second nature, and I couldn't hold him enough—neither could my wife, apparently, which relegated most of the one-on-one time I'd had with my son so far to the hours that Laila was sleeping.

I glanced at the dry erase board next to the door, examining the handwritten block letters there.

2:14pm. 20 inches. 7 pounds, 5 ounces.

Above the birth data were the words, *JACKSON DAVID RIVERS*.

After much deliberation, we'd decided to name him after my late BASE jumping mentor, a man who'd guided my progression from the windswept antennas along the Hudson to the rooftops of apartment buildings in the Bronx. Without him I'd have bounced at the foot of some tall object or another long ago, and while Laila didn't much care to hear about such details, both she and Langley liked the name.

More contentious was the selection of his middle name. I didn't want my son to share any of my attributes, to include the word David, but my wife had been adamant, and like any good husband, I consented to her will.

I watched my son closely, his face still mashed into a scrunchy bundle of flesh from his protracted stay in the womb. Earlier that evening I'd caught him smiling, a fleeting expression that had come and gone among many others during his first day on Earth. But the sight remained with me, punctuating my sprawling thoughts about his future and who he'd turn out to be, what passions he'd follow, and whether his mother's genetic contributions would be sufficient to outweigh my own, particularly the dark side I'd become all too acquainted with over the years.

The work phone in my pocket buzzed to life, and I carefully removed it to see *UNLISTED*, removing all doubt as to the caller.

I resolved not to answer the phone, then remembered that my team was out in the boonies right now. Their fate concerned me more than anything else my supervisor had to say.

Checking to make sure that Laila was indeed asleep, I accepted the call and brought the phone to my ear.

"Yes," I said quietly.

"Congratulations," Meiling Chen cheerfully replied. "How is your son?"

"In my arms," I said, "healthy as can be."

Then, unable to stop myself, I continued, "The doctors were concerned about his abnormally large cock, but I told them it's just good genes."

She responded humorlessly, "I'm sure that's exactly how it went down. How's your wife doing?"

I couldn't keep the pride out of my voice. "She was a champ the entire time. Finally sleeping."

"I'm glad to hear that."

"What's the status of my guys?"

"One dustup," she said dismissively, clearly accustomed to the implications of that word from overseeing radio updates from the OPCEN, "but everyone's fine. Have a good thread they're following up on, though I suspect it's going to take them quite some time to do so. We're still not sure if it will lead anywhere."

"Good. What about me?"

She was silent for a moment. "Enjoy the time with your family, David. You and your men aren't the main effort on this one."

Ah, yes, I thought, trying to imagine how Cancer was dealing with being in a supporting role with only a pistol to his name. Such a fate was unbecoming for a paramilitary team well accustomed to targeted killing operations, and I knew that when we were together again, I'd be able to gleefully fuck with him to no end on that point.

"So no hard time for my flight?" I asked.

"None at all. There's no rush to get you out there, if you want to go at all."

We said our goodbyes and I ended the call, mulling over her parting words.

With less than five months remaining on a CIA contract I'd never renew, Pakistan could well be the last mission I ever went on.

And while I no longer felt the unceasing drive to fling myself at death like I had for much of my youth, the fact that my guys were out there was another matter altogether. Leaving them to go on alone felt like nothing short of abandonment, a sensation that simply hadn't been on the docket at any other time since we'd been assembled.

Could I live with myself if I didn't join my men? Maybe, I thought, so long as all of them emerged unscathed.

But it would be another matter altogether if anyone got killed. In that event, I'd never be the same, never be able to relieve myself of the guilt no matter how much the rest of my team assured me there was nothing I could have done. The ripple effects of every decision in combat made any certainty in that regard nothing short of impossible to accept.

I looked at my son, who'd finally lapsed into a deep and motionless sleep.

Things were so much easier when I was a young, single mercenary. There were no considerations of family back then, no inhibitions that would prevent me from chasing the dragon of armed conflict all the way to the bitter end.

That had all changed, of course, and now I had my wife and kid—two kids, as of ten hours ago—to factor in. Laila was certainly supportive enough, if only because she knew my days as a gunslinger were dwindling. My team would never fault me for staying home, but I nonetheless found myself torn between my family, myself, and my job.

I set my phone on the table beside me, edging a vase of flowers out of the way.

Then I glanced from my son to my wife and back again. Both were sleeping peacefully now, both just as unaware of whatever may have been unfolding in Pakistan as I currently was. Neither they nor my daughter had any idea of what war entailed, and hopefully my children never would. Langley had already been the recipient of my repeated urging that she consider any and all careers that appealed to her, save those within the armed forces.

I'd have to avoid speaking of combat to both her and Jackson, I knew, for fear that anything I said could be construed as the same glamorization that made its way into so many movies and recruiting posters, game-day flyovers by fighter jets, and public praise of servicemembers. That entire ruse of turning trauma into glory kept the military industrial complex churning with fresh recruits that would, if they ever made it to war, later find themselves bewildered in a world of civilians they'd never be able to relate to again.

And yet the siren song was there, and very real, for those who wanted nothing more than to test themselves as a warrior. If either of my kids ever wanted to enlist, I'd have to do my damned best to talk them out of it with the full knowledge that nothing I said would ultimately matter in the least.

Then there was me.

I knew the score well enough by now on all of the above. War and its aftermath, the agony and the ecstasy, the thrill of battle followed by the long nights spent ruminating over whether or not I deserved to live after what I'd done. Perhaps worst of all, the crushing weight of processing oxygen into carbon dioxide after far better men had fallen in the unflinching injustice that was, always had been, and always would be combat.

Glancing around the maternity suite as if it held some answer for me, I was left instead with my own tumultuous thoughts. Laila was sleeping, Jackson was sleeping, and I didn't know when or if I would that night. My thoughts were eating me alive, mind dancing with conflicting possibilities, none of which seemed correct in the least.

I stared at my son's face, then the ceiling, and whispered one word to myself.

"Fuck."

4

"David will be here in five minutes," Reilly announced from the kitchen door. "Worthy just texted."

Cancer, seated at the dining room table, set down his vegetable samosa to check his watch. Quarter to five, which left them roughly ninety minutes to wait out rush hour before embarking on their next driving jaunt through Barakahu and the surrounding area in search of notable aberrations in communications activity. They'd been rotating sectors for a week now, three shifts a day with two team members in the van, and were no further in their search for Raza than they had been since the shootout in Qasbo.

"Make him a sandwich," Cancer decreed, picking up his samosa as Reilly vanished inside the kitchen.

And he was about to take his next bite when Tahir's voice boomed behind him.

"The fifth musketeer," the ISI officer shrewdly noted. "That will turn things around. Just what we need, one more American."

Cancer put his food down and looked up to see Tahir rounding the table, selecting a seat, and lowering his considerable frame into it before plucking an untouched samosa from the plate.

"What can I say," Cancer declared. "Five is better than four when you're putting your life on the line to clean up another country's mess."

Tahir bit off half his samosa, speaking as he chewed.

"But such a worthwhile risk, considering the landslide of vital information pouring into your precious van. What did we get from your one and only audio grab? A transaction of goats at the bazaar in Gorakh Hill, was it? Praise Allah that the humble ISI has access to such key intelligence. Where would we be without America?"

What Cancer should have said was nothing. He knew by now that he and Tahir were oil and vinegar, and could butt heads all day with no resolution to speak of. Here in Pakistan, much less Islamabad, they were indisputably on ISI turf.

Then there was the not insignificant matter of the safehouse, which trounced any the team had stayed in among their international forays.

Nestled discreetly among the bustling streets of an unassuming neighborhood, the home stood as an inconspicuous refuge, its outward appearance deliberately mundane to blend with the local architecture. Inside, however, the structure was robust, with reinforced doors and tinted windows ensuring privacy and security.

With five bedrooms, the safehouse was palatial in comparison to most others the team had occupied, and Cancer rightly feared that his team could just as quickly be exiled to some shanty on the city's outskirts. Tahir would gladly cite some administrative excuse or another, suffering alongside them out of sheer spite. Cancer had finally met his match in encountering someone who lived for conflict just as much as he did, and every shit-talking exchange between the two men—and by now there had been quite a few—nudged the team ever closer to a more uncomfortable fate.

Meeting Tahir's intense gaze, Cancer set his hands on the table.

Then he picked up his samosa, biting off a chunk and speaking with his mouth full as Tahir had. "With all of two minutes to make an audio grab before we got compromised, we're lucky to have that."

This elicited a mournful chuckle from Tahir.

"If we had staged farther from the mountains as I suggested, we would not have been compromised."

Cancer pointed out, "If we staged any further east than Qasbo, we wouldn't have been able to range the signals."

Their samosas now finished, both men reached for another one, their knuckles striking in the effort.

"Only because you are white," Tahir shot back, sweeping Cancer's hand out of the way to grab another samosa. "The ISI could have penetrated deeper into the mountains without being noticed."

This caused Cancer to smile, and he abandoned his attempt to procure more food.

"But would they have found anything?" he asked provocatively.

Tahir lowered the samosa from his mouth.

"Why would they not have? Your only advantage is technology, nothing else."

Cancer gave an ambivalent shrug. "Oh, I don't know...maybe because they couldn't find Bin Laden in Abbottabad, two hours from ISI headquarters."

"And what was he wanted for," Tahir responded, glancing at the ceiling as if trying to recall some distant memory. "Let me think...ah, yes, 9/11. One of the hijackers, Hani Hanjour, attended flight training at Freeway Airport in Maryland. Thirty minutes from CIA Headquarters."

"Big difference between one shitty flight student and the largest manhunt in the history of the world, but I take your point. Maybe both our countries are fucked."

Tahir bristled. "Speak for yourself. Pakistan was under British rule until 1947. Now we are a nuclear power—"

A new voice abruptly spoke from the entryway.

"Which made Kamran Raza millions before he was exposed. I wonder how much North Korea is benefiting from the information he sold."

Cancer smiled, rising from his seat and turning to see David Rivers setting his duffel bag down at the edge of the living room.

The two men shared a quick embrace, patting each other on the back before separating— and were then reunited as Reilly came out of nowhere and sandwiched both of them in a powerful bear hug.

"Welcome to Shangri-La," the medic cried as Cancer fought to push him aside. "We've got the whole band back together again. How's Jackson?"

David grinned and withdrew a glossy 4x6 photo from his shirt pocket, eagerly handing it over as Reilly examined it with the words, "Christ, he looks exactly like you. That's terrifying."

Cancer frowned. There was an unwritten team policy not to bring personal photos on mission for security purposes, and no one adhered to that more stringently than David himself. He took the proffered photograph from Reilly, thinking that if it showed a glowing family snapshot of Laila and the kids, he'd have to pull the team leader aside and make sure he hadn't lost his mind.

But the picture was only of a baby, a hideous pink thing that looked exactly like all other newborns.

"Cute, sort of," he managed, handing the photo back.

"You," Tahir said, pointing at David without getting up. "I immediately dislike you."

David strode into the dining room. "Well get used to it, because it'll probably only get worse from here."

"Judging by your shit teammates, I have no reason to suspect otherwise."

Stopping at the table, David said, "That settles expectation management for the time being."

Then, extending his hand, he said, "David."

"Tahir Qureshi, ISI."

They shook hands in an unflinching exchange that Cancer watched closely, wondering if the team leader's lack of diplomacy would make things better or worse. Probably the latter.

By then Reilly had retrieved a hoagie and offered it to David with the words, "Chicken tikka, fresh off the grill."

"Thanks," David replied, looking at Cancer. "Want to go somewhere and talk?"

The sniper shook his head. "This ain't my show. Head to the courtyard out back. Ian's on duty in the van. He'll get you up to speed better than I can."

And while that was the right call for a time-sensitive information dump, Cancer had another consideration in mind—he and Tahir had a debate to wage.

Ian heard the cargo doors to the van unlatch, and looked over to see David pulling them open.

"The prodigal son returns," Ian said, pulling his headphones off one ear to see his team leader enter with one of Reilly's sandwiches in hand, grinning broadly.

"How goes the surveillance?" he asked.

"Slowly," Ian said, leaning over in his chair to accept a half-hug. "You bring a picture?"

David dropped into one of the fold-down seats behind Ian's chair and the data console.

"You know I did."

Ian took the photograph, his eyes crinkling with pleasure at the sight.

"He's beautiful. Congratulations." Ian handed the picture back, followed by a heavy shopping bag. "Have some dates."

He used his boot to nudge a bucket filled with date pits toward the team leader.

"Chicken tikka, dates...you're going to send me back to Laila fat."

"Tell her it's sympathy weight," Ian said dismissively. "You've got a newborn. Time to start working on your dad bod."

David seemed to accept this logic, taking a bite of his sandwich and muttering, "Holy shit, this is good."

"Reilly's getting better. His tikka sucked for the first few days before he figured it out. Worthy filled you in on the way from the airport?"

"Yeah," David said, chewing. "Some guy from the Kirthar Mountains got summoned to a hotel outside Islamabad to wait for a ride to Raza."

Ian clarified, "Haris Shehzad. Some kind of logistician, as far as Chen can tell. He's staying at Indigo Heights in Barakahu, 17 kilometers from here."

"Worthy said the whole thing might be a ruse to pull us away from Raza."

"Could be. Shehzad has been stationary for six days running. Agency's tapped into his cell, hotel security, and traffic cameras, so if he moves, we'll know. If that happens, all we have to do is follow at a distance and track any phone vectors that Chen passes our way. Then run surveillance at his destination, see if Raza's there or not. If he is, Tahir calls in the assault force."

"The assault force of Pakistanis," David said, replacing his sandwich with a date, "so we basically sit on our hands until they clear the objective."

"You got it. Then we come inside to assist with site exploitation. If it's a command site like the audio grab indicated, there could be a lot for us to sift through. But that's about it. Not sure why you even bothered flying out here."

David spit a date pit into the bucket.

"Probably because I didn't think the mission would take long to wrap up. If there was a legitimate command site, you would have picked up on it during your surveillance runs. What's in these dates, crack cocaine?"

"Tahir says they're the best in Pakistan. And don't be so sure about the command site. Maybe it's beyond the sectors we've been screening. Or," he added, "maybe no one there is firing up their comms until some trigger is met."

"And the ISI is oblivious to all this?"

Ian folded his arms.

"They think we're looking for something off an ostensible Agency tip. Not sure if Tahir suspects we picked something up in Qasbo, but if he does, he's playing along well enough."

"Tahir," David muttered. "That guy's a live wire."

Ian nodded apologetically. "Yeah, he is. Basically a Pakistani Cancer in terms of being an asshole, but unfortunately for us he goes by the book. You won't find anyone with a better network of safehouses and deep-cover agents reporting to him. But as far as bending the rules goes...he's not our man. Wouldn't even agree to let us use captured rifles after we nearly died trying to defend ourselves."

"Maybe we'll break him in." David bit into his sandwich and mumbled, "What's our freedom of movement like?"

"We're golden in Islamabad and the suburbs. Cleared to take the van out by ourselves, and we've been doing it multiple times a day. Once we leave the metro region, though, Tahir better be at the wheel and have screened the route with his informants. Even that didn't help us last time."

"And for safehouse ops, we're running everything out of the van?"

Tapping the earcup of his headphones, Ian said, "Comms with Chen and all our intel, yeah. One of us stays in here 24/7. We have to be selective in what we tell Tahir and, by proxy, the ISI—"

Chen's voice emitted over his headphones.

"Any Suicide element, any Suicide element, Raptor Nine One."

"Hang on," Ian said to David, then transmitted back, "This is Angel. Send it."

David watched him closely as Ian grabbed a grease pencil and jotted notes on a laminate clipboard, letting Chen finish her message before replying, "Copy all, stand by."

He locked eyes with his team leader. "Shehzad just got the call—driver's coming to pick him up in thirty minutes."

"Time to find out if this is all a ruse or not," David said thoughtfully, rising to a crouch with the remains of his sandwich. "I'll round up the troops."

5

"He just turned off onto a local road," Ian announced from his data console. "Golf City Avenue, southbound."

"Golf City Avenue, southbound," Tahir echoed, guiding the van along the straight expanse of E-75 highway illuminated by headlights. They'd only been heading northeast for twenty minutes before the change of route was announced, and the transition onto a local road surely meant they were getting close.

David abandoned the passenger seat to climb into the cargo area with two words.

"Kit up."

Worthy activated his red lens headlamp from a fold-down seat beside the rear door, seeing the figures of Reilly and Cancer appear in a crimson glow as they did the same, and he hastened to unzip the kit bag at his feet.

The team's prerogative to maintain low visibility had lessened with the onset of nightfall, and their upcoming departure from the highway eliminated it completely—if they were exposed now, it wouldn't be by some vigilant policeman. Haris Shehzad's phone remained at the hotel, but the man himself was currently in a vehicle with two active cellular vectors that the team was following at a distance, and unless the entire movement was a very well-planned counterintelligence ploy, the team's odds of witnessing a Pakistani raid to kill or capture Kamran Raza were escalating by the second.

Worthy removed the concealed Kydex holster from his side, then transferred his Glock to a more substantial holster on a pistol belt loaded with four spare magazines. After donning the padded belt, he reached into his kit bag and removed his tactical plate carrier.

The vest was heavy, encasing soft armor sheaths on the front and back capable of absorbing small handgun rounds. Those sheaths padded twin armored plates that could sustain multiple 7.62mm hits before failing, and the remainder of the weight stemmed mainly from the attached water bladder, radio, and medical kit.

He felt the van slow and turn, the road rough as they left the highway. By then Ian was making his next announcement, echoed in short order by Tahir.

"Left turn at the fork, Zamindar Avenue eastbound."

Worthy slipped the plate carrier over his head, careful not to dislodge his headlamp, and lifted the stomach flap to affix Velcro waist straps into position.

The lightness of the stomach flap was the only aberration that violated the familiarity of this procedure, one that he'd conducted hundreds of times if not a thousand or more.

Ordinarily there would be three loaded rifle magazines in that space, while at present only their empty pouches remained. No one on the team had dared reconfigure their equipment to change that regardless of the current limitations in their weapon authorities. It was the plate carrier's most easily accessible space, hence its dedication for the highest-priority task of emergency reloads. And while the rifle mag pouches were vacant— save Reilly's, which were probably stuffed with candy bars—their presence would be desperately needed if events required them to employ captured enemy rifles.

"Right turn," Ian called out, "at the T-intersection. Minar Street."

Worthy turned on his radio, inserting his earpieces as it booted up.

Tahir said, "He is headed to the village of Bhanati."

"What's in Bhanati?" David asked, still donning his tactical gear.

"Absolutely nothing."

Worthy attached his night vision device to the mount on his helmet as Reilly spoke irritably beside him.

"No wonder we didn't find shit in Barakahu."

"Yup," Worthy commented, pulling his headlamp down around his neck. Then he put the helmet on and activated his night vision, ensuring the focus and eye relief were where he wanted them to be.

"So," Reilly went on, adjusting the massive medical aid bag between his boots, "the past week was a total waste of time." Then he lowered his voice so only Worthy could hear him. "We shouldn't be doing this bullshit anyway. There are plenty of outfits that specialize in surveillance, and we're not one of them."

Worthy removed his helmet and held it in his lap as he replied, "They're better at this than us, sure. But we're deniable."

David said, "Comms check in sequence."

Keying his radio switch, Worthy quietly said, "Racegun."

The rest of his teammates—everyone but Ian—spoke their callsigns in quick succession.

"*Suicide.*"

"*Doc.*"

"*Cancer.*"

"We're good," David concluded, and then Reilly was back to bitching.

"So what if we're deniable? You say that like it matters."

Worthy shook his head. "Did you even listen to the intelligence brief?"

"My eyes usually glaze over during those things. I nod every thirty seconds or so to make Ian think I'm listening."

"Then I'll give you the CliffsNotes. During the Afghanistan War we had enough American units in Pakistan to take Raza off the map. But with the Chinese strongarming the Paks to have nothing to do with the US, the Agency doesn't have the resources or infrastructure here like they used to. And the US can't risk a bunch of declared American intelligence officers getting rolled up. And India—"

"India," Reilly interjected, "doesn't want anyone helping the Pakistanis. It's Pakistan and China versus India and the Western world. I get that. I'm just saying, why not send a declared team from the Agency? What are the odds of anyone getting rolled up with an ISI minder glued to their hip?"

Ian spoke before Worthy could reply.

"Tahir, pull over wherever you can—he's slowing down, looks like they're getting close to wherever they're headed. We can still range him and I don't want us coming any closer for the time being."

Worthy felt the van come to a halt as he answered Reilly. "Apparently the odds of getting rolled up are good enough for the Agency to send five expendable dickheads, and even we can't get away with unilateral action here. Hell, the government doesn't even control most of the country outside of major urban centers. Letting Ian run his robots in the back of the van is the least of our worries. We're about four hours outside Kashmir, and the Indians and Pakistanis have been trying to figure out who controls it for a half century or so. We're sitting on a powder keg, man."

Reilly appeared lost in thought, face glowing crimson from his headlamp. "Kashmir...why does that sound familiar?"

Worthy blinked.

"Are you serious?"

"Do *you* think I'm serious?"

The pointman rubbed his forehead. Reilly was a master of all things related to special operations medicine—he could stabilize someone with multiple gunshot wounds and a collapsed lung at night aboard a moving helicopter—but with a startling array of matters not related to physical trauma, he had the memory of a goldfish.

"Doc," Worthy said, keeping his voice down, "we were right on the border of Kashmir during our China op. China controls a little, and the rest is split between Pakistan and India with a line of control that has a ceasefire violation every five minutes or so. The entire region is a game of chicken between nuclear powers, and a couple years ago you were three kilometers away from it. We could see the mountains from our hide site in China, man."

"Huh," Reilly muttered, tilting his head. "Thought I recognized the name."

Ian announced, "He's stationary. Grid to follow."

Worthy prepared his Agency phone, entering the sequence of numbers along with his teammates as Ian announced them.

An inverted teardrop marker appeared on his satellite imagery, and

Worthy panned in to analyze the structure where Haris Shehzad had just been delivered.

The compound lay stark and isolated amidst vast agricultural expanses and scattered outbuildings. High, unyielding walls encapsulated rows of rigorously aligned crops, imposing a rigid order on the natural landscape. At its heart, a large, two-story structure loomed ominously, its flat roof and considerable bulk casting long shadows over the tilled soil.

"It's big," David said. "What do you think, 4,000 square feet?"

Cancer replied, "Forty-five hundred, maybe. Who knows how many rooms are in there, or what their defenses are. The Paks better send a lot of shooters."

Worthy scanned the open space within the compound walls. The Pakistan Air Force Special Services Wing utilized a variety of helicopters for troop transport, the largest of which was the Mi-17. He selected the aircraft from a dropdown menu to generate a rotatable icon of the helo complete with rotor diameter, then dragged and dropped the icon at various locations to confirm landing zones.

Cancer must have been doing the same, because a moment later he said, "Clearing west of the building looks good for the drop."

"It'll support a single Mi-17," Worthy offered, switching helicopters on his phone software and repeating the process. "And they could land a Huey or an AW139 in the open ground to the southeast. Maybe a Blackhawk if the pilots are really good, but I wouldn't bet the bank on it."

He panned across the imagery to check the surrounding structures and terrain. "I'd advise a west-to-east trajectory for approach, egress to the south, and orbit over that patch of desert until the Commandos call them back for MEDEVAC or exfil."

"Concur," Cancer said, adding, "and make sure they have fast ropes in case there's any obstacles we can't see on the imagery."

"Got it," David replied, lowering his phone and moving forward to the passenger seat to bring Tahir up to speed.

Ian exchanged transmissions with Chen, the particulars indistinguishable from Worthy's position in the van.

But the urgency in the intelligence operative's tone continued to rise until he said, "Copy, stand by," and leaned back in his chair.

He called out, "We've got cellular, FM, and satellite comms activity lighting up like a Christmas tree from that compound. It's definitely a command site of some kind, and I'm picking up multiple references to High Tower giving orders."

Tahir spun in his seat to face the cargo area.

"My people do not move until you are sure."

"Raza is there," Ian replied. "The US passes positive identification, confirmed by the Agency, and we're requesting an immediate raid."

The ISI officer spoke flatly. "If this is a dry hole, the responsibility lies with you."

"Sure. You got it. Just make the call now, before Raza leaves. Please."

Tahir dialed a number on his phone, then began what sounded like a heated exchange in Urdu. Whether the conversation was confrontational or the harsh syllables of the language made it sound that way to the Western ear, Worthy had no idea.

David held his phone beside the ISI officer, answering questions when asked.

The outcome of this call remained uncertain until Tahir ended it, then looked over his shoulder with an expression of triumph.

"The 3rd Commando Battalion is launching from Tarbela. Three assault teams, 21 troops in total including medics. They should be wheels-down on the target in one half hour."

"Commandos?" Cancer asked with dismay. "What happened to Zarrar Company?"

"I do not choose the assault force."

The obvious problem was that Zarrar Company was the only dedicated counterterrorism element in the Pakistani Special Service Group, and sending anyone *but* them for a time-sensitive compound raid seemed like a deliberate undermining of the odds of killing or capturing Kamran Raza.

"What's 3rd Battalion's specialty?" David asked.

Tahir hesitated. "Mountain warfare."

The particulars of that skillset were about as far from urban raids as you could get, Worthy thought.

Reilly asked in a hushed voice, "You think someone in the ISI is protecting Raza?"

"Let's hope not," Worthy admitted, now scanning the imagery to find a location where the van could stage prior to the raid and, if at all possible, gain a vantage point into the compound to determine the locations of any visible doors and windows to pass along to the Commandos. "But this isn't a good sign."

Cancer was far more ambivalent.

"Not much we can do about it. They restricted us to fuckin' pistols, tied our hands, and told us to sit back and watch. So we'll sit back and watch, and they get what they get. It's not like the five of us could take down a target that big, anyway."

"Worthy," David said, "find us a route closer to the compound. Preferably on high ground so we can get eyes-on without exposing ourselves. When the Paks are done raiding it, I want to be in the door and collecting intelligence before the smoke clears."

"Already on it, boss."

6

The frigid night air of Pakistan was barely warded off by a lightweight fleece beneath my plate carrier as I approached the open cargo doors of the parked van, taking in the view through my night vision.

"How are we looking?" I asked.

Ian remained at the data console but was kitted up now, having been temporarily relieved at his workstation only for the time it took him to don a pistol belt, plate carrier, and conduct a radio check before resuming his duties.

"I can't make any sense of it," he replied with frustration. "But those rooftop antennas we saw are sending a lot of transmissions, and each one is using brevity codes they must have set up beforehand. I don't know what's in the works, but Raza's in the middle of it."

"And you're sure it's not a diversion?"

"They could divert us with a hell of a lot less effort than this. We're looking at the real deal, whatever it is."

I slapped the cargo door in response and circled the vehicle, approaching the front where the rest of my men stood in a row to gaze upon the compound below.

We'd parked on a hilltop at a distance, using a spotting scope to identify an array of antennas on the roof as well as a gate in the compound wall, the location of the south side door, and the orientation of windows on both floors, and confirmed that two possible landing zones were free of visible obstacles before relaying this information to the Commando assault force via Tahir.

The ISI officer clutched a handheld radio with a long-whip antenna, and I approached his side to inform him, "Ian still thinks it's legit."

"Oh?" Tahir asked, sounding unimpressed. "And are you going to share with me the reason why, or conceal it because I am Pakistani?"

"Their transmissions are coded," I said defensively. "We're not sweeping anything under the rug with shooters inbound."

Tahir grunted.

"Seriously," I assured him, though his silence told me he was skeptical in the extreme.

And before I could decide whether to reinforce my point or not, his radio emitted a crackle of static and a voice spoke in Urdu.

"They will arrive in one minute," he said. "No change to the plan. One team will make entry at the south door, one at the west door, and one through a window on the north side."

As I scanned the sky, a muddy shade of green apart from sporadic sheets of black clouds in my night vision, I heard Cancer say, "Eyes-on."

It took me another few moments to locate the birds, at present a pair of dark specks flying a few hundred meters over the landscape to my left.

"They're close enough," I said. "Switch to ground frequency."

Tahir rotated a dial on his radio as I focused on the target building with its dimly lit windows, watching for signs of movement. The quickest glimpse of activity was information that the assault force desperately needed, but as had been the case our entire time out here, the compound remained eerily still. It belied what I knew from Ian was happening within the building, namely a flurry of outbound and inbound communications whose purpose and intent continued to elude both us and the Agency.

Swinging my night vision toward the helicopters, I saw them dropping lower in the sky. I felt the momentary thrill that always preceded a ground raid, in this case misplaced enthusiasm considering we'd be watching the event from a distance and only allowed in once the Commandos gave us permission—and whether or not there was any intelligence left to exploit when that call occurred remained to be seen.

But as I continued to stare at the helos, I felt my spirits plummet.

There were plenty of specops aviation outfits that could land a helo on a dime and have it gone again, assaulters racing toward the breach, almost before the enemy knew what was happening.

But the Pakistan Air Force Special Services Wing wasn't among those ranks, or at least not the pilots they'd sent tonight.

A UH-1 Huey flew along a slow, lazy descent toward the southeastern field with a larger Mi-17 staggered in an echelon left formation behind it. Their gradual approach gave everyone on the objective ample time to flee or stage a defense as they preferred, and I had an overwhelming sensation of impotence at the former possibility. If we had rifles at this range, my team could merrily pick off runners as they fled from the south side of the building.

But still, no one emerged.

This meant one of two things, I thought, neither of them boding well for my team or the Pakistani Commandos. Either the transmissions stemming from the building were an elaborate counterintelligence ruse—a best-case scenario, at this point—or everyone inside was preparing to fight in place.

The Huey was first to land, descending behind the compound wall until I could only make out the murky disc of its rotor blades. A file of nine Commandos appeared seconds later, flowing toward the door while the Mi-17 set its wheels down to the west.

Before the latter helicopter's men could so much as run down the ramp, however, a pair of muzzle flashes appeared in the compound's second-story windows—two machine gunners, I knew instinctively. Their fire raked across the first row of assaulters as the Huey lifted off and dipped its nose in the pilots' frantic attempt to distance themselves from the objective before they were shot down.

The helicopter momentarily blocked my view, and by the time it cleared the eastern compound wall I saw that a half-dozen Pakistani Commandos had been felled while three survivors ran toward the building's southern entrance. Cancer could have easily sniped the enemy shooters at their first appearance, though both had since vanished from the windows either due to return fire or, more likely, the fact that they were relocating downstairs to fight the assault force head-on inside the building.

By then the Mi-17 had disgorged its troops, and another twelve Commandos split up on their approach to separate entry points. As one team slipped behind the building, the interior lights went dark, indicating that the inbound shooters had disabled a generator. But with six men down, the Pakistanis were already faced with a mass-casualty event. And while they had wisely abandoned their fallen to clear the building, such a massive loss seconds into their assault didn't bode well for the remainder of the effort.

I already knew what we had to do, my decision bolstered when Tahir looked up from his radio and spoke, sounding fearful as the Mi-17 thundered up and away from its landing zone.

"They are inside, but cannot fight through."

I yelled, "Load up," as I moved for the driver's door with the words, "I'll drive."

There would be no time for me to relay orders to Tahir if he operated the van and no guarantee that he'd follow them if I did, and every moment between now and our arrival increased the odds of more Pakistani Commandos falling injured or dead.

If there were any of them left, I thought.

Entering the van before Tahir could object, I fired the ignition and threw the transmission into drive, leaving the headlights off as I felt the vehicle rock with the entry of my team before the cargo doors slammed shut.

"What happened?" Ian asked from his data console.

"MASCAL," I replied. "Paks are bogged down inside the building. We're going in."

I accelerated as soon as Tahir slid into the passenger seat, gunning the van into a semicircle toward the dirt road we'd used to reach our vantage point.

The path curved downhill between mud-brick buildings, and I struggled to keep the van aligned on the road while moving at the maximum possible speed while Cancer shouted behind me.

"Unilateral direct action until we can get the Paks moving. Then we let them take the lead. Tahir, how many of the Commandos speak English?"

"Most of them. Three-quarters, at least."

"Good. We lead the Paks to the doorways and let them be the first in until the building is cleared. Once that happens, Reilly sets up a casualty collection point. Everyone else moves the wounded to him except Ian—you transition to site exploitation."

The intelligence operative protested, "What about monitoring the—"

"Set your bullshit to record and worry about it later. We need every shooter on deck."

"All right."

I whipped the van in a sloping right-hand turn, watching the headlights sweep across a field where rows of corn had been painstakingly planted. There was a protracted silence from the cargo area whose cause didn't require any speculation on my part. Cancer was reiterating to Ian that anything he found during the post-raid site exploitation needed to be concealed from the Paks if at all possible, and none of us had any cause to question that order. If the selection of a mountain-focused Commando unit instead of Zarrar Company was any indication, someone high up was on Raza's payroll and anything the Pakistanis obtained in the way of viable intelligence would be leaked in short order.

"Tahir," I said, "once we dismount, you get the van out and park it on the outside of a compound wall. We can't afford for it to get disabled."

He agreed readily enough, and as we reached the low ground, I asked, "What are they saying?"

The sound of panicked Pakistani voices had been issuing forth from his radio ever since the assault began, and Tahir informed me, "They are saying they will have to retreat."

"Nope," I said firmly. "Tell them help is on the way."

He did send a transmission, though whether or not he translated my message or relayed something else remained a mystery due to my ignorance of the Urdu language.

I spotted the compound ahead of us, and veered wildly off the road away from it.

"You are going the wrong way—" Tahir objected, cutting his statement short as I reversed the steering wheel to align the front bumper with the wrought iron gate between tall mud walls.

Rather than protest, he pulled on his seatbelt while I floored the accelerator.

Cancer announced, "Ten seconds."

Use as a battering ram was probably the last thing anyone at the Agency had in mind when outfitting the surveillance van, but when things went sideways on the ground—as they often did—you used whatever tools you had at your disposal.

And at the moment, our top priority was reaching the objective as quickly as possible.

The gate expanded in my field of vision until I could make out a single chain with a lock wrapped around the center beam of both doors. No match for a speeding vehicle, I thought, my assessment validated a second later as the van blasted through the framework with barely a shudder of the chassis.

The south entrance of the target building lay dead ahead, its door blown apart by an explosive charge, and I braked and swerved right to bring the van to a halt beside the row of fallen Pak assaulters.

My team exited in unison, the continuous chop of distant rotor blades barely audible over the din of gunfire and explosions within the building, and together we streamed toward the wounded and dead.

The closest Commando I found was sitting upright, shakily pulling a tourniquet over his left thigh.

I knelt beside the man and said, "We'll be back for you," then grabbed his M4 assault rifle and pulled the sling over my shoulder as I stripped magazines from his plate carrier and stuffed them inside my own pouches as quickly as I could. The first man from my team to enter the breach point would be whoever got there first, and I fully intended on that being me.

But upon rising, I saw that I hadn't moved fast enough—Cancer was already on his feet and moving toward the open doorway.

7

Cancer ran at three-quarters of a sprint, racking his M4's charging handle to eliminate any guesswork of whether the dead Commando he'd taken the weapon from had previously chambered a round or not.

Rotating his night vision upward on its helmet mount, he exposed his naked eyes in anticipation of the white light he could see beyond the breach point as he approached.

While the building's generator had been disabled, the interior appeared to be sufficiently lit by a matrix of rifle taclights from the Commandos that cast glowing beams in all directions deeper inside the building.

Then the southern entrance was before him, its door blown off its hinges by a Commando demolitions shot, and Cancer slowed abruptly before activating his taclight and slipping inside the building.

A dead Pakistani Commando lay just inside the breach, attired in camouflage fatigues punctuated by a black plate carrier. His body had been shredded by what must have been a belt-fed weapon—Cancer pivoted left to clear the nearest corner, then moved down the wall to see that he'd been correct. A fallen enemy fighter was sprawled beside a PK machinegun in a doorway of a room further down the first floor, probably one of the two who had fired from the second-story windows.

But that PK gunner hadn't anticipated the entry of a second assault team through the north window behind him, which accounted for his demise but not that of a second dead Pakistani Commando in the space between those two points. That told Cancer he'd find the body of another slain defender around the corner to his front, his eye movements assessing the tactical play-by-play that transpired in the opening seconds of the clearance before he came to a stop at the next open doorway.

Once he did, he saw the crumpled enemy body he'd been expecting, and beyond it, the Pakistani assaulters.

Two Commandos knelt at an open doorway in the next room, the pair representing the toughest sons of bitches on the playing field. They were part of the initial nine who had stepped off the Huey. Six of their number had been laid out by machinegun fire before entering the building, the remaining three made entry on the south door and lost another in the breach, and yet the dual survivors were fighting on.

Or at least trying to.

The opposite side of the doorway revealed another three Pakistanis, with two more visible at the threshold of another room they must have cleared by now. This was the team that had entered through the north window, Cancer knew, having sustained a single casualty in the interim.

All seven of those men were nonetheless frozen, their assault single-handedly halted by whatever forces resided in the yet-uncleared room. Dust and smoke billowed from the doorway; the Paks had been hurling frags inside, apparently without success, which indicated that the enemy within were well-entrenched, probably deaf by now but still in the fight.

David came to a stop a few meters away, Worthy appearing at the team leader's back as both took up positions on the opposite side of the door. Neither had much of a view beyond, Cancer thought, judging by the fact that David lowered his barrel to cede responsibility for the next move to him.

The sniper felt a hand touch his shoulder—Reilly or Ian, probably the former—and considered that while he knew what they had to do, a pair of troubling questions loomed in his mind. Where was the remaining machine-gunner, and what was the fate of the third Commando assault team that entered through the door on the west side?

He keyed his mic. "We're missing one assault team. Doc and Racegun, go back out and move to the westside breach point. Find 'em and get 'em moving."

Worthy shot him a thumbs up and moved back the way he'd come, leaving Cancer to resume his transmission.

"Suicide and Angel, the first two teams are stuck at a center-fed room. We're going to clear it ourselves—brownout, simo-frag, it's going to be point blank."

David was close enough to be heard at a near-whisper in silent conditions, but he reached for his transmit switch because the noise level at present was anything but.

"*Sounds like a party*," David transmitted. "*Let's do it*."

Cancer led the way out of the room and toward the Commandos, keeping his barrel down, taclight on, and shouting, "FRIENDLY, FRIEND-LY," as he moved.

They saw him immediately and didn't take aim, and he supposed that was a good thing—but they looked equally confused at his appearance with two additional Americans in tow. Had they received Tahir's message that reinforcements were arriving? Did they even know a CIA element was watching the objective ahead of their arrival? Cancer had no clue.

He swung well right of the smoke-filled doorway where enemy fighters clearly remained, circling the two Pakistani soldiers left over from the Huey touchdown and taking up a position on the wall behind them.

"Grenades," he yelled, holding out his free hand. "Grenades."

A Pakistani eagerly produced one of the devices, and Cancer snatched it from him—not a spherical M67 like the team usually carried, but rather an egg-shaped grenade with ridges circling the olive drab casing.

But that one frag was all the man had left to give. These Commandos had been tossing grenades in one at a time without making entry, and the fact that the enemy had thus far survived meant they had the benefit of substantial cover. The only solution was to "simo-frag," or whip in multiple grenades in near-succession, preferably after counting off a few seconds from the fuse delays, and then enter to finish off any survivors the instant the shrapnel stopped flying.

Holding up the grenade for the five soldiers positioned on the opposite side of the doorway to see, Cancer shouted for more.

The Commandos opposite the door rolled two additional grenades across the floor toward them, both plucked up by David and Ian.

Cancer ordered the nearest pair of Commandos to move back so the Americans could stack on the wall. Then he yelled at the Pakistanis to stay put—a room filled with enemy fighters hiding in zero-visibility conditions wasn't the place to test the tactical acumen of a partner force. Then, to his teammates, he said, "Two-second cook."

Cooking off grenades was a tricky business under the best of circumstances. Cancer yanked the safety pin and let it drop, holding the grenade to his side to let his teammates see.

Then he released his grip enough to let the safety lever or "spoon" fall free from the device.

At this point, the device should have been airborne at the greatest possible velocity—the slightest delay now meant instant death for himself, his teammates, and at least some of the seven Commandos now hunkering down and wondering who in the hell these white randos actually were. But instead of throwing, he held the ticking time bomb in his hand and silently counted *one thousand* before stepping forward and hurling it through the doorway at the two-second count.

Cancer ducked against the wall to clear the way for David to repeat the procedure, followed immediately by Ian, before all three men resumed their positions against the wall.

A deafening roar erupted as the trio of fragmentation grenades detonated in the room, filling the confined space with a violent ballet of shrapnel and shockwaves that tore through the air. The wall beside him shook, and dust and debris burst forth in a stinging cloud to his front.

Cancer took a breath and held it, the air thick with a metallic scent mixed with acrid explosive fumes, and then he advanced.

After clearing the doorway he instinctively reversed course, breaking right inside the room to find that his expectations of a full brownout were not unjustified. There was nothing to see at all but a uniform haze, and his second step ended when his shins struck the crouching form of a man's body.

Dropping his barrel until it alighted upon flesh, Cancer fired three times and kicked the man over, making way for him to sidestep the body only to hit the backside of an impossibly sturdy couch instead. The impact forced him in the opposite direction where his shoulder struck the wall, right boot clumsily descending on top of the dead or wounded opponent. Cancer established forward momentum the only way he could, stumbling over the man to find solid footing beyond and illuminating his taclight in a second-long burst that he abandoned when the glare was reflected back at him by the cloud of sand and dust.

A few more steps transpired, during which he heard the bark of David's M4 on the opposite side of the room. Then the muzzle of Cancer's barrel struck a flat surface, the first and only indication that he'd arrived at a wall.

Pivoting left, he began movement toward his second corner, seeking a deeper point of domination as the number one man. He kept his shoulder in grazing contact with the wall, the only way he'd be able to move straight without drifting one way or the other in zero-visibility conditions. His opposite leg skirted the backside of another couch, this one angled toward him from one grenade blast or another, forcing him to use his hip and considerable effort to shove it sideways before proceeding.

Multiple bursts of automatic fire erupted then as stunned enemy fighters regained enough composure to spray bullets across the room. One of these was directly to Cancer's front, and he dropped to a knee and shot five times as quickly as his index finger could depress the trigger.

His response succeeded in silencing the burst, though sporadic gunfire continued whether from his teammates or the enemy. Cancer dropped his barrel and fired twice more in a split-second estimation of where his last target had fallen given the sound of the previous fire.

Then he crouched low and continued moving, still seeking his next corner, his pulse hammering in his ears. He was still holding his breath, oxygen levels depleting fast as his left boot barked off a solid object that could only be a human head.

Dropping his barrel once more, Cancer blasted three shots before attempting to step atop the body. The tip of his boot snagged on some strap or piece of gear on the man's backside, sending Cancer flying forward in a prostrate fall that ended when his chest struck the floor, forcing the air from his lungs in one whooshing blast.

His first gasping inhale resulted in a choking intake of dust and debris.

Cancer coughed and tried to breathe through his nostrils instead, struggling to recover his footing and continue in a crouch as the gunfire died down, whether due to enemy deaths or merely their need to reload. A step and a half of movement transpired before his rifle glanced off a wall to his front, his forward momentum and oxygen-starved state causing him to stumble and knock his helmet against the surface.

Then he knelt and pivoted left, taking shallow breaths and orienting himself without the benefit of any vision to speak of.

The only person to take a second corner was himself as the number one man, and this room was many things but not triangular. Cancer was against the back wall, which left him with a clear field of fire to the far corner. He exploited this blind advantage to expend the rest of his magazine directly to his front, firing controlled pairs as he adjusted the angle of his barrel from down to up and back again.

His M4 bolt locked to the rear without any corresponding percussion of a body hitting the ground ahead of him, and Cancer conducted an emergency reload with a magazine pilfered from the same fallen Commando who had unwittingly provided the rifle.

After sending his bolt forward, he dropped into the prone and activated his taclight, hoping against hope that the dust cloud was beginning to rise and finding that it was. He could only see a few inches off the ground at first, just enough to find a dead man halfway down the wall and the backside of more furniture to his left. The haze was lifting with surprising speed.

"Prone," he transmitted, "get into the prone, cloud's starting to lift. I'm at the second corner, three walls are clear, I'm shifting to cover the middle."

That was all the advance notice he had time to give before slithering forward on his belly, clearing the side of the couch beside him and angling his barrel toward the yet-uncleared center of the room. In tactical terms this was a recipe for fratricide: David was at the corner to his front and Cancer was now aiming in the team leader's general direction, his transmission and taclight beam the only means of warning the team leader that bullets may be inbound.

But absurd objectives called for equally absurd improvisation. This was already a wild-ass target, Cancer thought—he'd shot if not killed several enemy fighters by now without actually *seeing* any of them, and that pattern was reversed the instant he spotted a figure in the center of the room.

The enemy fighter must have relocated to his current position at some point after the last grenade blast. He knelt with an FN FAL battle rifle, sweeping its muzzle erratically across the room in David's general direction. Cancer's quickest point of aim was the man's hip, and he took the shot before his opponent had any more opportunity to fire.

That sent the remaining fighter sprawling on the ground, exposing a thick beard that was uncharacteristically well-groomed for a combatant in this setting—a professional gunfighter, then—and more importantly, a sweat-drenched shaved head covered in grime that was like a beacon for the next pair of shots, both easy hits at the current distance.

A spray of pink and gray mingled with the dust particles still hanging in the air, and Cancer transmitted, "Center, right side, and back wall are clear. Suicide?"

David replied, *"My walls are clear, we're good."*

Rising to his feet as the hazy cloud in the room continued to ascend, Cancer took progressively deeper breaths and saw that plush couches and loveseats with hand-engraved wood framing lined the room on all sides. No rural Pakistan decor, but rather furniture that had been transported and arranged for the benefit of someone important.

Namely, he thought, Kamran Raza.

No wonder the remaining defenders had been able to survive as long as they had—all they had to do was take cover in the gaps between incredibly sturdy furniture and the wall, letting inbound grenades bounce toward the center of the room before exploding.

The inverted and obliterated remnants of what had once been a substantial center table were a testament to this fact, as was the pitted upholstery of the furniture, now askew from multiple blasts and charred black as Cancer made his way toward the door along with his teammates. He felt like he'd been inside this building for a week despite the fact that a couple minutes at most had transpired since he'd raced through the south entrance, yet another immersion into the eerie time expansion that occurred at certain points in combat.

David was the first to make it back to the doorway, shouting at the first Commando he saw.

"Clear!" The team leader made a chopping motion with his hand to indicate they needed to resume their clearance at once. "Go, *go!*"

Reilly stopped short of the exterior door on the west side of the target building, waiting until he felt Worthy's hand on his shoulder before calling out, "Friendly, friendly!"

The sound of explosions and automatic gunfire assured him that someone was having a hell of a fight inside—either his teammates, the Pakistanis, or both. And because no one on the objective apparently had suppressors, the entire ground floor was an earthquake of noise and chaos. Any distinction between incoming and outgoing gunfire was eliminated in one fell swoop as every shot coagulated into one deafening soundtrack amid the tooth-rattling echoes of grenade blasts, and Reilly strained to listen for a verbal response over the decibel cutoff of his radio earpieces.

When no one replied, he lifted his night vision upward on its mount and peered around the doorway and into the building.

Reilly immediately spotted a row of three Commandos stacked on either side of a hall where a dead man with an AK-47 lay sprawled on the floor. The Pakistanis had made precious little forward progress since making entry, having stopped a few meters inside the breach point. Two of them looked back at him without taking aim, their faces betraying no clue of whether or not they had any idea who this newcomer was. But the sight of Reilly's high-end tactical kit assured them that he was most certainly not an enemy fighter, and that was good enough.

After slipping inside, Reilly moved along the right-hand wall and stopped when he reached the rear of the nearest trio of Commandos. Worthy was already in position to his left, holding fast behind the remaining Pakistanis, and together they assessed what the hell was going on within a split second.

These Commandos had tailored the vast majority of their preparation to technical climbing and long-range engagements in the mountains, and what they faced now couldn't have been any further from that. Granted, it was clear enough they'd had some rudimentary training in urban combat —both files of men were stacked along the walls, not crossing past doorways, and maintaining a semblance of forward security down the hall.

But that was where their effectiveness began and ended.

Their discovery of opposing doorways on either side of the hall had brought their assault to a grinding halt, neither stack of Commandos in the hall willing to enter and clear their respective rooms for fear that their counterparts would remain frozen and render them vulnerable to enemy fire from behind. Whatever enemy fighters resided in the two rooms were now isolated from one another, having witnessed the fate of the fallen guard in the hallway.

Only a simultaneous entry into both rooms would remedy the situation, a fact known just as well to the Pakistanis as it was to Reilly. But the Commandos were nonetheless reluctant to commit to this basic maneuver out of a glaring lack of trust and, perhaps more so, experience. They probably looked like superstars running through a shoot house loaded with paper targets, but moving through a building infested with actual enemy shooters had a tendency to scramble the brains of all but the most experienced soldiers.

Reilly glanced at Worthy. "Looks like we're up. I've got the count."

No other conferral was necessary—Reilly's team had operated together long enough and through a sufficient amount of dire situations for their tactical decision-making to have reached near synchronicity. He and Worthy would have to be the number one man through both doorways at the same time while praying that the Commandos would follow close enough behind them to be of any assistance whatsoever once they made it into their respective rooms.

"Frags," Worthy shouted. "Grenades."

The last Pakistani in each stack procured one of the devices and handed them over without delay, eager to cede responsibility for further decision-making to the two Americans.

"*Prone,*" Cancer transmitted abruptly. "*Get into the prone, cloud's starting to lift. I'm at the second corner, three walls are clear, I'm shifting to cover the middle.*"

"Who's in charge?" Reilly roared over the sound of gunfire deeper in the building. "Leader, leader."

A mousey-looking Pakistani soldier with twin radios on his plate carrier answered the call, and Reilly tried not to let his disappointment show as he grabbed the man's shoulder and leaned in to speak. Had this supposed leader been promoted over the others out of raw skill, or because of nepotism within the Special Service Group? Time would likely tell, although the medic's experience with foreign militaries told him it was probably the latter by a long shot.

But the important thing right now was that the Commando held the attention of his men, and Reilly gestured to his teammate and ordered, "Me and him will go in first, both rooms at the same time. Have your men enter behind us, and this is the really important part—*right* behind us. Don't leave us hanging or we're all screwed."

He received a nod in return, followed by the man making a radio transmission that caused the twin stacks of Commandos to begin backing up from the doorways.

By then Cancer was speaking over the team net once more, the sniper sounding like he was panting for air.

"Center, right side, and back wall are clear. Suicide?"

"My walls are clear," David answered. *"We're good."*

The medic preempted a request for his status by keying his mic.

"Third team is stuck in a hallway just inside the breach, we're clearing their bottleneck now."

David responded, *"Copy, first two Commando teams are moving again, we'll advance our front line trace until we see you."*

That certainly beat getting shot in the face by a jumpy and overstimulated Pakistani, Reilly thought, and rather than respond, he pulled the pin on his grenade, keeping the spoon compressed. He saw that Worthy had done the same.

They advanced to assume the number one position in each of their respective stacks, grenade in one hand while the other kept their M4 aligned on the door, and Reilly called out to Worthy.

"Five. Four."

Reilly sidestepped against the wall, just shy of the doorway, as he continued the count in his head.

Three, two, one...

Here goes nothing, Reilly thought.

He and Worthy tossed their grenades into their respective rooms in unison, stepping back to assume a two-handed grip on their rifles and trying to hear what they could before making entry.

For Reilly, the only audible cues were the shouting of multiple men inside the room ahead, along with the scraping of metal before the detonation of both grenades drowned out everything else.

He'd been poised for one or more enemy fighters to come streaming into the hall, but none did. They must have determined their chances of survival were better if they took cover rather than race outside into certain death, and Reilly waited for the concussion to begin subsiding before cutting his gaze toward his partner. In his peripheral vision, he saw that Worthy was doing the same thing, and both men activated their taclights and stepped forward at the same instant.

The age-old question of whether to flow straight ahead once through a doorway or take a lengthier buttonhook to go the opposite direction was a hotly contested topic that ultimately remained the shooter's choice.

For Reilly, there was no debate under the circumstances—he couldn't trust the Commandos to enter with the split-second timing he could expect of his teammates, and he took his previous partial visibility into the doorway as a good-enough metric that the greater threat lay behind him. He swept his taclight's beam across the room's centerline as he entered, noting that the middle was too clouded with smoke to identify targets before pivoting right toward his first corner.

This was a sleeping quarters, flimsy metal bunks now cast askew from the grenade blast, one lying on its side and others leaning against their counterparts. Reilly hadn't yet completed his initial turn when his taclight both illuminated and blinded a man scrambling for cover, his side, arm, and scalp flecked with shrapnel injuries as he received a trio of 5.56mm rounds and tumbled sideways between the bunks. The medic's pivot was barely slowed by taking the shots; a moment later he was aiming at the corner, where he saw two crouched men.

Both were clutching the sides of their heads in the wake of the painful shockwave, one of them pressing the side of a pistol against his temple in a misguided attempt to safeguard his hearing. Reilly lit them up with six rapid-fire shots that felled both before swinging his upper body toward the center of the room—a flurry of additional shots echoed, the source distinguishable as friendly rather than enemy fire by virtue of the fact that he wasn't getting blasted by rounds.

The Pakistanis had entered the fray, Reilly assessed at once, continuing toward the two corpses in the corner while aiming to his left. He crouched slightly to peer between the two-layer bunks and was rewarded with the sight of two men further down the wall.

One had only his head visible and Reilly fired at that first, transitioning toward another fighter's exposed shoulders and shooting again without any indication of whether one or both engagements had been successful. Both men were gone from view as he took a final step toward the corner, clearing as much space as he could for the Pakistanis without stepping atop the twin corpses before him.

By then the fire had died down to sporadic pop shots, allowing Reilly to sweep the remainder of the space—the smoke from the grenade blast was dissipating, revealing a Commando against the wall to his left sweeping his taclight beam across the room. Dropping to his knee and then his belly, the medic aimed beneath the bunks only to find that clusters of knapsacks and duffel bags blocked his view before he rose again. Having assumed the most dangerous role as number one man, he now held the safest position in the room, nestled in the corner and sweeping his barrel over the fallen enemy to see that neither Shehzad nor Raza were among them.

Then the smoke cleared entirely, and Reilly saw that absolute pandemonium had erupted in the center.

For reasons that remained an unassailable mystery, one of the Commandos was on the floor in the center, rolling and grappling with an opponent in heated hand-to-hand combat as another Pakistani crouched over them with a knife, periodically stabbing downward as the enemy's body came into view.

The sight caused the Commando to Reilly's left to abandon his post and dart toward the fight, pressing the muzzle of his M4 against the enemy's head before firing a single shot that conclusively ended the battle.

Reilly hadn't moved, was almost frozen in place by the sheer fuckery of the sight before him. A single-room clear had somehow turned into a WWE Battle Royal, the three Commandos alive but fully exposed to both the doorway they'd just slipped through as well as the one across the hall, and none seeming to notice that disparity in the slightest as they diverged and slipped between the bunks, shooting sporadically at their fallen opponents.

The collective result was an illogical and virtually unsurvivable tactical catastrophe that had nonetheless succeeded Pakistani-style, and he had to forcibly stop the trio before they ran across the hall and interfered with Worthy's assault in the opposite room.

Reilly manhandled the nearest Commando toward the ground, angrily leveraging his amateur bodybuilder's strength with far more force than necessary to shove the man into a kneeling position to pull security down the hall.

Then he swept his own rifle across the gap to ensure he could make the crossing, and flowed into the open doorway through which Worthy had led his own Commandos seconds earlier.

Worthy was headed back toward the doorway to support Reilly's clearance when the enormous medic plunged inside the room in full battle mode, lowering his M4 when he registered it was empty save his teammate and the three Pakistanis.

"You good?" Worthy asked.

"Yeah," Reilly said, reloading. "Clear, ready to move, no Raza."

His voice was distracted, his gaze flitting around the space as he tried to process the same view that Worthy was still trying to make sense of. It wasn't the two slain enemies that stood out—that much was par for the course at the moment—but the rest raised questions as to what in the hell this building's purpose was.

The room was an armory, or at least it had been at one point.

A few aging rifles leaned against the rough walls, along with a rudimentary bench cluttered with basic maintenance tools and a tea set that had been abandoned by the former occupants. Ammunition crates were haphazardly piled in the corners, most of them empty or nearly so.

But the remaining wall space was practically filled from floor to ceiling with makeshift weapon racks, the wooden frames now empty. At full capacity it could have held a hundred or more rifles, enough to equip a small army and far exceeding what the enemy in this building could utilize if they'd stuffed in even a dozen men per room.

Reilly intuited the significance of this detail, glancing across the room before muttering a single word—probably a profanity, lost to a machinegun burst that erupted and then echoed deeper in the building.

Worthy hastily keyed his radio. "We've cleared the bottleneck, advancing now, no sign of Raza."

A moment of gut-wrenching suspense followed, sufficiently long for him to wonder if the automatic fire had claimed the lives of one or more of his teammates.

But David coolly responded, *"We haven't found him either, or Shehzad. We're at the base of the stairs. There's a machine-gunner on the landing. We threw a red chemlight, stop when you reach it."*

"Copy."

Turning to face his three Commandos, Worthy called out, "Back in the hall, left side, I'll take the lead. Machinegun on the stairs."

He took up a position at the doorway, noting that one of Reilly's Commandos was pulling security down the hall from the opposite room, and then leaned out to take aim himself.

Aside from the dead man between the two rooms, the hallway was clear up the right-hand turn ahead, where, Worthy noted with relief, a narrow plastic cylinder on the ground blazed crimson.

He transmitted, "Eyes-on the red chem, where are you at?"

"Just around the corner," David answered. *"You'll see us when you get there. Base of the stairs will be between your element and ours. We'll take out the machine-gunner and then you and Doc are the first up—the rest of the team will follow until we establish a foothold on the second floor, and then we send the Paks through. Our guys are briefed, just make sure yours pick up the trail."*

By then Reilly had mobilized his troops, taking the lead on the opposite wall as Worthy addressed the Commandos.

"I'll take lead. Everyone else move in a file behind me, right side of the hall. Wait until the rest of the Commandos head up the stairs, then follow them to clear the second floor. If you need to reload, do it now."

Reilly lowered his barrel to allow the pointman to cross the hall, taking up the number one man slot and proceeding forward with the remaining men behind him.

Upon stopping at the corner, Worthy transmitted, "Coming around."

"*Go ahead,*" David answered.

Worthy glanced around the edge before committing, and the sight that greeted him was somewhere between comical and tragic.

Three meters of wall space remained between him and the cutout for a staircase, just as advertised, but David had failed to mention that a dead enemy fighter was lying in the space past it, blasted to bits and sans weapon. That particular piece of equipment had been seized by Cancer, who knelt on the opposite side of the stairs with a PK machinegun in his grasp, its ammo box balanced across his thigh.

Stairways were a nightmare to clear in general, and never more so than when an enemy shooter with a belt-fed weapon was waiting at the top. But Cancer's solution to this problem set was a good one: Worthy felt far more comfortable advancing up toward the threat after a hundred rounds or so of 7.62mm rounds had blazed a smoking trail for him to follow.

David stood immediately behind the sniper, followed by Ian and, clustered deeper in the building, four other Commandos that Worthy could make out.

Rounding the corner and moving flush with the right wall, he stopped opposite the stairs and felt Reilly's hand alight on his shoulder.

Cancer addressed him in a low voice. "When this bitch goes empty, you're up."

Worthy responded with a nod.

Once he did, David reached down to grasp the canvas handle on the back of Cancer's plate carrier—it was intended to assist with dragging a casualty, but functioned equally well for yanking a teammate out of the line of fire when necessary. Cancer hoisted the PK into a modified firing position, buttstock tucked under his arm with the other hand on the carrying handle, and unceremoniously wielded it around the corner and up the stairs.

Earsplitting bursts of automatic fire erupted from both Cancer and his opponent, the latter's shots turning the wall at the base of the stairs into a churning froth of powder with incoming rounds that melted into the mud bricks before ending altogether. The enemy fighter was now on the losing side of a machinegun versus machinegun engagement where only one had the benefit of a fresh drum of ammo, and Cancer pressed his advantage by maneuvering his barrel in sweeping arcs both horizontal and vertical to ensure he was doing as much damage as possible.

Worthy was braced for his turn up the stairs, although the protracted fire made it seem like the chance would never come. Expended brass poured from Cancer's PK, bouncing and spreading across the floor in a never-ending torrent as the air grew ever more thick with the stench of oil and gunpowder.

Finally the ammo ran out, and the moment Cancer dropped the machinegun and David jerked him backward, Worthy pivoted around the corner and mounted the stairs.

The enemy gunner on the landing was dead several times over, his head and upper body little more than shredded pulp, the floor and wall behind him painted jet black in the glare of Worthy's taclight as the pointman neared the top of the steps with his team behind him. The sight was something out of a slasher film, and he had to force himself to look away lest he lose his focus at the terrible awesomeness of the kill.

A wall was before him then, extending to the right. Worthy transitioned his rifle to a left-handed firing position as he took the final steps, then dropped to a knee and spun in a 180-degree arc to gain a field of view as Reilly's knees pressed against his back, the medic performing the same maneuver while standing to bring a second gun into the fight.

The second floor spread before him, another hallway leading to doorways on both sides—one of these held the shadow of a human form that Worthy and Reilly engaged in unison at the moment a muzzle flash sparked from the enemy's weapon. A pair of supersonic bullets cracked through the air to Worthy's left before the man dropped to the floor, his partially exposed upper body receiving additional rounds until all fire went silent.

David and Ian rounded the corner then, taking up positions on the far wall and remaining stationary as Reilly called out, "Go, now."

A succession of footfalls thumped on the stairs as the Pakistani Commandos ran up and then flowed past the team and down the hall, their taclights sweeping the space as they advanced.

Worthy watched the Pakistanis flood into the rooms ahead, splitting into three- and four-man elements that vanished into doorways amid the cracks and pops of incoming and outgoing fire. He knew that an absolute shitshow was unfolding now as the Commandos negotiated what was likely their first real urban combat.

Their movements were sloppy and disorganized, devoid of the animal athleticism that distinguished experienced assaulters from everyone else in the world. But the Pakistanis had the advantage of numbers and a renewed confidence that the five Americans would back them up, and those factors alone seemed enough to turn the tables.

As the Pakistani assault teams began emerging and leapfrogging further into the second floor, David spoke over the sporadic gunfire.

"Two-man elements, let's clear."

Worthy rose and slipped forward with Reilly behind him, entering the first doorway as David and Ian moved down the far side of the hall.

And while the team's room clearances progressed as they normally would, the main objective was to ensure the Pakistanis hadn't left any enemy fighters alive to pop out at the assault force's six o'clock—nor had they, Worthy saw as he and Reilly cleared one room and then the next. While the first was a dry hole, the second contained a body far too shot up to represent a threat: Haris Shehzad, who'd been slain by the same Pakistani Commandos he'd unwittingly led to this objective.

Another room revealed a single Commando writhing on the floor, his injuries impossible to ascertain at a glance and not mattering to the team at present. Even Reilly abandoned the man as quickly as they'd discovered him. As a medic, he knew better than anyone that casualty treatment was counterproductive until the entire objective was secured.

It wasn't until the Pakistanis had stopped their assault entirely that the

Americans caught up to the rear of their formation, and while Worthy's team would nonetheless enter the remaining rooms before determining that no threat remained, the Pakistanis could be put to work.

Reilly yelled, "Leave the dead and get all the wounded inside the building. Casualty collection point is the first room past the south door breach. Start triage and I'll be down to assist. And get the helicopters inbound for medical evacuation."

The team made way for the Commandos to race past them, a presumed officer shouting instructions in Urdu. Once the last man had swept past, the Americans continued to clear the remaining rooms.

And while the Pakistanis had successfully eliminated all the enemy fighters save one mortally wounded man that Worthy dispatched with two rounds, the final room in the building represented the motherload the team had been hoping for.

"Last room clear," Worthy transmitted, "no sign of Raza. Angel, get to the room at the southeast corner, now."

Reilly followed that message up with a final order for the time being; with a mass casualty event on their hands, the medic now assumed all but absolute command. The rest of the team would act in a supporting capacity until he or David declared otherwise.

"Everyone else," Reilly said, "south breach point to assist casualty treatment."

Then he was gone, although Worthy moved to the doorway separating his room from the hallway beyond. He was unwilling to relinquish the space until the one man who desperately needed to be here arrived, and the answer to his radio transmission came in the form of Ian running down the corridor a moment later.

Worthy said, "Shehzad's dead, no sign of Raza."

Ian didn't seem to care, and Worthy stepped aside for the intelligence operative to enter the doorway and take in the entirety of what had been found.

There was the briefest moment of hesitation as Ian swept his taclight beam across the interior of the room, standing in stunned silence before regaining his composure in full.

"Go ahead," he said with authority. "I've got this."

Worthy had just begun to move toward the stairs when Ian added, "And for the love of God, keep the fucking Paks out of here until I'm done."

Ian twisted the back end of his taclight until it reached a fixed position, keeping the beam of light glaring continuously as he set the rifle atop a battered table and angled it diagonally to spill a harsh glow across the room.

There was nothing natural about abandoning his M4, nor in turning his back on a loaded weapon in a building that moments earlier had been filled with armed opponents, but he had minutes at best before the Commandos demanded entry, and speed took priority over all else. He scanned the room while removing his helmet, setting it beside the rifle and pulling a headlamp over his forehead to add a second white light to the upcoming effort. The beam mingled with his blazing taclight to cast stark shadows across the walls.

His attention was drawn first to a bundle of cables snaking out an open window, connecting the antennas they'd seen on the roof to a series of field radios stacked on one of the tables lining the wall. The frequencies were well outside the standard military bands, he knew, having already recorded them during his work in the surveillance van, and Ian moved quickly in the opposite direction, feverishly looking for any hard drives, laptops, or phones.

He found a surge protector filled with AC adaptor plugs, but none of the satellite phones that he knew had once been charged there were present. There was, of course, a chance that one or more would be found during a search of the enemy bodies—hopefully by his team, and not the Pakistanis—but he instinctively knew that wouldn't be the case.

Dust motes danced in the stark light as Ian snatched up a pile of papers, his first glance telling him they were encrypted logs of some kind, each entry in Urdu coded with precise shorthand that spoke of professional secrecy. He folded the stack in half and stuffed it in his dump pouch, moving on to what appeared to be briefing documents, their contents far more thorough. The dense paragraphs were broken up by individual lines of text, and if his intuition was correct, they were brevity codes and radio scripts to initiate the actions of field operators.

That wasn't good, he thought, and his findings thus far were merging into one undeniable conclusion.

He stashed the papers away in his dump pouch, searching further down the row of tables in an effort that, frustratingly, revealed exactly zero electronic devices whose contents could be deciphered by the CIA. Downstairs, the clamor of his team and the Pakistanis handling the casualties blurred into a muffled tumult of voices and footsteps, leaving Ian isolated in the thick silence of the second story as he located a series of photographs sprawled across another corner of the table. They were close-up satellite snapshots of security posts amid rugged landscapes, each page marked by coordinates along with arrows, symbols, and annotations in Urdu that Ian couldn't read but understood well enough.

This time Ian didn't stash them in his dump pouch. Instead he left them and transitioned to a partially torn, poster-sized swath of paper on the floor. Shredded holes at its corners told him it had been nailed to the wall, torn down at the sound of helicopters, and quickly abandoned when gunfire broke out and forced the men here into a desperate attempt to defend themselves.

It was a map, then, and while Ian couldn't conclusively state what the other side of the sheet held, he knew exactly what he hoped it *didn't* show. Because if he was right, then his team's mission had just gone from an increasingly important supporting role to the main event in a painstakingly orchestrated catastrophe of international proportions.

He knelt beside the map, pulse quickening. In that dim, cluttered room, Ian found himself at the precipice of a dark revelation, and he flipped the sheet over and examined the other side.

What he saw there verified his suspicions, confirming every minor realization that had steadily built to a collective realization that explained everything. Why Kamran Raza had moved closer to Islamabad, the reason for the command-and-control site, and the nature of the coded transmissions he'd heard and recorded from the surveillance van. Ian hoped he was wrong but knew he wouldn't be so lucky—his discoveries here irreversibly altered everything that he, his team, and the Agency thought they knew about the Pakistan mission.

He rose and removed every paper from his dump pouch, spreading them on the table beside the satellite imagery. Ian had planned on hoarding intelligence from the Commandos, spiriting anything of true exploitation value away from the site before they could discover it. But someone had done that before he could, and Ian instead resorted to photography rather than removal, grabbing his Agency phone to document the findings.

Right now, the Pakistanis needed to understand and process everything here as quickly as possible.

Ian took a picture of the map and then worked his way through the satellite printouts, checking his phone display after each shot to confirm every detail was visible. As he transitioned to the briefing documents, a panicked sense of urgency continued to rise within him—he had to send this information to the CIA as soon as possible.

But judging by the sheer quantity of transmissions he intercepted just before the raid commenced, it would have been a miracle if he wasn't too late.

Running footfalls echoed in the hall as David called out.

"Coming in."

"Come in," Ian said, not bothering to pause his picture-taking as the team leader entered and spoke.

"They found a hatch under a rug on the first floor. Led to a tunnel headed north. Raza must have taken off as soon as he heard the helicopters."

"He took off," Ian corrected him, snapping another photo, "as soon as the raid was ordered. Probably took a few bodyguards, plus maybe a key individual or two, and slipped out. He left the rest of his men to continue running the show until the Commandos arrived, and Raza let them get slaughtered to buy some time for himself—and his operation."

By then the team leader was opening a box in the corner to assist with the site exploitation. "What operation? Do you know?"

"I'm afraid I do."

Rather than ask for clarification, David gave a painful groan, turning to face Ian with one of the items he'd just found.

The combat jacket was camouflaged in shades of light olive, earth brown, and dark green, a slab of Velcro on the upper arm bearing a subdued Pakistan flag above a circular patch. That patch, Ian saw without surprise, had an upright dagger and star flanked by twin lightning bolts.

It was the unit symbol of the Special Service Group, which was easy enough to identify—both the jacket and its insignia were indistinguishable from those worn by the Commandos tending to their wounded and dead on the first floor, a fact that wasn't lost on David.

"My God," the team leader said breathlessly, his eyes wide and fixed on Ian's. "Did we just hit a military safehouse?"

And while David's concern was understandable, it wasn't warranted in the slightest.

He shook his head and replied, "No," eliciting a grateful look of relief from David. The expression faded, however, when Ian spoke again.

"It's much worse than that."

8

"Raptor Nine One, Suicide Actual."

Meiling Chen barely heard the transmission. The operations center was in an uproar, although that term in this context meant the nonstop hum of urgent conversations and updates being passed between both members of the individual staff sections and the staff sections themselves. Yelling would be counterproductive, although under the circumstances this was the next best thing.

She could barely keep up with the intelligence updates flooding across the array of screens on the front wall, and it wasn't until David Rivers repeated his transmission that she distractedly reached for her hand mic.

"Stand by."

David answered, *"Negative. There's about to be a major attack on—"*

"Kashmir?" she cut him off. "It's happening as we speak. And it's not one attack, it's six, all occurring simultaneously against Indian military positions on their side of the Line of Control. We're monitoring radio traffic indicating that the enemy dead are uniformed soldiers, and the Indians are already shelling villages on the Pak side in response."

By now her intelligence updates were as close to real-time as one could get without watching events unfolding on the ground. The relentless scroll of real-time translations, intercepted communications, and satellite feeds painted a grim mosaic of escalating violence. The military frequencies crackled with terse orders and desperate pleas for reinforcements, while government channels on both sides were heating up with approvals for increased mobilization.

At the front of the OPCEN, one screen showed infrared satellite imagery of artillery exchanges along the Line of Control, vivid plumes of fire and smoke marking the contested positions. Another was dedicated to sifting through social media chatter and local broadcasts, a cacophony of panic rippling through border communities as casualties continued to mount.

Chen's jaw tightened as she scanned the updates, every fragment of data a piece of a puzzle that her staff struggled to assemble while being power-less to stop it.

"It's not the Pakistanis," David transmitted, *"it's Raza. His men are in Pak uniforms. We've got maps, timetables, translations of the brevity codes Angel has been recording all night, and we're sending them over now. Raza escaped through a tunnel headed north. We'll have the outlet location for you shortly—you need to get us a fix on him, put all this into the press, and de-escalate the situation before it gets out of hand."*

She swallowed, feeling her shoulders sag at the weight of her next state-ment. "There won't be any de-escalation."

David's reply was dripping with sarcasm.

"If you're trying to support a nuclear war, you're doing a hell of a job."

Hand clamping down on the mic, Chen fired back, "It doesn't matter what the Paks say. No one's going to believe it, *especially* if the mastermind is one of their generals. They routinely orchestrate attacks by Kashmiri insur-gents on the Indians, and when they're not doing that, they're disguising their own soldiers as militia fighters to cross the LoC to do the same. There are already military and civilian casualties on both sides, and now that attackers have been killed wearing Pakistani uniforms, India isn't going to back down. Neither will the Paks, no matter what the truth is."

"The truth is the least of our worries at this point. Wars have been started for a lot less, and lengthy ones at that—look at Vietnam and Iraq."

"I don't need a history lesson," she replied curtly, although the team leader's comment wasn't unwarranted. When a country had a pre-established agenda for military action, what mattered wasn't the ground reality but controlling the media narrative.

And to say Pakistan and India had their own agendas for war would be a criminal understatement.

Chen continued, "The point is that Raza has already given India all the propaganda they need to escalate aggression, and that alone is going to force the Pakistanis to react whether they want to or not."

"We're in agreement there. But if we don't find a way to stop it, this thing will be a whole lot bigger than Pakistan and India."

Tell me something I don't know, Chen thought.

Pakistan was a nightmare for the US in every sense of the word—militarily, diplomatically, and politically—in large part due to China.

As America continued its pivot from the Global War on Terror to its fellow superpower in the East, the question of partners was of paramount importance. There was no more important ally against China than India. After all, Mongolia, Japan, South Korea, the Philippines, and Australia were already firmly within the Western orbit. And if India came fully onboard, then the US would have effectively surrounded her problem.

The fly in the ointment was that India wanted the US to have nothing to do with Pakistan—not reduced activity, not a discreet partnership, but nothing at all.

And while that ultimatum could be addressed in relatively minor matters with the use of deniable forces like Project Longwing, it presented a significant challenge in the geopolitical context. China was as loath to be surrounded by enemies as any other country would be, and their only recourse was to become a strong ally to a Pakistan that found herself suddenly abandoned by the West and was now all too eager to commit to this arrangement.

The ties with global superpowers left Pakistan and India, two nuclear-equipped countries whose blood feud dated back to the traumatic partition of British India that established both as formal nations, as the flashpoint for a possible conflict that could bring the entire world to war.

She keyed her mic and replied, "We'll be able to bolster our presence in India in order to monitor the situation, but further manpower in Pakistan is off-limits, as I've been assured in no uncertain terms by my superiors.

There's a reason we sent your team to locate Raza, and it's not because of your surveillance expertise."

"*We're expendable,*" David shot back, "*I get it. But this thing is already moving too fast for us to keep up, and it's only going to get worse. I've got a case of beer that says you'll be able to use the data we're sending to determine a follow-on objective if not two or more, and in a few minutes you'll have a grid location where Raza popped out of a tunnel. Get us the intel to capture him alive and you'll get a videotaped confession that will undermine Pakistan and India's justification for war no matter what either government says. But it's going to take more than my team.*"

"Even if we get that intel," she pointed out, "I can't marshal attributable paramilitary support your way, and neither can the DoD."

"*Exactly. You're telling me we're the only people in position to stay ahead of this, and I'm telling you that we're not enough. But we either double down now, or Raza is going to slip away and God knows what's going to happen.*"

Chen released a sigh of utter exasperation.

"Were you even listening when I said—"

"*I was,*" David interrupted. "*And I'm well aware of the deniability fetish. But there's a solution.*"

Chen was only half listening; instead, she was focused on a CNN broadcast with the headline text, BREAKING NEWS: KASHMIR IN FLAMES AS PAKISTANI MILITARY BREACHES LINE OF CONTROL, STRIKES INDIAN MILITARY OUTPOSTS.

The word was out on the global stage; there was no putting this genie back in the bottle.

"You think you have the answer?" she asked distractedly, still watching the screen.

But David's next transmission served to garner her full and undivided attention.

"*I damn sure do. You know the second Project Longwing team I'm not supposed to know about? You need to get them out here, now.*"

9

"Any second thoughts?" Cancer asked.

I shook my head, stuffing my hands in my pockets. "None whatsoever."

"It's ambitious."

"In the extreme," I acknowledged, breathing in the faint smell of oil and metal. "But it's the only choice we've got."

He shifted his weight, tapping the toe of one boot against the concrete floor. "Just remember you're the one who will have to explain it to Tahir, not me."

I turned my head to look at the two vehicles parked in the corner of the cavernous hangar in which we now stood.

One was a dark gray Hyundai H-1 van, a staple of businesses and passenger services in Islamabad. The ISI had provided it to us without complaint—with a war brewing, the loss of a vehicle from their extensive fleet was the least of their worries. A signature from Tahir at a motor pool near the Aabpara Road headquarters had secured our use of the van for as long as we needed.

The other was our surveillance van, Tahir's face barely visible in the driver's seat. He'd been brooding all morning, a prolonged temper tantrum caused by his government siding with the Agency's recommendation instead of his own. Though to be fair, he could refuse to leave the vehicle all he wanted—it would give the Americans he so disdained ample opportunity to discuss our next steps without him overhearing things he'd find out in due time.

And then, I thought, the real fireworks would commence.

Directing my gaze toward the open hangar doors, I told Cancer, "Don't tell me you're not excited to see his reaction. I don't know if he's going to spontaneously combust or try and kill us."

"Or himself, after he's done taking out our team."

"The options are limitless," I admitted. "No matter what, it's going to be interesting."

The hangar we stood in was nestled in a private terminal of Islamabad International Airport normally used to service business jets, government officials, and other high-profile travelers requiring privacy and expedited services. And while nothing about the sparse and utilitarian space screamed VIP—cables and tools were neatly arranged along the perimeter, with a few maintenance ladders leaning against the vast walls—the contained area was more than sufficient to serve our needs at present.

A blur of white noise underscored the stillness, the distant sound of aircraft taxiing, landing, and taking off echoing within the hangar. The constant sound was punctuated by a burst of laughter right behind me, and I looked over my shoulder to see Worthy chuckling in response to some quiet commentary by Reilly.

Ian stood beside them, silent and expressionless, hands stuffed into a fleece jacket that warded off the chill of an early December morning in Islamabad.

I wondered what was bothering him at that moment in time—there was always something with a man as smart as Ian—when the whir of jet engines became audible and then grew louder.

Cancer responded to this intrusion by issuing a stern decree to our team.

"Ten minutes, tops. One-on-one briefs with your counterparts, make it fast and furious. Then we're loading gear and moving out."

The whine of the jet engines crescendoed into a powerful roar outside, and I watched the tarmac and gray overcast sky until the sleek silhouette of a Gulfstream V appeared against the open hangar doors, taxiing smoothly toward us. Its engines hummed a steady, powerful beat as it approached, the sound reverberating around us.

There was nothing particularly noteworthy about the plane itself. It was painted a nondescript shade of white, its tinted windows betraying nothing of the occupants inside as it rolled forward with an air of quiet authority. The sight was a common one at international airports the world over, although this particular Gulfstream belonged to the CIA—more specifically, to the Special Activity Center's Air Department.

Its primary role was to conduct extraordinary renditions, transporting newly abducted terrorism suspects to various non-US countries that were more suited, to say the least, for detention and interrogation that bypassed the usual legal and ethical standards. Thailand, Poland, Romania, and Lithuania were the usual destinations, although I'd heard reports that Morocco and Jordan had lesser-known black sites eagerly provided in exchange for counterterrorism support and enhanced security cooperation in dealing with their own homegrown Islamic State and Al-Qaeda affiliates.

How many men had been transported on this particular Gulfstream, I wondered, hooded and shackled with no idea where they were being spirited off to? The bird had been in service for such purposes ever since 9/11, which meant, I imagined, that the total number was likely astounding.

And, with any luck, that count would be increased by one with the capture of Kamran Raza.

The Gulfstream slipped inside the hangar and came to a gentle stop, its engines winding down with a final protracted cry, and for some reason I found myself holding my breath. A side door behind the cockpit opened with a soft hiss, unfolding its clamshell steps as my team waited for the second team to disembark.

Daniel Munoz appeared first, a well-muscled sparkplug of a man carrying a padded rifle case with a hiking pack slung over his shoulder. He'd grown a beard since I'd last seen him, his eyes lighting up at the sight of my team as he trotted down the steps ahead of the next men to exit the bird.

In contrast to Munoz, I'd only had the briefest encounters with his next two teammates but recognized them nonetheless—considering the circumstances under which we met, their faces would be burned into my memory forever.

AJ Washington was the medic, his lean frame reminiscent of an endurance athlete and standing in stark contrast to the intelligence operative behind him. That was Logan Keller, and judging by his build he could give Reilly one hell of a run for his money in the gym.

The fourth man to appear was tall and intense in every way, with a stoic expression and piercing eyes that I remembered well from our last meeting in person. His callsign was Talon, a suitable choice given that his name was Brent Griffin. He was, in many ways, my polar opposite. Griffin was serious, pragmatic, and professional, while I was...well, none of those things.

But we both served as the ground force commanders of our respective teams, and that shared bond served as the pretext for a mutual understanding that began upon our first meeting, now seven months distant, amid the smoke of a Yemeni prison where my team rescued him and his men.

Or at least, most of his men.

Munoz alone had escaped capture by the narrowest of margins, instead winding up in the hands of my team and pleading for us to conduct a prison break to free the others. Up until that moment we'd had no idea there even *was* a second Project Longwing team, a ploy that Chen had concocted and then kept from us—and, upon the capture of Griffin's team, she'd happily written them off as expendable before sending my men to complete their original mission.

A final man appeared in the plane's doorway by the time Munoz reached the hangar floor, and the process of elimination told me it was Quinn Kendrick.

But instead of a pale white Irishman, I was met with a man whose skin bore the rich, earthy tones of the Mediterranean sun, his thick, jet-black hair gelled to salon-quality perfection. He locked eyes with me, then my teammates, and broke into a broad smile of dazzling white teeth.

My mind short-circuited then. I sure as shit recognized him, would never forget his face either, but what he was doing here remained well outside my ability to fathom at present.

Munoz arrived and clapped me on the shoulder, hard, then pulled me in for a compressing embrace with the words, "What's good, brother?" before releasing me and moving on to my teammates.

A quick reunion between the men from both teams followed, and I stepped outside the fray to greet Brent Griffin, who set down his padded rifle case and extended his hand in a gesture I should have anticipated.

No bear hugs, no backslapping, no semblance of joy, just a cold, firm handshake, a greeting that I returned as he spoke in a sober tone.

"David."

"Brent," I replied, still distracted by the final man to join the main group.

I eyed him as he closed with us, still beaming. At my look of confusion, he happily offered, "I'm the newest hire for Project Longwing. Even have the blade to prove it."

He flashed a sheathed knife with his free hand, the hilt evident, although I knew intimately the exact weight, balance, and even the serial number without having to touch it. It was, after all, an exact copy of the five custom-made Winkler knives my team possessed.

Jalal Hassan was Libyan-born and, at the time I'd met him, a master sergeant in the air force. My team lacked an assigned joint terminal attack controller to manage drones, fighter jets, and precision airstrikes, and when a deployment to Libya had demanded all three, Hassan had temporarily been assigned to us. Cancer promised the man his own Winkler knife if he turned out to be a rock star in combat, and Hass, as he preferred to be called, had turned out to be that and more.

I watched him pass, turned my gaze back to the plane, and saw that no one else would be coming.

"Where's Kendrick?" I asked.

Griffin gave a subtle shake of his head.

"Kendrick committed suicide a few weeks ago."

My stomach dropped. "Shit, man, I'm...I'm sorry to hear that."

It was a painful revelation to be sure, but one that shouldn't have surprised me as much as it did. There were twenty veteran suicides a day in America, all part of the continued fallout from combat going back as far as Vietnam. That fallout didn't magically disappear when someone took a contractor job with the CIA, and I tried to reconcile myself with the fact that the last time I saw Quinn Kendrick—an eager redhead fist-bumping my guys in appreciation before joining his team in a vehicle headed to safety at an Emirati base—would remain the last time I ever saw him.

I forced my mind to the task at hand, nodding toward the padded rifle case on the ground beside Griffin. "Any chance you brought extra for my guys?"

"We tried," he said grimly, "believe me. Paks wouldn't have it. It's a miracle they let my team bring ours. Give me the rundown."

I should have been doing that already, I thought, though my mind was still scrambled by the news about Kendrick.

Then I began, "All right, here's the deal. We'll need two split teams, one per van. Divide our guys so we've got a mix of rifles, job specialties, and ground experience in Pakistan. I'll lead the first team, and keep my pointman and medic on hand. Plus Munoz and Keller, so we've got an intel guy in the mix."

"So the second team is me, Washington, and Hass. Who else?"

"Ian," I said, "he's intel. And Cancer, my second in command. Sniper, but he's the guy you want on your side in a fight. Doesn't matter if he's got a pistol or a rocket launcher, he'll get the job done. Are your guys ready to go hot?"

Griffin observed the flurry of conversations occurring between the various job specialties on both teams, with Worthy briefing Hass, and answered, "We all took Ambien on the bird and slept for about twelve hours, so yeah, we're ready."

"Good, because after the Commando raid, the Pak government authorized us to conduct unilateral direct action under ISI supervision. The gloves are off, and the intelligence picture has developed a lot while you were flying over. Bottom line, we've got two objectives. Both need to be taken down asap, and since they're linked, the raids need to go down at the same time."

He was fully focused now, eyes glinting with sharp perception.

"What's the first?"

"Probably bullshit. Intel is thin. The Agency had a satellite snapshot of a truck near the outlet of the tunnel Raza used to flee, gone by the next satellite pass. Traffic checkpoint cameras tracked it to a duplex in Sector H-13, and we've since confirmed it's still parked there."

"That's it?" Griffin asked incredulously.

"That's it. Odds of Raza sitting on his hands wherever the truck stopped are close to zero, which means it'll be a dry hole. My split team will notify our ISI minder at the last second and take it down, more as a diversion than anything else—since I can't ditch Tahir, the Paks will know about that one in advance."

"I was told the ISI was committing a second minder to my team."

"They were," I said, "but we got a lucky break. They're too bogged down with Kashmir and the military escalation, so they don't have another minder to assign. That means Tahir's got to pull double duty, so your split team can take down the second objective without oversight."

The slightest trace of a smile cracked across one side of his lips, the most emotion I'd seen from him yet.

"Outstanding. What is it?"

"The hot spot we've been waiting for. We didn't recover any digital material from the Commando raid—Raza took it all with him when he fled —but Ian intercepted a fair amount of his communications with the surveillance van. Triangulated iridium comms and satphone service provider data both point to a boutique IT firm that sold last month. Small two-story building in Sector G-8. The Agency's been running exploitation ever since then and it's a gold mine. High-bandwidth internet, unusually large data transfer, VPN relays, high-capacity router activity with encrypted configuration, voice over IP, you name it. It's got all the workings for a central hub in a larger network, so the odds are Raza is now running the show from there."

"And that's what you want my split team to hit?"

"For sure," I said. "You'll have three long guns instead of two, and I want my intel guy on scene. No offense to Keller, but Ian's got working knowl-edge of the situation here and he'll be able to connect the dots faster than anyone else. We'll make it look like the CIA gave us a last-minute intel dump pointing to the objective, and I won't notify Tahir until you've gone through the door. No Pak interference, and anything you find gets compart-mentalized from the ISI. But we need you to take Raza alive."

Griffin looked more uneasy at this last proclamation. "Okay. We'll see if we can pull it off."

"You'd better," I told him, more forcefully than I intended, "because then we can tell him the ISI will get his wife and children out of the country if he goes on the record about staging the Kashmir attacks."

"What makes you think he'll roll over?"

"Because of what he did with his money from North Korea. Swiss bank accounts in his kids' names, payments to schools in London...all that got cut off when he was found out, but it's safe to say he puts his family first. And since we can't trust the Paks to roll him up, it's on us to find him. Once we do, there's an Air Department Mi-17 standing by to deliver him back to the airport. Then Raza is on his way to Thailand in the Gulfstream, Agency interrogators will work their magic, and within a few hours his videotaped confession will be all over the news. That's the first the Paks should hear about his abduction, and with any luck that'll be enough for them and India to pull the plug on this war whether they want to or not."

"I was afraid we were past the tipping point for that."

His fear wasn't misplaced, to be sure, but Ian had supplied enough hard logic for me to put Griffin at ease—somewhat.

"Don't be so sure. India's sent a lot of troops into the fray and hit the Pakistani side of the Line of Control pretty hard with artillery and airstrikes. Pakistan's been returning the favor, but so far everything is contained within Kashmir. Regional mobilization is ongoing, though, and civilians are being evacuated along the border. Biggest issue, though, is the internal political and military communications that were leaked to the press. Those ratcheted this situation up more than anything else."

"Yeah, I heard. And that's what I'm worried about. Both sides know what the other is thinking, and all signs pointed to escalation before diplomatic efforts broke down. Looks like it's a matter of time before this thing goes nuclear. Literally."

"I thought the same thing, but Ian says that if we can get Raza before the first strategic strikes, we might be able to pull the plug. Pakistan and India have yet to start taking out each other's logistics and command centers, and after that it'll be border engagements and urban bombardments. Nukes won't come into play until after all that goes down."

Griffin raised his eyebrows.

"Unless Ian's wrong."

"Yeah, unless he's wrong, but I doubt it. The Paks store their nuclear weapons in a disassembled state. Warheads are kept separately from the delivery systems, and the Agency's tracking all of them. If those devices start getting mobilized, we'll know ahead of time—"

My monologue was interrupted by Cancer, who appeared at my side with the words, "Time's up, boss. We've got to load their gear and get moving. They can get the target briefs on the way."

I checked my watch and gave Griffin a helpless shrug.

"Well, you've been in-country for ten minutes already. Let's do some raids."

10

"Stop right here," David said. "Target building is the flat roof around the corner to our left."

Tahir pulled the surveillance van to the side of the narrow street before killing the engine, and Reilly craned his neck to see around the cargo partition. The rooftop in question was barely visible above a row of trees.

He leaned back in his seat, allowing Worthy and Munoz to take in the sight from the cargo area. This was the most they'd see of their objective before initiating their clearance, because the surest way to scare Raza into flight was to do a drive-by in an anonymous van. While the general most certainly wasn't in the building, Tahir remained blissfully unaware of that fact.

And in the meantime, Reilly's split team had to keep up appearances.

"I'm oriented," Keller called forward to the cab, "systems are online. No traffic yet."

David replied from the passenger seat.

"Let's give it a few minutes. We're already going in blind, no need to make it worse by giving up our one advantage."

"You got it," Keller said, ostensibly fulfilling his duties as an intelligence operative with subservience. He currently manned Ian's surveillance console, supposedly monitoring the objective for radio or cellular traffic.

But in reality, everyone in the van was merely waiting for their counter-parts on the other split team to arrive at the *real* objective for today's festivi-ties. Reilly's raid, by contrast, was perhaps the first time he'd ever deliberately gone into a dry hole. At best they'd find the driver of the vehicle that had spirited Raza from the tunnel outlet to Islamabad, and the odds of that driver knowing anything about the general's current where-abouts were, indisputably, zero. It was far more likely that the building would be empty, and this entire thing would serve as little more than a distraction for Tahir's benefit.

Unless, of course, the duplex wasn't a dry hole at all.

Reilly exchanged glances with Worthy, finding nothing in the point-man's expression that indicated concern. Islamabad was broken up into five zones, each subdivided into smaller sectors. The current objective was in H-13, and their limited view on the way in barely resembled what they'd seen of the city so far.

Their target building was in the outskirts, situated amidst a mix of semi-urban and rural settings. The area had minimal commercial activity and consisted mostly of city blocks packed with small houses and open fields, none of which gave the slightest indication of hostile activity.

"So," Keller asked, turning to face Reilly with the headphones over one ear, "how do I look?"

Reilly gave him a nod of affirmation. "Your nose looks good. Can barely tell it was broken."

"Apparently you set the bone pretty well. Hey," he added, addressing Munoz, "remember the last time the three of us were together? In that truck...what did you guys call it?"

"The Franken-pickup," Reilly supplied. "Land Cruiser retrofitted with an anti-aircraft cannon."

"Right. That's some real Yemeni engineering right there. Yeah, I was in the back, you were on the gun taking out enemy vehicles two klicks out, and Dan—"

"I was driving," Munoz added. "A good setup, right until the cannon jammed. And, you know, the T-72 showed up."

"And that," Reilly acknowledged, hoping that particular encounter with an enemy tank wouldn't be a repeat occurrence in his time remaining under the CIA's employ.

He was momentarily afraid Keller would bring up another event from that drive…namely, the inquiry about his max deadlift. The question had occurred to Reilly almost immediately upon seeing the intelligence operative's physique, although he'd managed to suppress it for several interminable minutes before blurting it aloud, only to find that Keller had bested his personal record by twenty pounds.

But Tahir spared him the possibility of that particular indignity with one of his trademark passive-aggressive and anti-American comments.

"I am glad you are all happy to see each other. But with eight Commandos dead and five wounded the last time you said we would find Raza, I am much less enthusiastic."

It occurred to Reilly that the ISI officer was blaming the team because, simply put, the Pakistani Commandos had been unable to clear the building without American assistance. And while Reilly was happy to point out that fact and David would be more so, it was Worthy who deflected the accusation with considerably more tact.

"Raza was there," Worthy said. "And the outcome of that raid wasn't the Commandos' fault. Not really. Whoever chose them deserves the blame. Sending a unit that specializes in high-altitude mountain warfare to assault a hardened target building is like expecting an NBA player to win the Masters in professional golf. It should have been Zarrar Company on that target, plain and simple."

The pointman was coming up on the end of that declaration when Reilly's phone buzzed, and he checked the display to see the encrypted chat between the men of both split teams.

A new text had appeared, sent by the other team's ground force commander. Griffin had kept the message brief.

IN POSITION, STANDING BY.

Reilly barely had time to process this when a responding text appeared, this one typed by David.

GO.

Keller then played out the first of his two contributions to the unfolding charade, announcing in an urgent tone, "We've got a cell phone hit in the building, sounds like Raza is calling for exfil."

"Let's move," David said, quite convincingly. "We need to get in there before any more bad guys show up."

Tahir obligingly fired the ignition and accelerated the van forward.

Keller ditched his headphones and donned his helmet before joining Munoz in assuming a two-handed grip on his rifle, the last act before they exited the vehicle to bang their target. The action was a simple yet important one, a final measure of comfort that Reilly was denied, leaving him feeling utterly impotent and powerless. He wouldn't draw his pistol until he'd stepped out, and even that would be an anticlimactic reminder that his fully equipped HK417 was half a world away while he'd be clearing a building with a 9mm handgun.

The van turned the corner, and Reilly spotted the dented SUV that the Agency had tracked from Raza's tunnel outlet into Islamabad. Tahir brought their van to a sudden stop in front of the target building, which was Keller's cue for his second lie of the day.

"Update. The Agency just provided a time-sensitive target, the other split team is hitting it, no further information at this time."

"*What*?!" Tahir cried, but by then it was too late.

Munuz flung the cargo doors open and leapt outside, leading the way to the breach point as the rest of the split team poured out after him.

11

Ian clutched his Halligan tool, a ten-pound instrument forged from a single piece of steel that was like a sinister big brother to the crowbar. One end was forked for prying and pulling. The other had a flat, curved offshoot for similar purposes, albeit at a 90-degree orientation from the handle. It was flanked, however, by a pointed pick with a decidedly different purpose, and Ian swung that point at maximum velocity toward the upper right corner of the glass door.

A high-pitched pop erupted as the pick sheared through the pane, turning the entire surface into an opaque veil of hairline cracks. Ian raked the Halligan diagonally toward his feet, snagging the full-length blinds inside and pulling them down as the glass below the pick's path of destruction fell away in a glittering torrent of fragments. Once the tool made contact with the bottom corner of the doorframe, Ian hoisted it vertically, puncturing the corner of remaining glass and raking it free before stepping aside.

Hass slipped through the shattered doorway before the final shards had fallen, his HK416 at the ready, Griffin following behind him by the time Ian released the Halligan from his grasp and reached for his pistol.

There was an absolute sense of urgency. The building they were entering was situated near the intersection of a main road in the highly populated and commercially vibrant Sector G-8 of Islamabad, and the surrounding area was packed with markets, office buildings, and educational institutions. And while they'd parked the van directly opposite the door, at least partially blocking the view from the street, only seconds remained before the first of many calls were placed to notify the local police.

Ian's Glock had just cleared the holster in an exceedingly fast draw when the muffled patter of suppressed gunfire reached him. Despite the CIA's overwhelming evidence to the contrary, he'd been concerned that the boutique IT firm was just that—an IT firm—and these muffled shots were his first assurance that there was at least one armed opponent inside.

He entered the doorway with his pistol aimed at the center of a small lobby, then cut right toward Hass as he registered his surroundings. There was a reception desk with its swivel chair askew, and rows of server racks that stood tall and foreboding, packed into the space with blinking lights that created a dance of data. The hum of cooling fans was a constant, unnerving background noise, the air thick with the scent of stale coffee and electronic equipment.

A man in a navy blue security uniform had fallen dead beside the desk, his attire legitimate enough to convince Ian that this was, in fact, an IT firm. Nothing about the guard's security insignia and duty belt indicated a bloodthirsty terrorist mercenary, nor did the submachine gun that had tumbled from his grasp—Ian's gaze momentarily fixed on the weapon nonetheless, a prize he'd have to seize at the first opportunity.

He followed Hass right around the desk, flowing into an open doorway to find an empty room with a kitchenette. They exited as quickly as they'd entered, Hass in the lead and picking up the trail of Brent Griffin, who was now moving down a short corridor toward two side rooms and a set of stairs.

Ian made a brief departure from the stack to retrieve the guard's submachine gun, a Beretta M12 that fired the same 9x19mm bullets as the Glock he holstered now. But the 30-round magazine was a massive upgrade, as was the accuracy conferred by two pistol grips and a metal buttstock, and he rose with a far greater sense of effectiveness than when he'd knelt.

His rush to pick up the last position in the stack was nearly complete when two figures darted across the corridor and through the doorway opposite. Washington, the other team's medic, was followed by Cancer, both men having entered through a Halligan breach of a side window as Ian had done the same through the front door.

Both men reappeared as Hass and Griffin converged on the stairs, and the intelligence operative halted to allow Washington to take the third slot with his rifle. Ian should have been next, and he was about to set foot on the stairs when Cancer stopped him with a forceful grab and a single word.

"Gimme."

That was all the notice Ian had before Cancer snatched the Beretta submachine gun from his grasp, turned, and raced up the stairs in pursuit of the other three shooters.

12

Worthy ascended the staircase of the residential duplex, with Reilly close behind him as they followed the lead of Keller, Munoz, and David.

The clearance of the first floor had yielded no human presence, just a living room with dusty, neglected furniture, a kitchen with dirty dishes and nearly empty shelves, and one bedroom that was almost empty except for a broken chair and scattered belongings.

But the second bedroom they'd cleared was different, with threadbare mattresses packed tightly on the floor. It was a promising clue that pointed toward the building being a possible bed-down site for Kamran Raza, though by no means one that ruled out the presence of one or more civilians if not an entire family on the second floor.

Worthy reached the last stair, following his teammates into a hallway to find that the clearance was nearly complete. This level was smaller than the first, a detail he'd known since viewing the building from the outside but one he hadn't fully comprehended the extent of until now—there was a single door on either side of the hall, which ended in a set of stairs leading to the roof.

Then the stack divided into two, with each member moving the opposite way of the man to his front. The end result was Worthy entering a room with Munoz, and in the process obtaining his first confirmation that the residential duplex wasn't a dry hole at all.

That fact wasn't discernable due to human presence, for the room was empty. But what Worthy saw assured him that it hadn't been that way just minutes earlier. A tea kettle rested on a short table, flanked by two cups and positioned between dual windows that provided ideal vantage points onto the street below. This was unquestionably an observation post, and Worthy didn't need to feel the kettle to know that it was freshly steeped—the teacups beside it were still steaming, although it was the presence of a final object that assured him that they'd been intended for guards rather than civilians.

A single walkie-talkie rested beside the tea, forgotten by whoever had manned this position in the interests of providing an early warning to Raza. This room represented damning evidence that their target had in fact been here, the presence of a handheld radio and the SUV outside combining in Worthy's mind to turn the tables on everything his team had previously thought about the presumed dry hole.

This, the residential duplex, *was* the primary objective. The boutique IT firm that the other split team was in the process of raiding was a supporting effort at best or a red herring at worst. Raza wasn't there but *here*, or at least he had been—the only question that remained was whether they'd arrived too late or managed to isolate him in the only section of the building left to search.

Worthy stopped at the door to the hall and allowed Munoz to exit the room first, using the delay to transmit to the rest of the split team.

"Observer post, Raza was here."

Then he entered the hallway and sighted his next destination, the short section of stairs leading to a final door and, beyond it, the building's flat roof that they'd observed before the raid. If Raza hadn't fled already, then that's where he was, braced for a last stand with his security detail prepared to mow down anyone who appeared.

Speed and surprise were of the essence now more than ever, though the momentary delay incurred by placing the two rifle-equipped shooters in the lead was not only justified but critical to shifting toward this new and final portion of the clearance.

But David Rivers happened to be the closest one to the stairs, and in classic David Rivers fashion he was unwilling to forgo this happy coincidence to something as trite as tactical survivability.

The team leader aimed his Glock toward the door overhead, ignoring the cautionary shouts of Keller and Munoz. By now he was moving far too quickly for anyone to steal his position as the number one man, his figure nearly a blur as he took the steps two at a time toward the roof.

13

Hass was in the lead up the stairs, and both he and Griffin opened fire simultaneously.

Cancer heard the percussion of a human body hitting the ground overhead, although it wasn't until he reached Griffin's kneeling form at the top of the stairs that he saw the felled target: a Pakistani man dressed in the same security uniform as the guard downstairs, albeit with a Heckler & Koch MP5.

Hass crouched at the opposite side of the stairs and Washington fell in at his backside, mirroring Cancer's position as he pressed his knee against Griffin's backside. The kneeling lead shooters gave each other a quick nod before both pivoted around their respective corners.

Cancer followed suit, standing behind Griffin while aiming his Beretta submachine gun and firing five shots over the team leader's head at the sight of a man half-concealed within a doorway aiming a rifle in their direction.

The man below him did the bulk of the damage, however, stitching the opponent with subsonic 5.56 rounds and dropping him in place as unsuppressed gunfire abruptly rang out behind them before going silent—Hass and/or Washington had just taken someone out, and if the neighbors hadn't called the cops yet, they were now. Cancer looked over his shoulder to see

Washington doing the same, both of them checking the hallway to their rear before giving a shoulder squeeze to their respective number one man.

Griffin rose and moved forward with surprising speed, seeking to follow his shots through the open doorway as Cancer hastened to catch up. The other two-man element was now moving in the opposite direction with Ian in tow, both split-team elements fully committed by virtue of the hallway that created a T-intersection with the stairs.

He slowed in unison with Griffin a few steps before the doorway, after which the team leader sidestepped the enemy corpse and seamlessly entered without turning. Cancer made a counterclockwise rotation and moved along the wall to his right, visually clearing his first corner with a second's glance before rotating his aim and upper body toward the center.

The room's contents were reduced to a blur of obstacles and hiding places as he searched for targets, and Cancer only subconsciously noticed an array of multicolored light sources before a quiet *pop* rang out from behind a large, curved desk. A spray of drywall erupted from the wall to his front, and he simultaneously knelt and directed his barrel toward the noise.

His new lower vantage point now provided a view below the desk, where he made out a crouched figure that his Beretta MP12's front and rear sight posts neatly aligned with as he fired three blazingly fast rounds, then two more, the submachine gun subtly bucking in his grasp as he registered a confirmed kill.

Cancer rose to continue his clearance, finding Griffin halted halfway down the far wall and sweeping the room with his suppressed HK416. The area behind the desk represented a potential blind spot that Cancer sought to clear as soon as possible, and he did so to find the body of his slain opponent but no one else.

Hass transmitted, *"We're clear,"* and Griffin said, "Clear, site exploitation."

Only then did the room's contents come into full focus for Cancer, although the sight was just as bewildering now as it had been before he could take time to observe the details.

Numerous computer monitors were arranged atop multiple desks, the glow of their monitors casting eerie blue and green hues. Each screen was filled with cascading lines of code, real-time surveillance footage, and intricate digital maps. Behind the desks were server racks that hummed incessantly, their LED indicators blinking in a strangely synchronized rhythm. The air was almost frigid, with powerful air conditioning units working overtime to keep the sensitive equipment from overheating. Cables snaked across the floor, connecting various terminals and workstations in a tangled mess.

Before him was the large, curved desk behind which his opponent had crouched, the surface cluttered with state-of-the-art computer hardware. Multiple keyboards, mice, and touchscreens were arranged in an ergonomic arc, with a high-backed swivel chair positioned before the largest monitor—if the usual post-clearance search for intel was looking for a needle in a haystack, Cancer now saw nothing but needles. There was far too much digital data to sift through, and only Ian could prioritize what hard drives to take with them before the Paks arrived.

Cancer glanced down at the man he'd shot only to find it wasn't a man at all. Below him, an attractive blonde woman was twitching in the throes of death, her legs jolting slightly with postmortem spasms. She wore a blood-soaked fleece jacket punctured by all five of his bullets, her eyelids locked open to reveal frost-blue eyes staring at the ceiling, a CZ 75 pistol lying just beyond her grasp.

He was momentarily shocked by the sight, almost unable to process it; he'd initiated this raid fully expecting to capture a fat Pakistani general, and ended up greasing a hot blonde chick instead.

Between that disparity and the motherlode of computer and technological hardware before him, Cancer had officially entered into *what the fuck* territory.

Griffin seemed to have no such reservations, arriving at Cancer's side before glancing at the dead woman almost as if he'd expected to find her there.

"Katarzyna," the team leader said.

"Who?"

Griffin clarified, "Katarzyna Zajac." Then he gave a short laugh of disbelief, locking eyes with Cancer before he continued with emphasis, "You just killed Project Longwing's Target Number Three."

14

I reached the top of the stairs and flung open the door, hearing the thunder of footsteps from my teammates charging upward behind me.

My first steps onto the rough concrete of the flat rooftop cleared the way for them to follow as I conducted a 270-degree clearance. Worthy said Raza had been present in the building, and the only hope of a successful mission at this point was to find him up here. Capturing the general alive would require precise gunfire against his guards, which would be of particular difficulty for me with the Glock handgun I swept in a clockwise arc. I mentally cursed myself for not letting the two shooters with HK416s lead the way, and a moment later the admonition was replaced by a far worse revelation.

The rooftop was empty.

A sense of fury and self-loathing descended on me at once—it had been my decision to sacrifice this objective by allowing Tahir to notify the ISI in advance of our breach, and if I'd instead led him to the IT firm and let the other split team hit this duplex without interference, Kamran Raza would be dead or in custody this very second.

Then I was suddenly confronted with the thought that despite having a newborn at home, I'd impulsively refused to relinquish my position as the number one man, and charged up the flight of stairs with nothing more than a pistol. Perhaps equally disturbing was the fact that no thought of my family even occurred to me until now. My role as a father was so totally compartmentalized from my combat identity that it may as well have belonged to a separate person.

The remaining men from my split team spilled onto the roof as I lowered my pistol, breathing in cool air that carried with it the faint scent of wood smoke and street food. I felt detached from my body now, taking in the broader surroundings as if doing so would somehow reveal where our target had fled to.

Early afternoon sun bathed the city in a crisp, golden light. My northward view revealed the tall, rugged outlines of the Margalla Hills sharply defined against a vibrant blue sky. The distant hum of traffic from Srinagar Highway formed a steady, low murmur punctuated by honking car horns. I looked northeast to find the modern towers and white minarets of an enormous mosque, as well as the distinctive silhouette of the Pakistan Monument whose petal-like structure arced to form a semicircular orb that reflected the sun with glittering rays.

I traded my pistol for my cell phone when it vibrated to life, the display revealing that Griffin was on the other end.

The call jarred me back to another unfortunate reality—not only had I fucked up which objective should have been the primary one, but I'd sent the second split team into some kind of bait-and-switch decoy that probably resulted in them terrorizing a handful of IT techs in what I now knew was an entirely criminal action.

Bringing the phone to my ear, I said, "Raza was here, he escaped before our raid. Are you on your way out?"

By then I'd accepted it as a bygone conclusion that his split team had forcibly entered a civilian enterprise, which made his response all the more incomprehensible.

Griffin spoke quickly. "We killed Target Number Three, Zajac, the hacker. Intel motherlode, all cyber, Ian's collecting whatever hard drives he can but there's way too much for us to handle. Tahir needs to notify the police and ISI to cordon the objective and get over here asap to assist with site exploitation."

"Got it," I replied, ending the call without understanding how anything from Griffin's report possibly made sense given the remaining facts. If he were capable of humor—which, to the best of my knowledge, he wasn't—I would have demanded verbal confirmation that he was serious.

I turned to find my teammates spread across the roof, awaiting my guidance, and as if on cue, Tahir blundered through the door and onto the rooftop, holding his pistol.

He glanced at the cell phone in my hand and then made eye contact, asking the single worst question he possibly could in that moment.

"Did the other team find him?"

I watched the ISI officer in disbelief.

Here we were, having missed Raza by mere minutes because Tahir had reported the raid to an organization that had promptly leaked the information, and yet my team's minder was earnest in his inquiry, ignoring the obvious implication that the ISI had burned our objective long before we'd burst through the door.

The sum total of these factors made me want to punch him in the face, but I had bigger fish to fry: namely, fulfilling Griffin's directive and updating my men as soon as possible.

"Tahir, I need you to—" I announced, although that was as far as I made it before Munoz cut me off.

"Look!"

I followed his wide-eyed gaze to the southeast, initially registering only the unremarkable view of Rawalpindi. It consisted of densely packed buildings and bustling streets, a mix of residential areas, commercial complexes, and occasional green space, none of which would warrant the sniper's near-panicked expression.

Then my gaze ticked upward, and everything that had preceded that moment faded from my mind.

Four sleek, metallic objects streaked eastward across the sky, so distant as to be barely detectable. Their rapid, synchronized movement somehow defied explanation. At first I thought we were watching fighter jets, but their low altitude and unwavering trajectory were somehow different. They moved with a relentless precision, no smoke or exhaust in their wake although I now saw that a quartet of wispy plumes rose from the ground far behind them.

The realization hit me in a flash. These weren't manned aircraft at all, and the distinctive, elongated shapes and distant streaks of smoke could only mean one thing. The full gravity of the situation dawned on me then, my heart pounding as the truth crystallized in my mind.

Pakistan had just launched a cruise missile strike, and war with India had begun.

15

Meiling Chen made a final scan of the email directive on her central computer monitor, doing her damnedest to bring her breathing under control.

Then she stood and, noticing a slight tremor in her right hand, placed her fingertips on the desk before speaking.

"Listen up," she called, repeating the order at a near-shout when it became apparent no one had noticed her the first time.

Her second announcement had the desired effect, replacing the overlapping conversations in the OPCEN with the creak of office chairs swiveling to face her.

"Everyone's been understandably drilling down on their section's responsibilities, but we're going to level the bubbles right now. I want a full rundown of what we know and what we don't. Soren," she continued, addressing her communications officer, "the J6 desk is exempt—your only purpose in life right now is to get a fix on Raza's current location."

"Yes, ma'am," Christopher Soren began, his reply eclipsed as Chen continued her monologue.

"We sent our teams to go after Kamran Raza, Target Number Four. Instead they eliminated Target Number Three, Katarzyna Zajac. We know she was a Polish cybersecurity specialist turned hacker, poached by the Chinese before going freelance. We've tied her to data breaches in the DoD and DoJ, among others, and we know she vanished from Algeria the day that Erik Weisz was killed."

Chen forced a breath to steady herself—her pulse was hammering, the urgency of the situation bleeding into her voice in a manner unbecoming of someone who more than anyone else needed to be calm amidst chaos. Then she went on.

"But there have been no indications of Zajac's location or current activities until our men gunned her down in Pakistan a half hour ago, and the equipment and data found with her have made it clear that Kamran Raza's plan goes far beyond a border incursion in Kashmir.

"The Directorate of Analysis has thus far confirmed that Zajac intercepted Pakistani and Indian military and political communications. She selected messages from both sides that dealt with contingency plans for escalation, modified them to make it appear that war was imminent, and then leaked them to international media. That makes her singlehandedly responsible for the full breakdown in diplomatic negotiations, and it appears that was just the beginning—"

"*Raptor Nine One,*" David's voice rattled through the speakerbox, "*Suicide Actual.*"

She lifted her mic, dispensing with radio formalities.

"Make it quick."

"*Both teams are back at the safehouse, consolidated and standing by—*"

"Good," she interrupted, "because you're going to remain standing by. We've received Angel's initial data from Zajac's control room and I need him to continue transmitting the rest. Say nothing to Tahir—we've traced a call from the ISI warning Raza that your split team was inbound to capture him. We're using that communication to locate Raza, so until I personally confirm otherwise, both teams will remain at the safehouse. If there was ever a time for you to obey orders, this is it. Thousands of lives are at stake, if not tens of thousands."

For the first time in their working relationship, David Rivers displayed utter subservience.

"Will comply. Suicide Actual, out."

Chen resumed her speech as if the team leader had never checked in.

"It's going to take a full analysis of the captured data to determine the extent of Katarzyna Zajac's planned involvement, but we're getting a damned good idea based on the facts. When our shooters closed in, she barricaded herself in the control room and used her final minutes on earth to make her next move."

Her voice faltered at the last word, and she became suddenly aware of the eyes upon her. Everyone involved with international affairs was in full panic mode right now, and her verbal race to make sense of the situation had caused her to almost forget she had a captive audience.

"What we need to establish," she went on, preparing to concede her speaking role as she took a final glance at her computer screen, "are the specifics of *how* she did that and what the results were. I have to prepare a program assessment as an addendum to the Directorate of Analysis results. That report is going straight to the Joint Chiefs, so let's make this brief and to the point. Lucios, you're up."

Andolin Lucios didn't bother rising from his seat, alternating his gaze between her and his computer as needed to retrieve data that even he hadn't been able to yet memorize.

"Zajac had established access to the military's secure communications through spear-fishing attacks and targeting officers with entry to strategic networks. We can also conclude she knew exactly where and what Pakistan's first line of defensive measures were—Babur cruise missiles in Okara and Bahawalpur—as well as their pre-established list of targets in India. With the entire military on high alert, all she had to do was give the order."

The order, Chen thought, feeling struck by the incongruity between those two simple words and the utter hellfire that resulted.

"Which she did how, exactly?"

Lucios took a gulp of air, the first hairline crack in his professional veneer.

"Deepfake audio message sent over official channels," he explained. "The voice mimicked General Ahsan Malik, Chairman of the JCSC, and the audio was accurate enough to indicate she used advanced voice synthesis and AI algorithms to feign authenticity. As for the order itself, the message stated that India had launched offensive strikes and ordered immediate retaliation. Authority codewords and communication methods were by-the-book, and by the time the Pak government realized what was happening and shut everything down, it was too late to stop the strike."

"Next up. Specifics on the outcome of that deepfaked order. Jamieson."

Wes Jamieson didn't stand either, nor did he face her—at least, not fully—and it wasn't until she closely examined his features that she realized why. The normally grizzled combat veteran was visibly tearing up, although whatever emotions he felt at present were isolated entirely from his steadfast voice as he delivered his report.

"The first Pakistani launch was out of Sialkot, three cruise missiles directed against Amritsar Radar Station. Indian surface-to-air assets intercepted two of them, but the third struck the primary radar array. That operational disruption paved the way for the next salvo, four cruise missiles from Rawat. One was either shot down or malfunctioned near the border, and the rest reached their intended targets. We've confirmed one impact at Jammu Airbase, and two more at Pathankot Air Force Station."

"BDA?" she asked.

"Battle damage assessment is a munitions depot destroyed in Jammu, estimated to be a considerable ordnance loss but we don't know the specifics yet. A hangar housing in Pathankot was destroyed and the Indians are down three MiG-21s and two Sukhoi Su-30s, along with a main runway hit that's currently preventing the rest of their fighters from launching."

"Thank you," Chen managed, wanting to speed the brief along before Jamieson's emotions could get the better of him. "Let's move on to retaliation."

But the operation officer's voice remained steady as he glanced at his computer and responded, "The specifics are forthcoming, but India launched BrahMos cruise missiles against three strategic locations along the border. A Pakistani forward military outpost near Lahore was destroyed. No casualty count yet, most likely because there's no one there left to report. The second strike hit a military communications center in Sialkot, and the third impacted at Gujranwala logistics base. Nine missiles total, seven hits, and a full battle damage assessment isn't available because the Pak comms center is down."

"I have yet to see any intel indicating further missile strikes are about to occur. But given the nations we're dealing with here, I know there's a catch. So what is it?"

Lucios fielded that inquiry as if the answer were obvious. "All indications are that both governments are viewing the launches as a strike/counterstrike exchange. The Paks are scrambling to figure out how their forces fired first and the Indians are expecting another act of aggression. However, the stand-down is limited to their surface-to-surface assets."

"And there's the catch," Chen said. "Give me the ground picture first."

The intelligence officer's voice was abruptly tempered by precision as he leaned toward his computer monitor.

"Initial reports indicate that both countries are intensifying their military readiness along critical points of the Line of Control and the international border. The Indian Army is reinforcing its units in Punjab, positioning armored brigades and mechanized infantry to secure key transit routes and communication lines. On the Pakistani side, significant reinforcements are being positioned in areas like Lahore and Bahawalpur, including anti-tank and surface-to-air missile systems."

"Noted. Air and naval?"

"Both air forces are increasing sorties along the border and pre-positioning fighters and bombers at forward air bases. Submarines and surface ships equipped with cruise missiles are now underway from Karachi and Visakhapatnam—"

The shrill alarm of a phone on her desk halted his brief mid-sentence. The OPCEN staff was all too familiar with what that sound meant, and Chen damn well knew by now that she had better answer it by the second ring.

She lifted the receiver and said, "F2, Project Longwing."

The man who responded identified himself by last name only, which was enough. He was the senior intelligence coordinator for the deputy director, and Chen didn't have an immediate answer to the one thing he needed to know.

Placing the phone on mute, she called out, "Where do we stand on locating Raza?"

No response, and that caused Chen to snap her gaze toward the J6 section to find every one of its members too engrossed in their work to have noticed her.

"Soren," she shouted, gaining the man's attention. "You're up, make it fast."

The communications officer yanked off a headset and replied, "We're still following the outgoing call that the ISI used to tip off Raza about the split team raid. The correlating cell vector went dark when he fled but there's just been a new ping that the DA is exploiting. We should have more information in five minutes, maybe less."

Chen started to speak into the phone receiver, caught herself, and tapped the mute button before continuing.

"In the works, I'll call back with an update in ten."

Then she listened intently, processing the stream of information that was, mercifully, being delivered over the phone to give her a few minutes' head start before the official emails started flying.

But any gratitude she felt for the early notice faded as the man continued, the implications of his update going from hopeful to horrendous in the span of twenty seconds.

Chen hung up a moment after he did, and then relayed the contents of the call to her staff.

"Let's start with the good news," she began. "The data captured from Zajac's control room is being sped through the declassification process as quickly as it can be, and once that's done we can expect a White House press conference announcing that information to the world. But I've just been advised in no uncertain terms that due to Pakistan's lengthy history of deception operations, this may or may not help to de-escalate the situation. Bottom line, it's going to take Raza's capture and filmed confession to put the final nail in the coffin for stopping this war, and the stakes for doing that have just increased considerably."

She let that information settle for a moment, then said, "Which leads me to the bad news. That call was all the notice we're going to receive before the intel reports arrive."

For some reason her focus was drawn to Wes Jamieson. If he'd been on the brink of tears before he gave no indication of it now, although his head drooped in almost passive acceptance. What she was about to say was a bygone conclusion for him and perhaps everyone present in the Project Longwing OPCEN.

But Chen had to say it anyway, and when she did it was with a mournful sense of hopelessness.

"The Paks have begun assembling their nukes."

16

I took a drag off my cigarette, then leaned forward to tap it into the mason jar between my boots, a makeshift ashtray into which the last two butts had already been deposited.

Leaning back on the mattress in my bedroom at the safehouse, I looked at the flickering light mounted on the ceiling. Bringing the filter to my lips, I drew another inhale and blew the smoke upward. Cancer had loaned me a pack of his Marlboros, an incredible act of generosity for the sniper and one that I wouldn't forget anytime soon. Night was falling now, and I'd never felt further from capturing Kamran Raza.

I was taking my first break from radio watch in the surveillance van since we'd arrived back at the safehouse. Having waited a seeming eternity for Chen to alert me to some update in Raza's location, I finally decided to get away from the headset and collect my thoughts in private.

The search for our target was dire and had grown only more so since the opening hostilities between India and Pakistan, and I took stock of our situation for the tenth time in as many minutes.

Griffin's split team had left their objective with every pocket and dump pouch stuffed to the brim with hard drives, which left them unable to sneak any captured weapons past the Pakistanis. We could find a way to make do with our current equipment. Insurmountable odds were a hard-earned area of expertise for my team, but that counted for nothing until the general was pinpointed.

I heard footsteps approaching from the hallway, and was standing by the time Cancer entered my room.

He stepped close, speaking quietly.

"Just heard from Chen. They identified a spike in electronic signals, then geolocated it to intercept an encrypted call. It was Raza."

"Where?"

"Abandoned factory in northeast Rawalpindi. No telling how long he'll stay. We need to snatch him tonight. Air Department will fly in their Mi-17; there's a National Agricultural Research Center fifteen minutes from the objective where they could land an entire fleet if they wanted to. We self-destruct the surveillance van and ditch the one the ISI gave us, everyone exfils on the bird, and we're on our way home by zero-one, maybe even midnight."

I checked my watch. It was 9:16 p.m.

"How far is the objective from here?"

"Forty-five minutes, tops. And it's not huge by factory standards, but it's still two stories tall and about 5,000 square feet. We'll need both split teams to bang it. You know what that means."

"Yeah," I conceded. "No throwing Tahir off the trail this time."

Cancer nodded. "We need to deal with him. Now."

"All right, I'll do the talking. Plan A, I convince him to do what we want."

"And if he doesn't agree?"

I shrugged. "Then we hogtie his ass, bring him with us, and cut him loose before exfil. Either way, the ISI doesn't know anything until we're mission-complete."

The sniper gave me one of his trademark smirks, a surefire sign that he knew exactly what Tahir's response would be.

"I'll have the guys standing by for Plan B. You give the nod to Reilly, and he'll try not to give Tahir a concussion when we take him down."

"Brief the guys. I'll have a verdict in five."

Cancer stepped around me, snatching his pack and lighter from the mattress before giving me a final, "Sure thing, boss."

Then he was gone, leaving me to walk through the safehouse in search of Tahir.

I took no pleasure in what had to be done. Plan B would put my team on the run with Pakistani police and intelligence units being piled in with a terrorist outfit on our list of threats, and that was just on the tactical side of things.

The other consideration was that while Tahir was an ornery pain in the ass who was idealistic about his country and nothing else, he'd nonetheless done nearly everything we'd asked of him. There was no convincing him to betray the ISI, but I was going to give it a shot for five minutes and not a second longer.

I found the ISI minder in the living room, seated in the center of the couch and watching the Pakistani news on TV. His mood was palpable in both his grim expression and rigid body language—his country was going to war while he was stuck babysitting a group of Americans he'd never wanted to help in the first place.

"Tahir," I said.

"What."

He didn't take his eyes off the television, prompting me to retrieve the remote from the coffee table.

The news ended with the press of a button, inciting him to direct his intense gaze at me. His considerable shoulders and arms were tense, as if he was primed for a fight, and I continued, "We need to talk."

"Then talk."

Seeing that he wasn't planning on moving, I pulled the coffee table back from the couch and took a seat atop it, facing him at an uncomfortably close distance.

After swallowing, I said, "Someone in the ISI told Raza that we were coming."

Tahir scoffed. "Wrong. And we have bigger problems than Raza."

"No," I said, "we don't. Look, him inciting a border dispute was just the beginning. You want to know what we found on the second objective? He had a hacker balls-deep in Pakistani government and military communications. She'd been leaking diplomatic memos, some of them modified to make both sides think war was imminent. And when she heard our guys coming to find her, she gave a deepfaked order to launch cruise missiles against India."

His forehead wrinkled in disgust, and I could see from the look in his eyes that he thought I was delivering a heinous lie.

"I have heard nothing about—"

"You've heard nothing," I cut him off, "because the ISI hasn't told you. Believe me or don't believe me, but in a few hours this information will be all over the news."

Tahir leaned back on the couch, crossing his arms.

"If that comes to pass, I may believe you. But not a moment sooner."

"Well that's too bad, because we don't have time to wait. It's going to take a videotaped confession from Raza to end this war. He'll provide that just to get his family out of Pakistan, provided we can find him." I was, of course, unwilling to admit that we now knew *exactly* where he was, at least until Tahir had been restrained and stripped of his cell phone. "If we pinpoint Raza, we'll have to move fast. And we can't notify the ISI because someone there is protecting him."

He shook his head resolutely, although for the briefest of moments he broke eye contact with me to look down. I hadn't convinced him and in all likelihood couldn't, but I could see the first inkling of doubt creeping into his expression.

But he said only, "This is not true. It cannot be true."

I rubbed my forehead. "Tahir, the Agency respects a lot of things but information privacy isn't one of them. They traced a call telling Raza to flee the duplex before we hit it, and that call came from the ISI headquarters. There's a reason the US didn't notify your government before the Bin Laden raid."

"If they had," he replied angrily, unfolding his arms and leaning forward, "it would not have changed the outcome. I wanted to see him killed just as much as anyone in America."

"You did, Tahir, but your organization didn't. And here's another truth bomb while we're at it. The ISI knew where Bin Laden was hiding. I've heard that directly from my superior at the Agency. She wouldn't tell me whether that information was held by a three-man cell or the Director General, but the ISI knew. And as for Raza...maybe he's being protected from on high, or maybe he's got one corrupt secretary on his side. Right now, it doesn't matter."

For once, Tahir didn't want to fight over this or anything else. He looked utterly exhausted, though whether because of the news, our mission thus far, or me addressing things he'd previously considered but never spoken of, I couldn't be sure.

His rotund stomach pulsed in and out with breath. "Even if what you say is true, I am still an officer of Inter-Services Intelligence. I have served honorably for eighteen years, and I will not forgo my duty. I must do my job to the best of my abilities, and right now my job is to oversee your men and report back."

A shadow appeared in the doorway and I glanced toward the kitchen to find Reilly leaning against the counter, eating a sandwich while watching me closely for the word to tackle our ISI minder and take our presence in Pakistan fully off the grid.

"Tahir," I went on, "no one's questioning your competence. Or your loyalty. But a few hours ago we watched four Pakistani cruise missiles on the way to India, and we both know that order wasn't given by your government. The situation is already out of our hands, and it's only going to get worse from here.

"So forget about personal and national pride and start thinking about stopping this war before it's too late. And if altruism isn't good enough for you, then try the thought of your family dying in a nuclear holocaust. We don't have time. Updating the ISI is off the menu. My men are going to do whatever it takes."

I waited a beat to let my words sink in, then added, "So the question is, are you coming with us?"

Tahir looked down again, examining his lap, and then looked back up at me.

His voice was low then, just above a whisper. "You know where Raza is? Right now?"

"I have a feeling the Agency is getting close. Call it a gut instinct."

Tahir seemed to read between the lines of that statement, his stoic expression softening for the briefest second as understanding hit him. He knew everything I hadn't told him, that my men had Raza dead to rights so long as the ISI didn't interfere, and for the first time fully understood that his decision in the next ten seconds would spell the difference between full-scale war and, if all went according to plan, defusing the entire situation before it was too late.

I watched him closely, his brows furrowing as he drew a deep inhale.

"If I go rogue," he said, "no nuclear weapons will be needed—my family and I are dead. You underestimate the thoroughness of my organization."

Well that was it, I thought. I glanced at Reilly in the kitchen, prepared to give the nod that would result in Tahir's forcible apprehension and restraint. We'd only have a few hours at best before the ISI noticed he was missing, but if everything played out as I hoped, Raza would be in custody by then and we'd be boarding a helicopter for our trip out of Pakistan.

But before I could give the order that would escalate my team's status from well-heeled foreign advisors operating under ISI oversight to a criminal band of spies with a price on our heads, Tahir spoke again.

"However, David," he said thoughtfully, tilting his head in consideration of my offer, "perhaps there is another way I can help you."

17

Reilly scanned the darkened storage yard while his team walked, the distant hum of city traffic a muted backdrop. Griffin's men were stationed with the two vans now parked at the fringes of the lot while they kept a lookout for new arrivals.

The air was thick with the scent of diesel and dust as Reilly's team followed Tahir, who moved with practiced ease, his silhouette barely discernible in the dim light of a solitary bulb hanging from a nearby pole. He pulled a jangling keychain from his pocket, then stopped before a rusted padlock securing the largest storage unit in sight. Inserting the key, he clicked the lock open and rattled the shackle free.

He stepped aside, handing the lock to David with the words, "Secure the unit when you are done. Leave whatever you do not need."

Reilly took that as an invitation to kneel before the five-meter-wide sliding door, grasping the handle and heaving the movable partition upward, only stopping when he was certain the barrier wouldn't come crashing back down.

He was met with the smell of diesel and dusty concrete, the darkness within illuminated a moment later as his teammates activated flashlights. The sight of what waited inside the massive storage unit caused the breath to hitch in Reilly's throat.

A white Suzuki sedan faced them, with two additional vehicles backed in against the far wall: a dull olive green Hilux quad cab beside a faded blue Subaru station wagon with a roof rack. The paint of all three vehicles was marred with dust and dirt, bodies displaying dents and scratches, and at first glance the tires appeared worn but serviceable.

The remaining quarter of the storage unit was piled with duffel bags and hard cases that Reilly and Worthy descended on immediately to examine the contents. Ian held a flashlight over them, revealing AK-47s with worn metal surfaces, stacks of loaded magazines, additional boxes of ammunition, and a cluster of fragmentation grenades.

"Rifles," Worthy narrated to David and Cancer, "mags, ammo, frags—"

Reilly interrupted this with a titter of delight upon unclasping a particularly long hard case and seeing the unmistakable shapes within.

"RPG-7! One launcher, three rockets. I call dibs."

He rose and whirled to advance on Tahir. "What is this?"

The ISI minder seemed pleased with the reaction as he explained, "The ISI tasks me with running a network of informants and deep-cover agents. They do not provide the stipend or equipment to supply these men to do what they are asked. I learned this early on, and over the years have become skilled in acquisitions."

Ian asked, "So all this is off-the-books?"

"No accounting exists for the items because I gained them outside of official channels. Only a select few of my colleagues know about this as an insurance policy in the event that I go missing."

David looked puzzled in the ambient glow of the flashlights. Pressing a fist against his forehead, he said, "Jesus Christ, Tahir, why didn't you give us all this at the start?"

"At the start, I was not prepared to destroy my career."

"Destroy it?" Cancer sneered. "Hell, we're masters of discretion. The ISI will never hear a word from us, not about any of this."

"I should hope not," Tahir replied. "Because if you are around for them to ask, it will be because you are in prison."

And that cryptic bullshit, Reilly learned in the coming seconds, was enough to strike his entire team mute.

David broke the silence with the uneasy inquiry, "What's that supposed to mean?"

"It means," Tahir went on, "that I cannot be seen to willfully betray the ISI. I will report to them everything you said about Raza being protected, as well as the fact that you believed my organization would disrupt another capture attempt."

"I mean, you don't have to tell them *everything* I said."

"I will also report that as a result of this, you tied me up and left me to complete the mission on your own."

Worthy offered, "There's not much point in going rogue if you tell them we're going rogue."

Tahir shrugged. "The ISI is busy with India. They could not even commit a minder for your second team. This will give you time to do what you need to do—"

The generosity was too much for Reilly to handle, and he wrapped the man in a tight bear hug.

"You're a good guy, Tahir. I knew it the moment you came back for us in Qasbo."

The ISI minder wrestled free from his grasp, offendedly smoothing his shirtfront as he said, "I never left you. As I explained, I had to turn the van around—"

"Right," Reilly said. "Sure. But still."

David looked immensely relieved. "Okay. Thank you. We can work with this. Give us until ten tomorrow morning unless we call you first."

Tahir smiled and nodded politely, his face eerily lit by the flashlights like a father telling ghost stories at the campfire.

Then he lifted his wrist to manipulate his watch, a process that ended with a muted beep, before he looked across the assembled team members once more.

"You have two hours."

David stammered, "Two—what? You've got to be kidding me. Think about it, Tahir, we've got travel time, raid time, and time required to make it to our exfil. We'll need at least five to be safe."

Nodding as if he understood and accepted this logic, Tahir checked his watch and said, "You have one hour, 59 minutes, and 42 seconds."

There was a simple solution to this, Reilly thought, and it entailed what the team had discussed as Plan B: restrain Tahir and take him captive, to be released when exfil was assured and not a moment sooner.

Reilly began easing his way closer to the ISI minder in preparation for the order from David.

Tahir seemed to anticipate this, glancing at the medic and rolling his eyes.

"As I said, I have several colleagues who know about this supply. If I go missing, they will report the automotive information and you will be found. Either way, you will have to get rid of the vans by the end of my deadline. The only question is whether you can proceed with the weapons and vehicles I have so graciously provided, or proceed with none at all. The choice is yours."

Then he checked his watch. "One hour, 59 minutes, and 18 seconds."

"Call in the second team," David blurted, starting a timer on his own watch. "Rifles stay with us, the rest of the equipment gets cross-loaded evenly. Task org?"

Cancer responded, "Two per car, one from each team so each vehicle has a rifle that's worth a fuck. Worthy and Munoz on point in the Suzuki, Reilly and Hass in the Hilux, you and Keller take the surveillance van, Griffin and Ian take the other, me and Washington bring up the rear in the station wagon."

Reilly was already moving toward the equipment to divide the rifles, ammo, and grenades—the rocket launcher, he thought with unshakable determination, would remain with him—as well as to check the vehicle serviceability and fuel levels alongside Worthy and Ian. Then a subtle movement caused him to turn.

Tahir was calmly strolling away, hands in his pockets, sardonically whistling "The Star-Spangled Banner" as he disappeared into the night.

18

"Good spot here," Keller called out from the cab of the surveillance van. "I'm stopping."

"All right," I said, keying the mic to speak over the team net.

"We're stopping. Split Team One, proceed and don't get burned. We're standing by until we hear back."

"*Copy,*" Worthy replied. "*Moving forward for target reconnaissance.*"

I leaned back from the surveillance console to look through the windshield, watching the taillights of the Suzuki sedan glide past on the otherwise deserted nighttime street of northeast Rawalpindi. It had barely departed before Reilly pulled the Hilux to a stop in front of my van, taking point with Hass in the passenger seat.

We were in an industrial district that had seen better days. Closed factories and warehouses lined the streets, the exteriors faded and covered in graffiti. The sidewalks were dotted by piles of scrap metal and abandoned machinery, adding to the sense of desolation.

Grabbing the hand mic from its mount on the side of the van, I prepared to transmit. There wouldn't be much information from me and hopefully none from Chen, who was already tracking the fact that Tahir had cut us loose with spare equipment and vehicles. I checked my watch to evaluate the time remaining on the ISI officer's countdown before we had to ditch both vans and proceed on our own.

"Raptor Nine One, Suicide Actual. Be advised, we've got four vehicles staged a half-kilometer out and one moving forward for target reconnaissance. Currently fifteen minutes from the landing zone, with 32 minutes remaining before Tahir notifies the ISI that we're rogue. Unless there's any curveballs, we should be about ten mikes from breach, how copy?"

"*Understood,*" Chen replied. "*Good news is the White House press conference is beginning as we speak, so the world is about to learn that Zajac initiated the cruise missile exchange.*"

And while that much was all fine and dandy, I thought, I could tell from her words and her tone that the other shoe was about to drop.

"You said 'good news.' What's the bad?"

"*First curveball has already arrived. The Mi-17 will arrive at zero-one-one-five, but it doesn't have enough payload capacity to exfil all your men.*"

I took a breath, unwilling to accept the information. "Say again."

"*The helicopter is equipped with internal supplementary fuel cells to increase the range, and it carries a crew chief along with an interrogator and one Ground Branch medic. Once Raza is onboard, they advise room for an additional five personnel, but no more. That means your team will exfil as planned, while the second team completes the ground movement I'm about to relay.*"

Going from a helicopter exfil in half an hour or so to yet another leg of the mission was a gutting development to say the least, but what could I do at this point?

I said, "This would have been extremely useful information to have a few hours ago."

"*I agree,*" Chen added, sounding crestfallen. "*It's a failure in communications that I will adjudicate when able. Once the bird is away with Raza and your men, Talon's team will complete a vehicle movement toward Gujranwala, four hours southeast of your current location. By the time they make it there, we'll have the linkup set for their movement into Indian-administered Jammu and Kashmir or northern India itself. All formal border crossing points are locked down so it will likely involve a foot movement for the final leg to link up with Ground Branch.*"

After locating the area in question on my phone imagery, I transmitted,

"Stand by," before switching my hand mic for one tuned to the tactical net. "Talon, Suicide."

"*Go ahead,*" Griffin replied.

Time to drop this particular bomb, I thought.

"Bureaucratic fuckery is in full swing. Turns out the Mi-17 has internal fuel cells, so they've only got room for five on exfil. The only other option to get the hell out of here is a four-hour drive to the vicinity of Gujranwala, then a foot movement over the border to Kashmir or India. My call is that we load any wounded onto the bird and the rest of us stay together. Thoughts?"

Griffin was silent for a moment, but only a moment. "*Things might get dicey on a drive to the border. I concur.*"

I switched back to the command net. "Raptor Nine One, we will load any critically wounded team members onto the Mi-17. The rest of us will complete the ground movement."

"*Negative,*" Chen said. "*As I told you, your orders are to have your team conduct rotary wing exfil while Talon and his men make the ground movement.*"

"I heard you the first time. But unless someone gets hit on the objective, it's all of us or none of us. Talon and I are in agreement. Will advise on post-mission status and ETA to the landing zone."

After an extended pause—she was powerless to stop me, so it didn't matter much what she told me to do at this point—Chen responded, "*Copy all. Good luck, keep me posted.*"

"Suicide Actual, out."

Aside from the exfil, everything thus far was a positive development. We were minutes from raiding the factory, and news of Zajac's involvement was hitting the world stage in record time. That latter fact alone should begin to defuse the escalation between India and Pakistan, with Raza's videotaped confession sealing the deal for everyone involved.

Provided he was actually in the factory as advertised, I thought.

Before my mind could linger on that thought, Worthy transmitted over the team frequency, "*Suicide, we are drive-by complete, stand by for info.*"

"Send it."

"*Aside from the main door facing the street, we've got two windows per on the front and sides. We couldn't get around the rear to check, but it's a standalone*" *building and it looks like we'll be able to get a vehicle back there during the hit. Safe to assume there's another two windows and probably a door on the backside. Team One is moving to stage at the intersection southwest of the building."*

"Good copy," I replied. "Air Department bird is inbound, time on target is still quarter after one. That gives us 42 minutes to bang the objective and make it out with Raza before getting him on the Mi-17."

I used my red lens headlamp to consult a laminated notecard that I'd written on in permanent marker, my only means of keeping our task organization straight in my head at this point—we had five vehicles and two teams totaling ten men, which complicated my job considerably. Fortunately, the mix of job specialties was mostly equal. Unfortunately, Griffin's team had fully outfitted weapons while mine had, as Cancer had indelicately put it, shit.

The AK-47 beside me had a flashlight taped to the lower handguard, which was where the scope of modifications began and ended. And since the rest of my men lacked anything more sophisticated, we'd be little more than backup for our counterparts on Griffin's team.

"Current plan stands," I transmitted. "We drive in current order of movement, approach from the west. Split Team One takes the back, Two rolls to the far side, Four on the near side. Teams Three and Five hit the front. Immediate breaches, clearance runs clockwise on the first floor. No frags if we can avoid it—we need him alive. After exfil, we'll form up in the previous order of movement on the way to the landing zone. Any wounded get loaded onto the bird along with Raza, and the rest of us begin movement to Gujranwala...looks like Islamabad Expressway southeast to the N5. Questions?"

Worthy was the first to reply. *"One, copy."*

Then Hass, positioned with Reilly in the Hilux to my front. *"Two copies all."*

"Four, copy," Ian transmitted from the ISI van, which he drove with Griffin riding shotgun.

"Five copies," Cancer said. *"Let's do it."*

My second in command was at the rear in the Subaru wagon, piloted by Washington so the medics were split up the front and rear of the convoy.

I keyed my radio once more.

"Racegun, hold fast until we form up on your rear and give you the call, then lead us in. Doc, let's move."

Worthy leaned his head against the Suzuki's passenger-side window, watching through his night vision as a stray dog crossed the road just in front of the target building.

"Anything?" Munoz asked from the driver's seat.

"No," Worthy replied. "No lights, no movement. One dog."

"Armed or unarmed?"

"Definitely a civilian. Hold your fire."

Munoz's view was obstructed by a large, immobile cement mixer with its drum raised and supported by sturdy legs. They'd identified it in the course of their drive-by of the upcoming objective, and after making a two-block detour to loop back around, Munoz killed his headlights and glided the Suzuki behind the derelict machine to his right.

Now he had a line of sight to the four-way intersection ahead and, beyond it, the target building on the opposite side of the street.

They were now minutes at most from the rest of the convoy arriving behind them and the radio call to initiate the raid. Munoz was prepared to fire the ignition and speed the Suzuki forward and then in a left-hand loop to circle the back of the factory, or as close as he could get, before dismounting and moving to a rear entrance whether window or door.

But Worthy keyed his mic before any of that occurred, gaze fixed ahead as he watched new entrants arrive on the otherwise silent street.

"Two SUVs approaching the target building from the northeast," he quickly said, watching the distant vehicles glide toward his own vehicle and, by extension, the factory. "No headlights, they've got to be there to exfil Raza."

David's response was immediate.

"We're hauling ass—disrupt them the best you can until our arrival."

Worthy and Munoz were out of the car in a flash, advancing to take positions on either side of the cement mixer as the SUVs neared the factory. Worthy was in the process of taking aim with his AK-47 when he registered what was really happening here—the SUVs were flying down the road far too fast for a surreptitious nighttime pickup.

Worthy transmitted just as the trucks slammed on the brakes to arrive at the factory's front door in the most expeditious manner possible.

"They're not picking him up. They're here to kill him."

The inherent contradiction of this reality struck him then. Even the CIA had barely been able to locate Raza, and the only other people in Pakistan who knew where he was hiding tonight were his own people. Was the general being double-crossed?

All that mattered at present was capturing him alive, and Munoz opened fire just as the vehicles came to a halt, his infrared laser slicing across Worthy's night vision and shuddering slightly with each subsonic round fired toward the first windshield, then the second.

But an unsuppressed weapon would make far more of a statement at this eighty-meter range, and Worthy thumbed his selector lever downward to the full auto position. All he and Munoz could do was stall the otherwise imminent attempt on Raza's life and inflict the maximum damage possible until the other four team vehicles arrived to bring the fight up close and personal, and Worthy took aim the best he could before depressing his trigger.

The AK-47 jolted to life in his hands, its tremendous muzzle flash causing a near-total whiteout in his night vision for the duration of a five-round burst directed at the lead vehicle. His first break in fire revealed shadowy figures scrambling behind the SUVs, and he fired again, the wooden buttstock pressing against his shoulder in rhythmic succession.

At this point he'd have to trust Munoz to do the precision shooting. An AK was already an imprecise tool to say the least, and far more so when the shooter couldn't align its iron sights by virtue of night vision focused at distance. Worthy was at first shocked that he couldn't make out a single flash of return fire, but then he saw something far worse.

A half dozen infrared laser beams appeared in the darkness, sweeping across the intersection in disciplined arcs. Without a single muzzle flash in sight, the cracks of incoming bullets ricocheted off the cement mixer. Night vision *and* suppressors, Worthy thought—these men were both seasoned and well-equipped, and if they turned out to be Pakistani military shooters, then the team had just gotten themselves into a whole new world of trouble.

It was too late to back out now, and he poured a third burst of suppressing fire toward the vehicles before ducking behind the mixer as an incoming laser preceded the smack of bullets slamming into his only source of cover.

Then something very strange happened, likely just as much of a surprise to the enemy shooters as himself.

A compact sedan shot out of the space beside the target building, fish-tailing onto the street ahead of the stationary SUVs and speeding directly toward Worthy. The sight was almost too ludicrous to process, and there was exactly one explanation: Raza had a getaway car parked behind the abandoned factory, and at the sound of gunfire outside, he'd put it to good use.

Worthy's view of the SUVs was first blinded by the sedan's headlights, and then blocked by the car entirely as he fired at the engine block. Munoz managed to transmit the words, "He's on the run, headed toward you in the sedan," before the vehicle entered the intersection. If it proceeded straight it would run directly into the inbound team convoy, but the driver veered sideways instead, careening down the street to Worthy's right.

He was about to transmit that the car was now headed southeast from the four-way before realizing the update was completely unnecessary.

The Toyota Hilux containing Reilly and Hass came abreast of the mixer, braking sharply before swerving through the intersection in pursuit of Raza. Worthy had the briefest second to glimpse his adversaries scrambling to load their SUVs when his view was once again blocked, this time in more dramatic fashion.

His team's surveillance van blasted straight through the four-way and toward the factory, where the chirp of its tires responding to the parking brake preceded a sharp 90-degree turn that left the HiAce blocking the street at a perpendicular angle.

As the team's ISI van screeched to a halt in the far lane, it provided an opening for Cancer's Subaru wagon to pass. The Subaru cut sharply to the right, speeding off in pursuit of the Hilux and Raza's sedan.

Worthy quickly ejected his empty magazine and began reloading.

Meanwhile, Keller jumped out of the surveillance van. David followed him, stumbling slightly as he exited. The two men sprinted toward the cover of the cement mixer.

Finishing his reload, Worthy moved swiftly to his right, toward Munoz's position behind the cement mixer. He ducked low, making room for Keller and David to take cover where he had been standing moments before.

Griffin and Ian were already out of the ISI van and readying grenades, and Worthy saw the two SUVs speeding toward the roadblock. They were driving bumper to bumper toward the rear quarter panel of the surveillance van now obstructing their path, the first to ram it and the second to push the preceding SUV through the blockade.

He used the final seconds before impact to prepare his own grenade, or rather Tahir's—it was oblong with a ridged casing, and God only knew how old it was or whether it would actually detonate. He saw a flash of light through the surveillance van's driver's-side window as the embedded thermite charges of the self-destruct mechanism ignited within.

"Now!" he yelled, hurling his grenade over the mixer and seeing that Griffin, Ian, and Munoz were all doing the same.

His shout had barely faded when the lead SUV's bumper impacted the opposite side of the van, where it struggled to push through the weight of the heavily modified vehicle's surveillance equipment and its attendant power and cooling systems, all of which were in the process of being melted down.

Keller and David fell onto their assess and skidded behind the left side of the mixer, their baseball slides occurring to the soundtrack of SUV engines revving as they tried to ram the surveillance van aside. It was just beginning to pivot when the four grenades exploded in near-simultaneous thunderclaps, the flashes lighting the surrounding buildings in stark green through his night vision.

The lead SUV's partially visible silhouette was momentarily illuminated, then hidden by the ensuing smoke and debris as the sound of the detonations blended into a racket of destruction. Shrapnel scattered into the night, the force of the explosions shaking the ground beneath him amid a shower of sparks and twisted metal flying into the air. Maybe the SUVs were armored and maybe they weren't, but no one on Worthy's side of the fight was sticking around to find out.

Worthy and Munoz sprinted back to their Subaru wagon. As they jumped in, the remaining four Americans quickly climbed into the ISI van.

Munoz started the Subaru and immediately threw it into drive. Worthy rolled down his window and leaned out with his rifle as Munoz swerved the wagon around the cement mixer.

Once they cleared it, Munoz sharply turned the steering wheel to the right, cutting through the intersection. Glancing in his rearview mirror, he saw the ISI van following closely behind, mirroring their movements.

By then Worthy was speaking over the team net. "Teams One, Three, Four are clear of the target, moving to reinforce—need you guys to vector us to your current location."

Hass was just beginning his return transmission when Munoz straightened out the wagon on the road ahead and floored the gas pedal as far as it would go.

"First turns," Hass transmitted from the driver's seat, "right, left, right, left. Past that you're going to have to track our phones—he's still headed southeast, if we go much farther we're going to see PAF Base Nur Khan."

Reilly gripped the steering wheel of the Toyota Hilux, navigating the streets of the Rawalpindi industrial district at maximum speed as he offered, "That might be his plan."

Which would be just what they needed right now, he thought—to have a high-speed chase end at the gates of a major Pakistani Air Force installation. It was entirely possible that Raza had some prearranged military protection that would work in his favor, and if that was the case, every second mattered in interdicting the vehicle ahead.

Raza's compact Honda sedan swerving across the road ahead of him had seen better days.

Its rear window had been all but shot out entirely by whoever had tried to kill him at the factory, and one tail light had fallen victim to their fire. Reilly saw periodic smoke billowing from its hood, which meant there was a better than passing chance that Worthy or Munoz had hit the engine block.

But the Honda failed to die completely, its headlights cutting through the inky darkness and lighting up factories and warehouses before it whipped a right-hand turn at the next corner. It was these kinds of juking moves that had kept Reilly at bay thus far, the much heavier pickup faster in a straight line but far less nimble when maneuvers were involved.

Hass looked over his shoulder and said, "The Subaru's still behind us. We need to stop Raza before he reaches the airbase."

"I will," Reilly said, carving the steering wheel to follow his quarry. He'd always wanted to do a PIT maneuver in a real-world scenario.

And as he finished the turn, he saw that his chance may have arrived.

The Honda's driver had either deliberately slowed or the vehicle itself was giving out, more likely the latter, and Reilly assumed a laser focus in his determination to bring this chase to a close before it was too late.

He only dimly registered the faded graffiti and crumbling infrastructure on either side of them, feeling the rough texture of the road beneath the tires, each bump and pothole jarring him but failing to break his concentration. The Hilux's engine growled as he pushed it harder, weaving through piles of scrap metal and dodging discarded machinery that littered the sidewalks until his front bumper came abreast of the Honda's rear quarter panel.

Reilly spun the steering wheel toward the fleeing vehicle while maintaining acceleration, which caused the Honda's rear wheels to break traction. Then he *really* steered into it, pushing out the entire rear end and initiating a spin from which there would be no return.

The sedan flipped a 180-degree rotation across the street. It came to a halt facing the wrong direction as Reilly reversed his steering, first to avoid hitting the building beside him and then to angle his pickup's frame behind the Honda's rear bumper before he brought the truck to a screeching halt.

The pursuit intervention technique had gone as flawlessly as could be expected, checking off a major box on Reilly's bucket list, and he was in the process of grabbing his AK-47 and leaping out when a new set of headlights closed in from behind him.

He and Hass barely cleared the Hilux before the Subaru wagon slid to a stop with its front bumper against the Honda's, effectively sandwiching the target vehicle and preventing it from moving forward or back. Reilly raised his AK and prepared to round the sedan's passenger side, expecting his teammates to fan out around him with interlocking sectors of fire for the final snatch of Kamran Raza—or whoever had just suffered an insanely bad case of mistaken identity.

But the next few seconds made it clear that a coordinated snatch wasn't on the agenda.

Cancer was out of the Subaru in an instant and moving faster than Reilly had ever seen him, the flashlight taped to his AK-47 glaring its beam at the Honda as the sniper closed in before anyone else could so much as take up a position on his flank.

Cancer was no stranger to murderous rages. They were, by this point in his career, part and parcel of armed combat.

But the sudden end of the pursuit had triggered in him the same blood-lust that caused police to beat unarmed drivers who had just led them on a high-speed chase, to which was added the indignity of an unknown band of shooters very nearly killing the same man they needed to capture alive.

He was on autopilot as he darted toward the Honda's passenger side, flashlight glaring through the window to reveal the open palms of a surrendering driver and front passenger visible over the dash. Cancer held his fire, pivoting toward the rear window to find a third set of hands, these framing the wide-eyed face of Kamran Raza.

A millisecond's assessment assured him no one else was in the back, which was all the permission Cancer needed to wrap up this engagement in the most expeditious manner possible. Sure, he was feeling the same enraged exhilaration that a police officer would under similar conditions. Unlike a cop, however, there were no helicopters or civilians filming with their phones to dissuade him from making good on the ruthless instincts triggered by the chase.

The AK-47's designer had, in his infinite wisdom, engineered the selector lever to rotate from safe to fully automatic on the first click—it took sliding it down a second click to achieve single-shot mode, and Cancer didn't bother exerting that level of effort.

He opened fire on the front cab in a single protracted burst that simultaneously turned the front passenger window into a web of bullet holes and hairline fractures splattered with blood from the inside, and then shattered it entirely. With his view to the front two seats unimpeded, he saw that the passenger was slumped forward against his seatbelt, dead without a doubt.

The bullet-riddled driver was, however, still processing oxygen into carbon dioxide, albeit with great difficulty with the blood flowing out of his mouth, and Cancer took a half-step sideways before unleashing his final hellstorm. Headshots, full auto, at a range of two meters.

A one-second blast had the intended effect, melding the man's skull, teeth, and brains into one shredded and fragmented spray that painted the headrest, console, dash, and what remained of the far window into an abstract expressionist masterpiece.

Cancer didn't bother putting his smoking AK on safe—the magazine was empty anyway—before dropping it on its sling and wrenching open the rear door with one hand.

He drew his Glock with the other, briefly registering that Reilly, Hass, and Washington were fanning out around him before aiming his pistol at the last surviving man in the Honda.

The contrast between Raza's clean-cut military profile photo and his current appearance was staggering.

He was bearded now, and had gained considerable weight. Gone was the stiff-collared dress coat with medals and sash, replaced by a sweaty and rumpled dress shirt unbuttoned to below the collarbone. One wrist sported a gold watch as the lone visible concession to whatever he'd been paid selling nuclear secrets to North Korea.

Most striking of all was the sheer cowardice that Cancer observed— Raza was covering his ears with his hands, eyes pinched shut, body trembling in full-fledged spasms.

"Get your ass out here if you want to live."

There was no response, verbal or nonverbal. Cancer realized then that while he and his teammates wore dual radio earpieces with decibel cutoffs, Raza didn't have so much as foam earplugs and 7.62mm shots at close range were loud as *fuck*. A grin crept across the sniper's face as he holstered his pistol and replaced it with his beloved Winkler knife, leaning in to slice the seatbelt over Raza's shoulder and then at his hip rather than attempt to reach around the shaking man.

Cancer sheathed his knife once more, and it was time for the fun part.

He grabbed Raza's nearest wrist and pulled it away from his ear, locking the joint and using his opposite hand to drive the man's elbow into a straight arm position. That arm instantly became a lever that Cancer maneuvered with a combination of wrist lock and elbow control, sufficiently motivating the general to slide out of the seat and toward his assailant. The process was much more efficient than trying to simply muscle a 250-pound man out of the vehicle, and once Raza's sandal-clad feet touched the pavement, Cancer wheeled him sideways and lowered him onto the ground on his stomach with more force than was necessary.

He released a guttural exhale as the air was knocked out of him, the first sound Raza had made since his capture, and Cancer knelt while simultaneously retaining control of the locked wrist and grabbing the other. Looping a flex cuff around both, he cinched it tight to restrain Raza's arms fully behind his back before frisking the man for weapons.

The sound of a vehicle approaching caused him to look up sharply, though his concerns eased when Reilly announced, "Our guys." Hass was pulling security down the street in the direction they'd been heading before the PIT maneuver, and Washington was searching the Honda—or at least whatever he could without getting elbows-deep in gore.

Raza had no weapons, nothing at all on his person except for a wallet, and Cancer maneuvered him upright in time to see the ISI van pulling to a stop in the open lane.

The sliding door opened to reveal David and Keller in the cargo area, red headlamps glowing around their necks, and Cancer guided his quarry forward into their waiting arms as his team leader spoke.

"Load up," he called out, flinging Raza to the floor of the van. "We've got less than twenty minutes to make it to the LZ."

Griffin replaced Ian in the driver's seat, and the intelligence operative quickly rounded the ISI van to climb in through the side and pull the door shut behind him.

David and Keller rolled the general onto his back, then wrestled him into a sitting position against the far wall as the van pulled forward. It was the last journey this vehicle would take with an American at the wheel—given Tahir's countdown to notify the ISI and effectively sell them all up the river along with this vehicle, it would remain abandoned at the landing zone.

Ian took up a seated position beside Raza, setting down his AK on the opposite side and activating the red lens headlamp around his neck. Then he took final stock of the men in the vehicle as the convoy pulled away from what remained of the Honda.

Griffin was driving, with David riding shotgun and transmitting instructions to the remaining split teams. Ian removed his radio earpieces and exchanged a glance with Keller, the other intelligence operative in their ten-man element, who was kneeling behind the partition to the cab with his earpieces in so he could relay necessary guidance while overhearing the proceedings. Keller flashed his hand open once, then held up four fingers —nine minutes to the landing zone—and Ian nodded.

Then, after activating a button on his voice recorder, he turned his attention to Raza.

Ian began, "Your family isn't safe until—"

"What?" Raza nearly shouted. "I cannot hear."

The former general's hearing was and would forever remain impaired after Cancer went Tony Montana on the other two men in his vehicle.

Ian leaned in and said, "The ISI will only get your family out of Pakistan if you cooperate. In exchange for the safety of your wife and children, you're going to talk me through your entire operation from start to finish."

"What for?" Raza asked. "You saw the news. The Kashmir incursion *was* the entire operation."

So that was how this was going to go, Ian thought. If Raza wanted to play dumb, then he was going to take a little convincing.

Ian said, "I understand you want to minimize your involvement. But I've got a lot of time to hurt you before you're handed off to people who do that sort of thing for a living, and if you withhold information from me again"— he let the words hang for a moment—"I will."

There were two lies implicit in his last statement. First, neither Ian nor anyone on his team could torture Raza. The priority now was for a handoff and filmed confession of his participation, and any injuries he occurred before then would come back on the team tenfold.

And second, Ian didn't have the time.

He continued, "We already know what your plans were. And before you try to deceive me again, know that we took down your entire cyber site."

Raza looked at him in confusion. "My command post in Bhanati?"

He was referencing the location of the disastrous Commando raid. Providing a captive with information was a major intelligence faux pas, but Ian had no time to waste. "I didn't say your command post. I said your cyber site. Zajac."

"I have never heard of, or been to, a place called Zajac."

The intelligence operative swelled with feigned anger, though his thoughts at this moment were more underscored by confusion. Raza was either a world-class actor, or he genuinely had no idea what Ian was talking about.

He forced fury into his voice. "I'm talking about Katarzyna Zajac. And your cyber operation in Sector G-8."

Raza shook his head. "I do not know who this is. Or what 'cyber operation' you speak of."

Was he being genuine? Ian certainly hoped not, because if so, it spelled very, *very* bad things for the situation between Pakistan and India.

"I'll sum it up for you," he continued. "She hacked military and diplomatic communications from both countries. Leaked altered memos to escalate the situation. Last but not least, she gave a deepfaked order for the cruise missile launch, which resulted in retaliatory strikes by India. We've got her in custody"—another lie—"and she's already told us that you were the man in charge. We've confiscated and analyzed all her data to confirm that. Anything you say from this point forward that contradicts what we already know will result in consequences."

Nothing in Raza's dumbfounded expression indicated deception, nor, as Ian then found out, did his response.

"Whoever this is, she is lying. And her data is wrong. My role was to stage and command the offensive in Kashmir. That is exactly what I did, but nothing more. They were very clear about what my role should be."

"Who is 'they?'"

Raza looked at the floor of the van, an unmistakable look of guilt and shame penetrating his features.

"I do not know."

"You can't honestly expect me to believe—"

"I do not know," the general repeated, this time with a raised voice. "I was contacted by a man who set up a meeting."

"In the Kirthar Mountains?"

"Before that. Urak Valley. There were further meetings in Kirthar, however, where I received instructions. I dealt with several people. They paid me two crore, 14 lakh—"

"USD."

"Roughly 75,000 dollars. Paid each time, as a gesture of good faith. And they set up a bank account for the final payment."

"Which was?"

"Three million."

Ian's eyes narrowed, his heart beating faster with every word. "And you agreed? With no idea who your employer was, or what they intended to achieve?"

"What choice did I have?" Raza said, concluding the statement with a disgusted snicker. "The North Koreans were supposed to grant me asylum for our arrangement, but they ended all contact when I was exposed. My assets were frozen. I was forced to hide in remote shitholes, living like a *harijan*, a peasant, waiting every night for the helicopters to come."

"What about your ISI protection?"

"What protection? America was strong-arming my government to find me. I had no money. No one at the ISI would tie themselves to me."

"Until your employers stepped in."

"Maybe. I do not know. They told me to flee to the safehouse in G-8. Then they had me relocate to the factory in Rawalpindi."

"Both moves," Ian interjected, "kept you from being captured. So who tried to kill you at the factory?"

"The only ones who knew I was there," Raza said. "My employers."

"Why?"

"How can I know? They were supposed to pick me up and take me out of Pakistan. Forever."

Ian had a damn good idea of where Raza's next exile was supposed to be, but he asked the question anyway. "And your next exile was to be in…"

"Iran."

He considered that a moment. Pakistan's southwestern neighbor had much to gain from the war unfolding now—with two major powers weakened, Iran could strengthen both its regional influence and ties with China and Russia, fill any resulting trade voids with an increased demand for energy exports, and potentially assume a mediation role to position itself as a peace broker to gain diplomatic clout on the international stage.

But none of those benefits, Ian concluded, were sufficient to risk inciting such a conflict. There was simply no way Iranian influence would go undetected, and additional sanctions and trade embargoes would effectively cripple the nation. There would be total financial isolation, foreign investment would vanish, and both Russia and China would distance themselves in the quickest possible fashion.

Iran talked a good game about spreading Islamic influence and backed that up with extensive and multifaceted regional covert activities by their Quds Force, but ultimately its priority was strengthening its geopolitical and strategic position.

"The men you interacted with in this arrangement," Ian went on, "what nationality were they?"

"Only Pakistanis."

"Pakistanis, or Quds Force masquerading as Pakistanis?"

Raza shot Ian an incredulous look, one that bordered on pity.

"I have lived here my entire life. Two of them were Punjabi, three were Pashtun, and one was Sindhi with a Karachi accent. There were no Iranians."

Ian decided to probe another possibility.

"India funds and arms insurgencies and conducts espionage, including cyber espionage, within Pakistan. They have a larger military, higher defense budget, and better technology. Is it possible they incited this war to establish themselves as the dominant regional power?"

Keller extended two fingers and held them up for Ian to see, the final time hack before they arrived at the landing zone.

"Possible," Raza conceded. "They have a wide network of spies. But if they had such a plan, the ISI would know about it. We have our own sources, you see, and would have sought support from our allies long before a single cruise missile was launched."

His logic was sound, Ian thought, and the presence of Katarzyna Zajac seemed to contradict the already threadbare speculation. India's cyber capabilities were far too advanced to require outsourcing the role to a woman who was effectively a terrorist contractor. And even if they had, there was no alternate universe in which India would risk her capture by running the operation within Pakistan rather than on their own side of the border.

Ian didn't need time to assemble a list of which nations would benefit from such a war—Russia and China, as well as the United States by virtue of its military industrial complex. Iran, to be sure, along with a dizzying array of non-state actors and terrorist groups.

And while only members of the two latter categories would be sufficiently motivated to actually attempt such a feat, none of them had the means to do so.

Ian leaned forward and said, "If you're telling the truth, the attempt on your life makes sense. Whoever is behind this wanted you dead so everyone assumed you were the king instead of a pawn. Unfortunately, that means something bigger is going on. So, what could it be?"

"I have no idea," Raza stammered. "I know who would want such a war, but as for starting it? For being able to start it? There is no one." He thought for a moment, then shook his head slightly. "No one."

If Raza's intent was to deceive, Ian thought, he was successful. They were out of time, and anything of value the general could provide would be extracted by the men about to take control of him.

Ian said, "What I'm about to say is for you, not me. You're about to be handed off to professional interrogators. They're going to get the truth, all of it, and you're going to provide a full confession. If you do that, your family's out of Pakistan and safe for the rest of their lives. Listen to me carefully, because things could get very messy for you if you don't. Do exactly what they say. I don't have the equipment to catch you in a lie, but they do."

"My friend, I have not lied to you."

"I'm not your fucking friend."

Raza's expression fell into a deadpan look, then transitioned seamlessly to fear. It was the look of a man hearing the issuance of his prison sentence, only worse—there was no term of incarceration, no known location, and certainly no civil liberties, due process, or parole board. He didn't know where he would be taken or what was about to happen to him, but could assess well enough from his military experience that his journey would end at a black site from which he would never return.

The van came to a stop, and David pulled open the sliding door.

I accepted the voice recorder from Ian and pocketed it, receiving Raza as Keller stood him up. Placing one hand on the general's wrists that were bound behind him and the other on the back of his neck, I wheeled him away from the vehicle and assessed the flat green surroundings through my night vision.

Pakistan's National Agricultural Research Center was over a kilometer wide from east to west and close to two from north to south, all of it fields bisected by roads and not much else. We were in the northeast quadrant, far from the main buildings and the livestock station, and my team needed no guidance on what to do now.

The other three vehicles were either stationed or in the process of moving to occupy positions on the road on all four sides of the field, with Cancer's voice over my earpieces coordinating 360-degree security with the fully equipped shooters from both teams—save one individual.

Hass was already moving out across the field to our north, the antennas from his dual whip radios extended, an infrared strobe on his helmet marking his position for the aircrew with whom he now communicated.

I heard the helicopter approaching then, the thwack of rotor blades growing louder as I identified the Mi-17 approaching from the east, flying blackout with its navigation lights extinguished.

"Are you going to walk," I asked Raza, "or are we going to do this the hard way?"

"I will cooperate fully."

"Good. Let's go."

I marched him off the road, never easing my grip on his wrists and the back of his neck, until we both walked across the ridges of freshly plowed dirt.

Our destination was Hass, his strobe still flashing as he outlined a circle across the center of the field with his rifle's infrared laser.

After a few steps, Raza asked, "Where are they taking me?"

"No idea," I answered with total honesty. "But if I were you, I'd do whatever they say."

"So I have been told."

"You were told right. So if you lied about anything, now's the time to tell me."

Raza huffed a sigh. "I did not lie. Nor do I have any reason to do so, given the circumstances. My fate has been sealed."

"Don't be so hard on yourself," I said good-naturedly, my mood growing more buoyant with every step. "We had a hell of a time finding you. It was a good run, and if you weren't captured you wouldn't have made it out alive anyway."

"Death may have been preferable to what I face now."

I raised my voice over the sound of the helicopter descending to our right.

"Maybe, maybe not. Cooperate fully with your interrogators and I'll tell them to give you the best arrangements they can."

Which wasn't true, strictly speaking—the CIA didn't give a shit what its paramilitary contractors had to say once a rendition was complete, nor did I have any means of communicating with the shadowy types who extracted information in America's black sites around the globe.

But I figured Raza could use all the comfort he could get. Despite selling nuclear secrets and facilitating a war between his own country and India, he was well aware of his situation. I felt almost sorry for him, an emotion I'd not yet experienced for any enemy combatant. Maybe, I thought, the experience of witnessing my son's birth was making me soft. Entirely possible, because all I wanted now was to make it across the border and get back to my family.

I brought the general to a stop beside Hass, who took a knee as I told Raza to do the same.

"Close your eyes," I told him, and a moment later the bird pivoted clockwise, exposing its open ramp before flaring for landing.

A cloud of dust and loose dirt whipped across us as the Mi-17 touched down 25 meters to our front, and I looked away as the storm peaked just before the pilots throttled back the engine.

"Up," I shouted to Raza. "Let's go."

He stood and responded to my grip guiding him forward, the gusts of wind around us carrying the all-too-familiar scent of aviation kerosene along with the field's dirt. Hass walked on the opposite side of Raza, prepared to deliver a buttstock to the gut along with manual assistance should our charge decide that now was the time to resist his fate.

But our captive trudged forward without complaint. I watched the lowered helicopter ramp ahead, seeing the outline of three figures. One was the crew chief trailing his radio cable along with a tether, and just inside the fuselage, a tall interrogator wore an armored plate carrier and pistol. A man who must have been the Ground Branch medic was in full combat kit with a rifle slung around his backside.

The latter two men descended the ramp, their movements purposeful and swift as they approached and took control of Raza.

I handed Ian's voice recorder to the interrogator, then called out to the medic, "Sure you don't have room for us?"

"Five," he yelled back, "but that's it. No wounded, right?"

Hass had already relayed that much over the air frequency, but a good medic never took such things for granted.

"No wounded. Tell HQ that ten Eagles are en route to Gujranwala and will await further instructions. I'll check in when I can."

"You got it," he replied, joining the interrogator in maneuvering the general toward the ramp and into the red-lit belly of the helicopter. The medic looked far more lethal with his gear and rifle, but the lanky interrogator sure as shit represented the greater threat to Kamran Raza in the hours ahead.

Hass and I turned to jog back to the field's southern road, our journey temporarily suspended when the combat controller announced, "Down."

We dropped to our knees in succession. The whine of the Mi-17's twin turboshaft turbine engines increased along with the thudding chop of its rotor blades, and the mini-tornado of wind escalated into a gale force as the helo broke its contact with the earth. We were probably too far for it to knock us down from a standing position, but neither Hass nor myself wanted to endure the humiliation of being bowled over by rotorwash under the full view of our teammates.

Once the blast subsided, we stood and continued our jog to the ISI van parked on the road. I gave one rearward glance to see the helicopter lifting off the ground and rotating eastward before accelerating off, and then Cancer's voice came over my earpieces.

"All teams consolidate on the southern road. Racegun, Bulldog, Outlaw in the Suzuki. Doc, Suicide, Angel in the Hilux. Myself, Rain Man, Patriot, and Talon in the Subaru. That's our order of movement for now, designations are Teams One, Two, and Three in that order."

The remaining three vehicles reached the ISI van just before Hass and I arrived at the road. The Mi-17's noise was fading now, and we had to distance ourselves from the scene of the crime before civilians and police in the surrounding area, to say nothing of the military service members at the air force base six kilometers to our southeast, had too much time to react to the sound of a helicopter arriving and departing.

Our vehicles formed up, and all that remained was to load. We'd transferred our gear to the trio before departing for the factory raid in anticipation of self-destructing our HiAce surveillance van and abandoning the ISI's Hyundai H-1.

I moved to the Hilux, taking the passenger seat with Reilly at the wheel and Ian in the back.

Worthy transmitted, "One up."

"Two up," I replied.

Cancer concluded, "*Three up.*"

The convoy pulled forward then, with the Suzuki leading the way as I keyed my radio mic.

"Racegun, take us east on blackout until we clear the agricultural center. South once we hit the town, no main roads, don't switch to headlights unless we start seeing traffic. Work us west when able, brief halt before the Islamabad Expressway so we can transition to civilian configuration and go white light if we haven't by then. Expressway to the N5, then a straight shot to Gujranwala."

"*Good copy,*" Worthy replied.

I took a moment to consider that this was an astonishing victory by any measure—we'd come to locate Raza for the Pakistanis, and I'd made the case for the second team's deployment and received them in record time. Together we'd captured the general and killed Katarzyna Zajac, shutting down the escalation effort for the war and removing half of our Top Four targets from the battlefield. As if that weren't enough, we made it to the landing zone with time to spare.

Sure, I thought, war had broken out somewhere in the interim, but it was thus far limited to a handful of cruise missile strikes from both sides. The greater mobilization effort continued to delay any further hostilities, but Raza's confession aired on the world stage would put a stop to that, and if our luck held, it would do so before any more lives were lost.

Against this backdrop of progress, it was easy to forget that we still had to make it to our destination, a journey consisting of a four-hour road trip along with God knew what else once Chen finalized the exfil plan.

Still, I was elated by everything we'd accomplished, and shared that sentiment with my team in my next transmission.

"Solid work, everyone. And congratulations, we just stopped a war."

Then I added, "But the bad news is, I forgot to grab the dates out of the surveillance van before we torched it."

Worthy gripped the steering wheel of the aging Suzuki sedan, his palms tight against the worn imitation leather.

The car hummed quietly as it navigated the road out of the agricultural center and toward the streets of Chak Shahzad, which was lightly populated and featured a patchwork of modest houses and open fields, all of them cloaked in the inky darkness of a moonless night. His night vision device cast the world in a gradient of green and black hues, the sparse lights of distant houses glowing like spectral beacons.

Munoz stared at his phone from the passenger seat, evaluating the map imagery. "This road leads us straight into the village. We'll take the second right to head south—that'll give us parallel routes on both sides."

Worthy was about to respond when David came over the net again.

"*One more thing,*" he said, as if the thought had just occurred to him. "*We're off the grid and don't have time to fuck around on our way to the border.*"

The team leader paused, then added, "*Lethal force is authorized against anyone who tries to stop us, including Pakistani police and military. That may not be a lawful order, but it's an order nonetheless. We haven't lost anyone yet and we're not going to. I'm not going to let any of us get killed in action, or get captured and sent to prison unless anyone from Talon's team has a pressing desire to go back. If we have to operate in the black and Mayfly finds out, I'll take the fall.*"

Cancer transmitted back with a maxim well-known to military and law enforcement, which was ironic, Worthy thought, because his team leader had just authorized the slaughter of both.

"*Better to be tried by twelve than carried by six.*"

By then they were entering the village. Worthy's eyes darted from side to side, scanning for any signs of movement. His mind was a taut wire, strung between the adrenaline of the mission and the need for absolute caution.

"Next right," Munoz said, then asked, "Is David always like this?"

"Regrettably, yeah."

Keller spoke from the backseat. "Griffin's probably shitting razor blades right now."

"For sure," Munoz agreed, then turned to Worthy. "In case you haven't figured it out yet, he's one of those by-the-book types."

"What about you guys?" Worthy asked, making his first turn in Chak Shahzad.

Keller offered, "Let's just say I'd rather have your team leader calling the shots than mine."

"Yup," Munoz said. "My team has already been to a Yemeni prison, and I don't have any desire to see how a Pakistani one compares. Take the next left."

Worthy complied, wheeling the Suzuki through the intersection as he replied, "Yeah, well, let's hope we don't get any firsthand experience of an American one, either."

It wasn't just hollow rhetoric, he thought. David's order represented a massive escalation with potential political consequences, and Worthy wasn't nearly as flippant about that as his team leader, Cancer, and Munoz apparently were.

But when he asked himself whether the rules of engagement were worth not making it home, he reached the same conclusion as David.

"Right turn ahead," Munoz said, "then an immediate left."

The houses in Chatta Bakhtawar were modest, their outlines softened by the encroaching darkness. They were divided by a patchwork of crops, the entire landscape utterly still—but all it took was for one person to spot three cars driving without headlights minutes after a nearby helicopter landing. Worthy watched for window or rooftop spotters, seeing none as he complied with Munoz's directions.

Munoz looked over his shoulder and asked the intelligence operative, "So what did Raza say?"

Keller was quiet for a moment. "That would take longer to answer if you asked what he didn't say."

"Tough guy, huh?"

"Far from it," the intelligence operative said. "He sang like a bird, just not about what we thought. Said he was hired to stage and command the attacks across India-controlled Kashmir, that orders came from six Pakistanis providing payment and instructions, but that's it. No idea who was pulling the strings or why."

Munoz grunted in consideration of this. "Worthy, you've got a Y-intersection ahead. Take a left and follow the road for about a click." Then, to Keller, he added, "So what was the plan after the cruise missiles?"

Worthy was making his turn when the intelligence operative responded from the backseat, his voice exasperated.

"That's the thing. Raza had no idea. According to him, his role began and ended with the border dispute. His employers set up the safehouses, gave him the tip to flee before both raids, and were supposed to get him out of the country and into Iran."

Wondering whether his initial suspicions about Raza being double-crossed were true, Worthy asked, "Then who tried to kill him at the factory?"

"Had to be the same people who hired him. When it became clear that Katarzyna Zajac and her cyber post were down for good, they tried to kill him so he'd take the fall as the mastermind—at least, that's what Ian and I think."

So maybe his instinct was right, Worthy thought, although at this point it was hard to know anything about Raza's claims with total certainty.

They entered Burma Town then, the fields ending and giving way to tightly packed houses rising in the tiered construction of a century's worth of vertical building expansions. Impromptu power lines for electrical siphoning were strung over the road, and while there were no streetlights, a few windows remained lit. Worthy's vigilance spiked every time they passed the glow of an exterior bulb beside a house door.

He said, "Sounds like he lied his ass off."

"I think he was telling the truth," Keller noted, "and the fact that someone tried to kill him pretty much backs up his story whether he realized it or not. If he was a liar, then he was a pretty damn convincing one. Ian told him we hit his cyber operation, and Raza assumed he was talking about his command post in Bhanati. Thought the name 'Zajac' was a place, not a person."

"Maybe the Iranians staged the whole thing."

"Or India, or Russia, or China—but they didn't. None of them would benefit enough to justify the risk, and I'm certain of that."

"Extremist group, then."

"That hypothesis is consistent with Zajac running the cyber component. But none of them have the capabilities to pull it off. At least not since Erik Weisz was killed."

Munoz asked, "Then what the fuck happened?"

"I don't know," Keller admitted. "Neither does Ian."

"That's comforting."

Worthy eased off the accelerator as a pair of cats raced across the street to his front, then rolled back on the gas as Keller issued his reply.

"'Comforting' has never been part of this game, not as long as I've been in it. But the CIA hasn't finished analyzing all of Zajac's data, and with any luck they'll be able to figure out who was behind all this. The important thing is that White House press conference about the fake missile launch order is complete, and in a few hours they'll release a tape of Raza admitting to staging the border dispute. That should put the brakes on the war, and everything else is out of our hands. There's nothing else we can do."

Worthy commented, "Except make it to India in one piece."

"Except that, yeah."

Munoz scanned the street to the front and rear before transmitting, "Short halt."

As Worthy braked the Suzuki to a gradual stop, Munoz continued over the net, "Three hundred meters to the next left, after that we hit a four-lane straight to the expressway."

"*Copy*," David responded. "*Let's make this quick.*"

The process of transitioning to civilian configuration didn't take long. Worthy and Munoz handed their rifles and helmets to Keller in the back, and all three men removed their armored plate carriers. Once the gear was stashed beneath a drop cloth on the rear floorboards, with the exception of concealed pistols and radios, Munoz transmitted.

"One up," he said, and the passengers of the remaining cars did the same.

"*Two up.*"

"*Three up.*"

"White light, rolling," Munoz concluded over the net, triggering Worthy to activate his headlights and begin accelerating once more.

Now that they approached paved roads rather than the dirt-packed stretches through the villages, Munoz conducted his next directions over the radio.

"Left turn, south, then three hundred meters to Lehtrar Road."

Worthy had just cleared the intersection when he saw the lights of cars flitting past in both directions ahead.

"Right turn, west, fifteen hundred meters to the expressway."

Braking before Lehtrar Road, Worthy saw he'd have to wait for a gap in traffic to merge—Pakistan's colonial-era holdover of driving on the left side of the road was a real bitch sometimes—and it became clear from the staggered flow of civilian vehicles and cargo trucks that the convoy wouldn't make it across together.

"They're on their own," he said, shooting the gap between a motorcycle and an overloaded pickup before wheeling a westward turn.

Once he made it to the far lanes, he slowed just enough to avoid being rear-ended, then proceeded toward the Islamabad Expressway as he waited for the remaining team vehicles to join him.

It was immediately apparent that, as with most multiple-lane roads he'd traveled in Pakistan thus far, the observed speed limit was no speed limit at all. Angry motorists honked and swerved around the Suzuki, and Worthy was forced to speed up simply to avoid drawing attention.

"*Two is across*," David transmitted, followed a few seconds later by Cancer echoing the announcement for his own car.

Worthy checked his rearview to see the headlights of the Hilux speeding in the fast lane to close the distance before it merged behind him.

David said, "*Team Two is linked up. Three, how are you looking?*"

"*Hauling ass*," Cancer replied over the net. "*Hang on...all right, Team Three in position. Racegun, pick up the pace before we get shot for being slow.*"

Worthy was all too happy to comply. At this point, anything short of driving like a bat out of hell would be cause for concern if not alarm for the other drivers.

"Four hundred meters to Islamabad Expressway," Munoz transmitted, and he'd barely sent the message before Worthy spotted the expressway's on-ramp ahead.

And with it, the sight of police lightbars illuminated beside the road.

He braked sharply and whipped a left-hand turn as Munoz relayed the sight to their teammates via the radio. Worthy throttled the Suzuki down a single-lane street between buildings, seeing no outlets but asking nonetheless, "Where am I going?"

"Let's see, shit," Munoz muttered, keying his mic to think aloud, "we're on a one-way street headed for the one-way Service Road East. It heads the way we want to go, but there's no outlet to the expressway until the interchange in two-and-a-half kilometers."

By then Worthy was turning onto the Service Road, a perfectly straight route from which he could see the traffic on the Islamabad Expressway to his right.

"*So basically,*" David replied, "*we have to cross a bridge right at the southern tip of the airbase to make the on-ramp.*"

"Basically."

The irony of this situation wasn't lost on Worthy. Less than an hour ago, his team had been fearful of encountering the northern gates of the air force installation while chasing Raza's car through the streets, and now they would have to come within sight of the airbase's southern boundaries if they wanted to make it out of here.

Which had better come sooner rather than later.

He said, "No cops ahead; we've got outlets to the village on our left. I'm flooring it."

"Go ahead," Munoz agreed, and Worthy half-expected David to tell him to slow down for fear of detection from a vigilant cop.

But no such transmission came, which meant the team leader was in agreement. The law enforcement presence during their previous attempt to reach the expressway was probably the tip of the iceberg for what was to come in response not only to the shootout in the streets of Rawalpindi but also the abrupt and unauthorized helicopter landing a few kilometers distant.

Finally David came over the net.

"*Keep going pedal to the metal unless they block us from the front. If that happens, we draw them into the village and either lose them or take them out. Once we make it to the expressway, we're home free.*"

Worthy was piloting the Suzuki at the ragged fringes of his ability to brake for a sudden obstruction. He agreed with his team leader's assessment, although there was an almost crippling level of frustration at being able to see but not reach their intended route a hundred meters away, its traffic flashing through periodic breaks in the trees.

The Islamabad Expressway represented safety for three cars full of Americans trying to blend in, namely because roadblocks and checkpoints were a nonissue when the slowest car was moving at 60 mph. And once Worthy made it to that road, his team was only about ten minutes distant from the N5 Highway with much more traffic moving at a higher rate of speed, and additional civilian and commercial vehicles piling on as sunrise approached. And best of all, it stretched all the way to their next destination in Gujranwala.

But they couldn't make it to the N5 without the expressway, and at the moment the unanticipated delay meant they could be stopped by police any second now.

"There it is," Munoz said, then keyed his mic. "Bridge in sight, right turn heading west and it splits into the overpass. Coast looks clear for now."

The fact that they'd made it this far without disruption continued a winning streak that his team had very rarely encountered on their missions overseas, where they'd more often than not been beset by more horrendously bad luck than any group of men should encounter in a lifetime.

And, he saw as he swerved the Suzuki onto the bridge to find it void of anything but civilian traffic, everything was still looking absolutely perfect.

Almost unwilling to accept that their convoy movement was proceeding without a hitch, Worthy asked, "Our guys are still behind us?"

"Yes, you're golden," Munoz said. "Veer right onto the on-ramp after the bridge; that'll take us around to the expressway southbound."

Worthy complied, reaching the entrance to the on-ramp and gliding the vehicle in a clockwise curve that rose over the ground below. He was halfway up when he vaguely registered runway lights to his left, a sight that Munoz watched closely as he muttered, "What the fuck?"

But Worthy had no opportunity to see what he meant.

The view along the on-ramp curve suddenly revealed the brake lights of multiple stopped cars, and he slammed on the brakes for lack of options— there was surely a roadblock or checkpoint ahead, and no room to turn around. With his team now sandwiched between civilian vehicles aiming for the expressway, they couldn't even reverse out of danger, and the sum total of these factors meant that a gunfight was imminent.

The Suzuki came to a halt that threw him forward against his seatbelt, and the vehicle frame had just finished its rearward lurch when Munoz flung open his door and stepped out of the car without a word.

Worthy was transitioning from shock to outrage at the unannounced departure, an inexplicable offense exacerbated by the fact that a moment later, Keller did the exact same thing. Only then did Worthy realize they weren't alone. The occupants of every stopped car in front of him were lined up along the left rail of the on-ramp, staring northwest with seemingly absolute focus.

He looked left to find his view blocked by the rest of his comrades doing the same thing, and he begrudgingly exited the Suzuki while casting wary glances in every direction. The lack of 360-degree security, however subtle, ignited every fiber of PTSD within him, and only the nearby presence of civilians prevented him from voicing these concerns in the most profanely framed argument possible.

Then he heard the quick, barking growl of a distant explosion, and his hesitant march to the guardrail turned into a run.

He came to a stop beside Munoz and Keller, the rest of his teammates lined up to his left, expecting to see the fallout of an Indian cruise missile strike.

Instead, he felt all the air exiting his lungs in one fell swoop at the sight ahead.

Pakistan Air Force Base Nur Khan was spread out in the long clearing before him, the runway as perfectly aligned as if Worthy were a pilot coming in for landing. Parallel groupings of red and white lights led to the edge of the pavement, where a trio of lights marking the sides and center-line of the runway gradually converged for three kilometers before ending altogether.

Worthy swept his gaze across the distant blue taxiway lights to find the bulk of the military buildings and hangars along the western side of the base—which was where any sense of order imbued by the neat rows of regulation aviation lighting ended.

Streaks of tracer rounds arced in red, orange, and green as a distant gunfight unfolded. The sheer volume of fire that he could make out, even at this distance, was astounding. He could see the pinpoint dots of rocket exhausts streaking to and from various points, their flight concluding in mini-blasts concentrated against military vehicles scrambling to maneuver.

This was unreal, he thought. There must have been dozens of shooters on both sides, if not a hundred or more, and the thought caused a lump to form in his throat before things went from bad to worse.

A fireball of high explosives detonated at the entrance to a massive hangar, the blinding flash illuminating clusters of smoke that billowed from buildings and gates all over the main area of the base. He saw devastated guard towers and the smoking hulks of trucks before the blast receded, causing the tracer fire to once again dominate the darkness.

"That's our exfil fucked," Munoz said matter-of-factly.

Keller replied, "That's *everything* fucked," before going silent and prompting Worthy to fill the void.

"What does that mean?"

"It means," Keller said, "that Raza wasn't lying."

Worthy was incensed, growing angrier at the delay in response with each passing second. "Damnit, do you know what's going on down there or don't you?"

But the intelligence operative was slow to reply, his voice almost sluggish, eyes fixed on the chaos unfolding at the airbase. He stepped back from the guardrail and looked at Worthy. Keller's face was aghast, his eyes gleaming in the headlights of cars stopped along the on-ramp, their drivers and passengers still transfixed by the sight below.

"I know exactly what's happening."

19

The phone atop Chen's desk rang, and she answered it at once. The update would result in either immense relief or full-on crisis mode for everyone in the OPCEN, the latter of which had been perilously close at hand ever since the initial reports of a ground attack against PAF Nur Khan had arrived minutes earlier.

She quickly snatched the phone receiver and listened.

"I understand," she replied, her stomach plunging into freefall. Raza had been delivered to the Air Department Mi-17 roughly an hour ago, and at the time she thought it was the turning point that would stop a war.

Now, she couldn't care less.

Chen hung up the phone and stood at her desk.

"We have confirmation," she announced to the operations center, realizing that her next words would officially turn the tides on everything her staff thought they knew about Project Longwing's mission to Pakistan.

"The Pakistani government has privately admitted that they were in the process of fitting warheads to their Ra'ad Hatf 8 air-launched cruise missiles when the attack on PAF Nur Khan occurred. And one of these warheads was stolen." She took a breath, then concluded, "We have a loose nuke."

Her words seemed to freeze everyone in the operations center, with all but Jamieson assuming a deer in the headlights expression of shock as she went on.

"State Department engagement with the Pakistanis to authorize a DoD response is in progress. Sutherland and Jamieson, I want to know what the air and ground components of that response will be, in particular the timetable for employment, before the report arrives." That spurred both men into action as they turned to face their computers—Lucios had done the same, not so much as diverting his gaze as he answered her next question before she had a chance to ask it.

"Ma'am," Lucios began, "this contingency requires the immediate standup of a joint task force at the National Counterterrorism Center involving every relevant intelligence agency and DoD command. Whatever restrictions any of the above have in honoring civil liberties in Pakistan will be lifted in full. In my assessment, 90% of that will be window dressing— our best chance of locating the warhead will be by radiation-detecting satellites from the National Reconnaissance Office and Geospatial-Intelligence Agencies. However, those assets are very limited in number and will have to dedicate each pass on the most likely locations—which, given the size of the device, will be extremely difficult to determine."

"Out with it," she ordered.

Lucios referenced the specifics on his computer as he responded, "A Hatf 8 warhead is relatively small. 5.1 feet long and 1.6 feet wide, with a weight of 990 pounds. That means it's transportable in something as small as a station wagon with a good suspension, but since it will very likely be placed into a shock-absorbing case lined with lead to prevent detection by radiation sensors, it is far more likely to be moved in a van, pickup, or SUV, which in Pakistan means it will be all but invisible to the vast majority of intelligence collection methods. The warhead also has several layers of arming mechanisms that need to be sequentially activated in order to complete the arming process, so it can be transported in off-road conditions without fear of accidental detonation."

Chen considered this a moment, her eyes narrowing. "What about intentional detonation? Converting the warhead for use in a terrorist attack?"

"They'll need a small team of the right job specialties. A nuclear engineer to disable or bypass the safeguards that prevent accidental detonation, a missile engineer to modify the fuse, and an electrical engineer to reprogram the arming sequence. Even with the right people assembled—which I have no doubt has already been completed—the process will take days, not hours. My best assessment is that whoever has the warhead is solely focused on transporting it out of Pakistan to a more permissive area before attempting any modification."

Chen asked, "And that warhead's payload?"

"Twelve kilotons, ma'am," he replied. "Hiroshima was 15."

"Jesus," she whispered to herself.

Lucios's gaze ticked toward the ceiling.

"I assess that Raza was one compartmentalized part of the overall operation, used to incite the border incident and initiate hostilities between Pakistan and India. Zajac was another piece, utilized to escalate the conflict to the point that nuclear devices would be assembled and deployed to various missile silos, air bases, and submarine ports. Whoever masterminded this effort couldn't have penetrated a Pakistani nuclear storage facility, much less engineer multiple simultaneous raids required to gather all components.

"However, he knew Pakistan's contingency plans and the steps required to result in nuclear devices being deployed across the country. He determined that PAF Nur Khan was most within the capabilities of his available forces to stage a theft, and then set into motion the events required to bring the government to the threshold where these warheads would be mobilized."

The intelligence officer had just painted a grim, almost doomsday portrait of the situation writ large, and perhaps the most disturbing thing about it was that Chen couldn't find a single element to disagree with.

Instead she focused her efforts on anticipating her government's response. "I want to lean forward on the DoD response starting with aerial rotations. Sutherland, you're up."

As Project Longwing's Joint Terminal Attack Controller, the specifics of any and all US aircraft were Brian Sutherland's bread and butter. He didn't hesitate in the slightest, scanning the information on his computer screen to narrate an educated speculation so precise that Chen momentarily questioned whether the DoD report had already arrived.

"Based on available assets," he began, "there will be three classes of aircraft mobilizing from our fleets at Al Udeid Air Base in Qatar and Al Dhafra in the UAE, and four to five hours before they come on station. The first will be tankers for aerial refueling, likely establishing rotations over Karachi. Next up is surveillance. Manned platforms will include E-3s and E-8Cs to run signals and electronic intelligence collection, as well as targeting. For unmanned they've got forward-staged RQ-4 Global Hawks out of the UAE, likely bolstered by at least one Triton from Sigonella. Last is fighter support, and there's no shortage in the Middle East: F-15Es, F-16s, and F-35s."

She winced.

"Will a conventional bomb cause the warhead to explode?"

Sutherland began, "Ma'am, an airstrike won't result in a mushroom cloud—" before Lucios spared him the trouble in far more academic fashion.

"Nuclear weapons require extremely precise sequences to initiate a nuclear chain reaction, starting with the exact timing and coordination of conventional explosives that would be disabled or at worst detonated by an airstrike. Even if that failed, the mechanical safeties, environmental sensors, and electronic locks on the warhead wouldn't be correctly aligned for the arming process."

Chen said, "But it would still result in a 'dirty bomb' scenario, correct?"

"Yes, ma'am. Radioactive contamination would be localized around the impact site, with the extent of dispersion depending largely on the explosion's force and prevailing weather conditions. That's just one reason that an airstrike will be an absolute last resort—a conventional bomb could disperse radioactive elements more widely and complicate containment efforts. And there may be several decoy nukes in motion to draw our aerial surveillance away from the actual device. Bottom line, the DoD's priority will be recovering the warhead intact."

Jamieson knew he was up, and she saw the former Marine watching her in anticipation.

"Go," she said.

He spun to face his computer, speaking before his rolling chair had completed its rotation.

"JSOC's response is straightforward. It's going to be the Silver Bullet package, sent in two separate air movements. The first is out of Fort Campbell, and that's three transport planes to bring helicopters—two Chinooks for moving troops and two Blackhawks for combat support. Another plane will launch from Pope Field carrying a squadron-minus from Delta Force along with an NDT."

Chen raised an eyebrow. "And that is?"

"Nuclear Disablement Team." He squinted at his screen and added, "Bomb disposal experts, radiation safety officers, intelligence specialists, and a nuclear engineer. They'll stay back at the staging area to handle the warhead once it's secured."

She asked, "What's the estimated time for their arrival?"

"If the Pakistani authorities grant permission to use their airfields, Delta Force should be able to move out by vehicle around eleven a.m. tomorrow, local time."

"What about the helicopters?"

"The helicopters will take longer. They need to be partially disassembled and inspected before transport by C-17. Once they land in Pakistan, it'll take time to reassemble the helicopters and run pre-flight checks. They should be ready to fly around six p.m. local time, about seven hours after the shooters arrive."

Frowning, she said, "As impressed as I am by our rapid deployment capabilities, there are a lot of things that can happen in 26 hours, and one of them is the nuke leaving Pakistan altogether. Our next order of business is to determine where it's headed. Correct me if I'm wrong, but I'd say India is first off the list, with Jammu and Kashmir being a close second due to the influx of military forces. Xinjiang Province is out because China has too much to lose by being tied to a state-sponsored operation, however mistakenly. They won't let anyone cross their border."

When Lucios offered no immediate objection, she ventured, "Iran is a remote possibility, although I'd rank them a half-step behind China in avoiding any links to the events in Pakistan. A maritime option is also possible through the ports at Karachi, Gwadar, and Qasim, or anywhere along the coastline via offshore exchange. But Iran and the Arabian Sea are too far for anyone to reasonably transport the warhead, correct?"

Now Lucios did speak up, albeit only to verify her assumption.

"Fifteen hundred to two-thousand-kilometer ground movement from Islamabad."

She was about to continue the process of elimination when he stopped her altogether.

"However, we can't rule out a boat. Or an aircraft. If I were trying to move a nuclear device out of Pakistan, that's how I'd do it."

Jamieson interjected, "What about a ground movement west? It's a three-hour drive to Peshawar with two major highway options, which puts distance between them and the theft. Then they'd be in the former Federally Administered Tribal Area. Seven tribal agencies and six Frontier Regions, all of which have a rat's nest of smuggling routes into Afghanistan."

Chen could tell from Lucios's irritated expression that he was considering factors that the operations officer wasn't, and a moment later she found out exactly what those factors were.

"Afghanistan is the quickest way out," he conceded, "which certainly makes it low-hanging fruit. But our team's last mission uncovered nine figures' worth of terrorist funding that had already left the Congo. And given the private army Raza equipped for Kashmir and the size of the assault force required to overrun PAF Nur Khan, it's safe to say we now know what that money was intended for."

"But not all of it," Chen heard herself say.

Lucios nodded.

"Exactly. It probably took less than half of that sum to incite a conflict and steal the warhead, and whatever remains has been set aside to transport it out of the country. Whoever masterminded this didn't go through all the trouble to steal a nuclear weapon without a plan for exactly how to use it. Wes, you're right. He does want to put distance between the warhead and the theft. But not by highway, not in the big picture.

"My best guess is that the warhead is on its way to an airfield or port as we speak, and the rampant corruption in Pakistan provides more than enough opportunity for him to get it out on any number of air and sea vessels. Pair that with millions spent on a carefully orchestrated plan for its movement, and potentially, a highly sophisticated transport platform, and we can rule nothing out."

The chime of an incoming email distracted Chen from the deeply concerning monologue, and she glanced at her monitor to find an update to the military response plan.

"Wait one," she said distractedly, shifting her mouse to forward the message to her staff.

It only took a moment for her to scan the contents before blurting, "The DoD response is dead in the water."

"Ma'am?" Jamieson asked.

"The Paks aren't allowing us in—no ground, maritime, or airspace permissions have been granted."

Andolin Lucios was typically monotone to a fault. Now, however, his voice was alarmed, the normally pragmatic analyst nearly stammering, "Unless our mastermind has paid off the president of Pakistan, there's no reason for them to turn down support—"

"They're not turning down support," she said, now beside herself with exasperation. "They're turning down support *from us*."

Chen's eyes were wide as she met his gaze and continued, "China is leading the recovery effort."

The admission seemed to suck all the air out of the room at once, a vacuous gap ensuing as everyone struggled to process the implications.

And when she thought the situation couldn't get any worse, the speakerbox on her desk crackled to life.

"Raptor Nine One, Suicide Actual. Have you heard about the attack on PAF Nur Khan?"

20

Ian stood beside the tailgate of the Hilux, waiting to hear the return transmission. David was next to him, holding the radio hand mic, the mobile satellite antenna perched on the pickup's roof and aimed skyward. The recent ground attack at PAF Nur Khan was still fresh in their minds, and the lack of response from their headquarters was concerning, to say the least.

David spoke into the mic once more, his voice steady but urgent. "Raptor Nine One, Suicide Actual. I say again, are you tracking the attack on Nur Khan?"

Silhouettes of their team vehicles loomed in Ian's night vision, parked in a tight formation, their fronts facing outward into the cold night. Each was positioned for a swift departure along any of the four dirt roads connecting with the Islamabad Expressway, whose traffic they could see and hear a few hundred meters to their west. The distant hum of engines and sporadic honking added an eerie backdrop to their tense wait, the urban noise mingling with the occasional rustle of wind through the sparse trees surrounding the school grounds.

Each of the remaining team members was dispersed around the perimeter, scanning the darkness with night vision for the slightest indication they'd been detected. Their figures were barely discernible against the crumbling walls of the school, the trees, and an abandoned playground with dilapidated and rusting swing sets. The location was as good as they were going to get for this communications halt, which, along with everything else since they'd handed off Raza, was an unanticipated development.

The radio speaker abruptly relayed Chen's voice from the opposite side of the world. *"Confirm, we're tracking."* Then she continued, in an almost clinical tone, *"And the attack was to steal a 12-kiloton nuclear warhead that's currently in the wind."*

Ian felt an unsettling quiet take over his thoughts, as though the world had paused to absorb the gravity of the situation. The rustling of a nearby flag on its pole and the distant calls of night birds seemed to momentarily fade away, replaced by a profound silence. For a moment everything went out of focus, his head spinning with a vague dizziness, before the unsettling sensation vanished and his senses sharpened to the point of hyper-vigilance.

It wasn't that this was an entirely unexpected possibility—Keller had immediately predicted the purpose of the ground attack, and Ian agreed—but determining intent was a far cry from establishing whether or not the theft had actually been successful.

And now, Ian knew beyond a doubt that Raza had told him the truth.

David was leaning against the tailgate, mic held halfway to his lips but going no further. Ian wordlessly held out his open palm, and the team leader passed him the handset.

"This is Angel," he began. "Who stole it—what group?"

"We don't know."

"But the entire staging of a war with India was—"

"A ruse," Chen explained, *"to get the warhead transported somewhere it could be stolen with a little advance notice of national contingency plans. And, I should mention, to mobilize Pakistan's entire military along the Indian border, which leaves most of the country open to move the nuke by plane or boat."*

"Or vehicle," Ian mused aloud. "What about the western border?"

"Whoever did this," Chen continued, *"they've got the Congo funding. If you had millions or tens of millions with which to move that device, would you bother hauling it over the mountains and into the Middle Ages?"*

Ian's response was so immediate, and spoken with such conviction, that even as he delivered it, he questioned his motives.

"Because Afghanistan is the Wild West. Let's not forget that the Taliban inherited $7 billion worth of US hardware they've been selling on the international black market. So they already have connections with state and non-state actors, and the geographic proximity to transfer people and materiel west into Iran or north into the Central Asian states with equally porous borders. And if whoever stole that warhead didn't trust the Taliban, they could just as easily use ISIS-K, Al-Qaeda, Haqqani, and TTP, all of which have networks a few hours from the site of the theft."

He released the transmit button, wondering how much he actually believed in the likelihood of such a possibility. Was he making the case simply because it was the only thing his team could remotely influence and, therefore, a desperate attempt to project control over a fundamentally uncontrollable situation?

Ian could argue his case or play devil's advocate against it with equal skill, and ultimately he remained uncertain of what he believed, or why, when Chen responded.

"If that's the case, the warhead will go through Peshawar first."

"Exactly," he said. "Is that where JSOC is focusing their efforts?"

"JSOC is standing down. The Paks refused any US assistance. They're opening the door for China to intervene."

David snatched the mic.

"Then we'll have to go to Peshawar ourselves. That way we're in place for any intel developments, whether from US assets or you guys monitoring Chinese comms."

This thing was snowballing fast, Ian thought. His reflexive justification for an Afghan border crossing was already becoming cemented as the team's primary course of action.

Chen said, *"The only viable exfil I have for you is India. If you head west instead, I can't guarantee a pickup anytime soon, if at all."*

David spoke again, though not over the radio; his words were directed at Ian, delivered in a hushed tone.

"You really think it's headed for Afghanistan?"

"I do," Ian heard himself say.

The team leader keyed his mic and transmitted, "We're unattributable. You have nothing to lose."

Chen replied at once, *"You shouldn't be so flippant about a very real prospect."*

"She fucking serious?" David muttered, keying his mic to issue a heated response.

"It's a prospect that exists for a reason, and one you had no problem cashing in on when Talon's team got rolled up in Yemen. So don't give me the song and dance about how I should take this seriously. There's a loose nuke. Pakistan and China will be focusing on airfields and ports, and we're not in a position to help with those anyway. What we *can* do is get to Peshawar asap and stand by in the event the warhead is taken toward the Afghan border. We're the only American show in town, and apparently that's not going to change anytime soon. So use us."

David was coming to the end of his tirade when Ian's cell phone buzzed in his pocket. He withdrew the device, frowning when he saw the screen and then holding it aloft to David.

"All right," Chen replied. *"Given the urgency of the situation, if that's what you want to do—and it is your choice—check in when you get there. You are free to move."*

"Suicide Actual, out."

Then, setting the mic down, he asked, "Should we take it?"

It was a valid question. While the Agency phones were impervious to tracking, there were only a handful of reasons that Ian would receive this call, most of which involved the ISI's attempts to locate his team.

Then again, Ian thought, the ISI had bigger problems at present.

He answered the call on speaker, holding it between himself and David before speaking.

"Go ahead."

Tahir spoke with forceful intensity. "Have you heard about the theft from Nur Khan? Are you still in Pakistan?"

"Yes to the first," Ian ventured. "As for the second, maybe, maybe not."

"Good. Fine. Then stay here."

"Why would we do that?"

Tahir chuckled, as if relishing what he was about to say.

"Because the US is not sending its people. China is."

"So?"

Tahir went on, "Both countries have national security laws that limit their cooperation with a geopolitical adversary, especially intelligence sharing. But your teams are not bound by those regulations. I have already informed the Chinese of your team, and given the immediacy of the threat, they would like to use your men as a liaison element one step removed from formal channels. They will share relevant information from their aircraft, and in return the US helps them via surveillance satellites."

Ian's mouth went dry. "You've already been tasked as the go-between, haven't you?"

There was a slight hesitation before the ISI officer answered, "From the highest levels, yes."

"Wait one," Ian said, putting the phone on mute as a chilly breeze swept over him. "The Agency's not going to like us volunteering for that."

David gave an ambivalent shrug. "As long as the warhead is stopped, I don't give a shit what the Agency likes."

"Agree to it now, and tell them later?"

"Now you're getting it. And it's got the added bonus of getting us off the ISI's hit list for the time being."

"Unless this is a trap."

"Goes without saying," David admitted. "But it's worth the risk with a nuke at stake. Ask him the timeline."

The distant sounds of the Islamabad Expressway remained a constant hum in the background as Ian considered the implications of everything thus far. A few stars peeked through the gaps in the cloud cover, offering a faint glimmer of light in the otherwise dark sky, and he finally took the phone off mute and spoke.

"Tahir, what's the Chinese response and how long will it take to arrive?"

There was a pause as the ISI officer consulted his notes. "Fighter jets will be in Pakistani airspace in six to eight hours with mid-air refueling. Surveillance aircraft and UAVs in eight to ten, staging at PAF bases Mushaf and Kamra along with their tankers, and some form of counterterrorism force to bolster Zarrar Company. I do not have the timeline on them yet."

David said, "We've got some conditions. First, I need the protocols and frequencies to call in air support from helicopters and fighter jets, both Chinese and Pakistani."

Tahir hesitated, then replied, "Very well, but I cannot guarantee approval for airstrikes."

"They'll be approved if things get bad enough for us to need them. Next, we need to operate out of Peshawar."

"Why?"

"Because the Pak-Afghan border is our biggest blind spot, and the only one my team could feasibly respond to ahead of your forces or the Chinese. We'll need new vehicles and better weapons upon arrival in Peshawar, and transportation to get there. Preferably a helicopter."

Tahir gave a humorless laugh. "The ISI is fully occupied. At the moment I cannot get any cars or weapons beyond those I have already provided. And I cannot even get *myself* helicopter transport, much less you and your men."

"Come with us on the drive, then."

"You are that close to Islamabad?"

"Close enough to watch the attack on Nur Khan."

Tahir paused again. "I will be occupied for one to two hours. You can wait for me if you wish."

"If there's roadblocks by then," Ian explained, "you'll be held up by traffic no matter your credentials. We're going to get moving now. Meet us there."

When Tahir didn't respond, David asked, "Deal or no deal?"

"Deal."

Ian barely ended the call before David transmitted over the team net.

"Net call, net call. Nuclear warhead stolen from Nur Khan, possibly headed west. Zero US support allowed in-country. We're moving to Peshawar, Tahir's going to meet us there, we'll be liaising with the Chinese response."

It occurred to Ian then that since the updates with Chen and Tahir had occurred back-to-back, none of this information was attributable as ground force commander judgment versus official orders. He wondered when or if David would clarify that—none of it would be an issue with the men from their team, though Griffin and at least some of his men were another matter entirely.

David released his transmit switch for a second, pressed it again, and concluded, "Let's get moving. I'll field questions on the way."

21

"Fucking Mad Max out here," Cancer said, watching a motorcycle with two riders and a bundle of cargo speed past before threading back into the correct lane with a rusted sedan trailing by a few meters.

The vehicles had barely completed the maneuver when a panel van screamed past in the opposite direction, windshield reflecting the blazing sunrise as it moved fast enough to have easily killed everyone involved in the maneuver. It was sobering to watch ordinary civilians taking split-second risks that Cancer himself wouldn't, and to do so as part of daily life in negotiating the highway connecting Islamabad with Peshawar to the west. This reality was made all the more disturbing to him, he thought, in a country where vehicles drove in the left lane, the view outside alternating between open land and roadside towns, some of which were quite substantial in size.

"Look at the bright side," Hass coolly replied from the Subaru's driver's seat. "We're not in any danger of getting stopped by a checkpoint."

Washington was seated in the back next to Cancer, and the medic's outlook was considerably less rosy.

"True," he said in response, "but we're in a *lot* of danger of getting stopped by a jingle truck going 80 mph."

A fair observation, Cancer thought.

The N5 highway was dominated by enormous modified cargo trucks whose every surface from hood to body panels and tailgate was painted in bright colors, elaborate floral patterns, calligraphy, and religious symbols. Named jingle trucks for the sound made by chains and bells often attached to their bumpers, the vehicles were a ubiquitous sight across Pakistan and Afghanistan.

While such trucks played a vital role for transporting essential goods across the region, their size made them a force to contend with here on the highway. The N5 seemed to operate under the rule that there were no rules, save one: the bigger the vehicle, the more right of way it had. Even at just past five in the morning, everyone on the highway was committed to speed at the expense of all else, and there was a chillingly consistent lack of hesitation to veer into oncoming traffic if it afforded a local driver the slightest chance of passing somebody.

And the jingle trucks, Cancer noted, were the worst offenders.

Two of the vehicles sped by in the opposite direction, both drivers going full throttle on their way to receive or deliver cargo.

Hass asked, "What do you think the odds are that the warhead is moving toward the Afghan border? One in ten?"

"One in a hundred, maybe," Washington said. "But the odds go out the window if we find that fucker."

Cancer snickered. "We better find it, because it's going to be really embarrassing if we get killed a thousand klicks from the nuke when we could be approaching the Indian border for exfil by now."

He stopped himself from voicing further dissent, though he could have certainly gone on. And in a way, missing the exfil was the least of their worries—the goalposts on this mission kept moving, starting with the initial purpose of locating Raza. Somewhere in the middle, Cancer had unknowingly scored a touchdown by taking out Katarzyna Zajac, the first time a top target had been killed in self-defense, although any sense of accomplishment had evaporated amidst the cruise missile strike and subsequent theft of a nuclear device.

Griffin looked over from the passenger seat, his expression deadpan.

"If we get killed, it'll be for a purpose. If that warhead makes it to its intended destination, we're looking at a death toll somewhere between 9/11 and Nagasaki depending on where they detonate it."

As if to shoot down his team leader's attempt at justifying if not glamorizing the ultimate sacrifice, Hass said, "But if we die, it'll be while relying on communists. Not exactly what I envisioned when signing up for this outfit."

"Oh, come on." Griffin sighed. "China's not a communist state. Not really."

Cancer wasn't sure what to make of Brent Griffin. On one hand, the team leader seemed as tactically proficient as one would expect, and on the other, he seemed profoundly uncomfortable with coloring outside the lines. The other men in the car presented no concern. Hass had more than proven himself in the fast-and-loose methodology, and Washington exuded a vibe of being willing to race into the jaws of death at the slightest provocation that made Cancer feel warm and fuzzy inside.

But Griffin remained an unknown quantity.

Washington replied, "And here I was thinking that CCP stood for Chinese *Communist* Party."

"They've got the name," Griffin said, "sure. But traditional communism is a classless, stateless society where everything is communally owned. China, on the other hand, relies on private enterprise and foreign investment, and clearly they're no strangers to social classes and economic inequality. It's state capitalism within a single-party authoritarian framework."

Washington offered, "And that single party is led by a psycho."

"Xi Jinping?"

"Is that their president?"

"Yes."

"Then yeah, him."

Before Griffin could respond, Cancer said, "My team got a taste of his 'single-party authoritarian framework' when we were in western China. Plenty of concentration camps for Uyghur Muslims. That guy missed his calling with the Third Reich."

Then Hass chimed in, "Not to mention his anti-corruption crusade, which is pretty selectively focused on imprisoning or executing anyone who stands in the way of consolidated power."

Griffin was unmoved.

"China's more motivated than anyone to prevent the Pakistani government from being embarrassed. They've got the resources to prevent a nuclear warhead from leaving the country, and the geographic proximity to put those resources into play a whole lot quicker than America could."

Hass swerved the Subaru wagon into the right lane to pass a commuter bus, then back over before an oncoming jingle truck could make good on a head-on collision from which its driver didn't shrink in the slightest. "Boss, you seem a hell of a lot more comfortable relying on these people for intelligence support than I am."

"That depends on what you mean by 'these people.' Because yeah, Xi is evil. Putin is evil, and so is Kim Jong Un. But the people in China and Russia and North Korea are just as good as those in any free country, and let's not pretend we couldn't make the case that America hasn't had her share of evil leaders, too. Our politicians just have a different framework to operate in."

Washington tilted his head toward the roof of the Subaru, all but rolling his eyes as he responded.

"Come on, Griff. All this 'good and evil' talk is unbecoming from such a rational analyst. You don't have to be so dramatic."

"I'm not," Griffin replied. "That's what this is, what it always has been."

"In China?"

"In Project Longwing. Good versus evil, light versus darkness, pick your cliché. There are bad forces trying to do damage. Our job is to stop them."

So the man was an idealist, Cancer thought. It was an odd character trait to find amidst the men of a targeted killing program, and one that quite possibly stood alone from the rest of the participants.

Finally, however, the sniper couldn't take any more.

"Even if you're right about good and evil, I'd say my team has blurred those lines in the past. And I'm not just talking about our mercenary time. Which is why I'm glad we're on the ground in Pakistan."

"Why's that?"

Cancer smirked. "Can't be afraid to get dirty if you're going to play in the mud. My guys have bent and broken every rule in the book to make shit happen. And if there's a chance for us to stop this nuke, that's going to pay off."

Griffin said nothing, though Cancer didn't get the sense that he'd changed the team leader's mind in the slightest. No matter, he thought, because if the opportunity for further gunplay afforded itself amid such dizzyingly high stakes, then Griffin would see exactly what the original Project Longwing team was capable of.

And with a timing that couldn't have possibly been any more perfect if it had been scripted in advance, David transmitted from the Hilux.

"*Net call, the Agency got a satellite snapshot of a five-vehicle convoy leaving Islamabad on the N5 westbound; timing is consistent with warhead transport following the theft. They've also intercepted enemy comms indicating the vehicles include heavy security and high-priority cargo in the van at the center of the convoy, which should be about five klicks to our front. Vehicle composition from front to rear is Corolla, Mitsubishi pickup, HiAce van with the cargo, Land Cruiser, and Nissan Altima.*

"*Ideally we'd get them in sight and remain in a surveillance role until the cavalry arrives, but we can't trust the Pakistanis and Chinese aircraft are still two hours out. And if we get spotted, the convoy will lead us into a trap anyway. It's now or never. Mayfly just gave us authorization to engage, and we're taking it.*"

"Hot damn," Washington said with delight, reaching for the plate carrier at his feet, "we're in business."

David continued, "*I'll update Tahir after the fact. Let's pick up the pace until we locate that Nissan at the rear of the convoy, then we'll take them on the road. Here's the plan.*"

22

I pushed my upper body through the open rear window of the Hilux's quad cab.

The roar of the wind was deafening, and the sharp scent of diesel and dust filled my nose. My knuckles whitened as I gripped the window frame, bracing myself. The pickup jolted over a bump at high speed, making my stomach lurch.

Noise and wind pummeled me, grit from the road stinging my face and eyes. Taking a deep breath, I pulled myself further out, feeling the strain in my arms. My focus was on the pickup bed, loaded with our equipment and covered in a tarp.

I swung one leg out and found a foothold on the edge of the bed. As the vehicle swayed, I struggled to keep my balance, heart pounding. Slowly, I rotated my body until I was almost fully outside, clinging to the truck.

With my arms burning, I leveraged myself against the cab and roof, inching toward the bed. I reached for the edge of the sliding rear window—which was, regrettably, far too small for me to simply climb through—then muscled myself out and into the bed.

I landed hard on the tarp, the equipment beneath it doing little to cushion my fall. Gasping for breath, I crouched, ready to help my partner make his way back.

Ian was currently navigating the process with about as much grace as I had, which was to say none at all. His efforts were assisted, however, by my grabbing his shirt and hauling him into the back like a rag doll. My urgency was born of equal parts concern for life and limb and worry that any of the myriad cars around us was a peripheral security element for the convoy we were about to smash. If so, they'd have a hard time missing the two bumbling white assholes who'd just scrambled along the outside of a moving pickup.

But the only recognition of our feat came by way of a radio transmission from Hass in the Subaru behind us.

"That was like watching a couple chimps trying to figure out a unicycle."

"Fuck off," I replied, rolling to my side as Reilly accelerated and passed our point vehicle to bring us first in the order of movement.

Ian righted himself and called over the wind, "Thanks."

"Don't mention it."

He reached through the Hilux's sliding rear window to retrieve our rifles and plate carriers from the backseat. We stayed low, donning our gear in an awkward series of prone maneuvers to avoid being seen any more than we already had. I slung my AK-47 tight to my body and crawled across the tarp, sliding my hands over it until I located the hard case I'd been looking for.

Pulling the tarp off, I unclasped the case and flipped the lid open to find my contribution to the upcoming assault.

The RPG-7 was a fan favorite of irregular and guerilla forces, and for good reason. It was the Coca-Cola of shoulder-launched anti-tank rocket launchers, available anywhere in the world at extremely affordable prices. Its metallic tube was slightly longer than a baseball bat, the center section wrapped in scarred and worn wood, and it had a flared muzzle at one end and twin hand grips at the other. Normally an optic device would be attached, but this particular piece of equipment from Tahir's donation to our killing spree was limited to iron sights that I flipped upward and into position.

No matter, I thought as I greedily retrieved the launcher from its case, because sights were more or less optional at the range I planned on employing it from.

"Remember," I said to Ian, "stay directly beside me or the blast will—"

"I know."

Still lying down, I retrieved the first of our three rockets and slid its rod into the launcher. The point of the conical warhead would detonate on impact once I removed a mint-green plastic safety cap. I left that on for now because once it was off, so much as a pothole or errant bump of the rocket's tip would turn the Hilux and its occupants into a smoking fireball. Safety, as it turned out, was not high on the Soviets' list of priorities when designing the round.

Reilly transmitted, "*Eyes-on the enemy convoy, 300 meters to our twelve.*"

"That was quick," Ian noted as we arranged ourselves side by side, with him closer to the tailgate to engage the driver of the second enemy vehicle. I'd be busy dealing with the first, for which a perpendicular angle of fire was crucial. The RPG-7 had one hell of a backblast, and if it hit the cab, then Reilly would be severely pissed off at best.

The medic said, "*One hundred meters behind the rear vehicle, still have one car between us. Make sure you're staying down in the back.*"

And while Ian and I indeed remained lying down and out of sight from the surrounding drivers, this was my last chance to remove the safety cap from the warhead. If I forgot that simple step, the rocket would merely scare the shit out of the car's occupants, possibly spearing through one of them in the process and, if I was lucky, disabling the engine.

But I was looking to achieve effects that were a fair bit more dramatic, and felt myself rock backward as Reilly moved to overtake the last car remaining between us and the enemy vehicles.

"*Directly behind the convoy, waiting for a gap to advance. We've got to move fast—there's a town ahead, and once we reach it, I won't be able to create enough distance for the rocket to arm.*"

He'd barely finished that transmission before I felt the whoosh of a large vehicle heading the opposite direction, which must have given our driver the slice of open road he was looking for.

"*Here we go...past the trail vic...van...*"

I thumbed the RPG's hammer down into the cocked position. The Hilux swerved off the road and onto rough dirt as Reilly swung it as far abreast of my target as he could—the rocket would need a minimum of five meters' flight before arming itself. Then the acceleration stalled and our speed held steady as he sent his final transmission.

"Execute, execute, execute—"

Ian and I popped up at the same moment. He was already pointing his AK-47 at the windshield of the second enemy vehicle, a Mitsubishi pickup, by the time I had the heavy launcher atop my shoulder.

The profile of the black Toyota Corolla leading the convoy was directly to my front, the iron sights of my launcher shaky amid the rumble of our tires against rough earth. I managed to align my aim roughly with the front edge of the engine block, hearing Ian blast away with his rifle as I pulled the trigger.

I felt the launcher buck against my shoulder and send a quaking shudder through my entire body as it loosed its payload with an enormous roar, a trail of smoke marking the short flight to its target.

The rocket's nose plunged through the Corolla's front door panel, whose metal crumpled like paper under the force. A brilliant flash of light illuminated the car's cabin before smoke, dust, and debris momentarily obscured the view—but the wind whipped the cloud backward to reveal that the car had more or less disintegrated from the inside out, its frame twisted and buckling as it lost speed, its passenger door now cartwheeling along the road.

I saw the remainder of the convoy swerve to dodge their eviscerated point vehicle as I dropped the launcher off my shoulder and retrieved the next rocket to reload.

***

Worthy saw the flash of the rocket impacting the lead vehicle in the convoy a moment before Munoz steered their Suzuki into the rear quarter panel of the trail car.

The Nissan Altima lost traction immediately and transitioned into a drifting 180-degree slide past the windshield and into the opposite lane. By then Worthy had his AK-47 in hand and was leaning out the open passenger window, where his sole duty at present was to aim for the enemy driver as Keller did the same from the backseat, aiming out the opposite side. No matter how textbook a PIT maneuver was—and Munoz had not only executed the move with perfection but done so almost simultaneously with the RPG attack—it only temporarily disabled the targeted car. The Nissan would be back in pursuit the moment its driver recovered his wits, unless Worthy landed his shots and whittled the number of enemy vehicles on the highway down to three.

The PIT maneuver had slowed their car and caused them to drift out of their lane, and the Subaru wagon containing Cancer and three shooters from the second team sped through the gap in hot pursuit of the remaining enemy vehicles.

Worthy faced backward out his window, and was bringing his AK-47 to bear on the Nissan as best he could when he momentarily lost his stability —Munoz whipped the Suzuki to the right of the enemy point vehicle, now a skidding and still-smoking hulk from the rocket blast.

As he regained his aim, Worthy saw that there was no point shooting yet. The enemy vehicle was still in an uncontrolled flat spin on the pavement, and before he could assess when and if to fire without hitting civilian vehicles, a jingle truck whipped by the opposite way, its back end fishtailing slightly as the driver applied his brakes too late to stop the inevitable.

The truck struck the Nissan head-on, and the booming crunch of compressed metal preceded a cloud of dust blasting in all directions. Pieces of the car hurled through the sandy fog as Worthy abandoned the quickly receding sight, pulling himself back in the car along with Keller, who was, against all odds, laughing hysterically at the carnage they'd both just witnessed.

"Vic Five down," Worthy transmitted. The mobile attack had started off strong—they'd gone from a three-on-five vehicle engagement to three-on-three in the opening ten seconds, though the pair of remaining security vehicles would have to be dealt with before they could focus on the van and its cargo.

It only took him a moment to orient himself to the ongoing chase.

Cancer and Washington were visible leaning out the rear windows of the Subaru wagon directly ahead, their attempts at taking aim complicated by Hass, who piloted the vehicle with juking swerves in an attempt to land a PIT on a Land Cruiser that was aggressively defending against the maneuver. Beyond them Worthy could make out the HiAce van, an otherwise unremarkable sight that became the most sobering thing he'd ever seen by virtue of knowing what it held inside.

The enemy convoy was led by a Mitsubishi pickup that swerved wildly to avoid the sights of the RPG held by David in the back of the Hilux, which led the entire procession and was, by virtue of that position, the only one suited to bring the engagement to a close.

Griffin transmitted, "*Doc, start closing the gap.*"

Reilly applied the Hilux's brakes to slow the convoy and force the enemy point vehicle into the sights of David's rocket launcher, and Hass accelerated his Subaru wagon to execute the PIT maneuver on the Land Cruiser.

And seconds before the remaining two security vehicles could be engaged, everything went to shit.

The Mitsubishi pickup carved a sudden right-hand turn that took it between two vehicles in the opposite lane, and then into the open desert beyond the highway. Before Worthy could process whether or not this was intended as retreat or some roundabout tactical maneuver, the remaining two vehicles did the opposite.

Munoz slammed on the brakes to avoid rear-ending Hass's Subaru wagon, which was doing the same to prevent a collision with the Land Cruiser, whose driver was likewise avoiding an accident with the HiAce van that either had an activated parking brake or stopped so suddenly that it damn well didn't matter much.

Then the van was off the highway, carving a left-hand turn into the town on the south side, where it slipped between buildings with the Land Cruiser behind it.

The evasive maneuver had been deftly coordinated, leaving the American drivers scrambling to react. All three bailed off the road because to do otherwise after the sudden deceleration would be to invite a ten-car pileup among the frantic N5 traffic, and nothing else would matter unless that particular catastrophe was averted.

Worthy was flung forward against the dash—he'd removed his seatbelt in anticipation of firing from a moving vehicle—as Munoz brought the car to a near-stop moments before slamming into the Subaru, which Hass wielded like a butcher's blade by whipping a sharp turn to catch the road that the remaining enemy vehicles had sped down.

The Hilux had overshot that path long before, which left Reilly, David, and Ian out of the fight entirely. Munoz floored the accelerator and cut left to pursue Hass, whose Subaru wagon now represented their only hope of keeping eyes-on the fleeing van. This interdiction operation had now been distilled into a two-on-two vehicle engagement, though the odds of a successful resolution were getting longer with each passing second.

Griffin transmitted from the Subaru, "*Van is moving southbound into town. Teams Two and Three in pursuit. Team One, head that way and I'll talk you in.*"

Buildings seemed to fly past in a blur outside, painted in hues of orange and gold against the rising sun. Worthy caught sight of vendors setting up their stalls and pedestrians who barely had time to react to the speeding vehicles.

"*Watch your background,*" Griffin said, continuing to call the shots now that David was unavailable in every sense of the word. "*The van could be headed toward a defensive position or that Mitsubishi pickup could try to sneak up behind us, but no matter what there are enemy reinforcements on the way. We need to stop the van by whatever means necessary, get the warhead loaded into the Hilux, and make a straight shot back to Islamabad while we still can.*"

Cancer leaned out of the rear passenger window of the speeding Subaru wagon, his AK-47 firm in his hands. The engine roared, its sound bouncing off the tightly packed buildings as they tore through the streets in pursuit of the two remaining enemy vehicles.

Hass was at the wheel, with Griffin in the passenger seat monitoring Reilly's position via the tracking software on his phone as he issued directions in the hopes of vectoring the Hilux back into the fight.

But the backseat was where the action was, Washington aiming out the left side and Cancer the right, both men vying for a glimpse of the Land Cruiser that had vanished around a corner ahead.

The town was waking up now, and the streets were dotted with pedestrians reacting to the chase in progress. Men in traditional shalwar kameez carried, and in some cases dropped, their baskets of goods, women in brightly colored scarves hurried away from the streets, and children playing near the doorways of their homes looked up with fascination.

Then there were the civilian vehicles, battered sedans and pickups that Hass steered around while blaring his horn over shouts of alarm from the streets. By the time he whipped the Subaru around the corner, Cancer could make out his target ahead.

The enemy Land Cruiser was barreling down the street, weaving dangerously close to market stalls and pedestrians. Ahead of it, the Toyota HiAce van sped forward.

Cancer thumbed his AK-47's selector lever downward and, in unison with Washington leaning out the opposite side, opened fire on the Land Cruiser.

The sniper's specialty was precision long-range shots, to which there was a very fixed science. Firing at close range from a moving car, however, was an art born out of pure instinct. Each moment brought an entirely new sight picture and, with it, corresponding angles of fire, as Hass and the enemy driver juked their vehicles through the streets. All this occurred against the backdrop of civilians—a stray bullet hitting any one of them would represent exceedingly poor form.

Throw in a loose nuke, Cancer thought, and he was enjoying himself thoroughly.

Between his own gunfire and Washington's, the Land Cruiser's rear window shattered into splinters of glass—but that did nothing to slow the vehicle, which was still too distant to shoot out the tires with anything resembling accuracy.

Hass swerved to avoid a fruit cart, narrowly missing a collision as the vendor scrambled away. Ahead, the van and its security escort made a right turn, adding the screech of tires to an already jumbled mix of sounds. The men in both enemy vehicles were desperate to escape, a prospect that they had a very real possibility of achieving so long as they evaded until reinforcements arrived.

A pedestrian darted across the street, narrowly avoiding the Subaru as Cancer braced himself against the doorframe, feeling every jolt and vibration against the street below. He brought the AK-47 to his shoulder as Hass made the next turn in pursuit of their quarry, and this time the preparation paid off—the HiAce van had slowed in order to shoot a narrow gap between an abandoned vehicle and the adjacent building, which had cost both it and the Land Cruiser valuable progress.

The latter vehicle was now at the end of Cancer's sights, its rear window nearly destroyed.

Rather than sending more shots into the cab, Cancer dropped his point of aim and sent bullets at the rear left tire, the AK-47 bucking against his shoulder, fumes of gunpowder mixing with the morning air, rapid-fire shots ringing out loudly as ejected brass casings cluttered the road.

The blowout occurred soon thereafter, the wheel suddenly rimmed with nothing more than flopping black rubber, and the Land Cruiser swerved violently as the driver struggled to keep control while hemorrhaging speed. Cancer transitioned to the other visible tire and shredded that as well.

They'd now be able to pass the final security vehicle with relative ease, and Cancer dropped his magazine to the street before reloading for a final volley.

Hass veered left and accelerated past the slow-moving Land Cruiser. Cancer blasted rapid single shots at the driver's window, firing in a sweeping arc until his firing angle had just eclipsed 90 degrees. Then Cancer removed his right hand from the pistol grip and placed it on the AK's fore-end, swapping it for the left hand that he now moved to the pistol grip to resume shooting at an ever-increasing angle as Hass sped past.

The transition from right- to left-handed shooting had taken him perhaps two seconds, a time sacrifice that paid off and then some in the number of rounds placed through the driver's side of the windshield. Bullets did wonky things when passing through auto glass, but given the sheer volume of fire he'd laid down, it was a safe bet that whoever had been piloting the Land Cruiser was now well ventilated by 7.62mm rounds.

Once his target was out of sight, Cancer pulled himself back in the Subaru and reloaded before calling out, "We got him."

Griffin took to the air then, transmitting, "Vic Four down. Doc, go straight for two blocks, then right again. You should be able to cut them off at the T-intersection."

This time Reilly responded with his first positive message since confirming that the lead enemy vehicle was destroyed.

"Copy, I'm almost there."

Reilly gripped the steering wheel of the Hilux as he sped through the narrow streets of the Pakistani town, navigating the twists and turns with a precision born of necessity. Griffin's voice was urgent and insistent as he relayed directions, monitoring the Hilux's position on his phone.

"Doc, take the next left. The HiAce is trying to lose us in the maze of side streets."

The medic complied, swinging the Hilux sharply to the left. Its tires screeched in protest as the truck bounced over the uneven road, sending jolts through his body as he focused on the next instruction.

"Right at the intersection, then a quick left again. Van is moving fast," Griffin's voice came again, a lifeline in the chaos.

Reilly swerved the Hilux around one corner and then another, narrowly missing a vendor's cart that spilled its contents into the street. The pedestrians scattered, their shouts of alarm barely audible over the roar of the engine and the thumping of his heart. He glanced in the rearview mirror, seeing David and Ian steadying themselves in the pickup bed.

The peaceful glow of the early morning sun created a surreal backdrop to the high-speed chase as Reilly maneuvered to avoid civilian vehicle and foot traffic.

"Vic Four down," Griffin said. *"Doc, go straight for two blocks, then right again. You should be able to cut them off at the T-intersection."*

Reilly keyed his mic.

"Copy, I'm almost there."

He accelerated, the buildings blurring past. The Hilux jolted as it hit a pothole, but he didn't slow down. His senses were heightened, every sound, every movement around him amplified as he made the final turn. The radio crackled again, Griffin's voice tense.

"Van is still headed for the T-intersection."

Reilly's grip tightened, his eyes narrowing as he saw the intersection ahead. He pushed the Hilux harder, the engine straining. The streets were narrower here, the buildings pressing in close, creating a tunnel effect as he transmitted to David.

"Suicide, I'll pull up to the corner, get eyes-on, then ram his rear quarter panel for a sideways PIT."

"Copy," David replied.

This was Christmas all over again, Reilly thought. He'd desperately wanted to do a PIT maneuver for most of his career and got his first chance when Raza fled the abandoned factory. Now he'd get a second chance in as many days, this time when the stakes couldn't be higher.

He pulled the Hilux up to the corner and braked, looking right down the street to see if he'd arrived in time.

Sure enough, the van was speeding toward him right on cue. Reilly kept his foot on the brake, closely watching the HiAce's progress to time his transition to mashing the accelerator.

Instead he felt a massive concussion rattle the truck as a plume of smoke shot downward to his right, an unexpected development that could only mean one thing.

David, being the son of a bitch that he was, had fired their second rocket.

The projectile went low, streaking toward the street beneath the HiAce and detonating under the rear axle.

The explosion was deafening, a thunderous roar that echoed through the streets and lifted the van off the ground, its rear end disintegrating in a blinding flash of light and shrapnel. Chunks of metal, rubber, and shattered glass flew in all directions, twisted remnants of the axle spinning away from the epicenter of the explosion.

Reilly had the fleeting mental picture of the van exploding in a nuclear mushroom cloud that would kill both Project Longwing teams and take the entire town and a good chunk of the N5 highway with it. But the van only skidded uncontrollably, the front end still trying to move forward while dragging the mangled mess of the rear. It spun wildly, leaving black streaks of burnt rubber on the pavement before finally coming to a violent stop.

Swerving left, Reilly braked the pickup to a curving halt with his tail-gate facing the remnants of the van.

As his truck rocked with the movement of David and Ian leaping out of the bed, Griffin sent the next radio message.

"*Load the warhead into the Hilux—we need to get moving before any more bad guys show up.*"

Ian made landfall on the uneven street behind the tailgate, raising his AK-47 and racing toward the van's passenger side.

David was to his right and firing through the windshield as he advanced, covering Ian's movement amid the storm—witnesses who had seen the explosion from a distance were frozen in shock, and both Hass's Subaru and Munoz's Suzuki were gliding up behind the van in preparation to dismount and secure the site.

It would be a miracle if anyone in the demolished van had remained conscious, much less survived. Flames licked at the remaining fuel, creating small bursts of fire that crackled ominously as smoke billowed from the wreckage. He was advancing into a thick, acrid cloud that stung his eyes and choked his lungs, the air impossibly dense with the smell of burning rubber, oil, and scorched metal.

Ian saw the van's driver, dead, as he rounded the passenger side of the van with the heat around him rising ever higher with each step. The smart thing to do would have been to wait for the arrival of additional team members, but he made the split-second assessment that if anyone in the HiAce's cargo area was somehow still alive, then pressing the initiative before they recovered could well be the difference between taking gunfire and seizing a nuclear weapon before the enemy had a chance to fire a shot.

He skidded to a halt beside the van, fully intending to attempt opening the side door before chancing a window entry.

To his surprise, the van's sliding door moved back, but only by a meter or so before grinding into tracks mangled by the rocket explosion. That was space enough to enter, and Ian cleared the immediate cargo area for threats before panning his rifle sideways to see the rest and leaping inside.

He swung his aim to the far corner, expecting to find one or more security men, and instead found the space unoccupied by human presence.

But a rectangular tough box lay askew, roughly two meters in length
and one in width. It matched perfectly with the proportions needed to
encase and cushion a Hatf 8 warhead for off-road travel, though what
concerned Ian as he scrambled forward and began unclipping heavy-duty
clasps was the case's weight. Griffin had almost casually ordered them to
move the warhead into the Hilux, but the case would weigh a thousand
pounds. Despite having ten men to accomplish the task, there were only
two carrying handles along each side and one at the front and rear, which
meant a 160-plus-pound lift for the six team members who could actually
manage a grip. Just getting this thing out of the van, he thought, much less
into the back of the Hilux, was going to be a bitch.

Ian unclipped the final clasp when he was gripped by sudden concern
for a boobytrap of some kind. He attempted to shift the box only to find
that it wouldn't budge, and a visual sweep for any means of deactivating a
trigger inside revealed none.

Then, bolstered onward by insatiable fascination and awe, he lifted
the lid.

A half-burned American flag obscured his view of the contents, and he
pulled the desecrated banner aside to be met first with a pungent odor and
then the sight of what lay below.

The case was about a thousand pounds all right, but none of it
consisted of a warhead. Ian saw a tangled jumble of scrap metal, greasy
engine parts like alternators and carburetors, old tools and broken bolts
crammed into every possible crevice. He was instantly nauseous, whether
due to falling for the ruse, the heady scent of oil and rust, or both.

"No joy," he said quietly, only dimly aware that he was keying his
radio mic.

His mind was racing now. The only surviving enemy vehicle was the
Mitsubishi pickup that had fled into the desert and never returned. Was it
harboring the warhead while the van served as a red herring? Ian then
found himself wondering if there had ever been a warhead present at all.
Was the entire convoy a decoy? If so, were similar decoys fanning out in all
directions from Islamabad?

He had no answers, only a stark urgency to flee the area as quickly as possible. But the reflex was insufficient to overcome a shock-induced paralysis as he scanned the cargo area, as if his initial visual sweep had failed to notice the presence of a 12-kiloton nuclear device.

A hand alighted on his shoulder and shook him hard, and Ian looked back to see that David had entered the van behind him.

"Let's go," his team leader said breathlessly. "We've got to move."

Ian exited after David, the sights outside the van transpiring in sluggish slow motion amid his racing thoughts.

Munoz was already driving his Suzuki past the wreckage to take point, and Griffin's face was visible through the windshield of the Subaru wagon as it stopped alongside the van. Reilly was in the process of boarding the Hilux—apparently he'd dismounted to assist the van clearance, which had turned out to be an impossibly futile endeavor.

"In the back, in case we get followed," David called over his shoulder.

That was all the notice Ian had before his team leader leapt atop the rear bumper and pulled himself into the bed. And while Ian followed suit, it was with a sense of utter detachment from the reality of the situation. What were they supposed to do now, head toward Peshawar as if the disastrous spree of carnage had never transpired? He felt a sense of abject hopelessness at the very real possibility that after all this, they could be wandering into another pointless gunfight or worse, facing whatever enemy reinforcements had been waiting in the wings to attack any opposition to their movement of a rogue nuclear warhead on the N5, wherever it may be at that moment.

If that device was westbound at all, he reminded himself.

Ian crashed into the bed beside David, barely landing before the Hilux accelerated forward with Reilly transmitting.

"*Split Team Two, moving.*"

"*Three,*" Griffin said, "*picking up trail. Quickest route back to the highway, continue movement to Peshawar. Suicide?*"

"Concur," David replied in a jarringly neutral tone, releasing his transmit switch before his voice filled with fury and confusion.

"Ian," he continued, adjusting his position atop the tarp-covered equipment, "what the fuck just happened?"

23

I took another bite of my mid-morning breakfast, then traded my fork for coffee before turning from my seat at the bar.

Among the tables in the dining space were journalists typing furiously on their laptops, aid workers, and well-dressed and well-heeled clusters of people grouped by nationality—North American, South American, Asian —that could only be from their respective nations' consulates in Peshawar.

Uniting this diverse assemblage was an uneasy edginess centered on the state of current affairs. Everyone present glanced frequently at the TVs above the bar and spread throughout the dining room, all of them flashing images of troop movements and stern-faced politicians, their grave expressions matching the mood of the patrons. Every snippet of conversation that floated by involved discussions about the recent clashes and wild speculation about what might happen next.

I had desperately needed a public place where I could blend in as an American, and those requirements were met by only one establishment in Peshawar. The Frontier Lounge was billed as the *Star Wars* cantina for expats, and my first twenty minutes lived up to that reputation. Since taking up my seat at the bar, I'd counted four nationalities solely from the accents and languages around me.

"Mind if I join you?" a man asked in New York City English.

Make that five nationalities, I thought.

I looked over to find a Latino man in his late thirties, and took in his attire at a glance. Moisture-wicking button-down shirt, cargo pants, and pricey boots that had yet to see the dirt of Pakistan outside a major urban haven. That final detail ruled out his status as a freelance photographer or NGO field worker, and while he could have been managing the latter, he exuded the vibe of a staff member from the US Consulate.

"I'm waiting for some people," I said.

An easy smile crossed his face.

"I won't be long. It'd be nice to share a friendly word with—"

"Well would you look at that," I cut him off, nodding toward the door. "There are my friends now. Good luck finding that friendly word."

He took the hint and departed, casting a glance at the door as he left. No one had entered, and I turned my attention back to the plate of eggs, flatbread, and vegetables before me, poking at it with my fork before going for my coffee instead.

The warm flow of caffeine was the only comfort I had at present.

We didn't even know if the nuke was headed this way, only that the frontier between Pakistan and Afghanistan was the least guarded avenue and, consequently, the only one where our teams could have an effect beyond throwing in the towel altogether. The enemy convoy on the highway had been a glimmer of hope that we'd called the right spin of the roulette wheel, and now that hope had been erased in lieu of an uncertainty so great it was hard to put into words.

And now, I occupied a purgatory between a reunion with Tahir or, less enviably, being arrested by the ISI.

A solo meeting was the only option under the circumstances, which involved the not-inconceivable premise that the meeting could be a trap to bring the Americans back into custody. Particularly, I thought, after our ISI minder reported us as violating every international and diplomatic treaty under the sun.

Sending myself as ground force commander alone into this potential snare had been a controversial topic among the teams, but I'd made a strong enough case for me to handle it by myself. Griffin was more than capable of managing everyone, and Cancer was second to none as a right-hand man. They'd carry on just fine without me, but the truth was that tactical continuity was only the second of my concerns.

I was simply unwilling to order any man, whether from my team or Griffin's, to assume the risk of incarceration. If anyone was going to get hauled off to jail, then it was going to be me, and I'd do so without saying a word about the remaining Americans whose location, by design, I was completely unaware of. I hadn't even brought my Agency phone with me, instead packing only a burner in the event this linkup went off without a hitch.

A breaking news report caused me to abandon my coffee mid-sip, and I glanced up at the familiar face on the television screen.

Kamran Raza was freshly shaved, looking contrite with a somber expression. The wall behind him was beige, some harshly lit room in an Agency facility within the flying range of an Air Department business jet after his transfer from the Mi-17. I should have been happy knowing war between Pakistan and India was at this very moment being averted. Instead, the sight of Raza brought with it a feeling of sickening irony—I'd expected this video to represent the end of my team's involvement, a decisive victory for our assigned mission.

And now, I knew that Raza was but a minor player in a grander conspiracy to steal and smuggle a nuclear weapon.

That was my final thought on the matter before the front door swung open and Tahir strode inside wearing a backpack. I watched him for a moment before lifting my hand to flag him down. Only then did I notice that he'd brought someone with him.

The two men couldn't have been much more different, and together looked like a casting decision for a cheap buddy cop movie. Tahir was burly, intense, focused, while the Chinese official behind him—if that's indeed what he was—was slim and moved with a sort of languid grace, possessed by a calm assurance that he was a master of this domain and all others.

I took in his attire as he approached with a leather satchel over one shoulder, finding his pressed linen shirt and khakis to be a level of formality somewhere between the aid workers and the consulate officials.

His shoes hadn't seen the sands of Pakistan either, and I got the sense that field work was somehow beneath him.

Tahir arrived first, remaining standing as he asked, "Where are the rest of your men?"

"Somewhere safe," I replied, directing my attention to his counterpart. "And you are?"

The Chinese man slid onto the barstool beside me without waiting for an invitation, leaving his leather satchel slung over his shoulder. I noted honest-to-God manicured fingernails as he set a hand on the bar, his eyes half-lidded in a state of apparent indifference. Tahir remained standing behind me.

"You may call me Mr. Zhang," he said in a crisp Chinese accent.

"What's your position? Foreign affairs, state security?"

Zhang smiled faintly. "I serve my country in matters that require discretion. That is all you need to know."

"What I need to know," I corrected him, "is that you're legitimate and not some stand-in to get me to lead the ISI to the rest of my men. And so far I don't feel great about that."

Tahir interceded, "Mr. Zhang is your assigned liaison. He is a guest of the Pakistan government and to be afforded every courtesy. And I can assure you he is quite legitimate."

"Okay," I said, turning to face the so-called Chinese official. "Prove it."

Zhang glanced at the nearest television, still displaying Raza's confession, and then his eyes met mine.

"We have two BZK-005 long-endurance drones dedicated to this section of the Pakistani border alone. They are overhead as we speak and will be continuously replaced until I say otherwise. As are a flight of J-20s—"

"Stealth fighters?" I asked.

"Yes," he suavely replied, checking his watch, "for another ninety minutes. Then they will be relieved by a second flight that is currently refueling from an HY-6 tanker over Hotan. This is simply the immediate response, Mr. Rivers."

I nodded. So far so good, I thought. "Then talk me through the rest, because refueling over western China isn't going to cut it for sustained operations."

"Of course. We have additional J-20 and J-10C fighters staging at PAF Base Mushaf along with tankers and two KJ-2000s, which are airborne early-warning and control aircraft similar to your E-3 Sentry. Also a contingent of BZK-005 drones at Tarbela Ghazi Airbase due to its UAV handling capabilities, to say nothing of the full support of the Pakistan Air Force."

An impressive array of aerial power, I thought, provided he wasn't lying.

But if the force safeguarding a nuclear warhead was indeed headed this way or here already, I had the sneaking suspicion that the battle wouldn't be won from the air.

"Tahir mentioned a counterterrorism element."

He nodded. "A small contingent, yes. Currently airborne in a Y-20 destined for Islamabad. They will be in position by noon, with orders to assist any Pakistani ground response by advising and accompanying Zarrar Company."

"Your contingent," I asked, "who are they?"

"We call their unit Lotus Sentinel. They specialize in counterterrorism, hostage rescue, and counterproliferation of weapons of mass destruction."

I shrugged. "I've never heard of them."

"We do not publicize their existence. But trust that within China's borders, they have more experience than anyone."

To me, that translated into a couple realities.

One, they had no international deployment experience. That much was no surprise given the available information—or, to put it more precisely, lack of information—about China's special operations forces.

The second was what I addressed now.

"I'm sure your shooters are the cat's nuts when they're rounding up unarmed Uyghurs, but the people smuggling that device won't go down quietly. And they'll have more means for resistance than any dissidents to your president's power."

My comments seemed to glide through Zhang, who responded in a courteous tone.

"You may be surprised how determined some of those enemies of the state truly are, Mr. Rivers. And General Secretary Xi's prospects are secure with or without the help of our military. If Pakistan chooses to send Zarrar

Company and, with it, the men of Lotus Sentinel, I believe you will find them quite capable."

I nodded toward Tahir. "Let's have the JTAC info."

"The what?" he asked.

"Air support procedures."

"Ah," Tahir replied, unslinging his backpack to procure a sheaf of folded papers. "I have them here."

Accepting the packet, I flipped through it to find separate scripts for Pakistani and Chinese aircraft. They were interspersed with parenthetical notations for inserting magnetic heading and distance to target, along with elevation, description, location, marking procedures, location of friendlies, and egress azimuth. There were some minor errors in translation, particularly in the Chinese format, but I felt confident that Munoz and Hass, my two certified joint terminal attack controllers, could work with this.

I neatly folded the packet. "How would this arrangement work?"

Tahir replied, "I have reserved facilities at Badaber—you know it?"

"No."

Before Tahir could explain further, Zhang said, "PAF Camp Badaber, just south of the city. Very significant for your country, before you left Pakistan. Your Agency used it to communicate with Gary Powers before his U2 was shot down over the Soviet Union. It later became a major NSA listening post, as well as the center of logistics efforts for CIA support of the Afghan Mujahideen. I am told the base retains many American touches— your men should feel rather at home there."

I considered this information, knowing beyond a doubt that I was reaching the precipitous decision of whether to risk my men's involvement. Zhang certainly seemed legitimate, and Tahir's sincerity was nearly beyond doubt and bolstered by the fact that he hadn't yet put an APB out on the vehicles he loaned my team.

There were other factors to consider, not the least of which was collusion between an Agency element and Chinese intelligence. I'd have to clue Chen in on that, directly or indirectly, or risk facing espionage charges. Any information sharing of value could quite possibly reveal capabilities of US spy satellites that the Chinese may or may not have been aware of, and if they were genuine about a joint effort, the same held true for Zhang's unmanned aerial vehicles.

It wasn't a comfortable decision to make, though the prospect of a missing nuke did make it a relatively easy one.

"I'll commit a small intelligence and command element to Badaber," I said to both men. "The rest of my men will position themselves north of the city in case a ground response is warranted before Lettuce Centipede arrives."

Zhang looked momentarily confused, then angered.

"Lotus Sentinel."

"Whatever," I dismissed him. "Do we have an agreement?"

Tahir folded his arms.

"Yes, so long as any direct action is authorized by myself and Mr. Zhang from the command center in Badaber—where you will be present, David, whether you want to be or not."

Well there went my hopes of sticking Griffin with desk duty, I thought.

Grabbing a piece of flatbread from my breakfast plate and the packet of JTAC protocols from the bar, I rose from the stool and gestured to the door.

"Let's get on with it."

24

The Pakistani Army escort stopped at a door in the hallway, knocked three times, and then turned the handle at a shouted response from within.

Hass entered the room first, carrying his equipment as well as David's, followed by Ian with his own. The intelligence operative was only two steps inside, however, when the sight brought him up short. David and another man sat at a long table topped with communications consoles and sleek, modern computers, their screens filled with real-time data. The hum of advanced technology filled the air, but it couldn't overshadow the ghosts of the room's history.

Ian was well aware of Camp Badaber's historical legacy, but the remnants made the space nothing short of surreal.

The far wall held a large, framed map of Afghanistan whose outdated features dated it to the 1980s rather than the more recent American involvement. It was clearly a relic from the Soviet-Afghan War, marked with strategic points and routes that had once been vital to the flow of weapons and equipment to the Mujahideen.

On another wall, partially obscured by newer equipment, was a faded but unmistakable painted logo. It featured crossed US and Pakistan national flags over a broken hammer and sickle, and beneath it was a banner with the words *ECHO 89* and two rows of hand-scrawled words where the members of some long-forgotten CIA or NSA task force had made their mark. All were nicknames, and Ian scanned a list that included Mr. Coffee, Cat Farmer, Tiny Tim, and Squeaky Chair. Whoever they were, these men had been born in the '30s and '40s and were now in their eighties if not dead, having witnessed, and possibly assisted, the fall of the Soviet Union somewhere in the interim.

"Hey guys," David called from his workstation, pointing at two chairs and their attendant computers, "these are your seats. Ian, you're next to me. Hass, I need you beside Zhang."

Zhang, as Ian found when the man turned in his chair to face them, was of Chinese ethnicity and almost certainly an intelligence professional. There was something about Zhang's apparent comfort in the midst of such a covert operations center that removed any other possibility from Ian's mind as he and Hass set their equipment and weapons behind their newly minted workstations.

Ian strode over and shook Zhang's hand with a brief and cryptic introduction, and Hass followed suit in short order.

David told him, "Zhang will brief you on the air packages—China's got fighters and surveillance drones overhead, no intel hits yet. Tahir's outside supervising some radio nerds connecting us to the satellite receivers. Mayfly is up to speed, I already ran a line to our sat antenna outside. It's secure." Then he lifted a sheaf of papers from the desk beside him and waved it at Hass. "Air support formats for Pakistan and China, we'll have to set up your antenna so you can push these to Munoz over the air frequency. Which car did you guys bring?"

"The Suzuki," Hass responded, kneeling beside his pack to retrieve whatever materials he needed to manage air assets.

Ian did the same, and was in the process of extracting his ruggedized laptop when Tahir entered the room, halting abruptly at the sight of Ian and Hass.

"Ah," the ISI officer went on, strolling to his chair. "I see you two motherfuckers are still alive."

Ian nodded approvingly. "Your grasp of American slang is really coming along."

"I have been listening to you toilet mouths speak for long enough."

Taking the seat beside David, Ian noted that even the furniture in this room was a mix of past and present. Ergonomic chairs stood in stark contrast to the long table itself, an old, solid slab of dark oak whose surface was worn smooth by decades of use.

He had just opened his laptop to let it boot up—he'd have to figure out the power cord situation later—when David put a hand mic to his ear and attempted contact.

"Raptor Nine One, Suicide Actual on alternate frequency, stand by for Angel."

Then he asked Ian, "How are the guys?"

"They're safe." He chose his words carefully due to the presence of foreigners, but the remaining team members were spread across two locations. Both were on the north side of Peshawar, both occupying hide sites in the hills to survey key routes while maintaining distant surveillance on their vehicles in the event of an ISI search.

But if that were going to transpire, it would have by now, and the extensive precautions suddenly seemed to be born out of an embarrassing paranoia.

David listened to a return message over the satellite handset, then handed it over.

Ian took it, already dreading the painful game of telephone relay that would transpire from here on out because they couldn't put the radio on speaker mode in front of Zhang—or Tahir, for that matter.

"Angel here," he transmitted, making a scrawling motion with the opposite hand. David set a notebook and pen down before him, and Ian barely had time to pick up the latter before Meiling Chen came out swinging.

"*Listen closely,*" she began, "*everything I discuss from here on out will have the caveat of whether or not you can share that information with anyone outside your team. It's in everyone's best interests to facilitate a reasonable level of cooperation, and I want you to be the hinge point for that. But we have to safeguard the means by which we collect certain information, and the Chinese will be doing the same thing.*"

So Chen was well aware that three men from her team were now officially liaising with the Chinese, Ian thought.

"Of course," he said.

"First things first. I need the locations of your remaining men."

"My computer's booting up. I'll set up a splitter and send via data shot."

"Good. Next up, I do have one late-breaking update. This is for your team's ears only—we haven't received official word from the Paks yet, but the information was obtained by monitoring their channels."

"Copy," Ian said, preparing his pen.

"They captured a wounded fighter from the raid on Nur Khan. He was interrogated before dying of his injuries, and that interrogation revealed that the attack was planned and executed by Adrian Müller."

This mission kept getting stranger and stranger, Ian thought.

Müller was German, a former private military contractor with a decade's worth of experience fighting bush wars in Africa. He'd transitioned into terrorism for hire and been the tactical planner for a cruise line hijacking and a seizure of the convention center hosting the World Economic Forum. He was suspected in several other attacks, although his involvement had yet to be confirmed.

He was also Project Longwing's Target Number One.

Number Four was Kamran Raza, and Three had been Katarzyna Zajac, the hacker that Cancer had recently dispatched.

And since Target Number Two was a nuclear engineer named Mordecai Friedman who was likely waiting outside Pakistan to receive the device and convert it as needed for a terrorist attack, the true scope of this theft was coming into focus.

Chen wouldn't have missed arriving at the same conclusion, and he said, "So everyone in our Top Four is, or was, involved."

"At this point, it's safe to say that you're right, which brings us to the warhead. No one, to include us, Pakistan, India, or, to the best of our knowledge, China, has yet picked up any indication of where the device could be. I assess that is indicative of the fact that it's still in Pakistan."

Ian sighed. "I'm sure it is. No matter how they're getting it out, they'll have to conduct multiple vehicle exchanges and God knows what else to keep it from being found. If it's coming toward us or here already, it's going to be sent in the flow of jingle trucks moving across the border if not a foot, motorcycle, or ATV movement over the mountains."

"*Pakistan has sealed its borders, so more likely the latter. That would put the most likely avenues of exfil across the Durand Line.*"

"Agreed," he said, "either the former Federally Administered Tribal Areas or Northwest Frontier Province. Both have declared roads with a constant flow of jingle trucks, as well as geographically impenetrable terrain with trusted smuggling trails that have been in place for thousands of years."

"*Exactly. Which leaves us with 2,600 kilometers to cover. But the second that device crosses into Afghanistan, it will enter an intelligence black hole with an additional 3,000 kilometers of border access spanning five countries.*"

"Including Iran," Ian said solemnly.

Chen's voice was firm. "*We've found no indications of Iranian involvement, and no reason to suspect they'd dare to sponsor an operation this big.*"

"No, but an aggressive junior Quds Force leader looking to make a name for himself would definitely facilitate the transport. That's Iran's M.O., and they've got a long history of it—they don't sanction all the Quds Force operations, but when those operations work out, the government rewards everyone involved. Fast-moving boats racing in to capture Brits who are close to territorial waters and dragging them to prison for media reasons, all of it. I don't think taking the nuke to Iran via Afghanistan is a far-fetched possibility."

He set down his pen and awaited her response, listening to the murmur of Zhang, Hass, and Tahir engaging in animated conversation. David was silent, watching Ian closely.

Finally Chen said, "*It's not outside the realm of possibility. For now, I need you to stay glued to comms. My people will provide guidance for where to stage the other men on the teams once we receive their current locations, so send them asap. And be careful. While the Chinese have the same interests that we do at the moment, there's no telling who we can trust.*"

An understatement if Ian had ever heard one, he thought. Even if Pakistani government or ISI officials weren't on the terrorist payroll— which they most certainly were—the nation had a long and storied history of self-interest above all else. The US had funneled $3 billion to support the Mujahideen before and during the Soviet-Afghan War, and the most pessimistic estimates were that twenty percent had been stolen and/or sold into the black market through Pakistani corruption. That percentage had only gotten worse when the US entered the fray with 2.6 *trillion* dollars after 9/11, much of it funneled through Pakistan.

He signed off with Chen, set the handset down, and began to log into his computer when David interrupted him.

"So where's this fucking thing headed?"

"As I just told her, my best guess is Iran—"

"I'm not talking about the smuggling corridor," David clarified. "I'm talking about the destination."

Ian leaned back in his seat. "Oh. That'd be America."

"How do you know?"

A not-unjustified question, Ian thought. Usually he provided his best assessment, specified as such.

But for some reason, this was different.

He gazed at the Cold War-era logo on one wall of the newly reinstated OPCEN, then at the map of Afghanistan on the other.

Then he said, "I just do."

25

"Hey man."

Reilly awoke from a deep sleep with the words and sensation of a hand shaking his shoulder. He was dimly aware that he should have startled awake, reaching for his rifle a millisecond later. But instead he took the speaker's casual tone as an indication that it was merely time to swap shifts, although he sought to confirm that assumption verbally.

"Are we compromised," Reilly mumbled, "or dead already?"

It was Keller who responded, "Neither. It's a beautiful day."

"I thought we were still in Pakistan. Did they find it?"

"No."

"Is it the end of my rest shift?"

"No."

"Well then…"

Keller shook his arm again. "Come on, bro. Up and at 'em."

Reilly sat up and opened his eyes in that order, groggily blinking as he checked his watch and then surveyed his surroundings.

The first thing he noticed was that Keller had placed his AK-47 out of arm's reach—a wise call when waking up a combat veteran—and that the intelligence operative was kneeling beneath the rock overhang where Reilly had been napping.

Beyond the slope they'd occupied for the past few hours were the rolling hills north of Peshawar, with the noon sun casting a stark light over the rugged landscape of hardy shrubs and coarse grass. The air was crisp and clear, carrying a faint bite of the December chill, and the northwestern view featured undulating terrain that rose and fell like the waves of a frozen sea. In the distance, the mountains of the Pak-Afghan border loomed, their snow-capped peaks standing out against the clear blue sky. They formed a natural barrier, rugged and imposing, a constant reminder of the land's resistance to control.

And those mountains, Reilly knew, were in Afghanistan.

The scene was one of raw, untamed beauty, untouched by governments and empires that had tried unsuccessfully for centuries to conquer it.

He rubbed his eyes and said at last, "All right. What's up?"

Keller handed his rifle back, sounding all too eager to explain.

"Ian and Hass linked up with David. They're up and running with command, control, and intelligence from Badaber. They've got a Chinese intel guy with them. And Tahir."

Reilly cut his gaze to the olive green Hilux parked several hundred meters downhill. It rested on the side of a dirt road with its hood raised to present the appearance that one, it was inoperable to any aspiring thieves, and two, that the rightful owner would be returning any minute with a mechanic.

"If Tahir's there," he said, "then I guess offsetting from the truck was a waste of time."

"True, but it was a good precaution. Alternative if we were wrong was enjoying the view from a Pakistani prison by now."

Reilly supposed he should have been grateful they'd been spared the not-insignificant walk to the village of Abazai, where there was a possibility of vehicle procurement one way or the other.

Keller eagerly went on, "The Agency's crunched all the routes and possibilities for a western border crossing. Chen wants to push the split teams to Timergara and Swat, best spots for us to interdict if their assessments pan out and the locations are at least somewhat mutually reinforcing."

The problem with intelligence operatives in times like these, Reilly knew from working with Ian, was that they had a tendency to get intellectually excited about each twist in a mission. Nothing grated worse on the nerves of everyone else on their teams.

"Show me," he said.

Keller produced his phone, scooting closer so they could both see it.

"Current location is here, and we're going..." He panned across the screen slowly, allowing Reilly to take in the imagery. "Right here, to Timergara. One hundred and fifteen klicks, three hours. Split Team Three will be here, in Swat."

Reilly saw that the terrain became increasingly more mountainous to the north, split here and there by dried-out river beds.

"And Split Team Three?"

Keller repeated the process for Cancer's element, narrating as he swiped, "They've got a shorter route, ending up somewhere outside Swat. That puts them 80 kilometers from us, just under two hours by road."

Reilly shook his head. "Odds aren't great that either element makes it all that way without running into trouble."

"The odds," Keller replied, "are a whole lot better than they were five minutes ago. Hass is pushing air assets to Munoz, who's making direct comms with the platforms now. Chinese birds are running route reconnaissance for us."

Reilly eased into a kneeling position on the rocky ground, looking left from beneath the shallow cavern he'd been sleeping in.

Griffin and Munoz were seated behind two satellite antennas, the latter man with his long-whip FM antennas extended, scribbling furiously into a notepad with one hand as he held his hand mic with the other.

With a snicker of disbelief, Reilly said, "I've seen a whole lot of things in Project Longwing that I never thought I would. But having the Chinese supporting one of our ops has got to be at the top of the list."

Keller eagerly nodded his agreement. "Crazy, right? But at this point I'll take all the help we can get."

"Yeah, I get that," Reilly said. "But to sum this all up—and let me know if I'm getting anything wrong here—we've got three split teams, two of which are going deeper into the Wild West on the off chance that the bad guys head that way. Assuming, of course, that the warhead is still in

Pakistan at all. And if it's not, we've got an inordinately high chance of getting wiped out by some Pashtun militia over nothing."

"No," Keller replied, his voice resolute.

"No?"

"I'll lay it out for you. It's true that the majority of people where we're headed are Pashtun. But there's also tribes like the Syeds and Qizilbash that aren't. So the politically correct way of putting it would be that there's an inordinately high chance of us getting wiped out by some *frontier* militia over nothing. Frontier," he clarified, "not necessarily Pashtun."

Reilly's eyes narrowed.

"But about the rest—"

"Pretty spot-on," Keller said with admiration. "You're a quick study, Doc. Should have specialized in intel. Shall we get going now?"

"Yeah. Fuck it."

Keller gave him a cheerful slap on the shoulder.

"That's the spirit. Don't want to keep the Chinese waiting."

26

"We're moving," Cancer transmitted. _"Come on down and I'll brief you on the way."_

Worthy quickly replied, "Stand by."

"You got something?"

"Maybe," the pointman said, resuming his focus through the spotter scope.

The winter air bit through Worthy's gear, a sharp reminder of the season despite the clear blue sky and warm sun. His breath formed small clouds that quickly dissipated, the only movement in his otherwise still form as he remained in the prone amid the rock formations atop the hill where he'd spent the better part of the past hour on duty.

Black Corolla, gray Nissan Frontier, he thought to himself, peering through the scope to see if the pattern would repeat.

Munoz was the only fully outfitted sniper among the ranks of both teams, and since he wasn't about to hand over his tricked-out HK417, the tripod-mounted spotter scope was the only consolation prize that Split Team Two had received as a concession to long-range visibility.

But mounted on a tripod and set at 40x magnification, the optic was sufficient for Worthy to monitor the northbound traffic on a slip of Harichand Road visible at 2.03 kilometers through a dip in the hills separating it from his current position. The location had been selected with great care—the target road paralleled the N45 and M16 highways north of Peshawar, making it a viable path for anyone seeking transit to the mountainous, unregulated badlands between Pakistan and Afghanistan, all of them laced with more smuggling routes than any Western intelligence agency could possibly know about, much less monitor.

There remained the obvious problem that, barring any updates from Chen, neither of the forward-deployed split teams had any idea what they were looking for. Since she had yet to provide any meaningful guidance on specific vehicles, all that remained was to be vigilant for aberrations in the local traffic. An exercise in futility, Worthy knew, unless such an aberration happened to appear and be recognized as such.

And while the curving segment of road through his scope remained empty, he maintained hope that he was in the midst of discovering the clue that could tilt the warhead's odds of making it out of Pakistan firmly in the team's favor.

It was the vehicle spacing that first caught his eye.

Northbound traffic on Harichand Road had been exceedingly sparse, consisting largely of motorbikes and compact cars whose roadworthiness was questionable at a glance. So when a late-model Corolla glided past moments earlier, Worthy took casual note—but it was the appearance of a Nissan pickup following at a roughly 100-meter interval that made him question whether he was witnessing the beginning of a loose convoy. When trying to blend in with civilian traffic on remote paths, there was a fine balance between spreading vehicles out and remaining close enough for mutual support in the event of enemy contact.

And when another vehicle slipped across his field of view, Worthy's suspicion further swelled.

He transmitted, "Black Corolla, gray Nissan Frontier, dark blue Hilux, all northbound on Harichand. I think it's a convoy."

There was no immediate response, nor should there have been—Cancer was scrawling down the information, although Worthy found the inability to gauge his immediate superior's reaction disconcerting in the extreme.

But then came the next vehicle.

Through the 40x magnification of his scope, the jingle truck's garish colors and elaborate decorations stood out in stark contrast against the muted landscape. Its flamboyant reds, blues, and yellows would scream for attention anywhere else in the world but were utterly commonplace in the Pakistan-Afghan border region—so commonplace, in fact, that the only surprising element of the truck's appearance was that there weren't more of them. Its ornate patterns and jingling ornaments swayed gently, their movement almost hypnotic.

"Jingle truck," Worthy transmitted. "Similar spacing. This is it."

"You think a jingle truck is suspicious?" Cancer asked.

"I've been on shift for over an hour. This is the first one I've seen, it's moving at a clear interval behind the last three vehicles, and all of them are paralleling the highway northbound on a local road toward a spiderweb of routes leading toward the border—hold on."

Worthy took in the sight through his scope, then transmitted again.

"New vic, black Toyota Prado. That makes five, and that would be one hell of a coincidence if I'm not right. We need to get on this, fast—they're going to keep switching vehicles, and if that convoy splits up, we're going to be left throwing darts."

He looked up momentarily from his scope, blinking his eyes to obtain a fleeting reprieve from the otherwise nonstop focus.

The rugged beauty of the rolling hills was softened by the golden light of the December sun. Worthy was surrounded by rugged terrain and sparse vegetation dotted with evergreen shrubs and the occasional cluster of leafless trees, their bare branches reaching skyward like skeletal fingers, and with a final blink he resumed his view behind the spotter scope.

When the road remained empty save a heavily loaded motorbike threading its way southward, Worthy knew on a gut level that the procession had passed.

He continued, "I don't know which vehicle the nuke is in—hell, it's probably not the jingle truck because they can get a lot more mileage out of that one by stuffing twenty security guys in the back. But I'm telling you, it's with that convoy."

The weight of his words hung in the air, leaving a vacuum of suspense that would only be filled with a reply from the one man who could have made a definitive assessment in the first place. Cancer's intuition in combat was beyond reproach, but Worthy's was not. It wasn't that he'd predicted things that turned out to be wrong, but rather that he'd never predicted anything at all. Whereas Cancer was the closest thing the team had to a Magic 8 Ball, Worthy's strengths resided in being a pointman and reflexive shooter par excellence.

Cancer's voice was muted, any opinion indiscernible.

"*You sure?*"

Worthy hesitated, feeling anything but.

"I am sure," he responded.

"*Stand by.*"

The ensuing pause left Worthy all the time in the world to second-guess himself.

It wasn't that his observations were flawed, or that his suspicions were unwarranted. But America's humble boots-on-the-ground force to interdict this nuclear device consisted of ten men divided among three teams, a beyond-threadbare effort bolstered only by Chinese aerial support of dubious capabilities and intent. Any resources that were summoned to pursue a false lead could easily result in missing a real one elsewhere.

Finally Cancer transmitted back.

"*You better hope you're right,*" he began. "*I just had Bulldog throw a Chinese UAV on those vehicles, and that's going to cost us a lot of coverage elsewhere. But until someone has a definitive intel hit for us, our split team is loading up and following it north.*"

27

Chen swiped her keycard and pushed open the door to the OPCEN.

"We're approved," she announced, heading for her workstation as the door swung shut behind her. "Each of the three platforms will conduct a 90-second diversion for the sweep. Sensors will then return to the N5 and Torkham on their way out of sector."

She checked her watch. "Approximately eight minutes to time on target."

Lucios, seated beside her workstation with a tablet, replied, "Yes, ma'am, the seventh floor sent word. We're set up to receive the results."

Chen took her seat.

"Was the director there?" Lucios asked.

"His deputy," she replied, unlocking her computer. "How's the uplink?"

"Intermittent," he said, pointing to a screen. "We've had four outages since you left. The longest was 52 seconds."

She glanced at the screen depicting fluctuating signal strength, the bars jumping between mid-range and low. The unstable uplink from Hass's patched relay between the Chinese drone and CIA Headquarters was going to be a problem.

"The joys of under-the-table intelligence sharing." She grabbed her hand mic. "If we have another outage—"

"With the satellites this close, and depending on duration, it could be a showstopper."

"Wonderful."

Keying her mic, she said, "Suicide Actual, Raptor Nine One."

Her eyes shifted to another screen displaying timestamped data strings from the satellite array that showed the results of the scan. The timestamps were minutes old, reflecting the variable delay between the data capture, transmission to ground stations, data processing, and relay back to the OPCEN. Another screen showed a live feed from a Chinese drone, its camera focused on the four-vehicle convoy moving lazily northbound on a dirt road. The largest screen in the room displayed a map tracking the convoy's route toward Timergara and the border with Afghanistan.

David's voice crackled over the speaker. "*This is Suicide Actual, send it.*"

"Be advised, we have a high probability of confirming or denying whether the device is present in the target convoy within the next ten minutes, give or take, depending on uplink stability."

"*Good copy. If it's a no-go, I'll relocate both split teams to the primary staging areas. Tahir's sources are active around Peshawar, but we've got no fidelity from them or the ISI yet. Did your boss approve a kinetic operation if we get confirmation?*"

They would approve anything at this point, she thought.

"If we pinpoint the warhead, I have launch authority. Your teams have a blank check for any air support the Chinese are willing to provide. Stand by for updates."

"*Standing by.*"

Setting her mic down, she turned to Lucios. "Who's on the login to monitor the satellite data?"

"Outside the building, we've got the joint task force at the NTC, NSA, DIA, Joint Chiefs, White House Situation Room, and a bunch of compartmentalized programs I don't recognize. How receptive was the deputy director at your meeting?"

She shook her head. "The deputy didn't speak until his staff finished tearing me apart. I had to use every bit of leverage to get a two-minute scan on our convoy. Despite having the only teams on the ground, the seventh floor is focused on repeated sweeps of docks, airports, and border crossings, hoping the device turns up there."

Lucios didn't seem surprised. "The satellite packages are designed for fixed locations, not moving targets. Scanning moving traffic isn't efficient with current tech. The road network in Pakistan is—"

"Two-thirds the distance between Earth and the moon."

Lucios blinked. "I didn't know that."

"Neither did I, until it was pointed out in no uncertain terms. When I argued we have a drone providing geolocation fixes on the convoy ten times per second, they said that level of fidelity is barely enough to align the satellite's lenses on a moving target."

Lucios nodded knowingly. "Müller knows what he's doing. Keeping the device moving makes it nearly invisible. But he's had to conduct vehicle switches to counter surveillance, and that could have slowed him down enough to be in the area we're scanning. The convoy is still a possibility."

"Let's hope so."

Jamieson's booming voice filled the room.

"Time hack, ninety seconds to time on target."

Chen pressed on. "I've just fought hard to get this one chance. Tell me what I'm getting for that."

In truth, she didn't want to know. The twelve hours since the nuke theft had been an information overload, especially regarding the satellites now involved. Intelligence satellites worked in constellations—groups providing global coverage—that orbited the earth every ninety minutes or so. Despite this rapid revisit time, almost none were equipped to detect a single unlaunched nuclear warhead.

Lucios answered her question as simply as he could. "We've got three satellites in position, but only one, the SAR-NRD platform, has a real chance of detecting the device. The other two are likely to miss it due to shielding."

"What makes you think that?" Chen asked.

Lucios checked his tablet. "The first satellite uses Advanced Hyperspectral Imaging, which can detect exposed nuclear material. The second uses Quantum Magnetometer equipment, which picks up magnetic anomalies.

Both can be blocked by sufficient shielding, and I'm sure Müller has prepared for that."

"But not the third?"

"Correct," Lucios said. "It's SAR-NRD—Synthetic Aperture Radar with Nuclear Resonance Detection. It scans for the gamma radiation profile emitted by nuclear materials, and those gamma rays are highly penetrating. Müller probably encased the device in lead or a specialized alloy sufficient enough to defeat all known satellite capabilities, but SAR-NRD is highly classified. His shielding will reduce the intensity of gamma radiation but not eliminate it. If that warhead is present in the convoy, the satellite will detect it."

Jamieson interrupted, "Thirty seconds to time on target."

Lucios continued, "The SAR-NRD is our best bet. If Müller's shielding is anything less than perfect, we'll know soon."

"Hack," Jamieson announced. "The AHI satellite's pass has started its scan. QM is twelve seconds behind, SAR-NRD twenty."

"We're down," Lucios said.

Chen saw the status bar on the connectivity screen turn red, with the signal flatlining. Without an uplink, their satellites may as well have not been there at all.

"Time hacks for the SAR-NRD only," she said sharply.

"Time on target for SAR-NRD begins now," Jamieson called out. "Ninety seconds until it's out of range."

Chen's mind raced. Could they reconnect in time? "How long will the SAR need for a scan?" she asked Lucios.

"It depends on how quickly we can restore the link," he said.

"We only have this one shot," she muttered. "Do we already have background radiation levels?"

"Yes," Lucios confirmed. "Normal levels have ranged from 0.07 to 0.18 microsieverts per hour. Any reading above that will indicate the presence of a nuclear device, even if shielded."

"Thirty seconds remaining," Jamieson announced.

Chen stared at the screen, praying for the connection to come back. The red bar suddenly flashed to yellow, and the signal strength climbed.

"We're live," Jamieson said. "Eight seconds…five…two, one—SAR-NRD is out of range."

Chen exhaled shakily. After all her efforts, they were back to square one —no confirmation meant no authority to launch a ground raid. All they had was the intuition of a shooter who'd seen the convoy from two kilometers away.

"Listen up," she commanded. "The satellite data will take time to process. Meanwhile, let's focus on our other efforts. Soren?"

Christopher Soren responded quickly, though he sounded shaken.

"I requested targeted surveillance from the convoy's current and historical route the moment our ground team identified it. I expect to have a response any minute now—the Director of National Intelligence has lifted restrictions of any kind within Pakistan's borders, which means any ground-based, wireless, or satellite transmissions are being monitored through algorithms to flag communications with possible coded references. Anything that gets flagged is automatically triangulated to locate the associated mobile numbers and radio frequencies."

"Ma'am," Lucios cut him off, pointing to the satellite data screen.

Chen looked up, surprised that results had come so quickly. Lucios read the coded data aloud. "The AHI had a negative result, the QM missed due to the outage, but the SAR-NRD got a brief scan—gamma rays increased by 0.8 millisieverts per hour, consistent with a shielded nuclear device."

Chen felt an unexpected calm. They had confirmation, albeit limited. She grabbed her mic. "Which vehicle?"

Lucios shook his head. "It only had time for an initial scan within a 400-meter radius of the jingle truck. Could be any of them."

Better than nothing, Chen thought. She pressed the transmit button. "Suicide Actual, Raptor Nine One."

"*Go ahead*," David replied.

"The nuclear warhead is in the convoy. We're not sure which vehicle, but we have confirmation. Deploy both split teams immediately and avoid direct contact unless necessary. Advise the Chinese to reposition their aircraft accordingly, and tell Tahir to notify Zarrar Company for raid and recovery."

"*Copy all. Tahir can provide drone feeds to your OPCEN, and we'll maintain comms with him. I'm moving out to back up the other teams.*"

She responded, "Your other split teams have a two-hour head start on you, and if this thing isn't finished by the time you link up, then we've got bigger problems."

"*We've got bigger problems already,*" David assured her. "*Seven Americans in pursuit instead of ten. I may be late, but I'm not leaving them out there alone.*"

Chen had a momentary crisis of confidence. She could forbid David Rivers to leave the command center, and judged objectively against the tactical scenario, that was probably the right call.

But two other factors made her hesitate. The first was exactly what he'd said: his men were out there alone, and American backup arriving late was better than no backup at all.

And the second was that Rivers would go no matter what she said.

"Copy. Ensure all updates are seamless. Report back when you can."

"*Understood. We're out of here.*"

Chen had just set down her hand mic when the next twist of fate occurred.

"Ma'am," Sorenson nearly shouted, "I've just received the report from NSA."

28

I tossed my mic down and took one breathless second to process the situation.

Here I was, alongside two of my men, one Chinese intelligence specialist or whatever the hell Zhang actually was, and an ISI officer who'd reported my team as rogue operators the night before.

We were surrounded by relics of US involvement in Pakistan, which was about to gain one more illustrious chapter for better or for worse.

"The nuke is with the convoy," I announced. "Zhang, redirect all your aerial surveillance to follow it—we don't know which vehicle it's on, and if they split up, you'll have to cover everything. Likelihood of a transfer is high. I'm sending my other split team to reinforce the first in pursuit; they don't have the manpower to do the takedown but might be able to stall or isolate if we need them to. Tahir, your government is receiving official notification as we speak, but you need to get Zarrar Company airborne and en route right away."

Ian and Hass were out of their seats before I'd finished speaking, both hustling to the rear wall to recover our kit on the way out to the car.

Zhang leaned back in his chair, shooting me a skeptical glance.

"How can your Agency be sure?"

I threw up my hands. "You think they told me? I have no idea, but it's a definite confirmation. If you can't trust that, there's not much point in us running intel together."

"Very well," he conceded.

You're goddamn right very well, I thought. Turning my focus to Tahir, I found him analyzing me as if trying to see whether I was joking.

"Have you gone deaf, mute, or both?" I asked. "Can Zarrar handle this, or not?"

Tahir grunted. "They are more than capable."

"You're worried someone in the ISI will leak word to the bad guys."

He didn't answer immediately, his eyes ticking to the space over my right shoulder for one long moment of consideration.

"At this point," he said, "what choice do we have?"

I was thinking the same thing, and recovered the hand mic tied to my team's satellite frequency.

"Any station this net, Suicide Actual, emergency transmission."

"*Suicide, this is Bulldog.*" I could hear the wind whipping over the sound of Munoz's voice—the poor bastard was still in the back of the Hilux, keeping the open sky over his satellite and long whip antennas so he could maintain comms.

"Be advised, the warhead is with the convoy. Move to reinforce Split Team Three and don't stop until you're on their tail. Give me two mikes to hit them up on cellular and then call them with your ETA. I'm breaking down and moving north; it'll take us a couple hours to reach you, though."

"*Copy all, will comply.*"

Transitioning to my cell phone, I placed a call and was greeted by Cancer's voice after the first ring.

"You have good news for me?"

"The best kind. You're following a live nuclear warhead. Don't know which vehicle it's aboard, but it's definitely with the convoy. Continue pursuit at a distance and stay out of visual range per drone guidance, plan on interdiction courtesy of Zarrar Company with Chinese air support. Split Team Two is moving to reinforce, and my guys are leaving now from Badaber."

"Anything else?"

Classic Cancer understatement.

"One more thing. Tell Racegun he's never paying for a drink again—his instincts are the only reason we have a lead to follow."

"Yeah, yeah, got it."

I ended the call and rose from my seat, issuing final words to Zhang and Tahir.

"We're out of here. I'll leave the comms up and running so you have a direct line to my headquarters, callsign Raptor Nine One. Coordinate with them from here on out. If anything comes up, you've got my cell."

Zhang leaned back in his seat. "You will be too late to affect the situation."

"Maybe," I said. "Maybe not. But if my guys are going to be in the shit, it's not going to be with me sitting on my hands. Just get all your air support in play over the nuke. Airstrike is a last resort, but if the Paks drop the ball, I highly recommend that you blow that convoy to hell and back—better a limited radioactive event than that nuke getting away."

I was about to join Ian and Hass in kitting up when I heard the faint crackle of Chen's voice from the hand mic.

Lifting it without transmitting, I listened to her fervent pleading.

"Do not leave the command site, I say again, do not leave. How copy?"

I considered whether to leave her hanging and play it off like we'd already departed.

But there was an urgency in her voice that made me come up short. Someone above her could certainly overrule her decision to let myself, Ian, and Hass reinforce our men, however belatedly—but if that was going to happen, it wouldn't be in the fleeting seconds since I'd last transmitted.

I keyed the mic and asked, "What is it?"

She sounded relieved beyond belief to hear my voice, which was a first in our working relationship.

"Be advised, the NSA has just responded to our request for information. Müller is co-located with the convoy, and they've traced his communications with an outside party in the Qissa Khwani area of Peshawar."

"I don't see how that matters now."

"It matters because Müller has been receiving orders, not giving them."

"Say again."

"Müller isn't running this operation. It's someone else. That someone is

communicating less than thirty minutes due north from your current location. You can move to reinforce your split teams and arrive too late to make a difference, or you can potentially take out the individual responsible for stealing a nuclear weapon. What do you choose?"

A lump formed in my throat. This late-breaking development was almost too good to believe—if she was right, however, there was no question as to what I should do.

"The latter," I blurted.

"You've already told Tahir that you'll be heading north, toward the warhead?"

"Correct."

"Then don't change that story. Take yourself, Angel, and Rain Man north to the Qissa Khwani Bazaar and come back up on comms. By the time you get there, I should have a pinpoint location and, if we're lucky, authorization for you to conduct a capture or kill operation. If the enemy forces present are too great for you to handle on your own, you can maintain surveillance until a backup force arrives."

My gaze flitted over Tahir and Zhang, both pretending not to eavesdrop as they typed over encrypted chats to their respective commands.

Then I looked behind me, where Ian and Hass were standing with their rucksacks shouldered, weapons in hand, watching me as if to discern some reason for the seemingly meaningless delay.

"Copy all," I said to Chen. "Will comply."

29

Cancer listened intently to his phone, struggling to hear Reilly's wind-muted voice over the ringing in his ears, the rumble of tires across the uneven ground below, and, most concerning of all, the ever-fading cellular reception.

The view from the Subaru's passenger seat had been growing ever more ominous, the mid-afternoon sun blocked by patches of clouds that cast their shadows over the rugged landscape, highlighting the jagged peaks of the low mountains that loomed on either side. Patches of forest clung to the slopes, their dense foliage a dark contrast against the rocky outcrops. Occasional breaks in the trees revealed expansive vistas of the frontier region, a patchwork of scrubland and sparse vegetation stretching toward the hazy outline of the Afghan border.

"Got it," Cancer said into his phone, looking over from the passenger seat to relay the news to the other two men in the vehicle.

Both of them wore their plate carriers, having donned them when the nuke's confirmation within the convoy took their pursuit from casual surveillance to absolute necessity. Washington was at the wheel, the medic guiding the Subaru along the potholed and rocky dirt road. Worthy had been seated in the back since the end of his last driving shift, supervising their navigation with every update from Split Team Two.

"Reilly says the convoy is stopping at a village about a kilometer ahead. The road is about to swing east; we'll have to stop before it turns back north or we'll run into them."

No sooner had he finished speaking than a sharp right-hand curve arrived. Washington piloted the Subaru through it, and a wavering three-hundred-meter stretch opened up before the next curve.

"There it is," Washington said. "But if we stop, it's going to notify any peripheral security they've got set up to identify pursuit."

Cancer grimaced. "Don't I know it. But unless you want to ram this station wagon up their ass, we don't have a choice—"

"There," Worthy said, "trail uphill, left-hand side."

"Take it," Cancer ordered impulsively, barely even seeing the path before Washington careened the Subaru onto it.

The twin dirt tracks were wider than a car's, having been established by repeat traffic of what must have been much larger trucks. Now, however, the path was overgrown with weeds and shrubs that indicated the Subaru wagon was the first vehicle to traverse this stretch in some time.

A moment later, Cancer figured out why. The trail weaved uphill amidst ever more open terrain, the surrounding trees severed at the stumps from some long-ago clearance.

He spoke into the phone to update Reilly.

"We diverted west onto a trail a couple hundred meters south of the last curve before the village. It's not on the map, looks like an old logging road." Then, to Worthy, he said, "Tell me this reconnects with the main route."

"No idea," Worthy admitted from the backseat. "It's not even on the imagery. But based on the elevation, we're headed due west of the village. If the convoy's still stopped, we might be able to dismount and get eyes-on."

Washington offered, "I thought we had the drone for that."

"Sure," Cancer shot back, "right up until there's a vehicle swap beneath overhead cover, because I guarantee you that's exactly what's going to happen. The Chinese don't have enough eyes in the sky yet to follow more than a couple vehicles if the next convoy splits up, and not enough fighter jets to blow up every car even if they had the surveillance to track them. Müller's not stupid, and someone in the ISI probably tipped him off already. He'll have a plan for that, we just don't know what it is."

He returned the phone to his ear and said, "I need an updated ETA for your split team, Zarrar Company, and Chinese aircraft in that order."

Cancer lowered the phone from his ear, then checked the screen before accessing his map imagery.

Washington asked, "What'd he say?"

"Nothing. I just lost signal, so we do this on the fly."

The driver sounded incredulous. "'On the fly?'"

Worthy groaned. "Our team's motto is 'Fast and Loose.' Welcome to our world."

"Layout," Cancer began, panning his screen to narrate the findings for Washington's benefit as the path continued uphill. "Mid-size village in the low ground to the east side of the road, slopes uphill to tiered fields. Main road heads northwest; there's one subsidiary route to the northeast and another to the east. Looks like a 360 of smaller roads that are big enough for a single vehicle heading out to the surrounding mountains, and probably a few more that aren't on the map."

He looked at the rolling terrain, pleased that the logging trail had been cut in a direction that roughly paralleled the village. "Bottom line, they can get the warhead out of here in any direction they want—we need to see whatever the drone can't and identify which car the nuke is transferred to. Stop it if possible, and if not, get word to the others so they can direct the interdiction. And in the meantime, don't get caught—"

Washington's sudden braking brought Cancer up short, and he saw that however ancient the previous logging effort, it had come to a stop twenty meters ahead. The road ended in a circular washout of dirt and low tree stumps, just wide enough for trucks to turn around.

"Fuck it," Cancer said. "We're due west of the village, more or less. I'll move straight east and get eyes-on. Washington, you go southeast and do the same. Worthy, I want you at the northwest corner overlooking the main road outlet because that's their most likely egress."

Washington brought the vehicle to a full stop at the edge of a stand of pines, and the dismount was near-simultaneous—each man grabbed his rifle and took off at a run, leaving their rucks and the vehicle behind as a distant afterthought to the urgency of the task ahead.

Cancer sprinted downhill, each step calculated, his boots finding purchase on the forested slope. The scent of pine and earth mingled with the unpleasant tang of his own sweat amid his jarring steps, the plate carrier hugging his torso a comforting and familiar weight. He carried his AK-47 loosely in one hand, relying on hasty visual scans to alert him to the presence of any enemy security in the woods around him—this was a rare case where moving alone, much less at a rapid clip, was more than justified by the tactical situation. Pine needles brushed against his face as he threaded his way between the trees, hearing the forest echo the sounds of his movement and hoping to God that he was the only one who could.

He wondered if he'd arrive in time to see anything at all, because if he were Müller, there would be no refueling required. Given the available finances, he'd simply have clusters of cars spread out along his route and stop just long enough to transfer the device beneath overhead cover before proceeding in new vehicles and, better still, sending out decoy convoys like the one his team had smashed on the way to Peshawar.

After what felt like an eternity of hasty maneuvering that was in reality only minutes, the trees began to thin and Cancer found himself at the edge of the forest. He paused for a moment, his breath steadying as he crouched low behind a tree trunk. From this vantage point, he had his first clear view of the low ground ahead.

Terraced fields climbed the hillsides around the village, their green crops contrasting starkly with the tan stone buildings. Here and there, rocky outcrops jutted out, providing natural lookout points. Cancer's trained eyes quickly identified several potential sniper positions among them, some of which were amid the remnants of ancient fortifications—old stone walls and a watchtower that still stood sentinel over the village. His gaze shifted to the mountain paths leading out of the village, each of which would support movement for the warhead transport vehicle or any number of decoys.

The main area of the village was nestled in a natural basin surrounded by steep, rocky slopes, including the one descending from his current position. Stone buildings, many crumbling with age, clustered together along narrow, winding roads that twisted through the settlement like a labyrinth.

But the most distinctive visual feature of all was the central market area, currently obscured by a patchwork of large canvas tarps that had almost certainly been erected in the minutes prior to the convoy's arrival.

Beneath the tarps were a hodgepodge of vehicles too numerous to distinguish from one another besides a few outliers, namely the jingle truck. Cancer procured his compact field binoculars and oriented them to analyze the finer points of what was now occurring while hidden from overhead view.

A group of six men were struggling to transfer a coffin-like box through the open rear door of a white SUV that Cancer identified at once as a Mitsubishi Pajero, a common enough sight throughout Pakistan and the surrounding region.

This should have been easy, he thought—maintain his surveillance, direct Worthy or Washington to establish satellite communications, and relay the target vehicle along with its direction of departure to the CIA and, therefore, everyone in a position to stop it. A ground interdiction would ensue if Zarrar Company could handle that kind of thing, or in the worst-case scenario, a precision airstrike by a Shenyang J-16 or Chengdu J-20 would take the nuclear warhead out of play with little more than a minor radioactive dispersal far from civilian population centers. Game, set, match.

But of course, nothing could be that simple.

Cancer almost laughed at the sheer genius of the operation in progress. Except for the vehicles from the original convoy, he hadn't anticipated the rest and couldn't have come up with a more brilliant plan if his life depended on it.

He transmitted, "Net call, I've got eyes-on the village. And," he added, taking a final breath before translating the sight into tactical vernacular for his teammates, "we're fucked."

Worthy cursed under his breath.

His heart was pounding from the desperate sprint to his current position, which ended with immeasurable relief when he spotted the main road outlet ahead and took up a carefully selected position to watch it from the westward slope. After searching for any signs of movement from the village and finding none, civilian or otherwise, he'd been about to transmit that he was in position—and then Cancer had beaten him to the punch.

The sniper had just said they were "fucked" rather than "compromised," though there were a number of reasons that the former could be true without involving the latter. They were, after all, three men reacting to what was probably an asininely large enemy force with a live nuclear weapon, and doing so without the benefit of outside communications, backup, air support, or a proper counterterrorism force arriving anytime soon.

But none of those factors were new, and none required surveillance on the village to be painfully aware of.

And when Cancer's explanation came a moment later, it made perfect sense.

"I'm looking under a patchwork of tarps blocking the drone feed. The convoy is under it along with a bunch of other vehicles. Warhead is in a metal coffin, and they're putting it into a white Mitsubishi Pajero. Problem is they've got a dozen or so Pajeros just like it—my bet is they're going to move out in groups of two or three and then subdivide onto every route possible. The Chinese don't have enough birds to track more than a few, and by the time they do, the nuke will have been transferred into something different. Christ, there he is—I'm looking at Müller now."

Worthy scanned his surroundings, this time with a greater level of detail than he'd used in his hasty search for cover.

The most promising feature among the underbrush and debris of the forest was a downed tree to his left—it had fallen more or less parallel to the road, and had been down for some time. Its bark was weathered and cracked, encapsulating a roughly one-foot diameter and stretching a good fifteen feet in length. The branches had long since broken off, leaving the trunk bare and solid, attached to the ground only by a few partial roots.

It would have to do.

Cancer continued, *"I'm going to call the target vehicle's direction of departure. Whichever one of you two geniuses is farther from that moves uphill until you can set up SATCOM to relay all this, savvy?"*

"Copy," Worthy replied, now focused on the scattered rubble of new and old mudslides down the hill. No shortage of large rocks to be found—

his only limiting factor was which among them were appropriately sized and shaped for movement.

Washington transmitted, *"Copy."*

The next few seconds were occupied by a frantic visual search of the surrounding terrain that turned up nothing useful beyond what Worthy had already found. He faintly wondered which role fate would assign to him in the coming moments, and already felt reasonably confident it wouldn't involve setting up communications.

Cancer spoke with sudden urgency.

"Target vic is heading northwest along the main route, second in order of movement between two decoys. Patriot, you're on radio duty. Racegun, you got us into this mess, now stop these fuckers—I'm moving to you."

Worthy was on the move before the transmission ended, pushing his AK-47 back on its sling and forgoing any attempt to reply in the interests of managing the task now at hand.

He raced to the far end of the tree trunk, squatting to heave it upright and wrenching it perpendicular to the road. The remnants of dried root structure served as a pivot point, twisting and cracking as he rotated the linear obstacle into position.

Then he scrambled back across, darting up a slope of dried mud and pine needles toward his chosen rocks.

He remembered finding his father's dog-eared copy of *First Blood* at age ten, a prize that Worthy had squirreled away in his room and spent many long nights reading under a blanket by flashlight. It was his first introduction to Rambo and, in hindsight, probably at least somewhat responsible for planting the unconscious seeds of his current profession.

But even on first read, the description of a character using a stick as a lever to dislodge a huge boulder struck him as ludicrous. Worthy had by then spent years following his father, a hunting guide, through the forests and swamps of Moultrie, Georgia. His boy's mind found nothing fantastical about a former Green Beret evading dozens of men or downing a helicopter with a well-thrown rock, but the fictional physics of boulder movement seemed to have been conceived by someone who'd never actually spent any time in the woods.

And while the fact that these memories came to him now was absurd to say the least, nothing in his life since that point had changed his assessment on how he should approach the current problem set.

He abandoned otherwise tempting massive rocks in favor of those he could dislodge by hand—there was only time to add two or three into his impromptu roadblock. He selected those that would severely test his physical abilities to set them into motion but ultimately be tippable and round enough to let gravity do the rest.

The first required a Herculean deadlift to tilt, but only for a moment—it passed the point of no return and rumbled downhill, clattering to a stop behind the tree trunk as a weighted reinforcement while he moved to the next.

A second deadlift followed, this one only slightly less taxing than the first, before a second rock plunged toward the road. He'd hoped to have time for a third before making out the growl of vehicle engines approaching from the southeast and abandoning the effort altogether.

Worthy scrambled through the trees to find a covered position at the bend in the road where the first enemy driver would spot his obstacles. He hadn't made the route completely impassable, and certainly couldn't have on the fraction of a timeline he had available.

But slowing the vehicles should be sufficient for what he had in mind.

He knelt behind a large pine trunk, opening two grenade pouches on his plate carrier for quick access. After adjusting the AK-47 on his back so its cumbersome mass wouldn't interfere with his throwing ability, he opened the final pouch and removed Tahir's grenade, palming it in one hand and slipping the opposite index finger through the pull ring.

What happened next would depend entirely on how the enemy drivers reacted to identifying the obstacles in their path. There was no hope they'd assume it to be a minor inconvenience from Mother Nature—the second they spotted the tree trunk, any combatants worth their salt would know themselves to be in an ambush kill zone of one flavor or another. Their options then boiled down to ramming their way through, reversing back toward the village, or, least favorably for him, unleashing dismounted fighters to clear both sides of the road on foot.

And when he caught his first glimpses of a white Mitsubishi SUV through the trees below, Worthy knew he was seconds from finding out which course of action his opponents would take.

The sight of the first car brought with it a gripping intensity that nonetheless paled in comparison to that of the second, this one containing the stolen warhead. Both glided toward him straight down the center of the road, bumpers perhaps five meters apart, and were followed by a decoy car in trail. The three vehicles were indistinguishable from one another, he realized, each having the same roof racks and even wheels—it was a masterstroke of attention to detail from Adrian Müller, a man who clearly knew that the only way to defeat the super-sophisticated optics of surveillance aircraft was to overwhelm them with possible candidates for tracking.

He watched the lead vehicle approach the corner and come to an abrupt halt at the sight of the blocked path ahead. The second Mitsubishi braked then, three-quarters of the car framed so perfectly between a pair of trees that Worthy couldn't have planned this any better if he'd had hours to map out his position.

He yanked the pin from the grenade in his hand and hurled the projectile at his target.

Logically speaking, he knew that a frag wouldn't penetrate the metal box inside the car, much less detonate the warhead contained within. Still, there was something immensely sobering about throwing a live hand grenade toward a vehicle containing a live nuclear device, and the speed with which he pulled himself behind the tree went far beyond a rational fear of being spotted.

He readied a second grenade while peering out from behind the tree to assess the effects of the first—his main goal was to immobilize the middle SUV, fixing the warhead in place and allowing himself maximum time to make the enemy pay for any attempt to transfer it. If he could prevent them from doing so until Cancer arrived, the two of them just might have a shot of fending off further enemy reinforcements until Washington established satellite comms to permit an airstrike.

Pulling the pin on the second grenade, Worthy repeated the throw to hedge his bets, distantly wondering why the first hadn't yet detonated. Was the first Pakistani frag defective, did it merely have a longer fuse, or was his perception of time warped to the breaking point due to the stakes at hand?

Worthy had no definitive answer, although the coming moments assured him that Tahir most certainly hadn't provided a dud.

The target vehicle reversed out of position and was seamlessly replaced by the point car when his initial grenade detonated with a sharp blast that briefly lifted the front axle skyward, both front tires bucking off the ground in an explosion of sand and smoke.

He'd gotten his mobility kill all right, but against the wrong Mitsubishi.

Worthy took off like a shot, trying to gain a vantage point on the target vehicle and assessing almost immediately that he didn't have a snowball's chance in hell of catching up. At best he'd have a few seconds before it reversed out of sight, with nowhere near enough time and far too much space to put his final grenade into play.

He took aim with his AK-47 instead, tracking the flitting white ghost through the trees and firing a trio of shots at the hood, not to disable the engine—he wouldn't be that lucky—but rather to mark it as distinct from the dozen or so others currently on the move.

The final round cleared his barrel as the second grenade he'd thrown barked to life behind him, its blast drowning out the echo of the last and adding to it the warbling notes of warping metal and shattering glass. He felt a wave of heat and smoke wash over his backside as the target vehicle vanished altogether, and just as an upswell of rage at his failure rose within him, Worthy transmitted.

"Two SUVs reversing back into the village on the main route, lead one has the nuke and three bullet holes in the hood. Cancer, it's all on you now, I'm moving to support."

30

Ian exited the car alongside Hass and David, and together the three men stepped into the vibrant chaos of Qissa Khwani Bazaar.

The market was a sensory overload, the sidewalks brimming with local men in shalwar kameez dress navigating the sidewalks lined with parked cars and motorcycles on one side and on the other, tightly packed market stalls overflowing with colorful fabrics, fresh produce, and intricate handicrafts. Power lines ran over a street that was equally filled with civilians who parted only to allow the passage of the occasional vehicle before converging once more, the entire scene a humming throng of activity.

He'd barely stepped onto the sidewalk before a young child brushed against him, a pickpocket whose darting reach landed on the cool metal slide of Ian's holstered Glock.

That was enough to dissuade the boy, who darted away with a quick, apologetic glance.

"Seventy-five meters to the target building," David said. "I guess we're staying close."

No shit, Ian thought as they began to move. The sheer density of people made it difficult to maintain any meaningful line of sight, and he took a rearward glance to see Hass following behind them. He alone had a long gun, his HK416 buttstock collapsed and slung tightly to his side beneath a long shawl. His Libyan descent allowed him to blend in somewhat while David and Ian had no choice but to affect the appearance of expats in Western dress. And since there was no concealing the size of an AK-47, they were armed only with concealed pistols, extra magazines stuffed in their pockets.

The air was thick with the mingling scents of spices, grilled meat, and incense. Vendors shouted out prices and descriptions of their goods, creating a tumult of voices that blended into a constant white noise as the three men weaved through clusters of shoppers and vendors as they made their way toward the source of communications with Adrian Müller.

Their target building was innocuous enough. It was a tea house, a common enough sight across Peshawar, whose second floor was apparently occupied by the man they sought.

Chen had delivered her end of the bargain—in addition to the pinpoint location for the unnamed mastermind, she'd obtained authorization for a kill or capture mission. That latter detail was only as good as the three men's ability to execute it without being gunned down in the process, and the undoubtable presence of a bodyguard force rendered capture out of the question. At best they'd have a fleeting opportunity to shoot their principal target before beating a hasty retreat, and given how tenuous the intelligence was to get them here in the first place, they were lucky to have that.

There was an additional motivation driving them to succeed, because if the true mastermind of this nuclear theft escaped, he'd do it again. If not stealing a nuclear warhead, then some other heinous terrorist act of equal or, if at all possible, even greater audacity.

"Fifty meters," David said.

Ian scanned his surroundings with each step as he threaded his way in pursuit of David, considering how ingenious of a hiding place this was to manage communications for the overall terrorist operation. Buildings behind the market stalls rose two and three stories high, interspersed with narrow alleys that twisted and turned to form a labyrinthine network that may as well have been designed to confuse and disorient any potential visitors. Airstrikes were not an option, and apparently neither was a ground raid against the mastermind.

At best they'd be able to enter the teahouse as paying customers, then scout the stairwell and perhaps blunder up it under the pretense of being lost tourists.

That ruse would end the moment they encountered the first inevitable guard, after which their options boiled down to an apologetic retreat to wait for Pakistani Commandos who may or may not come, or an engagement and forward charge into whatever lay beyond. Given that David was in charge, Ian could guess which of the two would transpire.

And regardless of the number of enemy fighters present, they had to try.

David suddenly pulled his cell phone from his pocket, answering a call as they moved.

The suspense was palpable as Ian waited to hear the outcome of the conversation. Few things could be more unnerving than having the Project Longwing teams divided into three elements in order to cover two objectives. Communicating with one another over cell phones was the least secure method short of smoke signals, and yet they had no choice. Each split team was far outside FM range of the others, and none of the three exactly had the time to set up a satellite antenna.

"Got it," David said. "We've almost reached our target, will update when able."

Putting the phone away, he spoke as quietly as the crowd allowed.

"That was Reilly. The convoy stopped in a village, and Split Team Three went off comms after reaching it. Split Team Two isn't there yet."

Then, before Ian could process the information, David added, "Twenty meters ahead."

They continued to move between civilians, the market stalls to their left filled with every conceivable distraction.

Brightly dyed textiles in reds, blues, and yellows hung from canopies and fluttered gently in the breeze. Vendors displayed intricate handwoven carpets and embroidered shawls, while other stalls emitted the sizzle of frying foods as cooks dropped samosas and pakoras into hot oil, their aromas wafting through the air. The clink of metal utensils against large cooking pots punctuated the sounds of haggling as shopkeepers and customers bartered over prices, their voices rising and falling in a rhythmic dance.

Ian noticed a stall where a man had meticulously arranged an array of colorful spices in neat, conical piles. Beside this was a calligrapher sitting cross-legged on the ground, deftly applying ink to parchment to create ornate scripts that mesmerized passersby. There was a table loaded with pyramids of fresh pomegranates, oranges, and mangoes, and a group of musicians playing traditional instruments provided a soothing counterpoint to the energy of the bazaar as children darted through the crowd.

David looked over his shoulder and said, "Ten meters."

After a few more steps, David continued, "That's it, just ahead. Who's ready for tea?"

The son of a bitch was enjoying this, Ian knew, and in that moment he was hard-pressed to imagine David as a suburban father. In combat situations he was a reckless diehard who craved uncertainty, an aspect that the current mission had in spades.

Then the call to prayer began, a muezzin's voice rising above the market's din, creating a momentary pause in the activity as the band behind them abruptly stopped playing. Shopkeepers and patrons alike turned toward the nearest mosque, some beginning their prayers right where they stood. This brief lull gave Ian a moment to assess his surroundings in greater detail, but it also left the two Caucasian team members highlighted on the street even more than they already were. The market was ambivalent to this detail, remaining both a perfect hiding place for a terrorist and a potential trap for his hopeful assassins.

And amidst this backdrop, their target appeared.

Or perhaps "appeared" was too optimistic a word, Ian thought as a stream of men exited the teahouse in unison, forming a tight cluster around the central individual. While his body was largely obscured by those around him, he was notably taller. Ian caught a glimpse of his sharp and angular face; a thin beard traced his jawline, and his vigilant eyes scanned his surroundings. He had a black pakol hat worn slightly askew.

The eight men who surrounded him were clearly bodyguards, and included a mix of ethnicities. Each of them wore a backpack—radios, spare mags, and digital equipment belonging to the man they protected—as well as satchels slung over their shoulders that undoubtedly contained submachine guns.

They moved toward the street, where pedestrians were splitting in the path of a pair of SUVs in the oncoming lane.

In a flash, Ian put together the pieces. Cancer, Worthy, and Washington had just been compromised at what was almost certainly an exchange point for the nuclear warhead. At this, the mastermind knew beyond question that his carefully laid plan had a leak, and now he was trying to exit the area before he too was located.

"Take them on the sidewalk," David said.

Ian took no pride in what they were about to attempt.

He'd looked up atmospherics on the Qissa Khwani Bazaar during their drive over, and found that the site had endured more than its fair share of violence starting with British Indian Army troops slaughtering unarmed anti-colonial protestors in 1930. The event had triggered widespread protests and the furthering of both Indian and Pakistani independence movements, and more recently the marketplace had witnessed a suicide bombing that killed 25 people and, more recently still, an Islamic State attack that killed 63. The latter two events alone resulted in well over two hundred civilians wounded.

The people in this area would be devastated by further violence. But there would be untold death and an incalculable number of innocents wounded and forever traumatized if the mastermind escaped, and Ian reacted to David's order without hesitation.

The three men's reactions were smooth, unscripted, each knowing exactly what had to happen—Ian and David came abreast of one another and parted, allowing Hass to fill the gap and take the lead. Then the two men slid into a file behind him, effectively concealing themselves behind the teammate who could somewhat pass as a local and, therefore, allow them to get as close as possible before initiating contact. Hass picked up the pace, setting the trio on a perpendicular collision course with the enemy contingent now making their way to the street.

There were, however, several obvious downsides to this arrangement.

Hass would take longer to bring his HK416 to bear than either of his comrades with pistols, both of whom would need to come on-line and fire first. And since two white men amidst the Pakistani crowd would stand out like a pair of lighthouses to trained bodyguards, they had better act fast and do so against a backdrop that couldn't possibly have more innocent civilians.

But the strange twist of fate in which they found themselves was too good to pass up. The mastermind was about to cease communications with Müller until he'd reached a safe area, and that meant the CIA would lose him for the foreseeable future if not permanently.

Ian drew his pistol with one hand and a spare magazine with the other, keeping both low to his side while David did the same.

Then Hass passed between the final civilians as the bodyguards swept across his front, and the final sands of time and space between them and a hasty, unplanned attack fell through the bottleneck to the bottom of the hourglass.

Hass dropped low, pulling his shawl aside to make for his rifle. He was now entirely reliant on Ian and David, who took a step right and left, respectively, and fell to their knees.

The nearest bodyguards saw the flash of movement at once and pivoted toward the emerging threat. Ian's knees banged against the sidewalk, his spare magazine between them with the exposed bullet facing forward. He leaned back with his pistol aimed at the rightmost bodyguard, knowing the only way to avoid collateral damage in such a densely packed space was to orient himself in such a way that the target, and therefore the path of bullets, was angled overhead.

Amid the eerie wailing of the call to prayer emitting from loudspeakers atop minarets, Ian and David fired in unison, their opening shots joined a split second later by the whiffs of Hass's rifle suppressor.

31

Cancer's heart pounded as he received Worthy's urgent transmission.

"Two SUVs reversing back into the village on the main route, lead one has the nuke and three bullet holes in the hood. Cancer, it's all on you now, I'm moving to support."

Well wasn't this jolly good fun, he thought. A few minutes earlier he'd reported the nuke-toting vehicle to Worthy along with orders to stop it, and now the pointman was punting the order right back at him.

Cancer brought his run to an erratic halt, altering course ninety degrees to make a break for the road instead. He'd been racing to reinforce Worthy but that plan had apparently gone to hell somewhere in the course of two grenade blasts and a few scattered gunshots, all of which still echoed through the trees.

"Patriot," he transmitted to Washington, "forget about comms—if we don't survive the next few minutes, it's not going to matter. Parallel the west side of the village until you find me; we're about to have the fight of our lives."

"Moving," Washington replied.

Securing his grip on the AK-47, Cancer edged into a half-walking, half-sliding movement down the steep hillside. He could see the village ahead, which would have made this an ideal time for stealth save the upcoming span of seconds in which he would either kill the driver of his target vehicle or watch the warhead slip through his fingers yet again.

He scanned the forest's waning edges for the largest tree he could find near the road. With every step increasing the gradient of hill to his rear, retreat would be a painful if not impossible proposition, and he'd damn well better find something capable of absorbing the torrents of incoming gunfire that would surely follow.

A towering pine provided the only feasible option of a solid shield with a clear view of the approaching vehicles, and his final sliding descent ended with a hand braced against the bark. By then he could hear the revving engines of the two SUVs approaching to his left, and knelt while trying to steady his breath to controlled, measured intervals with limited success.

The first vehicle, a decoy, reversed past his position so fast that he barely registered it, its engine growling as it maneuvered back along the narrow road. Cancer pivoted around the tree, taking aim to intercept the second SUV as it passed his position.

Fully automatic bursts were something of a decadent luxury for a sniper, and something he craved on a soul level whenever possible. But the wild inaccuracy of such gunplay made the extravagance one he could ill-afford even at this relatively short distance. He only needed one perfect shot to do the trick, but between the moving target and the auto glass separating him from the driver, that translated into at least ten attempts—just over two seconds of firing as fast as he could pull the trigger, which was about the entire span of time he'd have the driver in sight through the trees anyway.

The target SUV whipped through the space before him, and Cancer opened fire the moment its driver's-side window crossed his point of aim.

His rapid single shots punched through the glass, and he glided the AK's thundering barrel sideways as the window shattered entirely on the sixth round to reveal the driver's head ducked low. The subsequent bullets drilled into the vehicle's A-pillar and windshield before it glided out of sight with little more than a few erratic jerks of the steering wheel.

Judging by the consistently fading sound of the engine, the driver had come through the attempt alive and well.

And before Cancer could so much as reload, gunfire erupted from the village.

He instinctively ducked behind the tree, expecting to hear the thunk of incoming rounds against the wood. And while a few bullets were indeed absorbed by the tree representing his only lifeline to continued existence, he was more concerned with the slightly more distant misses.

Or, to put a finer point on it, the *quantity* of misses.

Bullets cracked, hissed, and popped on either side of his position, as well as above and below. Dirt and pine needles sprayed upward, bits of twigs and dry leaves rained down, and the forest around him turned into a swirling vortex of supersonic flight trajectories coming to an abrupt halt on the hillside.

He looked at the steep slope behind him, a fraction of a second's glance more than enough to assure him that backward movement was off the table. So too were any lateral bounds to speak of—his current tree represented the best and only meaningful cover to his flanks.

That left moving forward, into the village, as his only remaining option. It was an unlikely one to be sure, but he hadn't survived more gunfights than he could count by ruling out possibilities.

Crouching as low as he could, Cancer peered out from behind the trunk.

The village sprawled in a haphazard layout of tightly packed stone buildings and narrow alleys that created a network of paths he wouldn't survive long enough to reach. White Pajeros streamed across the streets, while others remained parked—and, once these initial milliseconds of visual recognition had elapsed, he made out the dismounted fighters.

Most had taken up positions behind makeshift cover, but the bulk of movement seemed to be to his left. Armed men moved swiftly through the narrow alleyways, consolidating on the north side of the village and streaming toward the road for one unquestionable purpose.

Cancer pulled himself behind the tree as a bullet clipped a chunk of bark off the side, whiffing a spray of debris in his face.

"Target car made it past," he transmitted, "with its driver window shot out and some of the windshield. Bad guys are about to cross the road and flank south to drive me toward the market with all their tarps and bullshit.

Don't approach the village. I'm pinned; you two are on your own. Happy hunting."

Some distant instinct raised the consideration of whether to reload before exposing himself again, and Cancer suppressed the urge. The only question now was whether his body would be found with any rounds remaining in his magazines, and he was determined for that not to be the case. He couldn't advance, retreat, or even relocate, which left him with the one military tactic that not even the most ominous of enemy forces could take away.

Die in place.

And what the hell did it matter, Cancer thought. He'd already nearly been killed on almost every continent—Australia had yet to produce any meaningful terrorist groups to speak of—and usually for a lot less. If there was ever a blaze of glory worth burning in, then the attempt to stop a nuclear device was it.

He eased out on the opposite side of the tree trunk, visually sweeping for stationary targets providing a base of fire for the enemy maneuver element.

Not one but two caught his eye, both militants crouched behind a low mud wall across the road, their rifles trained on the forest edge where Cancer was hidden. The exchange of fire was mutual, both sides of the fight plainly seeing the muzzle flashes of the other, and responding with weapons that were no more or less accurate.

But while the fighters couldn't assess the impact points of their rounds amidst dozens of others against the wall of wood, greenery, and dirt on the hillside behind him, Cancer could make out each puff of dirt on the mud wall from his AK fire and adjust his point of aim accordingly. His first round impacted the base of the barrier, the second was halfway up, and the third and fourth chipped the top edge, with one or both ricocheting into a man who bowled over backward.

At that point Cancer should have sealed his victory by taking cover, but he stayed dialed in on the remaining fighter instead, tuning out the snap of incoming bullets breaking the sound barrier as he walked his rounds further sideways before scoring a single probable hit.

Then and only then did he duck behind the tree, now painfully aware from the impact of bullets against the ever more decimated bark that anyone on the enemy firing line who hadn't spotted his muzzle flashes before had now. So be it, he thought, because at this point he had nothing to lose by fucking their world up as long as his central nervous system remained in operation.

He had five to ten rounds remaining—reload? Not yet, and he eased out from the right side of the tree to find the most easily identifiable target, a man kneeling on the flat roof of a low stone building, fully silhouetted as he changed magazines. An amateur and one who paid the price for his inexperience with a direct hit from the half dozen that Cancer fired before his rifle went empty and he tucked behind the tree for his first reload, glancing left as he did so to assess the progress of the enemy's maneuver force.

The first men were spilling across the road, easy targets save for the fact that Cancer was still in the process of driving a fresh magazine into his weapon. But two of them tumbled forward to the ground nonetheless, an unexpected development that caused the remainder to take cover and return fire on the opposite hillside.

"*Almost to you,*" Worthy transmitted. "*I'll cover your withdrawal, give me a sec.*"

"Stay on the high ground, don't come downhill," Cancer replied, regretting the words as soon as they left his mouth.

"*You don't say. Just sit tight.*"

"Armchair quarterback," Cancer muttered, chambering the first round of his new mag and considering how best to pass the time. His only avenue of retreat would occur up the face of Mount Everest to his six o'clock, and if he was going to scale that beast, his greatest threat wasn't from the maneuver element further north but the stationary shooters directly across the road, waiting for him to pop out again.

So be it.

He rose to vary his firing position once more. He'd only gain a half-second advantage over someone who'd sighted in on his abundant kneeling muzzle flashes—fuck you very much, government of Pakistan, for sending him into the country without a proper suppressed weapon.

Angling to the left, he opened fire on a man with his rifle braced against a pickup hood, delivering three shots before spotting a burst of flame from the weapon of his previously unseen partner behind the tailgate. Cancer returned fire with another four rounds before ending the engagement, unsure if he'd wounded or killed either or both. For all he'd been able to see, every one of his shots probably missed.

Worthy transmitted, *"Patriot, where are you at?"*

No response, which meant Washington already bought the farm on his way to the fight.

By then, Cancer was kneeling once more to take aim off the right side of the trunk, firing at two man-sized shadows in opposite corners of an open doorway. This time he was relatively certain he scored at least one hit before return fire forced him back, and then Worthy's voice came over the net once more.

"All right, brother, I'm between you and the maneuver force. They're about to come back across. Get your ass up that hill, now—come straight back, keep climbing until I tell you to stop. You're out of time."

Cancer cursed under his breath, rotating his AK to his back on the sling. With Worthy's order ringing in his ears, he turned his attention to the steep hillside behind him and launched himself upward, using every ounce of strength and adrenaline surging through his veins.

The slope was unforgiving, a near-vertical climb of loose soil, jagged rocks, and tangled roots that were far more difficult to negotiate in this direction of movement than they had been on his way downhill. Cancer's boots scrabbled for purchase, each step a desperate struggle to gain traction. He lunged for the nearest tree trunk, gripping it with both hands and pulling himself up with a grunt of effort. The rough bark bit into the palms of his shooting gloves but he barely noticed the pain, his focus entirely on ascending the treacherous incline.

Gunfire cracked through the air, the bullets zipping past him with a deadly hiss. Some rounds struck the trees, sending splinters flying, while others thudded into the ground around him. The enemy fighters were relentless, their fire concentrated on his position as he climbed—he could hear Worthy shooting back at them overhead, though there was no telling if the pointman was engaging accurately or merely providing general covering fire.

Cancer moved with a frenzied urgency, his muscles burning as he hoisted himself higher. The forest around him was a blur of green and brown, his breath came in ragged gasps, the exertion and fear blending into a heady cocktail of adrenaline as he reached for another tree, this one a gnarled oak with roots that twisted and snaked across the hillside. Using the roots as handholds, he hauled himself upward, climbing on all fours when necessary. The slope seemed endless, every inch gained a minor victory in the face of the relentless assault from below.

The sound of gunfire grew more distant, the enemy's line of sight increasingly obscured by the foliage. But Cancer knew better than to slow down. He kept pushing, his body protesting with every movement. His fingers dug into the soil, scraping against rocks as he clawed his way up the hill with sweat pouring down his face, stinging his eyes and blurring his vision. He blinked it away, focusing on the next handhold, the next tree, the next step upward.

A bullet whizzed past to his left and cracked into a rock, sending a flash of red sparks. He pressed on, heart pounding, lungs burning, until he finally reached a small plateau, a brief respite in the unending climb. He collapsed against a tree, chest heaving as he tried to catch his breath. The forest provided a momentary shield from the gunfire, the thick trunks and underbrush creating a natural barrier that he only had a moment to enjoy before he heard crashing footsteps to his right.

Worthy grabbed the handle of his plate carrier and hoisted him upward.

"Come on, we've got to go!"

Cancer struggled to get his legs under him, and the pointman let go to appraise him for injuries with intense scrutiny that only lasted a moment.

"Follow me," Worthy said, and took off along the slope.

Worthy plunged through the forest, unable to shake his face-to-face with Cancer a few seconds earlier.

He didn't think he'd ever seen the man truly shaken before, and was in a state of abject shock to find the sniper rattled to his core—Cancer was pale, wide-eyed, seemingly uncomprehending of where he was or why. It was far from his first brush with death, though perhaps the effect of such encounters was cumulative rather than momentary.

"Patriot," he transmitted, "this is Racegun, transmitting in the blind. I've got Cancer, we're pushing south. Maneuver element is behind us. If you can hear this, go south and try to raise us on comms—"

"*Yo,*" Washington answered.

"What—did you just say 'yo?' Where the hell are you?"

"*Coming to get you two assholes. Make your way down to the road for pickup.*"

"For pickup in *what*?"

"*What do you think?*" Washington asked. "*I'm in a white Mitsubishi Pajero —I could blend in for days down here.*"

Worthy supposed that it was no dumber an idea than trying to make their way back to the abandoned Subaru wagon.

"Moving to the road now."

They navigated the treacherous slope, Worthy in the lead with quick glances back to ensure his partner was keeping up. The forest around them was dense, the underbrush thick with tangled roots and low-hanging branches that clawed at their gear. Sporadic gunfire continued a few hundred meters behind them as the enemy's maneuver force engaged likely and suspected hiding places for the two Americans now moving toward the road, and Worthy knew that the risk of a roadside linkup in broad daylight was miniscule in comparison to any other course of action—so long as they got it over with as soon as humanly possible.

He scanned the terrain for a suitable pickup point where Washington could stop briefly without drawing too much attention, somewhere that offered enough cover but was accessible for a quick escape. The urgency of their situation pressed on him like a weight, every second without a solution beginning to feel exponentially longer than the last.

Finally he spotted a small clearing just off the road ahead. It was partially shielded by a cluster of trees, with enough space for the SUV to pull in and out quickly, and was, as best as he could tell, free from any dedicated overwatch in the village beyond. He gestured to Cancer, who nodded, his focus sharpening as they approached the designated spot.

Worthy transmitted, "Patriot, we've found a clearing just south of—"

That was as far as he got into the transmission when a white Mitsubishi Pajero glided past, slammed on the brakes, and then reversed off the road and into the space before them with expert precision before coming to a stop with the engine running.

"This one?" Washington asked over the radio.

They sprinted to the car, and Worthy moved to the passenger door in a not-so-subtle assumption of the leadership role until Cancer had recovered his wits. The sniper didn't object, and Worthy yanked the door open to dive inside—he halted then, momentarily taken aback by the spray of blood and gore fanning from the driver's headrest, to the center console, to the throne he was about to occupy.

"Don't get any dirt on my seats," Washington said from behind the wheel.

Doing his best to suppress his revulsion, Worthy mounted the passenger seat and winced as his weight settled on the canvas and a warm, sticky ooze permeated the fabric of his shirt and pants.

By then Cancer was in the backseat, and both men slammed their doors as Washington hit the gas.

The SUV's tires kicked up dirt and gravel as Washington whipped a U-turn and sped away from the clearing, but instead of continuing south out of the village, he steered left, taking them deeper into the village and all the enemy forces it contained.

Worthy adjusted the AK-47 between his legs. "Where are you going?"

"Looking for the target car," Washington nonchalantly replied, wind whistling through a trio of bullet holes in the driver's window. "Saw it making this turn on my way to get you, unless you guys shot up more than one."

"Not me."

"Nope," Cancer said, his first spoken word since making it back up the hill.

"Okay then," Washington concluded. "So check it out—Müller doesn't know if the village is surrounded or covered by air support. I think he's keeping the nuke here while his decoys screen the routes, and once he's confident there's a straight shot that doesn't involve an ambush or a 500-

pound bomb falling out of the sky, he's going to push the target car out of here for good. We've just got to find it before then."

"Sure," Worthy conceded.

"A little navigation would help."

"Sure," Worthy repeated, finding his phone and accessing the satellite imagery. The village sprawled out on the screen, a maze of stone buildings, narrow alleys, and winding roads that made any attempt to anticipate the pattern of their target vehicle an exercise in futility. All they could do, Worthy decided, was traverse the key routes in succession and hope that Müller didn't have some makeshift garage in which to stash the car until the coast was clear.

"Head straight for another fifty meters, then take a right," Worthy instructed, his eyes flicking between the map and the road ahead.

"Got it," Washington replied, adjusting his grip on the wheel.

They navigated deeper into the village, veering between densely packed stone buildings whose crumbling facades loomed over the streets. The narrow roads were a confusing network of sharp turns and dead ends, each one a potential trap.

White Mitsubishi SUVs darted across the streets, their drivers executing abrupt turns and evasive maneuvers. Worthy and Cancer strained their eyes, checking for the telltale bullet holes in the hood and windows. It was a perfect decoy tactic, and Worthy felt a surge of frustration as they passed yet another identical vehicle.

"Next left," he directed, leaning forward to get a better view of the road.

Washington complied, the SUV's tires skidding slightly on sand and loose gravel as they made the turn. Ahead, a group of armed men ran across the street, their rifles at the ready. They didn't seem to notice the passing vehicle, too focused on their own objectives.

"This place is a goddamn maze," Cancer muttered from the backseat, scanning the alleys and doorways for any signs of the target car.

Worthy couldn't disagree. The satellite imagery provided an overhead view, but the real-world application was far more complex. The narrow alleys and sudden turns made it difficult if not impossible to predict the best route in real time.

"Another left up ahead," Worthy said, his voice tight with concentration.

They rounded the corner, and the central market area came into view, its large canvas tarps flapping over the streets. The market was deserted, save for the vehicles of the original convoy and a few armed men who seemed to be using the stalls as makeshift barricades. Worthy felt suddenly grateful that they'd inadvertently pulled a majority of the enemy fighters into the woods before conducting their search.

"Any sign of it?" Washington asked, his eyes darting between the road and the mirrors.

"Not yet," Worthy replied, frustration creeping into his voice. "Keep going straight."

The Mitsubishi weaved through the narrow streets, the scenery blurring past in a dizzying array of stone and mud brick. All around them, claustrophobic alleys twisted and turned with no apparent pattern.

"There!" Cancer's voice was sharp, cutting through the tension. He pointed ahead to where a white Pajero was just visible cutting across an intersecting road.

"Is that it?" Washington asked.

"Hundred percent," the sniper replied.

Worthy squinted, trying to spot the distinguishing marks and being unable to find how Cancer could have possibly done so. But the vehicle turned a corner before they could confirm.

Washington swerved, the car's suspension straining as they took the turn. They caught up quickly, and this time, Worthy could see bullet holes in the windshield.

"That's it," Worthy said, tension and relief mixing in his voice.

"Told you," Cancer replied. "Back off, and don't get too aggressive—for now, we just need to know which route they're taking."

They dropped back to a more discreet interval, tailing the vehicle until it disappeared at an L-intersection ahead. The stone buildings seemed to close in around them, the street they traversed narrowing to barely more than a single car's width as Washington made the turn in their next move on a chessboard of life and death.

Worthy scrutinized the next visible block of the village, his keen eyes taking in every detail. The stone buildings rose to either side like ancient giants, their walls weathered by time and strife. Not a soul was in sight, and he couldn't help but wonder if the village had been abandoned by its civilian residents or if they were merely hiding indoors, watching the unfolding mayhem from the safety of their homes.

"It's heading south," Worthy said. "I don't like this. Why would they be going back the way they came?"

Washington replied, "Could be part of their rotation, or—"

"Or," Cancer finished the thought, his voice low with the weight of experience, "they're leading us into an ambush. Break off pursuit at the next intersection."

Worthy was initially unsure of whether to agree or disagree. The target car glided ahead, neither accelerating nor slowing, and in the absence of any tangible threats, the looming danger of a loose nuclear device roaming the countryside seemed ample reason to continue assuming their current risk level.

But Cancer's instincts were always spot-on.

When the Mitsubishi ahead braked and turned right at the next four-way intersection, Worthy finally said, "Go left up here, we'll re-engage once the cavalry arrives."

Washington didn't reply, though his silence made it apparent that he contested the majority decision. Up until this point, it was clear enough that the medic was having the time of his life guiding their car on a hunt for a warhead with absolutely zero fucks given whether any or all of them died in the process.

Finally he said, "Yeah, all right," with palpable disappointment.

Worthy released a breath, feeling the tension abate in his shoulders for a fleeting second before the world shifted on its axis and time slowed to a nearly imperceptible crawl.

A jingle truck lurched into view at the intersection ahead, turning away to expose its open tailgate and, in the cargo area, two men in the prone with belt-fed machineguns atop bipods. Behind them were two ranks of fighters, one kneeling and the next standing, all wielding automatic weapons.

The truck was from the original convoy, he recognized at a glance, and so were the men inside. He heard his own voice from a few hours before playing back in his mind.

I don't know which vehicle the nuke is in—hell, it's probably not the jingle truck because they can get a lot more mileage out of that one by stuffing twenty security guys in the back...

Worthy's eyes ticked to his sideview mirror framing their only escape route, a narrow street leading to a one-way intersection they'd never survive long enough to reach.

Suddenly it all made sense.

The movements of the armed men in the village weren't random, as Worthy had initially suspected—they were moving to establish an ambush, a noose through which the target vehicle could lead them if its driver detected pursuit.

Worthy's heart hammered as he assessed the situation, the walls of the narrow alleyways pressing in on them in a suffocating and unyielding funnel toward death.

They were ensnared in an unsurvivable ambush with no way out, and Cancer's voice cut through the tense silence just before all hell broke loose.

"Well, shit."

32

I pulled the trigger from my knees, arms angled upward at the standing man before me, my Glock 19 barking in succession with Ian's.

The leftmost bodyguard I fired upwards at received the round head-on—he'd pivoted to face us, withdrawing a weapon from his satchel—and as an entry wound blossomed in his chest, I transitioned my aim to the right.

Our unsuppressed gunfire in the packed bazaar may as well have been a bomb blast, inciting total pandemonium in a split second as civilians fled in an outward circle amid a chorus of otherworldly screams. My teammates and the men we attacked had become the fistfight in the center of a swirling mosh pit, every noncombatant around us spreading to expand the engagement area.

The next bodyguard to find my aim had drawn an FN P90 submachine gun from his satchel and wielded it in my direction. I fired once, the round impacting above and to the right of his sternum on an upward trajectory before I drove my pistol further right to find my next target had already been downed by Hass.

Given the situation, it made sense to engage the group of men in the fashion named "family style"—I had no idea where the term had originated, or when—which meant firing a single round at each target in our sector, sweeping fully across before repeating the process in the opposite direction to achieve definitive kills.

But the milliseconds following our first shots revealed that we'd never have the chance to complete our ploy.

Four bodyguards were falling to the ground either dead or wounded and probably the latter. Two of those remaining had already seized hold of the man they protected and were hauling him at a sprint into an alley adjacent to the tea shop, which left another two for us to deal with—make that one, I thought.

A single member of the surviving security force was fleeing toward the street, his body moving with panicked adrenaline, feet frantically pounding against the sidewalk as he looked for an escape. Coward, I thought. It was a shameful display of fear that I would have loved to reward with a few rounds into his backside.

That possibility, however, was removed by the actions of the lone bodyguard who had stood his ground and opened fire with his submachine gun.

The P90 was used by elite protection units the world over to include the US Secret Service. Its bullpup structure afforded a surprisingly long barrel for its compact size, increasing the accuracy of the contents of its top-mounted, horizontally oriented magazine, which were, namely, fifty 5.7×28mm NATO rounds.

Those rounds were currently being fired at the rate of roughly 15 per second, impacting just to our front in a chattering fully automatic burst as the shooter walked his aim upward to slay his assailants the instant his weapon cleared the satchel at his side.

If he'd been using armor-piercing bullets, the ricochets alone would have killed us. The hardness and density of such projectiles meant they'd have a flatter trajectory, higher velocity, and would very likely remain intact after skipping off the concrete on which we knelt.

But jacketed lead cores tended to deform and fragment after contact with a hard surface, and the spray of white-hot metal fragments lacing into my thighs and stomach—please God, not the balls—were a testament to these basic realities of ballistic physics as Hass, Ian, and I engaged the man simultaneously, silencing his burst in a hail of gunfire.

I glanced at the retreating bodyguards, the last of whom were already nearly past the corner of the alley. Any misplaced shots from this angle would send bullets into the fleeing crowd, and I let them go with little more than a silent mental curse.

Still, the fact that we'd survived this long was a miracle.

Bodyguard protocol dictated that the closest members to an attack identify and engage the threat while those farthest haul their principal like a rag doll to a safe location. Successfully getting the jump on the formation meant that we'd downed all the men responsible for returning fire.

Gravity did most of the work for assuming a double kneeling shooting position, but rising from it was a bitch.

I snatched the magazine from between my legs, pushing off with both knees and executing a swift tactical reload as I conducted a momentary sweep for threats before glancing right at Hass and Ian. The fabric covering their fronts was peppered with tiny holes from which dots of blood were beginning to soak through—but both men had risen without falling down again, and I accepted the balance of probability that their many wounds were no more severe than the metal fragments now sizzling after shallow penetration of my own skin. I took off for the alley at a sprint.

The engagement had come and gone in perhaps five seconds, which was a world of time in Bodyguard Land where reaction time was measured in far lesser increments.

I lamented leaving the dead and wounded bodyguards behind, representing as they did the holders of five P90 submachine guns that would exponentially improve our firepower if we snatched them. And there was no telling what their backpacks contained, although I suspected there was an abundance of digital media and communications equipment that the CIA would have a field day dissecting.

If we so much as attempted the distraction, however, we'd find ourselves well-armed and likely with an abundance of intelligence but at a loss to find the terrorist mastermind being spirited to parts unknown, possibly with an ambush set in his wake.

It was that possibility that hung heavy in my mind as I slowed before the corner of the alley, hearing the call to prayer continue over the loudspeakers. The haunting, beautiful, and melodic chant prevented me from hearing anything in the narrow channel ahead just as much as the fading screams from the crowd.

I stopped at the corner and knelt to cover it, seeing as I did so that we were about to enter a shadowy channel littered with crates and trash, but seemingly no way out—and yet the retreating men were gone, a disparity that was explained when I spotted a single open door leading to the adjacent building.

Charging into the alley with little more than blind trust that my teammates were both behind me and could keep pace, I approached the door at a run before slowing a few steps out and kneeling to aim into the space beyond.

A P90 burst passed over my head and slammed into the wall beside me, answered by a pitiful trio of 9mm rounds that I directed at the blazing muzzle flash that extinguished almost immediately. It would be a Christmas miracle of immense proportions if any of my rounds had actually struck the shooter, and the fleeing shadow of a man disappearing through the doorway behind him assured me that had not been the case.

Worse still, the space between us was some type of convenience store, and one that had its aisle shelves thrown down to block my path.

I entered and threaded my way around the obstacles, each step a time delay that my target hadn't dealt with in his straight-line path through the store. Stunned Pakistani bystanders held up their hands as they crouched behind whatever cover they could find, which ended up being not much.

My footsteps were periodically met with the crunch of exploding bags of chips or whatever the fuck was sold here, and I approached the next doorway with a peculiar type of resolve. Any future gunfire could wound or kill me, but I decided then and there that it wouldn't slow me down. Whoever this asshole was who needed protecting, he'd sent my men to hell and back and he was going to pay dearly for that as long as I had a say in the matter.

I moved through the door to find myself in a stairwell, which was a nightmare development—I had to clear upward before mounting the steps three at a time, a process that ignited clusters of pain from the shrapnel wounds in my thighs and abdomen.

But as long as my nuts were intact I could deal with the rest, and although I hadn't physically verified that, I took it on faith that my continued movement was proof positive that they were indisputably still there.

As I advanced upward, I asked myself why the men who'd disappeared overhead didn't simply fight in place and await reinforcements.

The obvious answer was that they assumed there were a hell of a lot more men in pursuit. To them, they were on the receiving end of an elaborate and well-resourced CIA or MI6 interdiction effort, which was somewhat comical given the threadbare shoestring from which my Project Longwing team typically dangled while on a mission.

But there was a far more important question that needed answering—namely, where were they going?

The answer to that was obvious as well, although I lacked specifics at present. They had an alternate exfil plan that would end with a pickup at some unknown location, provided they could outpace their pursuers. It was up to us to prevent that from happening, although we were at a massive disadvantage due to having no idea of the paths they could take amidst the spiderweb of potential routes that they had no doubt carefully screened in advance.

Upon reaching the top of the stairs, I cleared the doorway to find that I was on a flat roof. The building in which I stood was linked to the next by virtue of a single wooden plank, possibly placed in advance by the same bodyguard who was dismantling their work before my eyes.

I shot twice at the man kneeling on the opposite roof as he thrust the board sideways, sending my only bridge sailing into the alley below. Both my rounds impacted the brick railing of the roof before the man was gone, chased by several more misses on my part as he darted behind a storage shed and out of view amidst a mass of poorly erected shacks, satellite dishes, and water tanks packed onto the rooftop.

After reloading I moved toward the edge, searching for any way to proceed as Hass and Ian spilled onto the roof behind me.

A two-meter gap separated my building from the next, and I looked left to find a similar board linking the structures further down—the bodyguards must have previously set up an alternate pathway, and one that remained intact albeit too far from my last enemy sighting to be a sure thing. At best I could hedge my bets by dividing my small force, and an instantaneous risk assessment came up empty on whether or not doing so would be a good idea.

"Ian," I said, pointing to the far plank, "cross that bridge and try to cut them off."

The intelligence operative took off at a run as I continued, "Hass, you're with me."

A moment of calm descended upon me, unsolicited. I was suddenly aware of the expansive sky above, a deep blue canvas streaked with the early hues of twilight. The remaining screams from below were spreading in an ever-widening periphery as marketgoers continued reacting to gunshots in a ripple effect that spanned outward, their cries underscoring the final note of the call to prayer hanging in the air. It was a poignant echo that seemed to hold the situation in a fleeting stillness amid cool air that was heavy with tension, every sound amplified as if the world were holding its breath in anticipation of the next moment.

I holstered my pistol and took two steps back before violently reversing and making a short, charging sprint toward the edge that ended with a soaring leap over the alley.

Reilly crouched low in the pickup bed, watching through the Hilux's rear window as they approached the village.

He could make out tan buildings with flat roofs clustered together. Ancient fortifications loomed amidst the dwellings, their high stone walls imposing against the horizon. Terraced fields climbed up the hillside east of the village, the vibrant green of the crops standing out against the forested landscape.

"*Any Split Team Three element,*" Griffin transmitted from the passenger seat, not for the first time, "*this is Talon.*"

As before, there was no response—they should have been coming into FM radio range any second now, and each unanswered transmission was more disconcerting than the last.

Keller slowed the Hilux from the full-throttle run he'd maintained ever since trying to catch up to their missing teammates, allowing the men to scan their surroundings for danger.

Or at least, three out of the four men.

Munoz was seated against the back of the cab beside Reilly, making no attempt to pull security, however discreet. Instead he continued transmitting to air assets in indecipherable JTAC jargon, flipping through the pages of handwritten script transcribed when Hass relayed the various communications protocols.

Reilly called out to him over the wind, "Thirty seconds out."

Munoz shot him a thumbs up without looking, the only indication that he'd heard the time hack at all.

Their latest update from the surveillance drone feed had been remarkably brief.

Munoz reported that the nuke convoy had vanished under a swath of tarps, after which three SUVs had attempted to transit the main road extending northeast. One was immobilized by methods unknown, and the other two retreated. There had also been a flurry of dismounted movement from the village into the forested hillside to the west, where Split Team Three had diverted onto a logging road that Reilly had seen flash by a minute earlier. The combination of these factors meant that Cancer, Worthy, and Washington were in a world of shit, likely being pursued on foot.

And since Reilly's split team only had four men, racing into the hills in an attempt to rescue their comrades was a desperate last-ditch maneuver that they'd only employ if absolutely necessary.

The best thing they could do, therefore, was seemingly the craziest option: drive into the village and disrupt whatever Müller's men were in the process of doing, and therefore make themselves the focus of the enemy's efforts rather than their missing teammates.

To that end, he had prepared the best he could. His AK-47 rested in his hands, the RPG-7 loaded with the final rocket lying beside him for easy access. David had selfishly fired the rest despite Reilly claiming dibs the moment they inherited Tahir's stockpile.

Griffin transmitted, *"Entering the village now."*

Reilly's view from the pickup bed revealed buildings that appeared frozen in time, their walls weathered and worn from years of neglect. A sense of eerie stillness pervaded the structures, which seemed a Pakistani frontier version of a Wild West town after the villains had rolled in from the mountains—no civilians, no enemy, no movement at all, at least here on the southern fringes.

The road twisted through abandoned homes with windows like vacant eyes, shadows dancing across dusty streets stirred by a faint breeze that carried with it a foreboding chill. Reilly's attention was drawn to the rooftops, seeking spotters or snipers and finding none.

And when the first sign of movement finally occurred, it wasn't what he was expecting.

A flamboyantly painted jingle truck turned through the intersection two blocks ahead and sped away from them. Reilly's view through the back window and windshield revealed it was filled to the brim with enemy fighters facing them across the short expanse of road.

Keller immediately slowed the Hilux as Reilly stayed low, trading his AK for the loaded RPG launcher beside him with the full realization that he wouldn't have time to employ it before the bad guys opened fire. He'd be far too late, and it would take only one of the belt-fed machineguns in the jingle truck of death to wipe out their vehicle and very likely kill them all in the process.

By the time he lifted the launcher, it became apparent that wasn't going to happen. For reasons unknown, the truck continued straight before swerving left at the next intersection and coming to a stop, its open tailgate facing an unseen side street.

And while there was no telling what other targets the village would hold, Reilly knew that a jingle truck loaded with enemy fighters was a one-time opportunity for his final rocket that far superseded any other concentration of opponents they were likely to find.

He stood in the pickup bed, bracing his upper body against the cab and aligning the weapon's iron sights with the flamboyantly colored freight box ahead as he cocked the hammer. As soon as that was complete, he pulled the trigger.

A muted, popping blast occurred, followed by the hiss of the rocket roaring out of the launch tube and soaring over the cab, then the street. Its flight trajectory was marked by a hazy trail of exhaust as the rod's gunpowder booster charge propelled the warhead for ten meters, after which the rocket motor ignited with a twinkling blaze, tripling the munition's speed for the short distance remaining to its target.

Reilly saw the vibrant colors of the freight box blur as the projectile cut through the air with precision, closing the distance between the Hilux and the jingle truck in a single heartbeat.

The rocket struck true, hitting the broadside of the jingle truck's cargo area with a blinding burst of light. A concussive force rocked the pickup as Keller brought it to a sharp stop to avoid the shrapnel and debris blasting in all directions like deadly fireworks.

Ducking into the bed, Reilly discarded the launcher and watched the aftermath of his attack through the rear window. He'd not only fired the round, but had done so with every intention of killing everyone inside; nonetheless, he was momentarily horrified as he watched the fiery inferno that lit up the street in a hellish glow. The enemy fighters inside had no chance as flames engulfed the truck, an uproar of screams and chaos filling the air as Reilly lifted his AK-47 and rose once more.

Two men spilled out of the open tailgate and rolled to the ground, both of them on fire and flailing like stuntmen. Reilly picked them off with controlled shots to put them out of their misery more than anything else, holding his fire when the scene before him somehow became even weirder than it already was.

A white Mitsubishi Pajero appeared from the side street ahead, swerving through the narrow gap left by the carnage of the jingle truck and turning away from them before roaring off to the north.

"*Thank Christ,*" Worthy transmitted. "*We're in the SUV you just saw.*"

Griffin replied, "*You hijacked the warhead?*"

"*No, there's a dozen Mitsubishis just like this—target vehicle is northbound, windshield and driver's window shot out and some bullet holes in the hood. That's the only way you'll be able to spot it. Follow us and we'll split up to cover the village.*"

Munoz flashed a thumbs up that he'd heard the message, and he began relaying its contents over the air frequency.

By then Keller was maneuvering the Hilux around the jingle truck, its cargo hold belching black smoke that rose lazily upward in a spreading bloom against the cloudy sky. The pickup shook as its tires rumbled over the pair of charred corpses, and Reilly took an insuppressible sidelong glance that he regretted even as he did so.

The acrid stench of burning flesh was thick in the air, flames licking hungrily at the twisted metal around the boxed cargo area whose floor was littered with almost unrecognizable bodies, their forms contorted in grotesque poses as fire danced across their remains. Dismembered limbs were scattered atop the carnage, a macabre scene from a nightmare painted in hues of blood and ash that Reilly tried to forget as soon as he saw it.

And although Munoz had borne witness to the same thing, he didn't so much as flinch—his voice was calm and steady as he continued his dialogue with pilots and/or drone operators whose work Reilly had yet to see. Was there still a single surveillance drone overhead, or had the Chinese managed to concentrate more air assets? There was no way to know for anyone but Munoz, and no interrupting a man so engrossed in his duties. If there was something important for the team to be aware of, he supposed Munoz would tell them, but until then they'd have to trust in the mysteries of his JTAC process.

The Hilux completed its semicircle around the jingle truck and continued into the village, at which point Worthy was back on comms.

"We'll take the main route. Talon, move to the parallel road and follow it north. Target vic will probably be on side streets, so that's our best chance of spotting it."

"Copy," Griffin replied, his transmission coinciding with Keller whipping a right turn so fast that Reilly nearly flew out of the truck.

As the Hilux was lining up on its new trajectory, Reilly saw that they weren't alone.

A pair of enemy fighters occupied adjacent doorways in buildings to his left, shooting as soon as the pickup rounded the turn. Their symphony of gunfire echoed through the narrow village streets as rounds pinged off the Hilux, flinging sparks while Reilly took aim and shot four times at the nearest gunman to achieve a single glancing hit.

The second gunman fell dead before Reilly could so much as transition his aim, felled by Griffin shooting out the passenger window with his far more accurate HK416.

Then they were past the threat, an achievement that was barely complete when Reilly spotted a white SUV glide toward him before cresting through an intersection two blocks ahead. An identical vehicle sped past in the opposite direction, disappearing as quickly as he'd spotted it. He hadn't made out bullet holes in either, although the scene had come and gone before he could be sure—Müller was a wily fucker, he thought. There was no way to react beyond adhering to the previously established plan.

Worthy transmitted, *"We hit the end of the village, doubling back now,"* as the Hilux swung left at the subsidiary road paralleling the main route.

More enemy fighters appeared ahead, blasting away from alleys and windows as Reilly and Griffin returned fire. But their best protection was doubling down on their status as a moving target with the gross application of speed, and Keller floored the accelerator to speed them through the various sectors of fire in their hunt for the real target.

When there were no more fighters ahead, Reilly turned and knelt to cover their backside against any shooters that spilled onto the street behind them—and instead, he saw a bullet-riddled white Mitsubishi Pajero fly past.

Keying his mic, he transmitted, *"Net call, target vic just passed behind us, headed northeast."*

Keller slammed the brakes and shifted into reverse, speeding the truck backward and ever closer to the enemy shooters they'd managed to clear without losing anyone to gunfire.

A second white Mitsubishi flashed through the intersection in the same direction as the first, and while this one bore bullet holes as well, it had a more distinguishing feature.

Cancer was leaning out the rear driver's-side window, orienting his AK-47 forward as Worthy transmitted his response.

"Copy, we're on him—you guys better get here fast. He's flushing out of the village, headed toward the mountain trails."

34

Ian took a deep breath and stepped onto the wooden plank bridge.

It wobbled under his weight, and he felt a gust of wind from the alley below. He kept his eyes on the opposite rooftop, his movements slow and steady.

The plank creaked beneath him, each step feeling like an eternity. Midway across, he stumbled, his arms flailing for balance. He quickly steadied himself, exhaling sharply, then picked up his pace, his focus solely on reaching the other side.

Finally he arrived, his boots hitting the solid surface of the rooftop with an overwhelming rush of relief. He quickly moved to take cover behind a low wall, drawing his pistol and scanning the area ahead. The rooftops of Qissa Khwani Bazaar were a maze of obstacles—old satellite dishes, water tanks, storage sheds, clotheslines strung with garments, and small brick structures.

And now, separated from his remaining two teammates, Ian had been thrown out of the frying pan and into the fire.

He needed a better vantage point to intercept the terrorists, if doing so was an option at all. Taking a deep breath, he made a bold and audacious sprint across the rooftop, darting between obstacles as his boots thudded against the concrete, the sound somewhat masked by the fading echo of the call to prayer.

His goal was to reach an old wooden ladder leaning against the wall of a small additional floor protruding from the rooftop, likely used as living quarters. Upon reaching it without being shot, he scaled the ladder swiftly, the rickety steps creaking under his weight.

The elevated overlook wasn't much good to him without a piece of cover behind which to hide, and the only option available was almost painful to look at: a raised metal ventilation duct just big enough to conceal him but probably insufficient to absorb incoming bullets. Moving behind it would preclude the ability to scan his surroundings in search of the remaining bodyguards and their principal, and Ian abandoned its relative safety in favor of moving to the edge.

He could make out distant voices and hurried footsteps that grew louder, and focused on the direction of the noises only to find a row of large water tanks obstructing his view. The voices were urgent, tense, and the clattering of feet on the rooftop told him they were moving quickly.

Ian could tell they were close, just beyond his line of sight as they moved through the maze of obstacles up here. Scanning the area to determine where they were headed, he concluded that it was a stairway access point that descended into the building across a short stretch of open ground. There would be only seconds to accurately place a bullet at roughly ten meters—far from an impossible distance when firing a handgun at a stationary silhouette target on a shooting range, but a practically endless expanse when his pulse was racing and the man he was trying to kill happened to be running.

The best way to hedge his bets was to assume the most stable shooting position he could. Ian lowered himself into the prone and angled his Glock at the edge of the water tanks, and he tried without success to control his breathing as he awaited his moment to fire.

A bodyguard appeared at last, heading toward the stairway exactly as he suspected with the principal in trail, still wearing his black pakol hat, then the final bodyguard. All three men moved in an oblique path that Ian tracked with his pistol's iron sights. As much as Ian would've preferred to take out the armed targets first, there was only a slim chance that he could land one bullet at this distance, much less take out three men before they disappeared for good. He'd only have one chance, and ignored the bodyguards to center his attention on the primary target.

Aiming just ahead of the principal, he brought the top edge of the front sight into focus and waited for the man to cross his barrel's orientation.

Ian's last act was to exhale fully, and he was only halfway through the process when his moment arrived.

Keeping his aim as steady as he could, he depressed his trigger to send one bullet screaming toward his target before chasing it with two more.

The terrorist mastermind staggered and fell, and Ian was in the process of adjusting his aim downward when the surviving bodyguards unleashed hell his way.

A primal scramble for cover ensued as impossibly fast bursts of P90 fire chipped the edge of the rooftop and sliced through the metal ventilation duct that Ian moved for, and then, upon reaching it, cowered behind. The incoming bullets were soon joined by those of the second bodyguard firing the same weapon, the gunfire moving closer with each racing heartbeat as Ian realized that without a principal to protect, these men had nothing to lose.

Their only goal now was to kill him.

He faced the embarrassing reality that he was pinned down by relentless gunfire alternating between the bodyguards as they maneuvered toward him. There was nothing he could do but lie flat—so much as easing his way toward the ladder would remove himself from his concealment and ensure a clear line of sight for their bullets to find their mark. If he moved, he would die.

Every second they got closer, tightening the noose around his position. Ian's mind raced for a solution only to find none. The realization of his hopeless situation sank in, the relentless gunfire heralding the bodyguards' advance as they closed in.

His lone advantage was that there was only one way onto the subsidiary rooftop on which he lay. That wouldn't amount to much when a bodyguard climbed the ladder only to aim a P90 over the top edge and spray with a fifty-round magazine, but Ian had to take whatever he could get.

Rolling onto his side, he faced backward and aimed his pistol at the top of the ladder. There was a chance he could get a lucky shot against whoever scaled it first, provided they scaled it at all—the smart play was for them to climb any one of a dozen objects on the roof to negate his height advantage, and he suspected they'd do just that.

Ian's pulse pounded in his ears, the sound of his own blood rushing an audible backdrop to footsteps moving to flank his position. This was interspersed with successive short automatic bursts that remained quite successful in pinning him in place. The raised vent he hid behind continued to disintegrate as the bitter tang of fear lingered on his tongue, his every muscle coiled like a spring. Ian knew that his vital signs were reaching the breaking point, sweat running down his back as adrenaline coursed through his veins. Now out of options, he braced himself for an imminent confrontation that could occur in myriad ways but would only end in one.

The sudden cessation of gunfire was almost as concerning as its presence.

There was a shuffling sound that he couldn't identify, followed by dull thuds that seemed dangerously close. This was their final maneuver, and the silence was soon broken by more running footsteps approaching his position—either additional bodyguards they hadn't seen or, more likely and far more concerning, enemy reinforcements responding to Ian's hasty ambush.

"Come on down," a voice called.

An obvious trap, Ian thought. These men had no interest in taking him alive and were now simply trying to get him to expose himself. He didn't move, resolving to take his chances in defending himself where he lay.

And then a second voice spoke, this one laced with anger.

"Angel, get your ass down here. You're clear."

That voice belonged to David Rivers, although Ian still couldn't allow himself to believe that he'd been saved. He adjusted his position and peered out from behind the vent.

The principal remained where he'd fallen, but the rooftop below contained the addition of two slain bodyguards whose maneuver toward Ian had been the last thing they'd ever do. Blood pooled beneath them, their backs pockmarked with 5.56mm entry wounds bestowed by Hass, who swept his HK416 across the rooftop in the search for emerging threats.

David stood a short distance away, wielding his Glock in the opposite direction as he shouted an additional two words.

"Now, fucker!"

"Moving," Ian called back, trembling as he pulled himself toward the ladder. He glanced over the edge with the full expectation that more enemy fighters would be waiting for him.

There was no one.

Ian holstered his pistol and scrambled down the ladder with shaky handholds, pausing at the corner of the rooftop shack to yell, "Coming out."

"Come out," David replied, and with that, Ian finally exposed himself in full.

His team leader was now crouched over the pair of dead bodyguards, collecting their weapons and stripping off their backpacks and satchels. David looked up and said, "Go do your intel shit. Make it fast."

Ian raced past him on a direct path toward the principal he'd killed moments earlier, crossing the ten-meter distance with running footfalls that ended when he stood over the corpse lying face down on the grimy surface beside the pakol hat that had tumbled off his head at some point in his fall.

One of Ian's three shots had struck the left shoulder blade on an angled, downward trajectory, and he rolled the corpse to see that there was no corresponding exit wound—the bullet had probably mushroomed upon impact with bone, then tumbled through his chest cavity before coming to a stop in or near the man's heart.

The face before him was ghostly pale, eyes wide open with an almost surprised expression. His hair was dark and slicked back, the features quite Pakistani—high cheekbones, sharp nose, and a thin beard that was well maintained.

Ian patted down the man from neck to foot, even pulling off the boots and hat lining in a search for anything of intelligence value that yielded nothing more than a pair of cellphones. He pocketed both and retrieved a compact camera that he used to photograph the man's face, first head-on and then from both sides to capture the profile.

Then he turned the mastermind's wrists to tilt his palms skyward, snapping photographs that a proper CIA analysis with the right software could use to generate viable fingerprints. The smell of sweat and dirt wafted up from the corpse, and Ian couldn't help but wonder where and when this man had intended to detonate his stolen nuclear warhead.

"I'm good," he announced.

David cleared the distance between them wearing a backpack and satchel, and threw down the other set for Ian to quickly don.

"Who is he?"

Ian threaded his arms through the backpack straps and responded, "I have no idea."

"Hass," David ordered, "cut off his hands for fingerprints."

The former Air Force Combat Controller was kneeling at the edge of a water tank, pulling security outward.

"Wait—what?"

David led Ian toward their third teammate as Ian slung a satchel heavy with the reassuring weight of a P90 submachine gun.

"I'm fucking with you," the team leader said. "We got our pictures, now let's go."

35

Cancer leaned out of the open window in the back of the stolen Mitsubishi Pajero, the wind whipping at his face as he scanned for targets. His AK-47 now felt like an extension of his own body, the familiar mass comforting in his grip.

The target vehicle was just ahead, weaving through the crowded city streets like a desperate snake trying to shake off its pursuers.

But Washington had his own vehicle well in control, refusing to relinquish visual contact for more than a few seconds. The task was growing easier by the second as the buildings became ever more dispersed, and Cancer knew they were approaching the village's outer boundaries. Having been unable to shake the two split teams prowling the streets, and with the majority of his dismounted force now scrambling to leave the hills west of the village where Worthy had successfully prevented the nuke from leaving, Müller had finally ordered the target vehicle to make a desperate, last-ditch effort to flee.

Finally the SUV ahead straightened its course and accelerated, and despite the fact that he hadn't been tracking their careening route on a map, Cancer somehow knew beyond all doubt that it was headed for the northeast trail out of town.

There was a flash of movement to his left, and he angled his AK-47 toward it to see a man edging past the corner of an alley while hoisting an RPK machinegun at the hip, its long barrel and round drum magazine unmistakable as the bipod legs swung free.

The target was Cancer's alone. Worthy was at the window on the opposite side of the vehicle, unable to see much less engage the emerging threat that was about to unleash a hellish burst of withering fire.

And while Cancer had been off his game for an unsettlingly long period of the unfolding engagement, there was no erasing his years of combat prowess. Lining up his sights with preternatural speed and fluidity, he fired a single shot.

The bullet punched through the man's sternum, creating a small circular hole that belied the gruesome effects of a 7.62mm exit wound that had just cratered his backside and probably taken a fair amount of heart tissue and spinal fragments along with it.

Cancer breathed a sigh of relief.

The engagement was like a warm, luxuriant bath for the sniper, who was now starting to feel much better after having resigned himself to death. Doing so at his ambush position hadn't been hard, or even unusual. Instead it was the frantic climb up the hillside, facing death at every moment, that had rattled him to his core. It was one thing to die fighting to his last breath, he decided.

But the likelihood of being shot while in retreat represented a degree of powerlessness over his fate that not even Cancer could ignore. Previously he'd thought that his only demon was the ever-increasing burden of survivor's guilt from a career spent watching his teammates fall dead while he survived.

Now, he knew that he was a control freak as well.

Slaying the enemy combatant nonetheless restored order to his world, a soothing routine that gave him sovereignty instead of the eerie circus sideshow bystander effect he'd felt when Worthy had to lead him off the hill. It was going to be okay, he thought. There were plenty of people left to kill, both here in the Pakistan frontier and elsewhere in the world, if he made it out. Life wasn't so bad after all.

His vehicle sped past the man, between a pair of ancient, weathered fortification towers on either side of them, and then they were out of the village entirely.

The hard-packed dirt road narrowed into a sandy trail weaving its way uphill, and Cancer glanced at the target SUV churning a cloud of dust thirty meters ahead.

Then he looked behind him, the task made difficult by both the Mitsubishi's suspension bouncing against the turbulent ground and the haze of sand generated by the enemy Pajero as well as his own, both speeding northeast. But he could make out the dim outline of the olive drab Hilux in hot pursuit, and with it came the certainty that the four men of Split Team Two would back up himself, Washington, and Worthy in whatever came ahead.

But the feeling was washed away entirely with the sound of gunfire behind him, followed by Reilly's voice over his radio earpieces.

"*We've got pursuers,*" the medic almost shouted, "*at least three cars, could be more. Whatever you do, don't stop.*"

That raised the stakes of the engagement considerably. The target car could simply slam on its brakes or, more likely, drive past a pre-staged vehicle ready to block the trail, and the seven Americans in pursuit of a stolen nuke would be unquestionably fucked.

The trail grew steeper and rockier as the chase continued, and when the target vehicle veered left onto a side path, Cancer knew that the enemy's most dangerous course of action was coming to fruition.

"They're going to hit us," he transmitted. "Roadblock followed by ground attacks front and rear."

Griffin quickly replied, "*Roger. Continue pursuit.*"

"Goddammit," Cancer replied over the net, knowing full well that he might be able to change David's mind, but not Griffin's. "Fine, but I'm not wrong about this. When the target vehicle stops or we get blocked, everyone needs to dismount into the woods as fast as we can. We'll already be in a kill zone, but the cars are a bigger target than we are."

"*Agreed, if we get stopped at all.*"

"We will. Count on it."

The forest closed in around them, the trail reduced to a channel barely wide enough for a single vehicle to pass.

This wasn't good, Cancer knew, although their chances of survival were reduced even further with the appearance of open sky ahead.

"We're headed for a clearing. That's where they're waiting for us, probably a local militia. They'll block the trail outlet and we'll be pinned."

"Maybe," Griffin conceded, *"but we can't back off now."*

The target vehicle blasted out of the woods and onto open ground, and then Cancer saw what he knew he would.

A Nissan pickup pulled forward to block the trail, followed by another of unknown make and model directly alongside it. There were a half dozen men visible in the Nissan's truck bed, all of them wearing a combination of civilian clothes and worn-out combat gear, their faces obscured by checkered scarves. They were local militia all right, and the least of the team's worries at present—with two trucks side by side, there was no ramming their way through and nothing to do but stop as the enemy converged from front and rear.

"Roadblock," Cancer transmitted, "dismount and—"

The muted clap of an unseen and inexplicable explosion ahead interrupted his transmission, and on its heels Cancer heard the incoming chop of rotor blades a moment before the sky split apart with the roar of a chain gun.

The two pickups disintegrated under a hail of withering fire and tracer rounds from overhead, disintegrating in fiery wreckage as metal and glass fragments flew in all directions.

Washington braked to a sharp halt as debris rained down on their Mitsubishi, which skidded into an outer periphery of sand and smoke. The shadow of an Mi-36 attack helicopter passed overhead, the twin bulbs of its cockpit windshields dipped low over the lance of a 20mm autocannon that trailed a thin stream of smoke.

It was followed by a second, identical bird, both vanishing over the trees as Cancer, Worthy, and Munoz leapt out of the car. Any fighters in the clearing would be setting a land speed record into the hills after their roadblock trucks turned into scrap metal, and the main threat now was the enemy vehicles that had pursued the team out of the village.

Cancer raced to the recently stopped Hilux, narrowly missing a car door as Griffin dismounted alongside Keller. Reilly leapt out from the bed, halting in his tracks as Munoz shouted.

"Stop, stop! Cover!"

And while Cancer didn't immediately understand the cause for the sudden order, focusing instead on the enemy point vehicle closing the distance along the trail, he and his teammates raced to the trees on either side of the path.

Peering out from behind his second tree trunk protection of the day, Cancer saw the first enemy vehicle evaporate in a fireball as the ground shook beneath him. The missile strike was followed by two more further down the trail, the forest illuminated in flashes of light as the subsequent explosions destroyed the enemy convoy in its entirety in the span of a few seconds. Echoes of the blast congealed like thunder, and were forgotten just as quickly as Cancer spun on his heels and charged toward the clearing only to find that Worthy had beaten him to the punch.

Worthy raced around the remains of the two pickups, the extent of devastation making it clear that no one inside had survived.

The Mitsubishi Pajero they'd been racing to follow was now stationary in the clearing ahead, an ostensible trap until he saw that it had been disabled in the same fashion as the security elements further back along the trail. But instead of being obliterated by a hundred-pound, air-to-ground, anti-armor missile, its engine block alone was reduced to a charred mass of metal, the effects of a smaller precision munition designed to reduce the threat of collateral damage.

With his teammates behind him and scanning for threats, Worthy raced to the driver's side of the SUV—it remained unknown whether there were one or more passengers inside, but someone had most certainly been at the wheel.

The rear side windows revealed no human presence, although as he proceeded he saw that both front seats were occupied.

It was clear at a glance that the passenger hadn't survived whatever shrapnel had taken out the windshield in its entirety. The body was slumped forward against the seatbelt, chest ripped open, although his head remained relatively intact, the profile of his face recognizable enough.

It was Adrian Müller.

More concerning was the driver, his head lolling on his shoulders, currently alive although from the looks of it he wouldn't be for much longer.

"Hands!" Worthy shouted, although the man didn't respond in the slightest. Nonetheless, there was untold intelligence value in an enemy survivor, particularly one who'd been directly entrusted with driving the warhead out of Pakistan.

Upon wrenching the door open, Worthy first checked the man's empty palms and then the rest of him, finding at a glance that he wasn't long for this world. Shards of glass and metal shrapnel jutted from his body, glistening in the faint light of the dying sun. A trickle of blood snaked its way down from a gaping wound on his forehead to his chin, where it pooled with the blood that had already seeped from a half dozen other wounds.

Worthy could see the driver's chest heaving with each labored breath, the ragged, gasping sounds punctuated by weak coughs that rattled from deep within his pained lungs. His eyes were open, but cloudy with a haze of pain and confusion.

"Where was the nuke headed?" Worthy asked.

The man looked sideways with great effort, finding the body of his opponent and gradually raising his face.

Clear blue eyes met Worthy's, blood bubbling from the man's mouth. His lips parted, resulting in a burble of dark fluid along with his sputtered last words.

"Fuck yourself."

Worthy's eyes went wide, a sense of alarm shocking him to his core. For one thing, the driver was not Pakistani or even Iranian, but Caucasian.

And for another, he had spoken in a southern American accent almost as pronounced as Worthy's own.

The man's head rolled sideways and came to rest with his chin on his chest.

Worthy turned from the car to find his teammates ringing the clearing in a loose semicircle, save one—Reilly was already behind the SUV, opening the rear door.

He stepped back and gasped. "There it is."

Worthy rounded the rear bumper to take in the sight that Reilly stared at in gaping awe.

The SUV's rear seats were folded down to turn it into a hearse of sorts, accommodating a bulky rectangular tough box two meters in length and one in width, sealed shut by heavy-duty clasps.

"You better confirm," Worthy said.

But Reilly didn't move, instead breaking the momentary silence with a voice that was dead serious.

"You found this motherfucker," the medic replied. "You do the honors."

Worthy hoped that his actions in the coming seconds qualified as that. There'd already been numerous confirmed decoys, and if the case was empty, he didn't know what he'd do.

He climbed inside the vehicle, squatting beside the box and disengaging its clasps.

"Fair warning," Reilly said, echoing Worthy's concern. "If it's filled with silly string, I can't be held accountable for my actions."

The pointman flipped open the lid with great effort, then propped it upright to appraise the box's contents.

Inside, the case was meticulously lined with thick sheets of lead, an obvious attempt to block any radiation that might be detected by intelligence assets. The lead lining was expertly fitted, forming a protective cocoon around the contents. Nestled within this shielded enclosure was high-density foam that securely padded a compact, cylindrical object.

It was smooth, its matte-gray surface marked with stenciled numbers and warnings indicating its origin and serial number. The nose was conical and the tail section tapered, and Worthy appraised the warhead's precise engineering. There were small access panels and reinforced casing that spoke of a device designed for maximum devastation. A faint metallic smell mixed with the scent of the foam padding, creating an atmosphere of cold, clinical danger inside the vehicle.

The warhead exuded a palpable sense of menace, its sleek form belying the catastrophic potential it held—and then, Worthy noticed the only other item in the case.

A beaded bracelet lay atop the foam, every bead black save one that, while the same rounded shape, had the appearance of a glass eye.

Worthy pocketed the bracelet, then climbed over the SUV's rear bumper and stood to transmit, "Nuke is in the car. Along with Müller, who died in the blast. The driver is toast, but he said a few words. He was definitely American."

Keller arrived without warning and began photographing first the warhead and then the bodies in the cab.

Then all three men looked up to find the source of a high-pitched roar.

A pair of fighter jets flying an echelon formation cut through the sky far overhead—unmistakably J-20s, easily identifiable from the swept triangular canards in front of the wings. Just when it seemed that there couldn't possibly be any more aircraft supporting them, two olive drab AW139 transport helicopters roared over the clearing and came to shaky hovers, a thick rope falling free from the open side doors of each.

"Here comes the cavalry," Reilly said, sliding his AK-47 to his back on his sling as Worthy did the same. The silhouettes of men from Zarrar Company slid down the ropes in quick succession, their first shooters making landfall and sweeping the area with M4 carbines.

Reilly, Worthy, and Keller held up their hands as the Pakistani counterterrorism troops spread out to cover the clearing, four of them moving toward the target vehicle with a fifth man trailing behind in fatigues of a different hue than the woodland camouflage worn by the Paks—a member of Chinese special operations accompanying Zarrar Company, and one of three Worthy could make out among the newly arrived men.

The quintet of foreign shooters raced toward the disabled Mitsubishi as their comrades spread out to defend the clearing—the threat of an enemy force converging to reclaim their prize was very real, although Worthy somehow knew that wouldn't be the case.

"Is it there?" one of the Pakistanis shouted on approach.

Worthy saw that the crew chiefs aboard both helicopters had dropped their fast ropes. The birds began their egress away from the clearing as he replied, "It's here, all right."

"Step away from the car."

Worthy, Reilly, and Keller had no objections to doing just that as the five men surrounded the vehicle, first clearing it for survivors and then, with more trepidation, rounding the back.

The Chinese operative was the first to gain a line of sight to the nuclear bomb, which he photographed using a handheld camera.

Then he turned to the three Americans and said, "You may leave now. Line up your men over there"—he pointed sideways—"and await helicopter transport."

"Yeah, all right."

Keller interceded, "You guys are welcome, by the way—just in case any of you were wondering about that."

His words elicited little more than resentful glances from the men, particularly the Chinese advisor who was the only one to respond.

"Go. Now."

Worthy led the way toward the northern edge of the clearing as Reilly muttered, "Ungrateful bastards."

"At least we're alive, and that's something." Then Worthy transmitted, "Net call. Everyone assemble on me, Doc, and Outlaw. They've got a bird on the way for us."

"*Copy,*" Griffin replied over the net. "*We're moving.*"

Keller asked, "What happened to your back? Looks like you rolled around in a vat of crushed tomatoes."

Worthy had almost forgotten that his passenger seat in the stolen SUV was drenched in blood and gore, and he responded with the words, "Ask Washington."

As they walked, Worthy saw two groups of Pakistani shooters dart toward the fallen fast ropes they'd slid down minutes earlier, unfolding large bags to remove them from what was surely about to become a helicopter landing area for the follow-on waves of troops now that the clearing was secure.

And, he thought with relish, one of those helicopters would serve to exfil both his team and Griffin's.

The three men came to a stop, and Worthy scanned his surroundings. Late afternoon sun extended shadows across the clearing, painting the rugged terrain of the western Pakistani mountains in hues of gold and deepening blue. Worthy suddenly realized he was cold, the plummeting temperature causing faint clouds as he exhaled.

Their teammates arrived seconds later, Griffin in the lead. "Any other instructions?"

"Chinese advisor just said to wait here."

The team leader walked a short distance away, checking his compass to determine a line of sight to the appropriate satellite before unfolding the arms of his portable antenna and holding it skyward.

Worthy heard him sending a transmission to Chen as Washington blurted, "Shit, I just remembered, our rucksacks are still in the car we drove up here—"

Cancer cut him off.

"Did you leave any sensitive equipment?"

"No."

"Neither did we. Let the militias have it, and let's get out of here while we can."

That logic seemed sufficient to defuse Washington's concerns, and Cancer turned to address Worthy.

"You said that driver was American?"

"Yeah."

"How can you be sure—"

"Because he sounded like me," Worthy interrupted, suddenly irritated at being second-guessed. "Southern accent, no question."

"Shit. Are you all right?"

"Why wouldn't I be?"

Cancer said, "I mean, you just witnessed the death of a NASCAR-watching, bible-thumping, wife-beating, sister-fucking illiterate who's got a half dozen hound dogs sleeping under a porch covered in rusted appliances. Must've been like watching yourself die."

Worthy's eyes narrowed.

"It was," he replied. "Too bad he wasn't from the armpit of America that is the polluted cesspool of Dirty Jersey who didn't know how to pump his own gas, thought it was normal for an entire state to smell like trash and sulfur, and spent his weekends at a beach littered with hypodermic needles and dead bodies next to a mob-controlled boardwalk." Raising his eyebrows suggestively, he added, "Then I would've considered his death a mercy."

Cancer gave an appreciative nod. "Thanks for pulling me off the hill."

"No problem."

The men of both teams were intermingled now, engaged in quiet conversation as Worthy searched for Munoz and then found him. "Hey man, was it you running those airstrikes?"

A smile crossed Munoz's face. "Of course."

Worthy clapped a hand on his shoulder. "Consider your team's debt from Yemen repaid in full."

Munoz started to respond when they heard more helicopters approaching from the east, and both men looked up.

Two Mi-8s soared over the clearing, the roar of their twin-turbine engines growing louder as they descended for landing. A Bell 412 flew in trail, barely clearing the treetops before touching down 75 meters to their front and spooling its power down.

By then the Mi-8s had made landfall with their rear ramps open, and the figures who streamed off the ramp were a hodgepodge. Worthy saw more Zarrar Company operators, who were easy enough to distinguish from their equipment, but there were also men in the familiar uniforms and gear of Pakistani Commandos and, most notably, a sizable EOD team.

That latter contingent carried rucksacks and duffels loaded with equipment, and six of its members were clad in bomb disposal suits that gave them a robotic appearance as they navigated the uneven ground toward the target vehicle.

Trailing them were Commandos working together to haul the real gear off the helicopters. There were disassembled components of high-strength steel that appeared to include stabilizing legs, a telescoping arm, unidentifiable metal framework fitted with multiple pivot points and reinforced joints, and thick coils of cable.

Munoz began, "What the fuck is—"

"Hydraulic lift," Worthy answered. "I think."

As this was occurring, a lone man exited the Bell helicopter and approached the teams, wearing not a military uniform but civilian clothes.

A representative from the ISI, Worthy surmised, and his suspicions were all but confirmed when he stopped before them and shouted over the sound of the rotors.

"Who is in charge?"

"I am," Griffin and Cancer replied in unison, with the latter man quickly correcting himself. "He is."

"You have all your men?"

"We do," Griffin said. "Just the seven of us."

The Pakistani pointed to the helicopter he'd just departed. "Load onto this aircraft. We will fly to Badaber to refuel and pick up the remaining three Americans. Then Islamabad."

Worthy led the file of team members toward the bird, and they collectively turned their heads sideways as the Mi-8s lifted off with a whipping hail of rotorwash and loose sand.

He was the first to board the Bell 412, where he found two rows of bench seating with additional outward-facing seats in the rear. Worthy took the far position and buckled his safety belt as he watched the remainder of the Americans load up— Keller beside him, then Reilly and Washington.

Then Cancer climbed into the back row and, following the usual protocol of JTAC and ground force commander remaining on the ground until the bitter end, Munoz and Griffin followed suit. The ISI man was last, slipping his way toward a rear outward-facing seat and donning a headset.

Looking out the window beside him, Worthy saw that the EOD men were now clustered around the wrecked Mitsubishi, while Commandos assembled the equipment that he had guessed to be a hydraulic lift for extracting a thousand-pound warhead.

Then the churning howl of the Bell's engines rose in volume and its skids broke their hold with the ground. The helicopter's nose tilted downward as it charged forward through the air, gradually ascending to treetop level before beginning a circular flight path away from the Afghanistan border ahead, and then leveling out facing south toward Badaber.

Worthy's final glance at the clearing revealed the pair of Mi-36 attack helicopters that had saved their ass from an ambush that almost certainly would have wiped the seven CIA paramilitary contractors off the map, and then his view shifted to the landscape of Pakistan.

The sun dipped low, casting an orange glow across the landscape that stretched endlessly beneath him. The sky was a deepening canvas of blues and purples, the last vestiges of daylight slowly giving way to the encroaching night.

Below, the land was a patchwork of craggy hills and scattered towns. The hills, weathered and ancient, looked like the crumpled pages of a forgotten book, their surfaces etched with the scars of time. Narrow, winding paths snaked their way through the valleys, connecting isolated villages that clung to the hillsides. Each town was a cluster of small, flat-roofed buildings, their mud-brick walls blending seamlessly with the earth around them.

Faint lights began to flicker on in the towns, small pinpricks of brightness in the growing dusk. Smoke from a hundred evening fires rose in thin, spiraling columns in the distance, adding a hazy veil to the twilight air.

Then Worthy looked out the far window where the stark, imposing silhouette of the Hindu Kush mountains rose, their peaks obscured by a blanket of clouds. The mountains stood watch over the rogue frontier that his team and Griffin's were now departing, a swath of badlands resistant to the control of man since the beginning of time, to which he would hopefully never return.

The helicopter's rotors beat a steady rhythm as Worthy pulled the bracelet out of his pocket, then showed it to Keller beside him.

"Any idea what this is?"

Keller took the item and examined it, his gaze focused on the single glass bead that looked like an eye.

"Sure," he said. "It's a *nazzar battu*, kind of like a lucky charm in Pakistan. Wards off the evil eye; it's supposed to give you protection."

Worthy chuckled to himself as he took the bracelet back and returned it to his pocket. "Guess it didn't work. I found it with the warhead."

"Really? Yeah, I guess it didn't help them much."

"Nope," Worthy muttered, musing aloud, "it most definitely did not. Three of our Top Four targets off the battlefield. Raza captured, the hacker and Müller killed. The only one we missed was that nuclear engineer."

"Right, Mordecai Friedman. Who will be on the run for the rest of his life. But we got the *real* Top Four."

"What do you mean?"

Keller met his gaze with a skeptical expression, as if trying to determine whether Worthy was joking.

Then the intelligence operative's expression softened. "Sorry. I thought Griffin told everyone after he made comms with the Agency—David, Hass, and Ian smoked the mastermind they went after in Peshawar." He shrugged. "Not much intelligence value from a dead man, but they grabbed some equipment and cell phones. Hopefully the CIA can piece together his identity and what he was going after. Because whoever he was, he didn't orchestrate that nuke theft for fun."

Worthy swallowed. "That's good. That's really good. I'm glad to hear it."

But some unbidden instinct within him felt uneasy at the news. He couldn't put his finger on it, but the conviction was no less powerful than the inner certainty that the warhead was aboard the convoy he'd seen slip past his observation post four hours earlier.

He tried to shake the thought.

"Mission complete," Keller said in a victorious tone. "Time to go home."

36

I stuffed my hands in my pockets and asked, "Why does this room always smell like printer paper?"

"I don't know," Griffin said. "I've never been here before."

The stoic team leader stood calmly in a tailored suit, his green contractor badge centered on his chest by way of a lanyard.

And while I wore the same badge permitting my access to select locations in CIA Headquarters, that was where our wardrobe similarities ended. I'd worn a suit as well the first couple times I'd been here, until my familiarity with what was about to happen had dropped my give-a-fuck-o'meter down to zero. Now I was in a simple button-down shirt that I'd debated tucking into my khakis, my sleeves rolled halfway up my forearms.

"Oh," I said with genuine surprise. "Then welcome to the Thunderdome, bitch. The escorts always dump you in this room and make you wait. I've squared off against Chen here before, along with her predecessor Duchess. Spoiler alert, get ready to be criticized for everything we did on the mission."

Griffin replied without enthusiasm.

"Sounds great."

"It will be," I added eagerly. "Nothing's quite as fun as having an office-dweller who sat in air conditioning the entire time we were in the shit play armchair quarterback and talk down to you like you're a child."

He squinted at me for a moment, then tapped his ear and waved his finger overhead.

A grin crossed my face. "You know what, let's hope the room *is* bugged. That way Chen can be impressed and delighted at my powers of precognition."

I leaned against the conference table, whose thick glass surface sat atop the faithful reproduction of a colored world map from the 1800s. The number of places I'd been on that world stage had increased by one, though by now I'd long since stopped counting the number of countries that I'd traveled to in the course of three careers spanning the military, mercenary, and paramilitary contractor realms.

Griffin's gaze danced across the wood-paneled walls around us as he said, "Call me crazy, but I would have thought some gratitude would be in order."

"As would I. Unfortunately, you're going to have to get used to this."

The door swung open on the heels of my response, and Meiling Chen entered in professional attire that rivaled Griffin's.

"Gentlemen," she announced, moving to the far side of the table, "please have a seat."

Her droll tone and slight movement struck me as ludicrous. After we'd hit the jackpot in Pakistan several times over, to include liaising between the Chinese and US in order to subvert numerous regulations that prevented either country from sharing intelligence with one another, she should have been doing backflips into the room.

As Griffin and I pulled out our chairs and sat down, I asked her, "Is the room bugged?"

"No."

I glanced at my fellow team leader and gave a helpless shrug.

She lowered herself into a seat. "Thank you for coming."

As if we had a choice, I thought.

"We're here to discuss your mission in Pakistan, as well as—"

"Haven't you seen the news?" I cut her off. "They have it on good authority that the nuke was stopped due to the superlative efforts of an ISI superstar. Tahir Qureshi, I think it was. I watched the recap of the Pakistani president giving him the Crescent of Bravery on CNN."

She watched me impassively, waiting to make sure I'd shut up before responding. "Don't be so quick to judge him. And on the topic of awards, I've gotten you both approved to receive the Intelligence Star."

"I don't know what that is."

"It's a valor award, for acts of extraordinary courage and bravery under hazardous conditions. Roughly analogous to the Silver Star in the military."

Nodding, I replied, "Cool. But unless every man from both our teams receives the same thing, I don't want it."

"Concur," Griffin agreed, letting the moment breathe before explaining, "It's all of us or none of us."

Chen suddenly looked like she was about to lose her mind.

"Do you know how hard it was to get two approved, much less ten?"

I said, "Not our problem. And now that we've got that out of the way, I've got one question for you."

By then there wasn't much to ask about the mission in Pakistan, nor any mission before that. The future, however, held my interest far more than the recent past that I remembered all too clearly—after a reunion with my team and Griffin's at Badaber, we'd been transported back to Islamabad.

And then the government of Pakistan had, quite unceremoniously, kicked us out of the country.

It wasn't like any of us wanted to stick around. But once the warhead had been recovered, the presence of ten Americans had become an inconvenience that both the Chinese and the Pakistanis wanted removed as quickly as possible.

We hadn't received so much as a thank you from anyone to include Tahir. By contrast, the Pakistani ISI and military people handling our departure practically treated us like we'd stolen the nuke instead of Müller's people. How much of this was due to a false narrative perpetuated by the Chinese and how much to simple xenophobia, I had no idea and didn't particularly care.

All I wanted to know was the question I asked Chen now.

"Where was the nuke headed for detonation?"

She hesitated. "We don't have specifics, but Müller's driver was an American member of an anti-government group. I'm not at liberty to say more than that, and while the Chinese have refused to share information on the other deceased fighters, it's safe to assume there were other US citizens present."

Griffin folded his hands on the table. "That's a smart play by Müller. Free labor, and the access and placement of domestic networks able to smuggle the device into America."

Chen nodded. "I agree that it's a smart play, and that America was the target." Her gaze flicked to mine. "But it wasn't the decision of the man you killed."

I felt a pang of dread at that moment, my first indication that there were larger forces at play.

"Why do you say that," I asked warily.

"The man you killed wasn't the mastermind. Target Number One is still out there."

"The man we killed," I said firmly, "was traveling with an eight-man bodyguard escort. If he wasn't the mastermind, then who was he?"

"A decoy. The mastermind, however, was there. We've confirmed that much through multiple communications intercepts after the warhead was recovered. And that means you saw him."

"I—saw him? How?"

"The man who fled your attack, the one you thought to be a bodyguard, was in fact the individual who planned and resourced the entire operation."

My stomach sank, and it took me a moment to process that information. Once I did, however, I appreciated the thought process that went behind this ruse. If anyone was going to be killed by a sniper bullet or a ground attack, it was going to be the individual surrounded by a protective detail. By disguising himself as a bodyguard, the man who escaped had increased his survivability tenfold.

I looked at the ceiling and sighed in reluctant concession. "I thought that guy was a coward. Now I realize he was a genius."

"A genius," Griffin said, unmoved by the information, "who engineered a war between two countries as a means to capture a single device, which means he's capable of similar operations in the future. Or worse."

"If there is such a thing," I added.

Chen swallowed.

"As best as we can tell, the events in Pakistan were his debut on the world stage. Whatever 'worse' may be in this case, it's safe to say he's already planning it."

Then I said, "Don't keep us in suspense. Who is he?"

"We don't have an identity yet. We do have a location, as well as reasonable intelligence indicating that he doesn't plan to leave there anytime soon."

"I'm assuming that it's a denied area."

"To say the least. Further specifics will be forthcoming during your next mission brief."

I stared at her for the exchange we both knew was coming and asked, "We're bouncing back overseas already?"

"Sometime after the New Year," she acknowledged. "The mission will require a train-up period."

"What for?"

"The infiltration method, for one thing. The actual execution is another."

My gaze dropped to the world map on the table between us. Here I was thinking that Pakistan would be my final mission.

Now, I knew that another remained.

And given the limited time remaining on my Agency contract, it would indisputably be my final one. I didn't know whether to feel spine-tingling elation or soul-crushing disappointment. On one hand, I'd lived for combat missions since joining the Rangers at eighteen years old.

On the other hand, however, I was a husband and father of two, and I'd vowed to my wife that my time as a gunslinger was coming to an end.

I looked sideways at Griffin, then forward at Chen, and finally at the ceiling between us before uttering the only response that came to mind.

"Goddamn it."

37

I stepped through the door and into my home, shedding my coat and the weight of the world along with it.

The smell of pine and cinnamon greeted me, a welcome and jarring contrast to the familiar scents of gunpowder, sweat, and sand that I'd become accustomed to before returning to the States.

Equally unfamiliar was the sight of the ground floor, which was the next best thing to a winter wonderland. My wife, my daughter, and I had really outdone ourselves this year, putting up our decorations the day after Thanksgiving in an annual event that I had christened the Rivers Family Festival of Lights. Our living room was dominated by a pine tree adorned with tinsel and ornaments that sparkled in the afternoon sunlight filtering through the windows, along with stockings, strings of lights, and various handmade Christmas crafts that my daughter had created in honor of her favorite holiday.

I could have told myself that this was the way of life I'd chosen to protect long before I had a family myself. Such sentiment would be a self-congratulatory reminder of the many sacrifices I'd made over the years, a tribute to the teammates lost along the way, and also a complete and total lie that I couldn't possibly deceive myself into believing for a moment.

The truth was that as idyllic as my home life now was, I'd continued a combat career out of far more selfish reasons than ensuring the American way of life, or out of the duty-bound sense of patriotism that had evaporated completely somewhere in the course of my first deployment. I liked gunfights and I loved adrenaline, and now I increasingly wondered how I'd fare in a few months when both were removed from the realm of possibility forevermore.

Nonetheless, I had three very good reasons for hanging up my spurs. Judging by the utter silence that greeted me on the ground floor of my house, all three of those reasons were upstairs.

I mounted the steps and emerged onto the second floor, moving for the open door of my daughter's room to find her lying on the bed, reading a book from the stacks at her bedside.

"Hey, Langley."

She put her book down, then practically leaped off her bed and raced over to hug me, a gesture that I knelt to accept head-on. Langley did this frequently, sometimes as a genuine display of affection but more often to increase her chances of parental approval in requesting one sugary treat or another that her mother wouldn't approve of at that point in time.

I asked, "Do you need anything?"

"No," she chirped. "I just love you, Daddy."

"I love you too, sweetheart."

We parted from our embrace, and she asked, "How'd your meeting go?"

I grinned, pulling out my phone and showing her the locked screen display—four missed calls from an unlisted phone number, the tally increasing to five as the device vibrated in my hand.

Langley nodded her understanding. "If you're ignoring them, it must have been rough."

"Yeah, girl," I said. "'Rough' is a good way of putting it."

I placed my phone in do-not-disturb mode and slid it back into my pocket. On the two-hour drive back from CIA headquarters, my willful refusal to answer every incoming call had been a source of mischievous comfort.

Now that I was home, however, any attempt at contact by Chen was an irritation I simply couldn't tolerate.

Langley eagerly asked, "Does your boss still suck?"

"Right now, a lot of things suck," I allowed, the closest I'd ever come to letting my daughter know that a terrorist mastermind was on the loose, God knew where to do God knew what. "But not the fact that I'm home. Is Mom where I think she is?"

"Uh-huh."

"Oh boy. I better get in there."

My next stop was at the end of the hall, and I eased open the door as silently as I could.

The room was darkened with blackout shades, lit only by the swirling panorama of colorful stars emanating from a projector. Laila was in the corner as I suspected, gently rocking from her seated position in a glider chair.

And in her arms was Jackson.

I advanced as she stood, bending her knees in rhythmic motion to keep our newborn son asleep.

She whispered, "How was your meeting?"

"Same as all of them," I whispered back. "How'd he do?"

"Went down right away. Up screaming a half hour later."

I held out my arms to accept the swaddled baby. Despite adopting Langley when she was five, it felt oddly natural to hold the warm little body I now took into my arms, assuming the bopping motion that Laila had maintained and adding my own personal brand of side-to-side rocking.

"Go relax," I told her. "I've got this."

She departed the room as quietly as I had entered, easing the door shut behind her.

There was something surreal about holding my son in my arms, particularly in the immediate wake of a mission. I had, I thought wryly, traded the wilds of Pakistan for a nursery, guns for stuffed animals, a rogue nuclear warhead for a newborn.

The silence in the room blanketed me in a warm, comforting tranquility. Although anything resembling peace would vanish the moment Jackson woke up, it was moments like these that assured me I'd be just fine after retiring from the CIA for good.

I sat down and watched his face in the dim light, his tiny features placid as I rocked the glider. Bringing life into the world was a far more profound experience than taking it in some far-flung land, the bursting swell of love for my children profound in a way that nothing else in my life ever had been.

Looking up at a beam of light from the door, I saw Laila come back inside. I assumed she'd arrived to recover some forgotten item—her phone, perhaps.

But then I saw the device in her hand, screen turned to face me as she leaned in and whispered in an urgent tone.

"Have you seen this?" she asked, showing me a *New York Times* article.

"Yeah," I said. I'd already all but confirmed to her that my men had been heavily involved in the Pakistan events that had now taken center stage in the global media, omitting as usual any mention of combat or imminent death, although she'd inquired without success about the minor wounds from bullet fragments across my upper legs and stomach. "ISI hero and the Pakistani Commandos stop nuclear theft, et cetera et cetera."

She shook her head adamantly.

"No, this was just released a few minutes ago."

I removed a hand from beneath Jackson's swaddled body and accepted the phone from her, ignoring for a moment both the headline and the feature photo and fixating instead on a thumbnail picture of the reporter— Alejandro Garcia, whose face I recognized well enough.

He was the man who'd tried to engage me in conversation over break- fast at the Frontier Lounge.

And while there had been a massive influx of media following the initial border attacks, the man's presence in Peshawar, and particularly at the linkup site for myself, Tahir, and Zhang, almost certainly indicated some form of advance notice from a whistleblower in the CIA who was very likely among the Project Longwing staff.

Then I looked at the feature photo, which showed a stream of men heading toward the open door of a waiting Bell helicopter.

Their faces weren't visible at the angle from which the photo was taken, although I could make out their identities well enough from their equip- ment and physical build. Worthy, Keller, and Reilly were in the lead, trailed by Washington, Cancer, and finally, Munoz and Griffin.

I knew at once what had happened.

No longer required to cooperate with America out of mutual concern for recovering the nuclear warhead, the Chinese had decided to cast their parting shot. The CIA had been called for comment immediately before the article went live online to the world, and Chen had tried to warn me. This development couldn't have been more troubling, I knew at once, though my concern only mounted when I finally scanned the headline.

When I did, my breathing came to an abrupt halt.

PROJECT LONGWING: THE MOST COVERT COUNTERTERRORISM FORCE YOU'VE NEVER HEARD OF.

"Mother*fucker*," I whispered to myself, then looked up to meet my wife's haunted gaze.

"David," she choked out. "Are we safe?"

It would have been the easiest thing to lie. It would have been kind.

"I don't know."

FINAL STRIKE:
SHADOW STRIKE #10

A secret mission, one final challenge.

For David Rivers and his team, this mission was meant to be the final chapter—an audacious strike to eliminate the world's most dangerous terrorist. But deep in the unpredictable terrain of Iran, they soon realize that the assignment is far more intricate than expected.

As they close in on their target, the team uncovers a devastating secret: their mission is just one piece of a much larger plan, designed to ignite chaos and fracture the very foundations of America. With time running out and Iranian militias closing in, they must execute a desperate, high-risk counter strike to stop a conspiracy that threatens the world.

Pushed to their limits, they face the possibility that not all of them will make it out alive. The team must decide how far they are willing to go to prevent a global catastrophe.

It's all amounted to this, one final showdown.

**Get your copy today at
Jason-Kasper.com**

ABOUT THE AUTHOR

Jason Kasper is the *USA Today* bestselling author of the Spider Heist, American Mercenary, and Shadow Strike thriller series. Before his writing career he served in the US Army, beginning as a Ranger private and ending as a Green Beret captain. Jason is a West Point graduate and a veteran of the Afghanistan and Iraq wars, and was an avid ultramarathon runner, skydiver, and BASE jumper, all of which inspire his fiction.

Sign up for Jason Kasper's reader list at
Jason-Kasper.com

jasonkasper@severnriverbooks.com